THE WOODEN ROSE

EVELYN GRIMALD

TARNEY BRAE CREATIVE ENDEAVOURS

For the ones who where there when this was just an inkling...

CONTENTS

1

$\mathcal{W}$alter Smythe did not mind one jot that it was raining. It was the sort of rain that lasted for days and was nowhere near bad enough to keep people from going about their normal lives but made everything that much more of a burden to do. People carried black umbrellas and tried to justify taking a cab or calling an Uber, though they knew perfectly well that the rain wasn't that bad. Among the trudging parade of gloomy people, unabashedly displaying a smiling, cheerful face, was Walter Smythe. He wore his nice blue slacks over his patent-leather shoes, a maroon sweater and white collared shirt with a dark leather jacket. His hair was gelled into place, and his rather round face was set in that smiling expression that got people grinding their teeth in annoyance. Over his head was a black umbrella.

He hummed quietly to himself as he walked the few blocks to where he had instructed his driver to wait for him. It wouldn't do to have pulled up to the soup kitchen in the flashy town car, even if you did see all sorts in New York City. Not when he was about to sign them a check that would keep them running until Christmas. Walter was one of those philanthropic types that gave simply because he enjoyed it. He did not care about tax benefits, or looking good among the wealthy set, or even about any publicity that would come from such things. He simply enjoyed seeing people smile.

And he was enjoying the rain.

That, probably, is what did him in.

The people huddled in alleyways or under blankets as close to buildings as they could get looked up at Smythe with a certain air of anger. Slowly, his cheerful mood sank as the stark reality of these unfortunate people hit him. Supporting the soup kitchen continue running would help them, but it wasn't quite the same as seeing these people well. He tried not to hand them each a ten-dollar bill, knowing that money wouldn't necessarily help these people. They needed clinics to get well or to deal with potential chronic or mental illness. They needed a place to live. They needed work. Not even he could provide that many jobs. Maybe for just one, though, he could manage to find training and work and—

Something shoved him from behind, causing Walter to stumble forward, dropping his umbrella to the ground, his smile finally falling. A young man with greasy hair and a dark jacket ran past, clutching a very distinctive leather wallet in his hand. Spluttering, Walter ran after him, yelling, "Stop! Thief!"

Being overweight and in his sixties, Walter soon desisted running, though he called angrily after the man. He had just wanted to *help* these people! A moment later and he stared in astonishment as one of the bulks of blankets that hid a homeless person moved to trip up the thief. A grubby-looking person—it took a moment for Walter to identify them as a woman—rose and lunged for the wallet, delivering a blow to the thief's head as she did so. She straightened with the wallet in hand, and the young man jumped to his feet, dazed but unharmed, and darted off before anyone could think to call the police on him.

Generous though he was with his money and sympathetic though he was to the plight of the people on the streets, Walter was not a stupid man. He knew full well that the woman who had snatched the wallet from the thief was probably someone not to be trifled with, especially considering that none of the other people nearby made a move to interfere in any way. In fact, two or three were hurriedly picking up their belongings and vanishing into the rain. Walter knew that there was little chance of getting his wallet back at this point. He also figured that it would be safer to turn tail and flee should this woman want to take him for more than the cash he was carrying.

The woman walked toward Walter, her posture straight and the grime on her face hiding any identifi-able features and giving her a dangerous look. He staggered backward, grasping for his umbrella in case he needed a weapon. Why hadn't he informed his office manager of his whereabouts? Why hadn't he taken the self-defense that his godson kept insisting that he take? Would he have time to reach the phone in his pocket before—

"Here," the woman said, holding out his wallet.

Walter froze.

She looked at him with serious eyes that held more pain than most people would ever see in a lifetime. They were stormy and strong and lonely, a sentiment echoed by her voice. It was like a bell, solemn and ringing through the rain, though the actual tone had been quiet. "Your wallet," the woman said, and Walter broke away from staring at her long enough to see that she was holding out his wallet, shaking it gently as she prodded him to take it.

Tentatively, Walter put his hand on the leather wallet and took it from the woman's grasp. He looked down at the object in his hand in wonder. A moment later, he looked up, "thank you" on the tip of his tongue.

His rescuer was gone.

Only hours later, as he was pacing over the Persian rugs that covered the exotic wood of his study floor with a cut glass of scotch over ice in his hand, running the events over and over through his mind, did Walter realize just how extraordinary the night had been. How often had he heard tales of people being mugged on the streets by desperate people? How often had he himself been warned that people weren't going to see him as a philanthropist but a target?

He hadn't believed them. Oh, he knew that there were criminals on the streets, that not everyone cared about the well-being of others, but Walter just wanted to help. He wanted to see people able to stand on their own. To get the support that they needed, not be failed by a cruel and heartless society.

Except...he couldn't stop feeling the jerk of his body as the young man ran into him with the intent to steal his wallet. It wouldn't have mattered hugely to Walter; he would have just canceled his cards and let the cash go as a gesture of goodwill. But that violation, that assault. It stuck with him.

As did that mysterious woman, helping without being asked. With hardly a word.

When had he ever heard of a mugging being stopped by someone equally as desperate, equally as alone as the mugger, and not even a reward asked in return? He had been saved from a considerable amount of trouble in sorting out the stolen cards and IDs, but he would have only been out a few hundred dollars' cash. That sort of money could have kept the woman in food for months. So why had she chosen to help him?

"I've got to find her," Walter murmured to himself, sipping absently at his drink. "I've got to help her."

He pulled out a pen and paper, both monogrammed *WS*, and started writing a description of the woman to give to the police. He paused. Dark-gray eyes, dark hair, voice that sounded like a bell. That was all he remembered. Surely there had to be something more. But no matter how many times he went through it, Walter couldn't remember anything else about her. It was as though blinders had been placed on his vision and his memory and he hadn't noticed anything but the way that she'd brought down the thief and the astonishment he had felt when she'd handed him the wallet. And the whole thing had only taken seconds, so there wasn't much material for him to run through.

He would simply have to go back there and ask around, see if he could figure out who it was that had helped him. Because she deserved his thanks, even if she didn't want it. And if there was one thing about Walter Smythe that people needed to understand, it was that he was a determined old man and he was going to give his help whether people asked for it or not. In this case, it never occurred to him that maybe this woman didn't want to be found.

It took him two days to organize a search party through his office manager, sending out notifications to the soup kitchen and requesting any witnesses to the mugging on that night. He went back to the street where it happened three times, all at different times of day to see if he could find someone who knew some-thing about her.

Each time, he opened his wallet and gave out money and received nothing for it. The homeless were unwilling to talk or they all had severe memory loss. Finally, a full week after the mugging, Smythe was inches away from giving up. He was interviewing a man with a thick, gnarled beard and eyes that looked right through you and was trying not to show his frustration.

"Why is it you're so eager to find this person?" the man asked after pocketing twenty dollars. He shifted slightly so that he could pull his ragged blanket over his shoulders and looked up at Walter with the sort of expression that demands an answer.

"Because she helped me. I want to return the favor," Walter answered, stuffing his wallet unceremoniously into his jacket pocket. He was getting grumpy at this point, and it seemed that this latest interview would lead him nowhere. "I'm not going to buy her out of the life, set her up as a mistress to one of my sons, anything like that. I just want to give her the chance to learn a trade and work, to set up a life for herself."

"And you think that she wants this?" the man asked, curling his lip into a sneer. He coughed quietly into his blanket.

Taking a deep breath and exhaling like a smoker who had long since quit, Walter shrugged. "I don't know. I just want to have the chance to offer it to her. But if you don't want to help, then it looks as though I'm wasting my time. Good afternoon." He turned to leave, his office manager standing by a car that was more than conspicuous in the street. He had learned the lesson of trying to be inconspicuous all too well.

"Wait," the man called out.

Suddenly more hopeful than he had been in the

last few days, Walter wheeled about, raising his eyebrows expectantly.

The man appraised Walter carefully. He jerked his head backward in a nod of acceptance. "I can tell you where she'll be, but you have to do everything else on your own."

"Where?" Walter asked eagerly, pulling out a piece of paper and his monogramed pen, nearly trembling with excitement.

"Corner of Pelham and Esplanade," the man answered. "She normally haunts that area. But be careful. She's not someone to be trifled with. And if you choose to go there, I would suggest not dressing like you own the world. Some of the people around those parts won't take too kindly to that."

With a flurry of enthusiastic thanks, Walter pressed another twenty-dollar bill into the man's hand and rushed off to the waiting car. His office manager, a skinny man in a well-tailored suit with dark hair swept back with nary a strand out of place, slid in next to him. Walter relayed the information given to him and told the driver to head over to Pelham and Esplanade but park a block or so away. He didn't want to scare this woman off, after all.

"Mr. Smythe," the manager said, "I don't think it's a good idea to be going right now. You should take the warning that this man gave you seriously."

"What? Oh, don't worry about that," Walter answered. "Graham, you're a good manager, and you'll probably go far, but when it comes to things like this, I know what I'm doing."

"Like you did when you got mugged?" The words came out quietly, with a breathed apology a moment later, but they still stung.

Walter shrugged. "I have to believe that people are generally good. It will all be okay," he said firmly.

Graham didn't say anything.

The street corner where this woman was to be found wasn't too far away, and almost before the car had even stopped, Walter was bounding out and hurrying over to the area where people were gathered, Graham reluctantly following behind. Derelict buildings flanked the corner, though one corner store was trying to hold on. The green space where the few people were gathered was mostly scraggly grass and weeds, but it was better than nothing.

The intruders stood off to one side, Walter searching the people for any sign of his rescuer. He spotted a couple of people arguing, another standing by, and he started with surprise as he realized that the woman he was seeking was one of the arguers. She was holding her hands slightly raised, her feet spread in a balanced position. She looked as though she was going to fight her assailant.

Without even a pause to consider his own safety, Walter rushed forward. "Excuse me! Miss! Excuse me!"

The people not involved in the argument took one look at Walter and turned to face him, quietly watching, then must have seen Graham strutting along behind him and bolted. It took only a couple of minutes before the entire area was cleared of people but for the three that Walter was currently standing before.

The woman, now that he had a better chance to look at her, was fairly fit for someone on the streets. She was of average height, but her frame—though skinny, as most of the homeless were—was trim and reasonably well muscled. Her hair was brown and tied back in a severe bun, though several strands had escaped. She sported one black eye and a bruised lip, and blood spots stained her clothes.

"Can I help you?" the man with whom she had been arguing asked.

"Oh, I want to talk with her," Walter said, pointing at his target. At that moment, Graham walked up to his boss's shoulder, looking so annoyed and harsh that the two men took one look at him and followed the example of the other people. They scampered. The woman was about to do the same, edging away, looking around for the best possible escape route.

"Wait, please," Walter said, holding up his hands to show he meant her no harm.

"What do you want?" she asked, her voice smooth and cultured, a slight shock to Walter.

"You helped me. I mean, about a week ago, you gave me back my wallet," Walter said, noting that she stepped away at the words "you helped me." He knew that there was some sort of taboo in the streets about helping people, especially in the way of investigations.

"What of it?" she asked, taking another step back and putting her hands up again as though she was expecting a fight.

"I wanted to express my thanks," Walter said. This made her pause, and then she laughed. It was a dry, cynical laugh that sent shudders down Walter's spine, and he found that he was the one inadvertently backing up.

"I doubt that you went to all the trouble to find me, a week later, just to say thanks," she said. "So what is it you want? You think that I can do something else for you? Get you drugs, maybe? Sleep with you? Well, you've got something else coming if that's what you think—"

"No, I wanted to offer you a job," Walter blurted, the words coming out so rapidly they could probably barely be understood. She paused. He recognized that this was perhaps his only chance to win her over and tried to explain everything as quickly as possible.

After a moment, she shook her head and held up her hand. "Slow down," she said. "I can't understand you."

"I want to offer you job training in whatever field you want. A chance to get off the streets and make a life for yourself. I can't guarantee that you'll get work once you've completed the training, but I want to give you the opportunity. If you don't want to do anything with it, fine," Walter said, looking tentatively at her.

"Why? All I did was get back your wallet," she said, lowering her hands. This, as far as Walter was concerned, was a good sign. She didn't look as though she wanted to fight and run away. He might actually have a chance.

"Exactly. You gave me back my wallet, which was noble in and of itself, fully aware that I was someone who could probably do without. You didn't even think about it; you just did it because it was the right thing to do," Walter said. "I want to reward that."

"You don't even know who I am. I could be a drug dealer or something worse," she countered, though her gaze seemed uncertain.

"Are you?" Walter asked, ignoring the way that Graham tensed at his side.

"No," the woman admitted.

"Well, then there we have it," Walter said, smiling.

She looked hesitant, as though what he was saying couldn't really be true. But he didn't vanish, and she didn't walk away. Eventually, she held out her hand, looking frightened. Walter understood that, at least. He wasn't giving her a surefire way to get off the streets. He was giving her a chance to get herself off the streets. And not only was that not easy, it was altogether possible that it wouldn't work out at all. But, perhaps despite these misgivings, she held out her hand and Walter shook it.

"I'm Walter. Walter Smythe," he said, pulling her gently in the direction of his car. She went, still tense and wary but willing.

"Gwen Townsend," she answered. "If you want to

run a background check, look up Lieutenant Gwen Townsend, formerly of the army."

"You're military? How did you end up here?" Walter asked. Gwen picked up a small rucksack lying off to one side, then looked at Walter uncertainly. He smiled his friendliest smile. He led Gwen back to where his driver waited. He opened the door of his saloon car for her, and she hesitated a moment before sliding inside. The car smelled of fresh leather and wealth, and she fidgeted uncomfortably, obviously trying not to touch anything for fear of getting it dirty.

"Life," was her reply. Walter didn't probe any further.

They rode in silence for a few minutes, eventually hitting the Manhattan traffic and slowing to a crawl.

"So what field do you want to train in?" Walter asked, the shock of having Gwen be military subsiding as his excitement in this new project took over. "You can do anything you want."

"Anything?" she asked, drawing her eyebrows together.

Walter nodded, his round face splitting into a wide grin. "Anything at all."

"I've always...," she started, then frowned and shook her head. "No, never mind."

"What? This is no time to back out now."

"It's just not practical," Gwen said. "If this is going to be something to do for the rest of my life, it needs to be practical."

"Miss Townsend. Gwen. If I believed as you did, I

wouldn't be here today. My entire fortune and life have been built on doing things that are certainly important and innovative but not practical. Finding you, offering you this chance—that was far from practical, but it was absolutely worth it. Trust me." Walter leaned forward, searching her face for a hint of what it was that she could want to do with her life.

"I've always wanted to cook. In a restaurant," she said finally, ducking her head and refusing to meet Walter's gaze. So she missed when he leaned back in his eat and grinned like a little boy at Christmas. He knew exactly what he was going to do.

"It just so happens that I know a chef. He runs a cooking school out of a restaurant—the Wooden Rose —and he owes me a favor," Walter said. Clearly startled, Gwen looked up at him, perhaps checking to see whether he was serious. After a few moments, Walter saw something rare and wonderful. She smiled.

2

"Danny, if you overcook that duck again, I'm going to give you the sack right now," Alaric Bennet growled, standing behind one of the sous chefs in the kitchen. To his pleasure, the man started to sweat just a bit more, though that could have been from the heat of the grill.

"Yes, Chef," the man answered, using the towel hung in his apron strings to wipe his face. His stringy blond hair stuck out in curls from under his hat, and he looked at his boss nervously. The head chef of The Wooden Rose, a five-star restaurant in the middle of Manhattan, was a dangerous man to cross. So Danny took a pair of tongs and turned over the duck breast, giving it another dash of extra virgin olive oil, all the while keeping his boss in the corner of his eye.

Alaric ran a tight kitchen, of that there was no doubt. It probably helped that all of his staff were slightly terrified of him. They could talk with him, sure, maybe even make a joke, but in the back of their minds was that niggling sense of fear that they might be the next to find a new job. He preferred things that way.

He wasn't an imposing person, at least not in the literal sense. He wasn't overly tall, and despite the fact that he was in great shape physically, he wasn't extremely handsome. Attractive, sure, with his sharp, angular features and the dirty-blond hair that constantly got in the way of his vision, forcing him to push it back in what people would call a "stylishly tousled" manner. But his expression was almost always set in a scowl, and his eyes were dark and brooding. Most of the women—and some of the men—on the restaurant staff figured that if he were to smile every once in a while, he would be much better to look at. And maybe, just maybe, he wouldn't yell at them quite so much.

Despite the shortcomings of his personality, he was a great chef. A fantastic one, even. Which was why The Wooden Rose, one of the best restaurants in the center of the city, had snared him. That and the manager was the only one able to keep him in any sort of check.

"Clumsy idiot!" Alaric snarled as one of the younger kitchen assistants bumped the chef while holding a plate of pissaladière. The savory pastry nearly slid off the plate before the assistant was able to save it. Alaric snatched it out of the poor girl's hands and stalked off, muttering to himself. He replated the appetizer and set it on the bar of food to go out. Turning, he spotted the assistant by the cutting boards, trying to prove her worth as she cut up celery into even pieces. Alaric nearly went over to grab her by the elbow and give her a lecture on walking out of people's way when someone tapped him on the shoulder.

"I think you should relax a moment," the manager and owner said. He was a man of about forty-five with glasses that constantly slid down his nose, a smile that was easy and sincere, and salt-and-pepper hair that was straight out of a magazine. Fifteen years older than Alaric, the two got along like brothers; each balanced the other out, and when no one else was willing to talk, there they were.

"I *should* get this kitchen into running order. Everyone seems off their game tonight. I had to remind Cecil twice that he needed to beat the butter before adding the other ingredients for the gratinéed mussels," Alaric grumbled. But he followed the man over to the storage area for dry goods and obligingly leaned against a wall. "How's the house, Jack?"

"People are smiling and enjoying themselves," Jack answered, holding up an apple and checking it over before taking a bite. A little juice dribbled down his chin as he continued, "The Morgans are back and wanted me to thank you on the salmon in lemon sauce. It was well done."

"At least some people appreciate food," Alaric muttered, secretly mollified at the praise of his dish. He watched Jack take another bite of apple before picking one up and doing the same, unaware of how hungry he had been until he'd started eating.

"How are the preparations for the school coming?" Jack asked. He needed to know; otherwise, he wouldn't have asked because immediately, Alaric was angry and snarling again.

The chef began to pace back and forth in front of his friend, forgetting his apple as he waved his arms about. "I have far too much work to do, and you know that full well. The final applicants need to be informed of the required materials they need to purchase. I have to finish getting together the menus for each week's presentation. Then there're the ingredients to be ordered. The garlic from Modena hasn't come in yet, and the truffles were powdered, not whole! On top of that, I have a restaurant to run, so my kitchens are going to be twice as crowded and not nearly as efficient. Lauren is going to be going on maternity leave just as the classes will be wrapping up, and—"

"You know that it's all worthwhile, Alaric. You run this school every year, and you complain about it all the time, but it always turns out well. Really well. Where else can these prospective chefs get a chance to learn and train under someone so talented at an actual restaurant?" Jack said quietly.

With a humph, Alaric slumped against the wall again and finished off his apple. "You're just saying that to appease me," he snapped.

"No. If I were doing that, then I wouldn't acknowledge that sometimes, you're a real ass. Now, I have to get back to the floor, and you have, as you so rightly put it, a kitchen to run. But in half an hour, I'm coming back here to force you to take a break. You will sit outside and eat the coq au vin that table five sent back because it was slightly cool," Jack said. He didn't bother waiting around for Alaric to argue but threw his apple core away and straightened his tie, weaving his way through the kitchen and stepping through the doors to the restaurant floor.

This, Jack thought as he smiled at a couple sipping a glass of red wine, was his element. This was where he belonged, just as much as Alaric belonged in the kitchen. Among the people, the conversation, the lighting, and the atmosphere. He wanted nothing more in his life than to give people a plate of good food and somewhere to eat. It hadn't been for lack of trying that he had discovered he couldn't cook. So he'd brought in Alaric and took care of everything else.

Jack wandered slowly through the restaurant, managing to give off an aura of efficiency and ease simultaneously achieved. He stopped at table fourteen to inquire about the appetizer of stuffed mushrooms and directed the sommelier to table three, where an old man and someone who looked to be his daughter were musing over the wine list. Then he spotted someone he knew.

"Mr. Smythe," Jack smiled, putting extra pep in his

step for the man who had found his superb head chef for The Wooden Rose. "How are you?"

"Jack! Things look like they're doing well?" Walter asked, pushing away the menu he had just picked up. Jack noted this and smiled all the wider. It was going to be a good night when Walter Smythe came looking for a fantastic meal. The man was a great boon for business and publicity, and he always tipped well.

"As ever. Things usually pick up just before the school season starts. We never announce it, but somehow people always know that the kitchens are about to get new talent. Once the courses begin, I imagine that things will drop off slightly. The first few weeks are tough on the students," Jack said.

Walter laughed, the sound echoing slightly and making people look over at the wealthy man and the restaurateur.

"Well, Alaric will whip them into shape in no time," Walter said. He looked up at Jack with a suspicious gleam in his eye and leaned forward. "Actually, I wanted to talk to you about that."

"Oh?" Jack said.

"Do you have one more spot open in your school?"

"A charity case, Walter? Some poor chef stuck in a low-end restaurant but destined to make it big if only he had the chance and the training?" Jack teased. Walter Smythe's charity cases were famous, especially where his acquaintances were concerned. Nearly everyone owed him a favor or something of the sort, and he often used them to get people into better positions. So Jack wasn't terribly surprised that Smythe was asking.

"Actually, a retired army lieutenant helped me the other night, and I'm returning the favor. She needs a new career, and cooking was her dream. So naturally—"

"You thought of Alaric and The Wooden Rose," Jack answered. He heard a slight rise in volume from the direction of the kitchens and shook his head. If he were to accept this mystery student from Walter, Alaric would not be happy. The only students that ever attended the culinary school went through a tremendous series of tests and trials. The application itself was seventeen pages long. And there were three rounds of applications and interviews. Alaric took only the best, and of the three hundred that applied, seven were accepted. A spot at the school was highly sought after. Nothing less than the best was even allowed in Alaric's kitchen. "You know Alaric won't like this," Jack warned.

"Ah, but you can do something about that. She only needs a chance. One of the other sous chefs can give her extra help if need be. Jack, come on. You owe me one," Walter said.

"Fine," Jack sighed, allowing himself a moment of weakness as he let his shoulders slump. He never would have refused Walter though. Somehow, the man had an uncanny ability to grasp who would do well where. An instant later and he was just as straight and smiling as before. "But I'm sending Alaric after you if he comes out swinging."

"I wouldn't expect any less." Walter laughed. "Now tell me what I'm going to have tonight, and tell someone to bring me a glass of your best, richest red wine."

Jack went to do as he was told, smiling affectionately as he relayed the orders to each of the necessary people. Then he went back to the kitchens, where he found Alaric chewing out the new busboy.

"If you need to get into the dishwasher, fine. But don't go interrupting people while they are cooking! My duck is ruined because of you, and you can be sure that the price of those birds will come out of your paycheck. Now—"

"No, it will not," Jack said. He stepped in next to the busboy and raised his eyebrows at Alaric. "You don't have the right to threaten my employees' salaries, Alaric. You can fire your crew, yes, but everyone else is mine. And no, he is not part of your crew. Now get back to work," he told the boy, and to Alaric, said, "It's time for your break."

"I have to start a new set of duck breasts," Alaric grumbled, turning away from his manager and reaching for a pan.

"No. One of your assistants—Danny, in fact," Jack said, spotting the assistant listening in, "will be starting the ducks. You are going to grab that coq au vin and come with me."

~

Deciding that obeying was better than arguing, Alaric did as he was told and snatched the plate of cold chicken off the counter, picked a fork out of the set of clean dishes, and marched after his manager, still fuming about his ducks. Instead of going into the storage area, Jack lead Alaric to the loading docks, where Jack started pacing.

Without a word, Alaric sat, his long legs hanging over the edge of the docks, and started shoveling food into his mouth, knowing that the sooner he was finished, the sooner he could get back to his kitchens. There was only another forty-five minutes before the restaurant closed, and in another hour or so after that, he could go back to his apartment and sleep off the annoyance that the day had brought.

"Damn it, Alaric, you can't go around terrorizing the employees like that," Jack sighed, putting his hands on his hips as he paced. Eventually, he stopped and sat next to the head chef. "You can terrorize your kitchen crew, sure, but that's because *you* hired them and they knew full well what they were getting into. You can terrorize your students just the same. But if you start on anyone else, then I'm going to have to put you on probation."

"You can't do that," Alaric retorted, the fork halfway to his mouth. He took a bite and spoke around the food, "You need me."

"Yeah, I do. The Rose is a great restaurant because

you are a great chef. But I will find someone else if you continue to do this to me," Jack said.

Alaric gave a sort of appeasing sound and put the half-empty plate of food on the raised deck next to him.

"There aren't many people that put up with you."

"I know," Alaric said, shrugging. "But I can't help it. I'm a perfectionist, and when people can't even follow instructions, it gets on my nerves."

"Gets on your nerves? I'd say that's a bit of an understatement. Seriously, you're going to have to figure out something to keep your temper under control. I don't know, take up boxing. Get laid. But figure something out, soon. Because otherwise, I'm going to make it a condition of your employment that you take anger management classes."

"Seriously? You would make me see a psychologist?"

"Yeah," Jack said. "But only if things go too far. You have until the end of the term for the culinary school to get things sorted out. I don't care how, just do it."

"Fine," Alaric snarled, wanting to throw the plate he had just set down against the ground. He knew that would only prove Jack's point, so instead, he wrapped his fingers around the edge of the loading dock and glared at the building across the way.

It was an old industrial building that had been bought up a few years back and made into an apartment complex. The apartments cost a fair amount, being in the city center, but they were nice, and Alaric had never heard of any trouble that went on there. He had even considered buying an apartment there himself, simply because it was conveniently close to The Wooden Rose. He had been talked out of it by his girlfriend of the time, Marcie. She had wanted him nearer her law office, so he lived a couple miles from his restaurant. He still regretted it.

"Looks like someone's moving in," Jack said. Alaric blinked and looked at the back of the building. Indeed, there was a van there, and a couple of people were moving boxes and small pieces of furniture into the building.

"That'll be the last apartment let, then," Alaric said. So much for his chances of moving in. "I wonder who it is."

"Someone who wants to be close to the culture, perhaps" was the reply. Alaric shrugged.

He shivered, realizing that the cool air, ripe with the possibility of rain, had cooled off the heat of his anger. He grabbed the plate and stood, brushing off his apron. "I have to get back to the kitchens."

"And I have to get back to the floor. Oh, by the way, your friend Walter Smythe is out there. You should probably go and have a word with him."

"What's he having?"

"The mussels. With a red wine."

Alaric winced and shook his head. "He always was an eccentric sort. But he's a good person. Without him, I'd be far away from The Rose. I wonder what sort of charity case he's gotten into now," the chef said, opening the door to head back to the kitchens.

Jack sighed and put his hand on the door, closing it before Alaric could get a chance to walk back inside. Alaric narrowed his eyes; Jack only closed the door if he didn't want this being overheard by the kitchens.

"About that," Jack said.

"Oh no. My kitchen staff is full. I don't need anyone else, and not even Walter Smythe is going to change my mind about that."

"Your kitchen staff isn't what's going to be changed," Jack said. He leaned against the brick wall of the restaurant and stuffed his hands into his pockets, not meeting the gaze of his chef. This was bad, Alaric knew. "He wants to get someone into the school."

"The slots are full," Alaric said flatly. "You told him that, right?"

"Of course. But we both owe him a great deal, and I know that you've had more students than this in the past. So…"

"Tell me you didn't agree," Alaric said, his voice suddenly gone soft. "Tell me you didn't let him foist some sous chef in a two-star restaurant in the slums of Queens into my *selective* class."

"I didn't let him foist some sous chef onto you—onto us," Jack said. Alaric sighed in relief and Jack swallowed before going further. "I let him foist a retired army lieutenant onto us."

"*What?!*" Alaric yelled, the sound echoing in the loading area and making the people across the way pause in the middle of moving a box. "You let him put some completely untrained military man in my cooking class?! Someone who has no idea how a restaurant is run? With no idea of the proper skills? Do you have any idea how insulted the other students will be? They expect to be working with people who understand what cooking is, not someone who thinks that it might be fun to learn! Do I even get a say in this?!"

"No," Jack replied, calm as ever.

Alaric cursed. Loudly.

Alaric's voice carried very well. The people across the way had stopped moving completely and were undoubtedly looking to see who was yelling so much.

Jack winced and rubbed his forehead. "You know that Smythe wouldn't have asked if it didn't matter. And I've already said that one of the kitchen assistants will give extra lessons each evening after the kitchens close. They'll get paid overtime too."

Alaric hissed in displeasure. "I will not let one of my people get caught up in this. No, no. *I'll* stay behind and do the extra lessons. But don't come blaming me if this lieutenant loses his nerve and skips out on this. It wouldn't be the first time that one of Walter's charity cases has gone seriously wrong."

"Fine. But Alaric," Jack said, turning the doorknob and staring his chef straight in the eyes, "if I hear of any wrongdoings, you're going to be out of here faster than you can say 'chef.' Understand?"

"Whatever you say, boss. No, I'll treat this person just the same as I'll treat anyone else who makes a claim in my kitchens." Alaric pushed past Jack and stalked back to the warm kitchens, where the manager imagined the staff was going to feel the brunt of his anger. Sighing, he wished that he hadn't given up smoking and shook his head before returning inside.

Graham, as usual, wasn't pleased. Walter hadn't realized how difficult getting Gwen set up for her new career actually was. As a result, he'd given Graham the charge of the mission, sent Gwen to get cleaned up, and taken himself out to dinner at The Wooden Rose. Graham began to organize a month-to-month apartment near the restaurant where Gwen was to work and hoped that when she came back from the showers, she would at least smell a bit more personable. He doubted very much that she would achieve anything more than that. So when she returned, wearing an old pair of his sweatpants and a black T-shirt that made it very apparent she wasn't wearing a bra, he coughed in surprise and immediately turned to his work.

Because she cleaned up well. Very well.

Her skin had been dirty and grimy when she'd arrived; now it was pale and clean. Her hair had been stuck in clumps and the color of mud on a damp Tuesday. Now it was a lustrous light brown and was pulled back from her face in a tight bun. Her skinny frame was more apparent, especially now that she was wearing clothes two sizes too big, but that only made the fact that she had lithe muscle attached to her more visible. The only thing that detracted from her looks, simple yet appealing, was her expression.

Gwen retained the stoic look on her features, but her eyes told the story of someone who had seen far too much. There was sadness in her eyes and also wariness and pain. The black eye that she sported was even more obvious because of it, though her split lip was less swollen. She stood there, completely out of place in the office of Walter Smythe but looking as though it wasn't an unfamiliar feeling. She was an enigma, and Graham had always liked puzzles.

"I don't think we've been properly introduced," Graham managed to say after he reminded himself that she had just been picked up off the streets. Staring was impolite. He forced himself to remain calm and cool, scolding himself for thinking that she was nothing more than another pretty face, another charity case that would be his job to mop up when it went wrong. "Graham Ruskin. I am the office manager for Mr. Smythe."

"Gwen Townsend," she answered, her posture straightening slightly as though she was about to salute or give a sharply barked "sir." Graham looked down at his computer screen, pushing any thoughts about anything other than his immediate assignment far, far away.

"Right. Ms. Townsend. Mr. Smythe would like me to get you set up with an apartment, preferably near the restaurant where you will be working. You will be given some money to buy furniture and clothing and whatever else you will need. I already have some men out at the chosen building, getting things organized. Until the time that you complete your training, you will be given a weekly allowance that should be sufficient. A bank account has been set up in your name, and you will receive, in the mail, all of the documents that you will need. Do you have any questions?"

Gwen hesitated for a moment before shifting nervously. "Why is he doing this? It's costing him a lot of money and putting you out of your way. I don't..." She trailed off.

If he had expected anything out of her, this charity case that his boss had adopted, it certainly wasn't that. Most of the people he dealt with were more than willing to take Walter's money and start a new life or take it and relapse into the way things had been. He didn't remember a time that the recipient had questioned why. Graham looked up from his desk and put the reading glasses he was wearing onto the computer keyboard. He met Gwen's hesitant, wary gaze and tried his best to give her a reassuring smile. From the way that she seemed to tense up, it didn't work very well.

"Mr. Smythe is a generous man. He believes, wholeheartedly, that since he has been given wealth, he should do something to help those who do not have it. He does not simply give money away but always searches for someone that he thinks might be worthy of receiving a second chance. Sometimes, it doesn't work out. From what I hear, though, you helped him when it did you no good to do so and when it was obvious that he was just another rich man in the wrong part of town. That must have meant something to him. So why is he doing this? For you, I think it's because he believes you are a good person," Graham said.

Gwen blinked, clearly surprised.

Then, reminding himself that this was just another homeless person, someone who couldn't live up to the rigors of society, Graham looked down again and picked up his pen to jot something on a piece of paper. "Just don't prove him wrong."

"Yes, sir," Gwen said softly, sharply, as though Graham were her commanding officer. Graham had seen her records. He knew she had worked as an interpreter—a glorified translator—for the equivalent of two tours in the Middle East. She had been honorably discharged and now she was glaring at him and blinking back tears. As far as he could tell, this cooking venture could go very well, or very badly. Graham hoped, for her sake, that it went well.

3

Two weeks later, after reading every cookbook with tips she could get her hands on—mostly from the used bookstore at the corner—and cooking as many things as she had time to make (her neighbors were quite pleased with this), Gwen stood outside The Wooden Rose, staring her enemy down. *I've been to war. I've faced boys with trigger-happy fingers and men who know the best way to kill with a single stroke. I've driven in convoys that have been subject to IEDs. I've argued with soldiers in different languages, winning each time. I can damn well take on a single restaurant.* She straightened her posture, made sure that her all-black "uniform" of slacks and a plain tank top under a button-up blouse was creased properly and looked acceptable, then walked up to the door and pushed her way inside.

It was eleven o'clock in the morning, and The Wooden Rose didn't open until five. But still, the doors were unlocked, and sitting at a cluster of tables in the otherwise empty house were seven other people. All of them were wearing some form of slacks or trousers in dark colors and a plain shirt, but all of them looked far more at ease than Gwen felt.

"You must be the last one, then," one of the men said. He was sporting a bow tie and shaved head, and he took his time in looking Gwen over with his dark eyes. She knew what he was doing: assessing her, sizing her up. Enemy or ally? She met his gaze evenly. This part of the day, at least, was something she understood. After a few moments, the man looked away. Gwen sat down in a chair a couple over from the man and didn't say anything to him or anyone. It looked as though no one else was really willing to say much either, so she wasn't out of place.

After a good ten minutes of everyone waiting, the doors opened again, and a man walked in. He was wearing jeans and a T-shirt under a worn jacket and had the look of someone who was awake far earlier than normal. He grumbled in and walked past the students, all of whom were thinking that he was another student. But when he stood at the door to the kitchens and said in a rather annoyed voice, "Well come on, then," they jumped up to follow.

The kitchens were silent, even slightly eerie. Gwen had expected them to be busy, full of the noises of sizzling and chopping, of people and energy. Giving a huff as he turned his back on the stoves, this mystery man gestured to one of the stainless-steel countertops in the center of the room. The students gathered around.

"All right. I imagine you all know why you're here. I am Alaric Bennet, head chef at The Wooden Rose and also your teacher," he said, looking around and meeting each student's gaze, cementing his authority. As before, with the other student, Gwen held his gaze until he looked away. It was this that let her see him frown, ever so slightly, as he broke eye contact.

Gwen surveyed her fellow students with interest, wondering what special talents they must possess to have brought them here. Unlike her, who had managed to make it into the school with little more than luck.

There were four men and four women, so it broke down fairly well. Of the men, the black man with the shaved head and bow tie looked the most confident. There were two that looked completely average, one with brown hair and one with blond. The last was an overweight man of Asian descent who looked as though he indulged in his food a little too much. Gwen smiled slightly at that, though he was likely a good cook for it.

The women were all different, more so than the men. There was Gwen herself, with her plain brown hair and steel-colored eyes. There was a petite woman with wispy dirty-blond hair cut in a pixie style. A third was tall and willowy, with long features and a nose slightly too small for her classic Indian face. The last was squat and had her eyebrows drawn together in a fixed expression of determination. There were no visible tattoos and no annoying piercings.

"Since we'll be working pretty closely together in the next couple of months, we'll need to know everyone's names. Go around, say your name and the job you last held," Alaric said, eyes flashing with interest. Gwen's heart dropped into her stomach. She straightened her shoulders; she refused to be ashamed of her past. Or at least what everyone but the dead knew of her past.

Shaved Head went first with, "James Warren. I was a sous chef specializing in seafood at the Golden Dragon."

"Bob Kasey, head chef at Jimmy's Tavern, over on First Street," the average-looking blond man said.

"Tom Kavanaugh, chef at Young Spices," the average-looking man with brown hair said.

"Robert Wallis, chef at Karma, the Indian restaurant off the park," the overweight man said.

Alaric frowned for a moment, his expression darkening.

The women went next, first the small blond with, "Allison McKher, sous chef at Kippers on Third."

"Sarah Rahid, chef at Martin Alder's," the willowy woman said.

"Jennifer Yaxley, sous chef at Bellton," the squat woman introduced herself.

Then Gwen straightened her shoulders, met Alaric's gaze without a hint of fear and said, "Gwen Townsend, Lieutenant, US Army."

Alaric twitched his lips into a smirk of surprise. Gwen kept her expression stoic. He had known she was coming—of course he had. Walter would have informed him. But the fact that she was former military might have surprised him a little. She read the challenge in his gaze and knew he would try his hardest to prove that she was somewhere she didn't belong. She would prove him wrong.

With the introductions out of the way, Alaric explained the schedule—each student would be working at The Wooden Rose five days a week with lessons during the day—and showed them the menu. Then, obviously loath to waste any more time, he began whipping this motley crew into shape.

"Chop that celery finer," Alaric snarled at Allison. "The knife isn't going to kill you if you know how to use it properly."

"If you don't add more oil to the pan, soon that duck is going to catch on fire!" he shouted at Tom.

Each student received his or her fair share of abuse, including James and especially Gwen. By the time they were allowed a break, it was two in the afternoon and all of them were sweating. Alaric allowed them half an hour for lunch, saying they could very well eat the ruined dishes they'd made; it would make them learn faster. As soon as he was out of sight, having chosen to go eat out at the loading docks, they all collapsed against the counters or breathed a sigh of relief.

"I feel like I'm back at cooking school," Sarah

complained, rubbing her head. "I haven't been yelled at this much since I don't know when."

"I mean, I heard rumors that Bennet was tough, but I never expected that he was this bad," Robert said, looking at his slightly charred chicken breast. Under the pressure of Alaric's fiery tongue, everyone had apparently fared worse than they normally would have. Except Gwen, who wasn't afraid of the temper but hadn't yet gotten around to the level of greatness that the other students were obviously used to.

"I know someone who used to be a kitchen assistant here, and she said that Bennet was probably the most terrifying guy that you could ever deal with," James said. He alone had managed to make an eatable meal, though from the way that he was wincing, it hadn't been done up to snuff.

"What about you, Gwen?" Jennifer asked, half-heartedly pushing her chicken around on her plate. "What do you think?"

Gwen considered. "He wasn't nearly as bad as my commanding officer. If you were late out of bed or couldn't do the training right, you would know about it. And so would the whole complex."

That brought about a chorus of laughter, though James merely smirked and raised his eyebrows.

Sarah leaned closer to Gwen, smiling. "What was it like, being in the army? You must be thinking that we're a bunch of wimps, tired and complaining about only half a day's work."

Gwen swallowed the bite of food she was chewing

and shrugged. She knew what it was like to have to eat food worse than this, and she wasn't going to pass up the opportunity for a meal, no matter how bad. "I was just an interpreter. They didn't train me nearly as hard as many of the soldiers. Still, you'd be surprised how much you can manage. Half the people I served with were whining like crazy the first day of training, and they made it through. But you will get used to it. Eventually."

Again people laughed and, for the first time in a long time, Gwen felt as though people liked her—that was, until Alaric walked back into the room, saw how little everyone but Gwen had eaten (she surreptitiously mopped up the last of her sauce with a bit of bread), and began to chew them out. If they weren't willing to eat their own food, he said, how could they expect anyone else to do so?! Gwen was certain that his voice echoed for minutes afterward, though it just as easily could have been her ears ringing from the shouting.

They worked until four and got an hour off to go do whatever before the restaurant opened. Gwen chose to run across the street and take a quick shower, reveling in the luxury of warm water on her skin instead of blisteringly cold rain. She changed into something a little less sweaty but equally subdued and went back to the restaurant, making it there fifteen minutes before it opened. And if she thought that classes with Alaric were something to behold, watching him run his kitchen was a terrifying, mesmerizing experience in of itself.

The kitchen staff was obviously skilled and knew the drill, but even so, it was like watching a well-oiled machine. The students were the only ones who got in the way, stuck as they were with ingredient preparations. Alaric shouted frequently, mostly trying to get people to move faster as the orders came in, yet there were moments when he was quiet and pensive, watching the sizzling brussels sprouts in an iron pan while he tenderly sautéed them or plated a dish with expert precision, rubbing a clean towel along the edges of the plate so that the customer only got perfection.

Then the evening wore on.

The busier the kitchens got, the more people began to make mistakes. The more this happened, the more frustrated Alaric got. His acid tongue was beginning to whet itself on the nearest target, which was, more often than not, one of the students. Even Jack, the manager, was unable to curb more of his employee's anger. Though when Jack was around, Alaric was slightly quieter.

"If you burn one more dish," Alan snarled at Sarah, who had been promoted to roasting some vegetables for one of the stews, "then I don't care how qualified you are, I won't let you back into my kitchen."

"I'm doing the best I can, Chef," Sarah barked out in reply, looking harried and upset. "I need more olive oil, and the burner keeps sticking on the highest setting."

"Good cooks know better than to blame their equipment," Alaric hissed. Gwen watched all of this as she moved her knife across the cutting board, the strokes even and swift. Knife work was something she was familiar with, at least.

"She's right though," Gwen said as Alaric turned to storm away. He acted as though he hadn't heard her, but Gwen was certain that his face grew slightly red from anger. She nodded at Sarah. "You're right. I've been watching you work."

"Thanks, but the chef is right. I shouldn't blame my equipment, just learn to compensate," Sarah muttered, keeping her head down as she tossed the vegetables in the pan. Gwen blinked. Had this cook, who had just said that she was doing the best she could and acknowledged that it wasn't her fault, just lay the blame on herself? Gwen didn't understand. No soldier would be able to blame themself if the gun was faulty. Though that was why they had such stringent equipment checks. She shook her head, returning her attention to the parsley she was chopping.

Eventually, the night ground to a halt, and the temperature of the kitchen seemed to change dramatically as the last burner was turned off. All the people in the kitchens, students and staff alike, let their shoulders slump with relief and started the cleanup. People rubbed knots out of their shoulders and, as the kitchen returned to its sparkling state, left one by one until only the students remained.

"All right," Alaric said, looking over the people in his tutelage. They were pleased to know that he looked tired as well, though there was an air of satisfaction about him. "All right. You did well enough. Now go home. You'll be here by noon tomorrow, and we'll start this process again."

The students nodded to each other, smiling weakly as they stretched and wandered over to their coats. Gwen was about to put on hers, more than ready to get a good night's sleep, when Alaric called her name.

"Yes?" she said, turning.

James and Allison stopped as well, obviously curious, but one piercing look from the head chef told them to get a move on. They did so.

Finally, only Gwen and Alaric remained. "Did you need something?" she asked.

"You are supposed to be getting private lessons," Alaric said. Gwen felt her belly tighten. She had nearly forgotten that Walter had told her she would be getting extra lessons to catch up. She was desperately tired and wanted to go home and sleep. Instead, she hung her coat back up and rubbed her eyes before stepping forward.

"Yes. Sorry, I forgot," Gwen said.

"If you aren't willing to put in the work, just say so," Alaric snapped.

Gwen stiffened, ready with a retort. "I never said—"

"Because you don't belong here, and we both know it. You aren't a chef, and maybe—*maybe*—you might be one but not because you went to my school. This is for people who have worked their asses off from the time they were young to get where they are now. Not for people who come back from fighting and say that they deserve everything and more, simply because they were doing good for their country."

"Now, listen here—"

"So you had better put in the work to get caught up to where my other students are, or you can get out of my kitchen right now," Alaric finished, drawing his brows together and curling his lip in a look of anger and disgust.

Gwen clenched her jaw and took three deep breaths to keep from punching the man. Fighting to prove her place in the army had been one thing, but this was something completely different.

She clapped her heels together and straightened to attention, her gaze fixed on a point on the far wall. "I'm willing to do the work, sir!" she barked.

Alaric scowled. He had probably hoped that she would just give up and go home, leaving him to his life, but she was a veteran. He had to remember that she had to be determined or she wouldn't have gotten as far as she had. But that didn't mean he couldn't break her. He just needed to work a bit harder. Gwen ignored the tightness in her throat.

"Fine," he said. "Then let's get started."

Three hours later, at nearly two in the morning, Gwen staggered into her apartment, feeling as though she had just been through a day of intensive training. Her shoulders hurt, and she was certain that there was still sweat trickling down her back. Her head was swimming, and she was doing her very best to control the urge to put her fist through the wall.

This was just as bad as her first days of training. She felt out of shape and full of indignation at the quips and snide remarks made at her expense. She was certain that she wasn't wanted and that people thought she couldn't handle the work, but she was going to prove them wrong. Prove Alaric wrong. Now, it wasn't so much a way to get started on a new life but a gauntlet thrown to prove herself. And she would do it, no matter the cost.

Still, as she dragged her feet through the door and exhaled in relief at the click behind her, Gwen had to admit that she was tired. It didn't help that she was still malnourished from her life on the streets. It would take time and a whole lot of calories to build up her strength again. For now, though, she would settle on a nice, long sleep.

A red blinking caught her eye, and Gwen stared in surprise at the answering machine to the phone that Walter had insisted she get installed despite also giving her a cell phone. She had a message. Who could possibly be calling her? She didn't even *know* her phone number. She certainly hadn't handed it out to people. Tentatively, she pressed the play button and waited for the message to begin.

"Hello, ah, this is Graham," the message began. Gwen raised her eyebrows but did nothing. "I am calling at the request of, ah, Mr. Smythe... He, erm, wants me to make sure that your first day at the, ah, school went well..."

There was a pause on the machine, and for a

moment, Gwen thought that was all and she could safely go to bed. But then, "And well, I don't mean to pry or be rude, but you haven't pulled out any money from your bank account. I just wanted you to know that, ah, that money is for you to use...however... Well, I'm sure you're busy, but if you would call back, tomorrow maybe, that would be great." He proceeded to give the number to the office and rang off rather awkwardly, as though he wanted to say more but couldn't. The blinking red light went away.

Gwen played the recording again and wrote down the number, choosing not to read anything into the message Graham had left. If she were vain, she would think that he was trying to express an interest in her. But she wasn't, and she was pretty certain that he wasn't, so that was that. The mention of the bank account was strange though. She didn't think that Walter or his office manager would be monitoring her spending habits—though when she mulled it over while lying on her bed, it made sense. He was trying to make sure that she was a good investment for his money and that his initial judgment wasn't wrong. She hadn't needed anything though. Walter had been extremely generous in furnishing the flat and purchasing a wardrobe and groceries.

The more she thought about it, the more she waffled between it being an odd statement and perfectly sensible. When the answering machine started taking on the shape of a floating genie head and spouted information on the best possible method of sautéing broccoli, Gwen dropped into a deep sleep.

It did not stay that way.

First, there was the corridor, dark and filled with rubble and rocks that might cause a noise if someone placed his foot wrong, barely wide enough for a single person to go through at a time, let alone a whole squadron. But that didn't matter to Gwen because she could see exactly where to place her feet in the green-tinged light of her night-vision goggles. She held her position with practiced precision, and her gear was a comfortable weight, which kept her pleasantly warm in the cool desert night. She was an interpreter, attached to a group in the midst of a war zone, heading to a supposedly routine meeting with an informant. Her friends—soldiers, all, and armed accordingly—were with her, one in front, four behind, all briefed and prepared.

Routine flew out the window.

There was a noise, and her commanding officer halted the group with a raised fist, the air suddenly filled with tension as Gwen and the others checked their weapons, ready to fire at a moment's notice. They scoped out the area, looking at eye height or just above, waiting for enemy militants to appear with weapons or explosives in hand. Only the threat wasn't from above.

A meow filled the air, and Gwen flinched, looking down at the cat, which had shifted some of the rocks. It was a feral cat that had once been a family pet by the way that it wound about Gwen's feet. She tried to shake it off as silently as possible, but the creature was persistent. She was growing more desperate now as the squad started to move forward again. She had to get rid of the cat without making noise or the enemy would know they were coming.

She heard her squad mates move again, trying to get around her as she stepped over and around the cat, which persistently tried to get her attention. One of them—Damon, her best friend—stepped in a spot that hadn't been cleared. He was three people behind Gwen, and it was that distance alone that saved her life.

There was a click, and before anyone had time to react, the air was filled with the roaring of a thousand machine guns. A lion inside your head, screaming to get out. Fire seemed to come from everywhere, so powerful that Gwen was knocked off her feet and fell on her gun, pinning it to the ground. She tried to move but couldn't. Something was keeping her down, immobile, completely useless. Her commanding officer yelled something incoherent, his words lost in the terrible ringing that filled her ears. Gwen did her best to move to his aid.

She couldn't get herself unpinned before the air was filled not with fire but with bullets. Muzzle flashes blinded her through the goggles, and she did her best to see where her commanding officer was so that she could help him, give him any support she could. She was an interpreter. Trained in combat, sure, but she carried no gun. No weapons. Still, she had to try. She spotted him and gave up struggling; what was the point when his lifeless eyes stared at her, blood dripping slowly from his mouth and the various bullet wounds that riddled his body? She closed her eyes and blacked out, unable to cope with the realization of what had happened.

The scene replayed itself in Gwen's head, over and over until the image of her commanding officer lying dead before her, her friends dead behind, and her squad mate's body pinning her to the ground were all that she saw behind her closed eyes. With a scream of terror that made it perfectly clear she couldn't take any more, Gwen woke, sitting straight up in bed and returning to reality.

Reality, though, was more than she could handle at the moment because it meant that what she had just seen wasn't a dream. It had really happened, and she was really the only survivor of an attack gone wrong, honorably discharged and given a ribbon to "ease her way."

She buried her head in her hands, entangling her fingers into her hair as the tears came. They always came, great, gasping sobs that shook her entire body and made her tremble with the need to scream out and beat something to a pulp. The scars she had retained from that event were more than the few burns and scrapes from the blast. They were written on her soul, unable to heal.

She had never seen what had happened after her

commanding officer had died, but a briefing from a general had made it seem as though the militants hadn't stopped to check that the soldiers were dead. They'd just left, not bothering to secure the site or claim their victory. All they'd wanted was the destruction and death of those they'd seen as their enemy. It had certainly been achieved. Gwen had been rescued when the major at the base hadn't heard from the squadron in over an hour. She had been taken to the medical tent, then to the hospital in Germany before being moved to one in the States. She hadn't left for three months.

Now she was sitting on a bed paid for by someone who believed she was honorable, worth saving. Gwen knew the truth, and though she might pretend otherwise, her incompetence was like a bad stench that followed her around. She would do her best, but despite her determination, people would come to realize what she was and what she was not. Certainly Alaric already had.

4

"Today, we are going to be making one of the specials on The Rose menu," Alaric said, pacing before the students like a general preparing his troops.

Gwen didn't enjoy the comparison but, like any good soldier, kept her mouth quiet and her eyes gazing straight ahead. Her posture was straight, and her hands were folded behind her back.

"Gratinéed mussels."

There was excited murmuring from James and Sarah, who both had worked extensively with seafood in the past and knew how to prepare mussels. Gwen had, in her cooking experiments the last two weeks, attempted to work with them but hadn't gotten very far past the simple cleaning and broiling stage. Cleaning, though, she could do—or so she thought.

Alaric sent Allison into the storerooms and brought out buckets of the shelled creatures. They were obviously fresh and gave off a distinct smell of the ocean and the fish market. Alaric took the buckets and slammed them on the counter. "All right, the recipe for the dish is over there." He jerked his head toward a wall where various recipes had been hung. "Ingredients are in the fridge and storerooms. You have an hour to create a meal with the mussels as the main course. We have some of our kitchen staff coming to eat lunch here, and they will taste each meal and tell you which is the best. That person will have the honor of acting as sous chef tonight."

There was silence for a few moments as everyone took in the stakes and waited for Alaric's command.

He raised his eyebrows at them and said, as if he had been expecting them to act on their own, "Well, get to it!"

The kitchens became, suddenly, a flurry of action and noise, each person dashing off to the recipe board or the storerooms to grab other ingredients for the different portions of the dish. Gwen didn't bother with that, though she didn't know the specifics of the recipe or even what she was going to do. She walked over to the buckets, grabbed a clean bowl, and took a large handful of the mussels before moving to her workstation to begin cleaning them.

She had learned from experience—and the horrified look of one of her neighbors—that mussels needed to be properly cleaned and set to soak so they could disgorge the sand that was invariably trapped inside. Normally, in a kitchen, the mussels were already cleaned and prepped for the chefs, but she doubted Alaric wanted to make it any easier on them. So she stood with her hands under a faucet, using a scrub brush to diligently clean each mussel and putting it in a bowl of water while the other students rushed about, adding butter to saucepans, blending ingredients, and creating wonderful things. Time ticked on.

"Forty-five minutes left," Alaric said just as Gwen put her last mussel in its bowl. She took a deep breath and walked over to the recipe board, where she found the piece of paper that everyone had been staring at. She paused, considered, and blinked. That was *it?* Apart from cleaning the mussels, it was a fairly easy task.

"What are you doing?" Alaric hissed, coming up behind her. "Can't you even figure out a simple recipe?"

"I was thinking about what to do with the mussels," Gwen said flatly, knowing better than to rise to his bait. She was used to the harassment of her peers and her superiors. Alaric would not get the satisfaction of seeing her crack.

"So you can't even combine flavors properly? What sort of cook can't even get the right flavors together?" Alaric sneered, dropping his voice to a low murmur as Robert walked past. Gwen said nothing and moved away, going to the fridge and getting the ingredients she needed for the mussels as well as a shallot and onion plus a bottle of brown ale. Without looking at

Alaric as she returned to her workstation, Gwen began to cook with only forty minutes remaining on the clock.

Maybe it was her training under pressure or the fact that she was so new at this, but Gwen didn't bother to think about the clock; she simply cooked as best she could and trusted that things would sort themselves out. With twenty minutes remaining, she put the mussels—now shucked and prepared with butter, garlic, and bread crumbs—under the broiler and added a thickening agent to her soup. She strode across the kitchen and grabbed half a loaf of French bread, continuously watched by Alaric and occasionally the other students.

Most everyone was concerned with their own dishes, but a few—such as James—were quipping with a few of the others, trying to get them to mess up or break their concentration. Gwen, with her workstation as far away from the storerooms as possible, nearly completely isolated from her peers by Alaric's design, was able to ignore the talking and jeering.

The students she could ignore, but Alaric was getting increasingly on her nerves. He would walk by her station every few minutes, staring closely at what she was doing as she pulled the mussels out of the broiler and dumping the briny liquid, which remained in her soup along with some parsley. He seemed to have learned not to say anything, but he made it perfectly clear that Gwen wasn't working up to his standards and if she didn't improve, then he would have to take it up with someone else, namely Walter. The frowns and anger that Alaric seemed to radiate weren't helping either. Gwen, as she began plating, was starting to get frazzled.

Alaric let out a quiet bark of laughter as she put her first mussel onto the plate. It fell from her fingers onto the dinnerware with a clatter, the shell sliding about a bit. The mussel itself wasn't harmed, but Gwen had begun to shake, jumping between anger at the silent insinuations that Alaric was making and the fact that she knew, of all people, she was the one who was going to make the mistake.

What had she been thinking? What had Walter thought when he'd put her in this high-end cooking school? Did he think that she could make it, compete with people who had been cooking since they were little? She was a soldier, an army veteran, and good at little else but following soldiers into war zones so she could translate for the locals and their enemies and following orders. Even that had been taken from her due to her incompetence. People were *dead* because she hadn't been able to do one simple thing.

"Two minutes," Alaric called throughout the kitchen, waking Gwen up. She noticed that her hands were gripping the edge of the counter quite perilously —for her or the counter, she didn't know—and her plate had only one mussel on it. She finished doing her task and couldn't help but feel relieved when Alaric called time. Gwen let her shoulders fall from their typically straight and tight position and did her best not to look at the plate.

A moment later and she straightened her shoulders again and did her best to look as pleased as the other students as they came together to discuss what they had made. Alaric didn't let them pause long enough for much chatter, as the kitchen staff had arrived. Gwen followed the other students and stood in a line before the kitchen staff.

"What lovely food do you have for us today?" Danny asked, grinning at the slightly nervous students. "I'm starving."

"You had better be, to taste everything." Cecil snorted. The other staff laughed and grinned and only settled down when Alaric appeared, all of the students' dishes on a dessert tray, ready to eat.

"All right, no claiming your dish until the very end. In fact, to avoid prejudices completely, you all get to go back to the kitchen and clean up the mess you made. I want to see it sparkling by the time I've finished with this lot," Alaric snapped. Rather than argue, everyone headed back to the kitchens.

"Ugh," Jennifer said as they returned to the kitchens and saw the mess. "You know, Bennet isn't the easiest person to work with. He's criticized my methods far more times than I can count, and I've used them for years. It's making learning things very difficult. Not to mention that we have to do all the menial work around here."

"You signed up for this," James answered, his voice

taking on a sharp snap. "If you don't like it, you can leave."

Jennifer bristled at this but said nothing, choosing instead to exchange a look with the sympathetic Sarah and start on putting her used dishes in the dishwasher. Gwen started on her own work and was settling into the familiar rhythm of it when Allison joined her. The small blonde woman looked slightly uncomfortable, but her jaw was set, and there was no doubt in Gwen's mind that she had come over here for a purpose.

"How do you think the challenge went?" Allison asked. She started scrubbing the counters hard enough that her knuckles were turning white.

Gwen shrugged. "Well enough, I suppose. Mussels are sort of new to me. Not that I'm as good at this as you are, considering my career background."

"You're managing," Allison said shortly. Then she sighed. "In the army, you learned hand-to-hand combat, right?"

Gwen thought of the hours training with her squadron, the countless times that she had been thrown to the ground when sparring with some of the men until she could fight back. She had been taunted and harassed and made to feel as worthless as any woman in a "man's profession" could be. Until she'd learned to hold her own, that was. She still had the scars from some of her training sessions to prove her worth. "Yeah," she said. "I learned a fair amount."

"Do you think that you could teach me?" Allison

asked, blurting out the words as if she was afraid of holding them in.

"What? Why?" Gwen asked. She flinched at her own words and shook her head. The look that Allison threw to the men in the room was enough to tell its own story. "Yeah, I mean, most of the stuff I know is pretty advanced and specialized for, er, war. But I can definitely teach you some basic self-defense tactics."

"Really?" the small blonde woman said, looking into Gwen's eyes for the first time. \

Gwen nodded.

"Thank you! I mean, really, thanks. I know that you're probably super busy with the school and whatever else, but this means a lot."

"Sure," Gwen said. "We don't have a whole lot of time to work on this though. Except mornings and weekends, that is."

"Mornings and weekends are great," Allison said. She plunged her hands into a bucket of soapy water, emerging with a sponge, which she then proceeded to squeeze as if trying to kill it. "I want to learn as much as possible."

"Uh, all right, then," Gwen said. "How about Mondays, Wednesdays, Fridays at, say, seven? Then we can do a longer session on Saturdays."

"Seven? That's a bit early, don't you think?" Allison balked, suddenly appearing more nervous than angry. The realization of what she was doing seemed to have sunk in a bit.

"Well, classes start at noon, and I don't want to

devote only a little bit of time to this. We can do seven to nine and still have plenty of time to get ready for classes," Gwen said. "I mean, if that's all right. I don't want to...well, you can pick your schedule."

"No, that's good. I can do it. I need to do it." Allison nodded and started asking another question when Alaric returned. Allison scrubbed viciously at the counter, her cheeks reddening. The kitchen was pretty clean, but Gwen doubted it was anywhere near sparkling.

"Is this the best you can do?" Alaric growled. He looked around the kitchen and focused on Gwen and Allison, the only two obviously working close together enough to be having a conversation while working. "Do you think that this is a social club? Think that you can just talk instead of doing work?"

"It's my fault," Gwen said before Allison could even consider blushing further. "I was asking a question about the best use of white wine in cream sauces."

The head chef could find no fault with this answer—cream sauces was what he had been working on with Gwen the night before—and settled for an irascible mutter under his breath. "You can finish this later," he decided, pointedly ignoring the subtle grins that the students exchanged. "The 'judges' have decided," he said, curling his lip slightly.

For a moment, looking at the displeasure on his face, Gwen felt a rush of hope that maybe, just maybe, she had won. But that was quickly suppressed, and she followed everyone back out of the kitchens, as demure as before.

The kitchen staff all sat around, joking and talking with one another in a way that was missing dreadfully from the rapport among the students. With them, it was all about competition and winning the attention of Alaric rather than tackling the tasks in a friendly manner. Gwen missed the camaraderie of the army and knew that she wanted what the people on the staff had: secure senses of self and a lack of cruel competition.

"All right, all right, settle down," Jack said. Gwen blinked, not having noticed him before. He must have slipped in after they'd gone back to clean the kitchens. "We have some critiquing to do."

"We'll start with the mussels and risotto," Alaric said, indicating a dish that looked as though many people had tasted it but not eaten. So it went with each and every dish. Some, like the risotto, were too dependent on a citrus or savory flavor, not letting the mussels speak for themselves. Others relied solely on the mussels to make the meal. All were good, including Gwen's, and yet there could be only one winner.

"Who made the mussels with the stuffed bell peppers?" Cecil asked. James took a step forward, unabashedly smirking, though he had the decency to duck his head. "Well done" was all that was said, and that was that.

"You'll be working alongside Danny," Alaric said. He looked at all the dishes that sat on the table and was silent for a moment, as if considering something. Then he shook his head and looked up, drawing his brows together as he examined at the students. "I thought you had a job to do," he said. That was enough to have everyone scrambling back to the kitchens.

"We're never going to hear the end of this," Jennifer muttered to Robert and Gwen, eyeing James as he traipsed back to the kitchens, definitely sporting a bounce in his step. Gwen shook her head and shrugged. There was always one like James. He wasn't a bad person, but he definitely took a bit more stock in himself than others did. Her best friend, Damon, had been like that, cocky and sure of himself, but the most loyal companion that anyone could have wanted.

There was a pang of bone-crushing pain in the center of Gwen's chest, and she faltered for a moment, leaning against the doorframe into the kitchens.

Gone.

Her fault.

There was nothing she could do about that, but it still hurt like being shot. And right then, Gwen wished that she had been shot. Her breath wouldn't come, and she saw the destruction that she had caused rather than the kitchens. Her commanding officer, Damon, everything.

"Gwen?" Allison's voice broke the vision, and Gwen took a deep breath, fixing her gaze on the small woman as if taking to a lifeline. "Are you all right?"

"Yeah. Just tired," Gwen said. "I'm fine. Let's get this done."

Allison shrugged, nodded, then they got to work.

Jennifer's prediction had been right. For the rest of the day and evening, James moved around as though he had been awarded some high honor or been asked to shake hands with the president on national television. Bob, Tom, and Sarah took to calling him Your Exaltedness behind his back, and before long, it was a name that stuck, eventually being shortened to Yex. Even the kitchen staff picked it up, and James only started hearing it once it was shortened. He took to it immediately, causing some sniggers behind raised hands.

Gwen, for her part, did much better that night than she had since starting the classes a week ago. She was able to keep up with all the orders and only made a mistake when she handed someone sunflower oil instead of extra virgin olive oil. She was beginning to think that things were going to work out all right, that maybe she wasn't as hopeless at this as she had thought—and as Alaric had made her believe.

When the time came for her private class with Alaric, though, the good evening seemed to vanish. Before he even spoke, she could tell that he wasn't happy with her. Had it been her mussels? The critique had made it seem as though people enjoyed the soup, though it was a bit rich, and her actual filling had done well. But Alaric hadn't said anything, and from the way that he was glaring at her, she didn't think the chances were great that he would be giving her any compliments.

"Are you going to keep trying to incinerate me or are we going to start working?" Gwen asked after two awkward minutes of standing at a workstation, trying to think of something she could do without Alaric's direction. Everything was clean, and she didn't think they would be working on cream sauces again, so she went with mild insubordination.

"What?" Alaric hissed, narrowing his eyes.

"Now, hold it." The third voice made both Gwen and Alaric jump, though Gwen came out in a fighting position and Alaric simply clenched his fists. Jack had walked back into the restaurant, obviously having forgotten something, and was now looking between the two as though they were dangerous beasts. "Alaric, you can't go treating people like this."

"I don't know what you're talking about," Alaric said, shooting a warning glance at Gwen. She held her tongue, knowing what would happen if she spoke out against her "boss" with his.

"I came to get my jacket, and I see you about to go on a tirade," Jack said, crossing so that he stood directly in front of Alaric. "And don't you dare deny it because I know exactly what you on a tirade looks like. You are going to chew her out because she's not your ideal student and because I 'forced' her on you. But you know perfectly well that, if not for your outspoken jibes this afternoon, her dish would have fared better with your staff than those overseasoned peppers. You don't think that someone who hasn't trained for years can do this, and you want to prove it."

"Jack, I'm just trying to figure out what to work on tonight," Alaric said, frowning. "You're reading far too much into the situation."

"Am I?" Jack asked. He rounded on Gwen. "Has he been harassing you about not belonging in his kitchen?"

Yes. "No, sir," Gwen said, replying as would a soldier. It was an age-old tradition, just like saying "I fell" after getting into a fight. Her battles would be fought by her and her alone, if there was even a battle to be fought. As far as Gwen was concerned, Alaric was justified in voicing his opinions about her. She wasn't even sure she belonged at The Rose. After all, little more than three weeks ago, she had been wandering the streets.

"Are you lying to me?" Jack asked. It wasn't a question but a statement of fact, and Alaric knew it. The manager's eyebrows were raised in surprise and confusion, and Jack looked between Alaric and Gwen, trying to understand. Alaric's jaw ticked, and he stared hard at the wall beyond Jack's shoulder, just as confused as to Gwen's answer.

She had every right to complain against him, considering all that he had done. And, granted, he had been in the wrong on some of that. Her mussels certainly had come out very well, especially in comparison to some of the other dishes. And there was no doubt that she worked hard, meticulously pursuing a task until it was perfected. There was even a sort of flair for the work that was getting harder and harder to deny. But that didn't mean that Alaric wanted her in his kitchens.

He didn't like being told what to do and who to hire, even by wealthy philanthropists to whom he owed a favor. He wanted her out and not completely for the reasons he was giving her. The other students were beginning to admire this former soldier, looking to see what sort of life this woman was creating. She was certainly gathering enough attention from Danny and Cecil, not to mention the joking statements from her peers. Even Jack was on her side. There was nothing that could give Alaric any reason for disliking this, but he did. He didn't like how much attention she was getting, and he didn't like that his thoughts revolved around her whenever he was in the kitchens, teaching. He noticed that he had gone out of his way, twice, to explain a concept that all the other students knew so that she could understand. Alaric especially didn't like that he was beginning to enjoy her company.

Jack looked once more at Gwen, as if he could force an answer out of her, then shook his head and let out a deep breath. "All right, fine. I won't press the issue. But Alaric, remember what we said about an outlet? This doesn't count."

"Wh—" Alaric started, then remembered. He tightened his jaw and jerked his head in understanding at

Jack. He thought that Alaric was taking his anger out on Gwen instead of getting into boxing or counseling or whatever it was that he was supposed to be doing. The very thought was insulting.

"Good night," Jack said before going to his office and returning a moment later with his jacket. "Oh, and Gwen, you might want to call Walter. His assistant has been bothering me about wanting a status update."

"Yes, sir," Gwen said, again acting the soldier.

Jack paused and answered her with a soft smile, "It wasn't an order, Lieutenant."

"Right," Gwen muttered. Then Jack was gone. Alaric sighed and pressed the bridge of his nose between his thumb and forefinger.

"I should—he's right," Alaric said. "I have been giving you a hard time."

"I've had worse," Gwen answered solemnly, causing Alaric to look at her and meet her gaze. She had the look of pain in her eyes that he had seen on people who had just lost a friend. He blinked, and the look was gone.

"Still, you haven't been as dreadful as I've made it seem. Frankly, in a week or so, you'll be on par with most of the others. Your mussels were...very good," Alaric said.

"Thank you," Gwen said. She said nothing further, her eyes trained on the counter before her. She didn't look to be shy about taking a compliment, so Alaric had to assume that he was the one making her uncomfortable. Maybe she didn't like him. Maybe she was feeling pleased with herself at his grudging acknowl-edgment. He scowled.

"That doesn't mean you're going to be able to stop working," Alaric growled, a stiffness in his shoulders.

She nodded. "What should we—" she started, stopping at the sound of a very shrill and terrified scream.

"What was that?" Alaric asked, turning around as though he could find the source of the noise in his kitchens. Gwen didn't bother looking, just turned swiftly and ran to the door as if her life—or someone else's—depended on it. Alaric ran after her. She shoved open the door to the loading dock and went through, scanning the area first.

What Alaric saw sickened him. Allison was standing with her back against the loading dock, wrapped in her jacket, her hands shaking and her keys jingling as she shook. She, like Jack, had returned to pick up something she had forgotten and, unlike Jack, had run into trouble with some of the local thugs. They were people who preyed on the rich who got caught on their own, and they were the more vicious among those who wandered the streets.

There were two of them, one holding a knife, the other crooning to Allison. Gwen didn't seem to hesitate, didn't even seem to register that Alaric had come through the door as well or that neither of the attackers had noticed her. She simply acted, jumping off the dock and landing before Allison in a slight crouch.

Alaric felt his heart beat loudly in his ears.

Gwen held up her hands to fight as the two men looked at each other, leered, and continued forward. "Stop," Gwen snarled, the sound similar to the one that Alaric often made but much more dangerous and vicious, much more uncontrolled.

"I don't think so," the man with the knife said.

5

Gwen could hear Allison whimpering softly behind her, and she was fully aware that Alaric was watching everything, completely frozen. The two thugs advanced, hoping for an easy score despite the fact that they were now outnumbered.

"Stop," Gwen said again, sliding slightly deeper into her fighting stance just in case things turned violent.

"Why should we do that?" the man with the knife asked with a sneer. His friend held out his hands as if he was a magician on a stage, only this stage was far more dangerous than they knew.

"Because if you don't, then my friend will call the police, if he hasn't already. Because we have your faces on the security cameras pointing at this very spot and because I have friends in very high places," Gwen said. If that hadn't woken Alaric up and forced him into action, then she didn't know what would—perhaps a full-out brawl would get his attention. Though if she could avoid fighting, she would.

The two men exchanged glances, probably deciding whether it was worth the risk. They obviously weren't dealing with an easy target. This one was willing to fight back and could keep her head under pressure. The likelihood of them walking out of this one was growing smaller every second they hesitated. Finally, after exchanging some sort of silent communication, they turned tail and fled.

Gwen held her stance for another thirty seconds, then relaxed and turned to Allison. The woman was still staring, wide-eyed, at the spot where the men had been. She was shaking and looked as though she would burst into tears at any moment. Her breath was ragged and hiccuping sobs were beginning.

"Allison," Gwen said cautiously, holding out her hands in a peaceful gesture. "Allison, it's okay, they're gone. They're gone, and they won't come back. It's okay, you're safe."

Allison flicked her eyes to Gwen's, a good sign given the circumstances, and Gwen stepped closer, wrapping her arms around the woman in a protective, comforting hug. Shooting a look at Alaric over Allison's shoulder—she was now crying openly in Gwen's arms, her fingers clutching at Gwen's shirt in desperation—Gwen mouthed "kitchens." He nodded.

"Come on, Allison, we're going inside," Gwen said, turning Allison gently in the direction of the ramp that would lead them up the loading docks and into the back door. She didn't do anything as her brown hair started to come undone and as her arm began to throb in Allison's grip. All she did was make sure that the terrified woman knew that she was safe, among friends. Alaric ran his fingers through his own mussed hair and followed the two inside.

As soon as Allison was given a stool and a glass of amber brandy, she lost her control. The sobs became body-shaking shudders of terror, and tears streamed openly down her face. Alaric looked at Gwen in deferential desperation, seeming completely at a loss as to what to do. The brown-haired veteran, for her part, simply let Allison cry on her shoulder, eyes staring straight ahead as she patted the blonde woman's hair. She was seeing something else entirely, looking at a completely different pain.

"Th-thanks f-for this," Allison spluttered after a good ten minutes. She wiped her eyes with a shaking hand and refused to look up. "I d-don't know wh-wh-what would have happened if y-you hadn't c-come."

"You don't need to think about that now," Gwen said. "You need to focus on the fact that it's over. It won't happen again. You're safe." These words came from her mouth as though she was simply repeating something someone had told her as she tried to make sense of things again. Gwen caught Alaric's eye and saw a questioning look there, one she had seen many times before. He was wondering what had happened to her, why she had left military life. Gwen knew that she didn't look as though she had been detrimentally wounded, and she didn't display any overt signs of suffering from PTSD. But there was a tinge to her relationships with others that reeked of secrets and shadows. Somehow, they all started to look at her like Alaric did.

Gwen looked away.

"Are you all right to go home?" Alaric asked after another few minutes of silence. Allison lifted her head and looked at Gwen with horror in her eyes, like a young child told she must leave her parents. Gwen glared at Alaric, who at least had the tact to wince. She handed another tissue to Allison and ignored the irascible head chef.

"You can come with me," Gwen said. "I just live across the way. I have a spare camp bed and everything."

"Really?" Allison asked quietly, rubbing her eyes once again with the corner of her sleeve. Gwen nodded and rose before putting on her jacket and linking her arm through Allison's.

Gwen hesitated a moment. "Unless we need to..." She looked at Alaric, an unspoken plea in her eyes.

He shrugged. "Go on. We'll keep working tomorrow," he said and picked up Allison's untouched glass of brandy. Gwen nodded and left, just like that. No goodbye, no acknowledgment, just a nod and she was gone.

Gwen led Allison to her apartment in the building across from the back of the restaurant. She half supported the still-trembling woman up the stairs and had to fumble for her keys to let the pair into the apartment. Allison relaxed visibly once the door was closed and looked around, no doubt desperately clinging to her surroundings in an effort to escape her trauma. What she found obviously confused her.

The flat was furnished in very simplistic styles, but everything was wood and of high quality. It was stylish, perfectly organized, and clean and did not suit Gwen at all. Just one look made it perfectly clear that this furniture had been bought for the retired lieutenant by someone else. That did not change the fact that everything was clean to the point of sterilization. There were no personal touches but for a few framed photographs of desert landscapes on the walls. It was, understandably, militaristic.

"Come on," Gwen said, moving toward the kitchen. "We'll make you a cup of tea." Allison followed along and looked relieved when she saw that the kitchen, at least, was obviously used and well cared for, though it was as clean as everything else. There were pans hanging from hooks on the wall, tools in ceramic jars along the backsplash, a spinning rack of spices, and a knife block that was top of the line and well used.

Gwen put the kettle on to boil and got out a pot and the appropriate tea leaves. The simple, essential act seemed to push the last of Allison's tremors away, and she sat on a stool, watching her host with the sort of weariness that comes after a great shock. Gwen calmed down as well with the act of making tea. She pulled her hair out of its tight regulation style, shrugged out of her jacket—which she promptly hung up—and rolled up her sleeves.

"Why didn't you beat them?" Allison asked once Gwen handed her a cup of tea.

"What?" Gwen said, surprised. "Those idiots in the alley? They went away and aren't going to come back. Isn't that enough?"

"No," Allison answered with surprising vehemence. "No, I wanted them to lie there, hurting, on the ground, for what they did."

Gwen didn't answer immediately but stared into the depths of her cup of tea. "I used to think like that too. Wanting to cause pain for every wrong done to me, two- even threefold. But that's not justice, that's revenge. And revenge is what causes wars. Wanting to cause hurt because you were hurt is natural, but it is also wrong. You have to understand this."

"But you would have hurt them if they attacked you?" Allison asked, looking up at Gwen with a pitiful, desperate need in her gaze.

"Yes. That is self-defense, not attacking them simply because I could have. You're going to need to learn this if I'm going to teach you," Gwen said. She drained her cup of tea like it was something much stronger and put the cup delicately in the sink. "Now come on, let's get you to bed."

"You could have hurt them really badly, right? If they'd attacked you?" Allison asked, repeating her question and emphasizing her need to get revenge in some way, if only in her mind. Gwen kept silent for a moment, thinking that she knew too many soldiers who had been just like Allison. They were often separated so they couldn't cause too much trouble, but there was a lot of that sort of thought in the military. The hardest part was that they were often good men, fiercely loyal and completely dependable.

"Not now, Allison," Gwen said stiffly, remembering her squad mates' faces as they lay on the ground, dead. "You can sleep in my room. I'll sleep on the couch. Don't argue; just do as your told."

"All right," Allison answered, lowering her head and rubbing the back of her neck. She followed Gwen to the bedroom, which was decorated just as the rest of the flat, only a single picture of the desert showing anything about the woman who lived there. Gwen gave Allison a pair of pajamas and the necessary toiletries and then went to make up her bed.

She slept easier on the couch than she did in her bed, the stiffness of the cushions remnant of the ground that she had slept on for so long, after her return from the Middle East and during her time in the desert. The night terrors that haunted her weren't about the night that had ruined everything but the time afterward, when all she could hear was the major who had rescued her saying over and over again, "It will be okay." She heard it, and superimposed over the major's concerned features were those of her commanding officer, looking at her with pain and a single line of blood trickling out of the corner of his mouth.

When Gwen woke, it wasn't because the dreams were so terrible—nothing was as terrible as real life—but because there was a noise. She rose from the couch, grabbed the knife she always kept nearby, and listened. A moment later, she put the knife away and walked to her bedroom where Allison was lying in her bed, the covers wrapped around her form as she sobbed. Gwen sat gently on the edge of the bed, and without prompting, Allison allowed Gwen to hug her.

Then, because there was nothing else to say, Gwen murmured, "It will be okay."

She sat with Allison for another hour, quietly murmuring and slowly slipping away when the woman fell back asleep, her hiccuping subsided. By this time, it was nearing four in the morning, and Gwen knew that she would not be able to fall asleep again. She was fully aware of what waited for her if she closed her eyes, and the shame of having to hear the major repeat the words she had just spoken to Allison would tear her apart. She couldn't deal with what had happened before that either. The other combat situations in which Gwen had participated—even as an interpreter, these situations were inevitable—were also clamoring to speak out, tired of being shut up behind That Night.

Gwen disentangled her fingers from her hair when she realized that she was about to do serious damage to it. She looked at the sleeping form of

Allison—now deeply breathing, not likely to wake anytime soon—and made up her mind. It was time to start running again. Before joining the army, Gwen had hated running. It was only after being forced to do mile upon mile of the terrible exercise that she'd begun to appreciate the rhythmic movement of her feet, her mind concentrating on not slipping and where to put her foot next. She could think, if she wanted to, but more often than not, it was a way to let her mind go.

She tied her hair back into its regulation style, put on her running clothes, and laced up her trainers. Then, without another pause, she was gone. As soon as she hit the pavement outside of her building, she began running. Her feet ate up the ground in an uneven stride, but the familiar sensation returned. She relaxed and let her thoughts go away until she was just Gwen, free and easy.

Alaric groaned as he rolled over in his queen-size bed to reach the incessantly ringing phone. He hated that thing and only kept it in case someone needed to call him during his day off to let him know that something had gone wrong at The Rose. He did *not* keep it so that people could call him at six in the morning. Who got up at six in the morning anyway?

Without bothering to check the number, he answered, his voice gravelly from sleep, "Mmm, 'llo?"

"Alaric?" the person on the other line said, sounding familiar.

He squeezed his eyes shut and buried his face in his pillow for a moment before lifting it up and putting the phone back to his ear.

"Allison?" he growled through a yawn. "What's going on?" Alaric figured that demanding to know why she was calling wasn't the best plan, especially not after what had happened last night. And he had given all the students his number in case something came up and they needed to call. He just really didn't want to be a sounding board for a woman who was feeling vulnerable, a big part of why he didn't currently have a girlfriend.

"Um... I don't mean to bother you so early," Allison started.

Too late.

"But, er, I went over to Gwen's last night, like she said, and uh, when I woke up this morning, she was gone. I looked everywhere, but she didn't leave a note, and I don't think she took a cell phone with her, and... it's been an hour."

"Right," Alaric said, his mind finally starting to work despite the late hour. "I think I might know someone who might know where she is. I'll find her."

"Thanks. Sorry for waking you up," Allison said. Alaric replied with a monosyllabic grunt and hung up before flopping over onto his back so that he could sit up properly. He rubbed his eyes with the heels of his palms and took a deep breath, grumbling inwardly at the way the cold air ran over his bare skin. He knew that he should call Walter Smythe, should be more worried about the fact that Gwen was not at her apartment, but there was something holding him back.

It was as if there was someone whispering quietly in his ear, telling him that as soon as he started to worry about Gwen's well-being and about the fact that she was gone so early in the morning, he would start to care about her. Care *for* her. Already he had been forced by his conscience to admit to being hard on her. He had already conceded to the fact that she wasn't a terrible cook and that she could even be a decent one. He had begun to think about her as one of his students, as someone he was proud to teach and mentor. What he couldn't do was let things get further than that.

Sighing, Alaric fingered his phone and remembered the promise that he had made to Allison. He would find Gwen in an uninvolved manner, but he would find her. Alaric dialed the phone.

Unsurprisingly, Walter wasn't awake at 6:15 in the morning, but his office manager—a man whom Alaric actively disliked—was awake. The moment that Alaric mentioned Gwen was missing, though it had only been an hour, and that one of the other students was worried, Graham became more than business-like and started organizing a rather extensive search.

"There are a couple of places she could be that I know of. One is the street where Mr. Smythe ran into her the first time, but I don't think she'd be there because she had abandoned it by the time we found her at the intersection near the—"

"Whoa, whoa, slow down," Alaric said, running his fingers through his hair and wishing desperately for coffee. "What do you mean she had abandoned it?"

"I mean that she wasn't living there anymore. We found her about twenty minutes away, at an intersection near an overpass. I'll check there. I honestly don't know where else she would go, but you can check the street near the soup kitchen," Graham said. He rattled off an address that Alaric noted, his mind shocked, then the office manager hung up, leaving Alaric holding the phone to his ear.

Living there? Alaric couldn't wrap his mind around the concept. Gwen had been living there? As in on the streets? As in homeless? He knew that Walter liked to do charity work, but he'd figured that Gwen was just his latest project that he'd picked up from a veterans' center or through a friend or something. Not that he had actually picked her up off the street. Somehow, that made her all the braver and more capable to Alaric.

Gwen wasn't just some deadbeat trying out cooking. Cooking was her only chance at making a new life for herself. She had risked everything—though she might not have had much—to pick herself up off the streets and become something else. She was rebuilding and working her ass off to do it. If that wasn't admirable, Alaric didn't know what was. It made his heckling and yelling seem so petty.

Shivering, Alaric came to his senses and wrote down the address that Graham had given him before it was completely forgotten. He dressed in a pair of jeans and a dark sweatshirt and grabbed his car keys. It was time to go hunting.

The soup kitchen was nearly the whole way across town, and Alaric doubted very much that he was going to find Gwen there. Why would she go back to that place when she was rebuilding and recreating her life? If he were her, he would go somewhere different, somewhere new. Before Alaric had even driven a mile in his car, he turned around and headed in a different direction.

The truth was that he didn't know enough about Gwen to try and figure out where she would go. Without the compass of the soup kitchen, he had absolutely no idea where she could be. He only knew that so early in the morning, there were few people awake and that if she had wanted to seek out company at all, she would go to one of the farmers markets, maybe near her apartment or The Rose. Did she want company? He couldn't say, but it was a start.

Alaric knew of several farmers markets that were close to The Wooden Rose, but there were two near Central Park that were the best. He picked his favorite and drove there, hoping beyond hope that his instincts were right. The Morningside Park market was a beautiful thing, especially for someone who appreciated food and the quality of ingredients. Farmers and sellers from many places came and set up their booths, selling fresh produce, interesting breads, local jams, wines, and more. Alaric had been there many times to pick out just the right tomatoes or get freshly baked bread when he wanted to make a meal for himself or for someone else. He knew that The Wooden Rose had people who came and picked out the ingredients each morning, and he wouldn't have been surprised to see them there.

"Bennet!" a haggard voice called, making Alaric look up. Waving at him from his perch on top of a crate was a man who looked ancient enough to be anyone's grandfather but with weathered skin and a twinkling eye that said he knew his strength. He was Alaric's favorite farmer because he always dealt fairly and had good carrots.

"Morning, Joe," Alaric said.

"I got some great peppers, just in," Joe said, jabbing a finger at a collection of beautiful plants. Alaric was tempted but remembered why he was there.

"Actually, I'm not looking for produce today. I was wondering if you'd seen someone. A woman, a few inches shorter than me, brown hair, looks like she could beat the stuffing out of you if she had the inclination," Alaric said. He described Gwen without thinking and winced at the way his words sounded, no matter how true they were.

"What, you mean Gwen?" Joe asked, raising his bushy white eyebrows and jerking a thumb over to the point where the market dwindled into the park. Sitting there, her back to the world, staring out over the green space, was Gwen. Alaric was more than surprised to find her there. He hadn't known if she would seek out people or even head in the direction of the park—it was more than a few blocks from The Rose—and there she was.

Seeing Alaric's surprise, Joe shrugged. "She's been down here a few times before, tried to get work for one of the farms. Was fair good at it, too, but for the nightmares and flashbacks. She had to stop when she nearly fell off a delivery truck after a bad one. A shame too. She didn't even make it two weeks on the job."

"Nightmares," Alaric said. He didn't know Gwen had nightmares. Though he doubted she would tell him, of all people, if she did. Even so, maybe the nightmares had gone away. Maybe she had gotten everything sorted out. "Thanks, Joe." Alaric jogged over to where Gwen was, and before he could convince himself otherwise, sat down next to her.

Gwen jumped slightly as he did so, then watched him calmly. "What are you doing here?" she asked, looking confused but not annoyed. It was clear she was simply curious as to why he was there; she had no idea that Graham was going to turn over the city looking for her, that Allison was worried about her. Alaric realized that she didn't even consider that people would care about her enough to do something when she went missing. For that, he pitied her.

"Allison called," he said, knowing how easy it would have been to simply say he had been at the market. "I called Graham, and the pair of us went out looking for you."

"Oh," Gwen said, looking out at the park again. In the early-morning light, the slight wisps of hair that had escaped her bun were illuminated like a halo. She shrugged. "I suppose I should have left a note. I went on a run and found myself here."

"You went on a run," Alaric said, frowning.

Gwen nodded. "I used to run all the time, in the army, in Beirut, after the—" She stopped and shook her head, her lips pressed tightly together.

Alaric remembered the nightmares Joe had mentioned. Could this unmentioned thing be the cause? He didn't know and didn't care to press.

"I was feeling restless, so I started running again. I stopped here to watch the sunrise."

"How early did you get up?" Alaric asked in disbelief. Sunrise was still latish in the morning, spring having only just barely started, but still. To have run from The Rose to Central Park and still have time to watch the sunrise?

"Four, I think," Gwen said simply. "How did you find me here?"

"The farmers market is the only place in the city that I know of that's awake this early in the morning. I figured that if you were looking for company or people or whatever, you might end up here. This was my only idea though," Alaric said. "That reminds me, I'd better let Graham know that you're okay. He seemed pretty worried."

"He doesn't want to lose Walter's new pet project," Gwen said without malice. She knew what she was to Walter and didn't resent him for it. That was quite the feat. Alaric texted Graham and put his phone in his pocket. He didn't know what else to say to her, didn't know how to have a conversation with her. Gwen was his student and, up until that point, had been one he didn't particularly like. But even the few things that he had learned—that she had been living on the streets, that she was plagued by a fierce streak of independence that left her without friends, that she had a past she didn't talk about—colored his view of her. Still, he wasn't sure if that was a good thing.

"Have you had breakfast yet?" Alaric asked. "I know this great place a couple of blocks from here that opens early for all the commuters. They serve a pretty decent cup of coffee too."

Gwen said nothing for a moment, then in a swift movement that was graceful and capable, rose from her spot on the wall and nodded. "Sounds good."

6

The little place was just a small coffee shop that served breakfast from sunup to noon. It was charming, with mismatched furniture and quiet, simple music playing in the background. You ordered by flagging down the only waitress in the place, a cheerful, beautiful woman of dark skin with a smile that flashed constantly. She would take the order to the single chef, her grinning jokester of a husband, and then she would bring you whatever it was that you had ordered.

"What'll you have?" Alaric asked, looking around to see what the other clientele were having, as there were no menus. "I don't think there's anything fancy, but it's nice."

"Just some toast and a fried egg, maybe," Gwen said, rubbing her hand over the simple wooden table as if appreciating the craftsmanship.

"You need to eat more than that," Alaric growled.

"You just ran from The Rose on no breakfast, and I'm pretty sure that you could use a bit more weight on you. Especially after—" He broke off, not wanting to mention that he knew about her previous living situation. "Just get pancakes or something."

"All right," Gwen said, rolling her eyes. Alaric knew that look; it was one that he saw on all his students when they judged his mood. They all knew better than to argue with him when he was feeling like this, and Gwen was no exception. After all, she had seen him in many moods during the nights in the kitchen, and by now, all of the students lived and worked by the Bennet-o-meter.

When they waved down the waitress, Alaric ordered a full breakfast, and Gwen ordered, "Pancakes or something, please."

She received a glittering smile from the waitress and a muttered "smart-ass" from Alaric.

They waited in silence until tea was brought, and then Alaric forced himself to talk. "You know, I really am sorry that I've been giving you a hard time—"

"I wish you would stop apologizing," Gwen said, a hint of frustration in her tone. "I've had to earn my way before. It's nothing new."

"So what, you think I'm groveling, trying to get into your good favor or something so you'll give a good report to Walter? I'm apologizing because I'm sincerely sorry," Alaric grumbled, feeling his own temper rising.

Gwen curled her lip slightly but said nothing, instead looking darkly at her tea. "So why did you want to be a chef?" Gwen asked, apparently choosing to change the subject rather than continue to press and get them both into another argument. Alaric saw her shift in her seat, her expression an inch away from angry. He swallowed a mouthful of hot coffee and tried to force his overprotective instincts down. They weren't helping.

"Honestly? Because my dad wanted me to be a lawyer." Alaric shrugged and watched Gwen carefully, trying to judge her reaction. When she didn't flinch, he continued, "My dad is the latest in a long line of lawyers, some of which were working for very powerful people. It was sort of assumed that I would continue in the family business. I would be successful and rich and have whatever the heck I wanted. Except for a life."

"So you, what, worked in a kitchen during your rebellious teenage years and decided that you would be a chef?" Gwen asked. Her voice was teasing, but the intent seemed sincere. She really wanted to know.

"No. I spent time with my mother while my dad was at work. She was a wizard in the kitchen, taught me all that I knew. I was much closer to her than to my dad, and I figured that I would much rather follow in her footsteps than his. Of course, I did work in many kitchens during my 'rebellious teenage years.' You can imagine how thrilled my dad was when I told him I wanted to go to cooking school. He nearly took my head off," Alaric said.

Gwen nodded, a slight smile of understanding

flickering over her lips before it disappeared. "Parents tend to do that," she said.

"Well, I did it anyway, paying my own way through school, since he certainly wouldn't do it. Then I decided to prove to him that I could be just as successful working as a chef as a lawyer. I got world-class status and went to show him, but he didn't care. I still deviated, and that couldn't be reconciled," Alaric said. He stopped, not wanting to talk about what happened later, about the shouting match and exchanged blows that had occurred, about the horrified look on his mother's face when she'd gotten back-handed by his father for getting involved, about how he had been effectively disowned and walked out with burning resentment in his heart. He had only exchanged a few tense phone calls with his father since, and that was still a sore spot that he avoided with desperation. Yet he had told Gwen much more than he had told anyone else, including Jack. Perhaps it was the quiet way that she listened or the pene-trating stare of hers, or maybe he just knew that she wouldn't pity him because she had dealt with worse.

"The family business is always fun," Gwen said, shaking her head gently. Alaric sipped his tea and raised his eyebrows in question. She tucked a flyaway strand of hair behind her ears and shrugged. "My dad was a deadbeat. He walked out on my mom, my younger brother, and me when I was seven. We moved in with my uncle, my mother's brother, and he raised both me and my brother. I adored him. He ran a used and rare bookshop and often went out hunting for books, bargaining with people until they gave in. I often went with him to get away from my brother—he was reaching the pesky age that siblings get—and I didn't learn until later that I was being groomed to take over."

"If you adored him, why give up the job and join the army?" Alaric asked. There was a slight pause in the conversation as the breakfasts were brought with a smile from the waitress. Gwen didn't answer immediately but poured some syrup on her pancakes and speared one with her fork and knife. She ate a bite and chewed as if it was the most wonderful thing she had tasted. Alaric snorted quietly as he spread his beans over his toast. The food was good, but it wasn't *that* good.

Actually, now that he thought about it, Gwen ate all of her food like that, savoring each bite and eating all of it. Everything she made and was allowed to eat for lunch or dinner or whatever, even the things that didn't turn out as well, she savored.

"I got stupid," Gwen said, shrugging. "I was sixteen, and I started looking for my dad. There's nothing quite like the stubborn curiosity of a teenage girl. It took a whole lot of interviews with his old associates and a lot of phone calls that led nowhere, but I found him. It took a year and a half, but I found him. He was staying at a sort of common living center for veterans. He was in bad shape—drunk, struggling with life—but he had all these people surrounding him who would have supported him through fire and hell. They had, in fact. I wanted that."

"But your uncle didn't like it," Alaric said, watching with a new fascination as Gwen nodded and picked up another bite of pancake.

"He wasn't thrilled with me for going to find my dad, but my mother was devastated. It took my brother yelling at me and calling me an insufferable, selfish bitch that really drove it home. I accused him and the rest of them of trying to make me something that I wasn't. It wasn't pretty, and eventually, we all stormed away with serious breaches in trust. I figured that if I couldn't trust the people I had lived with for years, then who could I trust? I remembered my dad, and so I joined the army. Turns out I have an aptitude for languages, so they sent me to war."

"Just like that?"

"Just like that," Gwen said. She finished her first pancake before speaking again, this time with a note of sadness in her voice. "I did reconcile with my family after my first tour, but things were never quite the same. I had what my dad had. Friends that stood by me through hell, who I trusted with more than my life. I had all of that but no real relationship with my family. I haven't talked with them since—"

"Since?" Alaric asked, disregarding the slight tremor in her voice as she broke off, occupied as he was with cutting some of his sausage into manageable pieces. He looked up to see her focusing on her own breakfast. It must have just been a trick of his mind.

"It's just been a while," Gwen said, her voice flat and dark, signifying that the conversation was at an end. Alaric nodded in what he supposed was understanding, though he couldn't really understand any of what Gwen was going through. He was about to say something when his phone rang, the sound slicing through the tension and giving both a suitable distraction.

Alaric snarled in annoyance at the device and pulled it out, glowering at the number and excusing himself in a huff. He went outside and talked on the phone for a couple of minutes before returning, tossing the phone roughly to the table and slumping down into his seat. Gwen ate her pancake in silence but had an obvious look of question on her face.

"Your watchdog wants you to check in," he said, curling his lip in distaste.

"My watchdog?" Gwen asked.

"Graham," Alaric explained.

Gwen sighed and put her fork and knife onto her plate. For the first time that morning, she looked as though she had run many miles on little sleep. "He's not my watchdog, and he needs to figure that out," Gwen said. "He's called a few times in the past week, just wanting to check in, to chat and see what's going on so that he can tell Walter. He's nice, but it's getting on my nerves a bit."

"You should probably call him. He did put together an effort to nearly tear the city apart this morning," Alaric said.

Gwen nodded. "Can I borrow your phone?"

Alaric handed over the device, and Gwen fumbled with it for a few moments, obviously unused to the new technology. Eventually, she figured it out and managed to dial Graham's number. She rose and, following Alaric's example, walked out of the restaurant to pace around while she talked to Walter's office manager.

Alaric did his best to finish his breakfast, but he couldn't focus on the food before him, no matter that it was good. All he could do was watch as Gwen paced back and forth, then paused, sat on the bench outside the restaurant, stood again, and paced once more. Her conversation ran over ten minutes, and Alaric was beginning to wonder what she could possibly be talking about. He watched as a flash of surprise flickered over her features and then growled to himself and resolutely forced himself to think about his meal.

Why did he care so much? It wasn't as though they were friends and she would tell him what was going on. Sure, they had shared their respective stories about their childhoods and learned more about each other through that conversation, but that meant nothing. Alaric was certain that he was nothing more to Gwen than a teacher, and she shouldn't be more to him than a student. He had been wrong about her cooking and about her character, and now that he knew he'd been wrong, he was suffering for it.

He couldn't help but attribute her skill to her determination and bravery in starting a new life. He noticed the little things that she was wont to do—like eating as though she hadn't eaten for a while—and put such meaning behind it. Alaric gave up on eating when he realized what his problem was.

He liked her.

He found her intriguing and interesting, and there wasn't any doubt in his mind that he found her attractive. But this was different for him. All of his previous girlfriends had been so flat and dull, though they had seemed mysterious at first. They were no amateurs in the art of seduction, and it was because of his last girlfriend that he lived where he did.

Gwen was different. She didn't ask of anything from him, though she accepted his help when offered. She didn't try to seduce him; Alaric doubted that she was even interested. She was just...Gwen. An enigma, a fascinating woman with an iron core. She seemed content within herself and yet willing to put effort into changing, and—

Alaric straightened as Gwen returned, looking annoyed.

"Everything all right?" Alaric asked, pushing the thoughts he had just been having from his mind.

"He's...I don't know. He just wanted to know where I'd been and whether things were all right. It was all very routine, and I'm sure he's not a bad person, he just, ugh," Gwen said, waving her hands vaguely. She handed Alaric back his phone and didn't make any move when their fingers brushed. Alaric was certain that he had been the only one who felt a shiver. "I don't know why I don't like him all that much."

"If it's any consolation, I find him to be an annoying bastard," Alaric said. Gwen looked at Alaric pitifully for a moment, her eyebrows drawn together in a confused, questing expression. Then she smiled. It was a full smile, open and joyful, with a breathy burst of laughter attached to it. Alaric shook his head, his dark-blond hair falling over his eyes. He brushed it back and realized that he didn't really care why Gwen was so interesting to him. It was enough to accept that she was. So he laughed with her.

Gwen shook her head and covered her mouth before leaning back in her chair and smiling at her plate of food. "I shouldn't laugh," she said behind the smile. "He's not a bad guy."

"Most days," Alaric said. He signaled the waitress for the bill, and Gwen took the moment to relax into her chair. She sat in silence while Alaric paid, and then the two finished off their tea and went out to find Alaric's car.

"Thanks for breakfast," Gwen said. "It was nice."

"I told you pancakes were good," Alaric said.

Gwen snorted good-naturedly and climbed gracefully into the passenger seat. Inside the car, the sounds were muffled, and the silence that hung between the two was obvious. Gwen didn't seem to mind much, but Alaric kept shifting uncomfortably, feeling Gwen's silence as oppressive.

"I... I don't mean to be...well, an asshole, but how

did you go from the army to…" Alaric trailed off, suddenly ashamed of what he was trying to ask.

"To the streets?" Gwen asked. She didn't seem surprised by the question.

"I didn't find out until this morning. A, ah, friend at the farmers market told me, and I won't ask if it makes you uncomfortable," Alaric said. He couldn't bring himself to tell her that Graham had been the one to let the information slip. He tightened his hands on the steering wheel of his car and stared fixedly at the traffic to hide his expression. He needn't have worried. Gwen was leaning one elbow on the window frame and looking out at the city around them, calm, if a bit solemn.

"It's fine. Actually, I figured that Walter or Graham would have told you earlier, but I guess not. It's just that I was so used to the military lifestyle that holding a normal job didn't really fit. I wasn't used to the real world, and so I lost my apartment, and I didn't really have anywhere else to go. The streets were hard, but it was sort of familiar." Gwen didn't mention why real life seemed wrong. He could guess though. It probably had something to do with the nightmares, with the flashbacks. Things that had kept her from lasting long at a job.

"But it's not so bad now?" Alaric asked, turning into the parking lot of The Wooden Rose and driving across the street to the building of apartments.

"Actually, this is more like the military than you'd think. Everything has to be just so, and you are one hell of a drill sergeant," Gwen said, giving him a light chuckle. Alaric simply stood, stunned. She replied with a smile and opened the door. "Thanks for the ride. I'll see you in a few hours."

"Uh, right. Sure," Alaric said. Before he could blurt out a question about taking her on a date, the door was closed, and Gwen was jogging up to her door. She looked back once, and then she was in the building and gone.

Alaric sighed, his shoulders releasing their tension. He put his head to the steering wheel and growled at himself. This wasn't working. He didn't know what "this" was, but it wasn't working. He knew he should head back to his own apartment and take a shower to get ready for class later, but he was too distracted, and The Rose was so close. Alaric turned the car back on and drove over to the parking lot, choosing to get out and go work on the menu or try out a new recipe or anything other than think over the pleasant feeling that spread through him with the image of Gwen.

Maybe Jack was right; finding a girl could be the solution to his anger management.

It was much easier for Alaric to put his untoward thoughts about Gwen aside when he was directing his kitchen. He still faltered when he caught sight of her in the corner of his vision, but that was fixed when he snapped at Danny or one of the other students. Especially James.

James was, by far, the best cook out of all the students, but he was cocky and annoying, boasting openly to anyone who got too close. The usual kitchen staff had complained to Alaric more than once, and the other students avoided James as best they could. Only Gwen was able to put up with him, and that was because she ignored him most of the time. Tonight, he was talking about his skill at one of the local defense studios, as he had overheard Gwen and Allison reviewing some of the concepts Gwen had been teaching.

It was almost two weeks after the incident that had driven Allison to tears, and the small blonde woman was proving to be an avid learner when it came to fighting. She had gained confidence in her stride, and her skill in the kitchen was improving as well, almost to the point where she rivaled James. The tattooed man hadn't liked the competition and so was doing his best to become top dog once again. It was becoming really annoying.

"Seriously, you should come sometime," James said, tossing some brussels sprouts in a roasting pan. He looked over at Gwen, who was sharing the station next to him and smirked. "The owner is a master in all sorts of fighting styles, and since I've been doing so well in Karate, he's moved me on to—"

"James," Gwen said, taking her tongs and flipping the duck breast just as it was turning the perfect golden brown Alaric kept pushing them to get. "Stop, please. I'm teaching Allison self-defense, not looking for a fight."

"You haven't been in the fighting circuit for a while, then? That's all right," James said, doing his best to make it sound as though he was being pitying and understanding. "Everyone gets rusty."

Gwen put the pan back on the stove with a loud clatter, her face flushed, from anger or from the heat of the kitchen, it was hard to tell. Alaric moved in their direction to break up a fight if need be. He surreptitiously watched the pair while standing over Bob's station, making the man sweat in consequence.

"Seriously, James, just stop. I get enough of your bragging about cooking. I don't need it anywhere else in my life," she snarled. Gwen drew her eyebrows together enough to make it very, very clear that she was barely holding on to her temper.

James was oblivious. "Fine," the man shrugged and began plating the sprouts.

Gwen turned her attention back to the duck breasts and sprinkled some basil over them.

"I was just thinking you might be interested. No need to bite my head off."

Gwen clenched her jaw, and exchanging a glance with Robert—who had started watching, just like the other kitchen staff—Alaric hurried over. It was too late.

Gwen straightened and looked James straight in the eye. "If you want to challenge me, go ahead. You could use a decent bit of humility knocked into you."

"Whoa." James held up his hands, a smirk dancing over his mouth. "Relax. There's no need to go all super-soldier on me."

Gwen snarled wordlessly, her temper snapped. She pulled the duck off the stove and plated it as quickly as she could before shoving the dishes over to Sarah, who had been preparing the rest of the meal. Then she stalked in the direction of the storage areas. Alaric frowned and followed. No one was supposed to get angry in his kitchen but him, and when it came to Gwen, he was more worried than he should have been.

"Wait," Jack said, putting a hand on Alaric's shoulder as the head chef approached the storage area. He was far enough back that Gwen didn't notice him, and his friend and manager stopped him from going any further. "Let her cool off a bit. She's going to need it."

"What?" Alaric asked, rubbing the towel at his apron strings over his forehead. He heard a loud thunk and turned, wide-eyed, to look at Gwen. She was pacing back and forth, her hands clenched into fists at her sides. In the freezer door, a stainless-steel sheet that was tough but pliable, there was a dent that looked as though it had come from a fist. Alaric swallowed and turned back to Jack. "What do you mean?"

"Just let her cool off and then have her come out to the floor. There's someone she needs to talk to," Jack said. With another gentle pat on Alaric's shoulder, the restaurant owner left. Alaric took a deep breath and looked to his kitchens. Danny was bantering good-naturedly with Tom over a salmon steak, and Jennifer was smiling as she chopped carrots into fine pieces. Things were running smoothly, and so he turned behind him to the storage areas.

"Hey," Alaric said, fingering a bottle of wine as though he had come back to grab an ingredient instead of check up on Gwen.

"Sorry about the freezer," she said, stopping her pacing to lean against the wall.

"It's fine," Alaric said. He paused, then giving up on the wine, went to stand next to her. "Is everything all right?"

"Yeah," Gwen said. "I just figured that I was done having to prove myself to idiots like James when I left the military. Especially when it came to defending myself."

"I thought that you said you were used to having to prove yourself," Alaric said.

"Well, yes, but with jerks like that, it's different. They have no right to demand that I prove myself, and they still do, just to get a kick when they figure out that they're better than you. I've met far too many people like that, and it's been getting on my nerves for a while," Gwen said. She took a deep breath and held it for a few seconds before letting it out again. "Sorry. I didn't mean to get all annoying on you."

"You're not annoying," Alaric said before he could stop himself. He was thankful that Gwen replied with a sarcastic yet thankful smile rather than anything else. "Feeling better?"

"Yeah," she said. "I'll get back to the kitchens now."

"Actually, Jack said there's someone out on the floor who wants to talk with you," Alaric said.

Gwen raised her eyebrows in question.

"Probably Graham or Walter. I wondered how long it would take before one of them showed up to check on you."

"Right," Gwen said. She pressed her lips together and shook her head. It was fairly plain she didn't want to deal with them right now, but it was her duty and so she did. She pushed herself off the wall and moved through the kitchens, smiling at people who smiled at her and seeming like she belonged there. Alaric couldn't help but follow, completely ignoring the looks he got as he walked through the doors to the floor.

He paused, though, just at the entrance to the kitchens, scanning the crowd of people at The Rose for any sign of Walter or Graham or both. He saw nothing. Gwen approached Jack and exchanged a few words with him before moving across the restaurant to a table in a secluded corner. She made it to about five feet away before freezing, her breath catching in her throat.

"Hello, Lieutenant Townsend," the man said.

"Major Dalton," she breathed.

7

*M*ajor Dalton was a quiet-looking man with a pair of eyes that were calm and belonged on the features of a favorite uncle, not someone of his standing. Gwen knew, though, that in an instant, those eyes could turn into wells of fury and that his kind, pleasant looks would become wrathful. Sitting there before her, she wished that he would look at her with anger rather than the pity he offered. She couldn't move, completely frozen by the shock of seeing him again. Somewhere in the back of her mind, Gwen was planning escape routes, her training telling her that now would be a really great time to flee.

"Lieutenant," Major Dalton said, rising and bridging the gap between Gwen and himself.

Gwen retreated.

"Gwen, hold on," the major said, holding out his hands to show her that he meant no harm. He took another step forward, and Gwen, adrenaline beginning to run through her so that her vision narrowed and the sounds of the restaurant melted away, stepped backward again.

"Is everything all right?" The new voice startled Gwen, and she turned, bringing her hands up in a defensive posture, sliding into a fighting stance. Alaric put a hand on her shoulder, and she shuddered, instinct telling her to pull backward and reason telling her that he wouldn't hurt her. She listened to her instincts and pulled away, causing Alaric to blink.

He looked between Gwen and this unknown man and raised his eyebrows, the first signs of temper showing on his face. Gwen needed to be back in the kitchens, not out here, having a conversation with someone that she didn't want to see. She did not wish to talk with Major Dalton. She did not wish to remember things better left forgotten. Especially not with Alaric here, looking over her shoulder like a protective friend. If she could call him that.

"I am Major Jonas Dalton," the man said, holding out a hand for Alaric to shake.

Hesitantly, and glancing at Gwen, maybe to gauge her reaction to this, Alaric shook the proffered appendage.

"Lieutenant Townsend—Gwen—and I go way back," said the major. I got a call the other day from a Walter Smythe, telling me that Gwen was working at the restaurant. I guess I was the closest thing to a job reference they had. I came here to catch up."

"Catch up," Gwen said, the words sounding

disjointed and alien in her mouth. She gaped at Dalton, unable to believe that was what he wanted to do. Alaric shifted his feet as though he was going to step in front of her and take care of this, but Gwen shook her head subtly. She was relieved when he did not move. The relief was palpable when he did not retreat either, remaining close enough to Gwen that she could reach out if she needed.

"Yes," Major Dalton answered. He took a deep breath and let it out slowly, fixing Gwen in his care-worn gaze. "I don't like it when my people drop off the grid, Gwen. No one's heard from you in over a year. Your family has stopped calling. I was almost sure that you had—" He broke off, choking at the words that threatened to escape.

"Had what?" Gwen asked quietly, daring him to say what was on the tip of his tongue.

"It doesn't matter; you're here and doing well," Major Dalton said. Alaric frowned.

"Had what?" Gwen repeated, her gaze narrowing and her voice going hard as steel. Somewhere in the back of her mind, she knew that they were creating a scene. She was meant to be in the kitchens, keeping her head down, not out here confronting her past for an entire restaurant full of people to see. She half hoped that Alaric or Jack or anybody would tell them that this could be done elsewhere. Still, this needed to be said, if only to wipe that pitying look from Dalton's eyes.

The major kept Gwen's gaze, not backing down

from the challenge. It was this that made the words that much more terrible when he said them, not even bothering to whisper. "Had killed yourself."

Gwen made a noise in the back of her throat somewhere between a gasp of surprise and a growl, and she curled her lip ever so slightly. She shifted, and Alaric acted, his movements jerky, surprised.

"Gwen," he said, stepping in front of his student and whatever monster she knew herself to be. "Not here, not now."

Gwen straightened, returning her posture to military perfect instead of fighting ready. She glared openly at the major and then ducked her head to Alaric. "I have to get back to the kitchens," she muttered as an excuse, then fled past where Alaric stood, watching her departing figure until she disappeared behind the doors of the kitchen, staring as if she might take her anger out on the freezer door again. Gwen huffed.

"I'm sorry about that," Major Dalton spoke again. Alaric turned, looking at the man. He wasn't that much taller than Alaric, and he wasn't built up like action movies depicted military types to be. He was fit, of that there was no doubt, but his power came from the quiet authority he exuded and the confidence that he knew his place and his strength and how to use both. "She's a good person, was one of the best soldiers I ever had the honor of working with. But ever since she lost her squad, she's been volatile. She wasn't even meant to be in a combat situation, but it happened."

"Lost her squad," Alaric said, drawing his eyebrows together. "Volatile," he continued, a tone of disbelief in his voice.

"She...she hasn't told you?" the major asked.

Alaric felt that saying "*told me what*" would be far too obvious, so he just shook his head, suddenly very curious to learn everything that this major knew about Gwen, the quiet and capable woman who worked in his kitchens.

With a sigh, the major took his seat again, picking up the glass of wine that sat by his plate. He swirled it around and stared into the burgundy liquid. "Ah."

"She's a good cook and seems to have things together, but she's definitely quiet about anything... personal," Alaric said, realizing in that instant just how true his words were. Gwen was able to talk with people easily, and she occasionally told stories about her own life, but there was nothing personal in them, nothing that could reveal anything about herself. And that was beginning to be a problem for Alaric.

"I would say that it would be better to wait for her to tell you," Major Dalton said, putting down his wine glass again. "But I know her far too well to believe that will happen before...before it may be too late."

"She doesn't seem suicidal," Alaric said.

Major Dalton shook his head and gave a wan smile, about to respond.

A burst of laughter from one of the guests in the restaurant startled Alaric out of his focus on the major. He had the kitchens to attend to, and while they could manage on their own for a bit, there were better places to have this conversation. The fear that Major Dalton would go away before Alaric could find out what he wanted was pulsating behind his temples. He sucked in a breath and, breaking all of his personal rules about interacting with guests, especially when he was working, sat across from him.

This man seemed to understand the step that Alaric was taking and, in the same breath, understood the motives behind it. His calm, comforting presence made it seem okay, and Alaric leaned forward.

"Gwen has changed a lot since the last time I saw her," Major Dalton said. "She has put on weight, and there's a definite energy in her that wasn't there before."

"But," Alaric prompted.

"But I've seen her at her best, and she's nowhere close. I...would like to talk with you about this, but you have a manager looking for you, and I think that there are better places for this conversation," Major Dalton said. He spoke with the authority that made it apparent that his words were not a request while also allowing Alaric to breathe a sigh of relief.

The chef stood and nodded to the major, running his hands through his hair as he tried to come to terms with what had been said. He took another breath for his own sanity and held out a hand to the major. "It was nice to meet you."

"You as well," Major Dalton said. He slipped a business card into Alaric's hand. "I'll be in the city for another three days. You can reach me at this number. If...you want to talk."

Alaric nodded in acknowledgment and answered with a smile that only touched one side of his mouth. He turned toward the kitchens where, as the major had said, Jack was poking his head out of the door, watching Alaric.

"Oh, and chef," Major Dalton said before Alaric had made it three steps.

Alaric turned, raising his eyebrows.

"You've done more than you know. For her."

"I don't think it was me," Alaric said and returned to work.

His skin had cooled down in the interlude from the kitchens, and he grinned at the rush of heat and noise that came over him. There was the sizzling of meat in pans, and his students and one of his sous chefs were at the cutting stations, chopping vegetables and focusing on their tasks with fierce looks and slight smiles. This was where he was meant to be. Among the activity and the heat, moving from place to place as he checked on multiple dishes at once, cooking everything with just the right touch, just the right amount of attention. He had people who looked at him with respect and the right amount of—flattering—fear. He belonged here, in the kitchens of The Wooden Rose.

Gwen, on the other hand, did not belong like Alaric did. She fit in well, accomplishing her tasks with precision, even art, and she was far past the stage of overcooking or undercooking a dish. She created concoctions out of flavors that suited one another, and the extra training that Alaric had been giving her was obviously paying off. But there was a seriousness behind her eyes that made Alaric painfully aware that she wasn't content here, that there was something plaguing her and making her press her lips more tightly together as she cleaned vegetables under a spray of water. She looked as though she was grieving and, worse, as though she was in pain.

Alaric wanted to fix that. He wanted to make her belong in the kitchens because she had talent that could shine if it was nurtured properly. She could be content there, more than content. She could be happy. Yet something held her back.

He shook his head and lunged for an unfulfilled order slip before heading over to his own workstation, where he began to pull ingredients together. Every now and again, he looked up, snapping orders to someone who seemed to be slacking off or was making a glaring error, but mostly he worked in silence, thinking. He thought about why it was that he felt the need to protect and help Gwen, why her pain mattered so much to him. Alaric knew it went beyond the normal student-teacher relationship. He was, like it or not, her friend. He only had a few friends—namely, Jack—and the fact that Gwen was one as well shocked him. It wasn't what he had expected, but it was nice.

With this newfound friendship came a sense of duty and loyalty. She was hurting, and he was going to help. He hoped that she would come to him on her own, but given what the major had said and the way that Gwen had pulled away from him, as if he was intruding on something dark and secret, he doubted she would willingly approach him. It was then that the business card seemed to begin burning a hole in his pocket.

He only managed to corner her at the end of the night, when they were about to begin their extra training. Gwen waved to Allison as the blonde woman left and walked to the freezer to grab a few spring berries just as Alaric was walking out. He brushed by her, and it was like his entire body was aware of the touch, burning and causing him to want to follow her and demand more.

Okay, Alaric thought, swallowing as he hurried into the kitchens to get out a pan, *not just friends, then.*

Gwen returned a moment later, looking a bit worse for the wear.

"Are you okay?" Alaric asked.

She looked at him, as if knowing that the question spanned far more than being tired. She opened her mouth to answer then paused, shrugged, and moved over to the stove.

"It doesn't matter," Gwen said. "I just wasn't expecting to see him here."

"I hate to be that person," Alaric said, watching as Gwen bathed the frozen berries in a cold-water bath and put them in the pan before stirring them to cook the juices out for a syrup. "But do you want to talk about it?"

Gwen gave Alaric an incredulous look and raised her eyebrows. Then she started to laugh. It was infectious, and eventually, Alaric joined in, though he managed to keep an eye on the berries.

"Add the honey liqueur and yeah, I know," Alaric said. "But I'm not really all that good with...that sort of thing."

"I'm sure that you're a hit with all those sobbing women out there," Gwen said, tipping the liqueur into the mixture with a flick of her wrist that Alaric was sure he hadn't taught her. She stirred the fruit around and turned up the heat, watching as the berries started to simmer down.

"Yes. I've been certified by the Sobbing Women Society to lend my professional advice," Alaric said. "I would add something else to that syrup, if I were you. Maybe—huh, I wouldn't think that nutmeg would work with that."

"Honey and nutmeg are a great combination. I used to put nutmeg in all the pies I made when I was a kid," Gwen said, shaving a few flakes off the nutmeg.

"I'm sure you made plenty of pies." Alaric reached around him for a lighter, which he then handed to Gwen. She shot him a look, and he shrugged.

"Actually, I made a round total of two pies in my

life," Gwen said. "Both were for my brother's birthday, until he decided that it was much cooler to go out with his friends and buy a cake. But they went over pretty well, at the time."

"You should be a baker," Alaric said. He smiled as Gwen flicked on the lighter and held the flame to the bubbling mixture in the pan. The liquid flared, the alcohol catching fire while the sugar merely caramelized, not hot enough to light. A moment later and the fire was out, and Gwen stirred her spoon through the liquid once before turning off the heat and moving the pan to a cool burner.

"I don't think I have the patience for baking," Gwen said. "Besides, I think I'm doing pretty well here. I don't want to go about changing careers and learning something new all over again."

"That and I think that the French baking masters are a bit…angrier than me," Alaric said, watching as Gwen began to mix the ingredients for crepes, stirring the syrup occasionally to keep the juices from solidifying. She whipped everything together and heated a cast-iron crepe skillet before putting a great dollop of butter in the middle. She began pouring out the thin pancakes and frowned at the thick, lumpy result.

"I don't get it," she said, putting the bowl of batter back onto the counter. "I did everything right."

"Here," Alaric said, stepping forward and reaching for a tablespoon. He scraped the pancake that Gwen had made out of the skillet and handed her the spoon. "Now reheat the pan, spreading the butter out evenly."

Gwen did as she was told. Alaric stepped behind her to get to the batter, swallowing as he brushed against her. "Take the spoon and take the batter. See how thick it is? You want it to be almost like water. Add some more liquid... There you go. Now pour a dollop into the pan."

Gwen took the spoon, served out a portion of batter into the pan, and watched it spread evenly, sizzling over the melted butter as it did. She waited almost patiently until one side was cooked enough and, with a questing glance at Alaric, who nodded, took the skillet and flicked it with her wrist. The crepe slid out of the pan and into the air, falling back down and landing half folded.

"So close," Gwen said, hurrying to straighten out the crepe.

"No, that was good," Alaric said. "Though you could have used a crepe spatula." When Gwen looked at him with an astonished look, he nearly flushed and looked away. Normally, he was harsh and abrasive, growling at the simplest mistake until Gwen got it right. That was the point of these evening sessions, after all. It was too late to back down, so Alaric continued, trying to justify what he had said. "When I was learning to make crepes, it took me months of working to get that flip just right. I even know some people who use a flat silicone spatula, like with normal pancakes. It's...what?"

Gwen averted her gaze, focusing on making

another crepe, using the spoon to spread the batter out. "Nothing."

"No, that was definitely a look," Alaric said, growling slightly.

"It's nothing," Gwen insisted. Alaric huffed in response, reaching toward the syrup and stirring it with a ferociously wielded spoon. Gwen shook her head.

"All right, there's definitely something going on," Alaric said, slamming the spoon to its rest. "What is it?"

"It's just that you're not normally so, well, nice," Gwen said. "Do you know that everyone, including your kitchen staff, is terrified of you?"

"They're not—"

"They are. Even James knows not to mess with you, annoying though he is," Gwen said. "But we're used to it. We can judge how well things are going by how angry and vocal you are. The louder and more colorful your curses, the better the night. The darker, more sullen you get, things aren't doing so well. I'm just not used to you being quite so understanding."

"I thought we had a great *understanding* conversation over breakfast a couple of weeks ago," Alaric grumbled.

Gwen flipped the crepe she was making, failing again to get it to sit properly. This one tore slightly as she fixed it, and she frowned. "Well, yes, but that wasn't while we were cooking. In the kitchens, things are different," Gwen said. "You expect things to be done right. Anyone who doesn't live up to your standards is told."

"You make it sound as though I'm some sort of cruel professor who sends little girls crying from the room." Alaric frowned.

Gwen laughed and turned off the stove before pulling out two pristine plates and putting the crepes on them. She took the syrup and drizzled that over top before spooning the remaining berries into the middle. With a fork, she deftly folded the crepe over itself and handed a plate to Alaric.

"I figure if we get to make dessert, then we should at least get to try it," Gwen said. She smiled endearingly, and it was hard to refuse her. Alaric certainly wasn't able. He growled half-heartedly and took his plate to an empty counter before leaning against it and contemplating his dessert with a fork poised in the air. He knew he didn't look particularly happy.

"Wait," Gwen said, reaching for the liqueur bottle and the lighter. She drizzled the honey liqueur over the dessert. For a few seconds, the magnificent flames licked at the air before dying out. The crepe had taken on a crisp golden color.

"I don't normally condone setting desserts on fire," Alaric said, cutting into the crepe with his fork. "But I think I'll make an exception."

"I always thought it was sort of fun, watching things catch on fire. No one ever seemed to be concerned, not in the kitchens. I thought that was one of the best things about being a chef. I've been waiting to try it out," Gwen said.

Alaric nodded and stuffed a bite of crepe in his mouth. He chewed slowly and then gave Gwen a slight dip of his head. She fairly beamed.

"The rate that you're going, these sessions are almost a waste of time," Alaric admitted.

"So you don't want to continue them?" Gwen asked. It was asked innocently enough, but Alaric froze all the same. He knew that it was rather pointless to continue making both of them tired, keeping them up late to work on something that needed no help. But he didn't want to stop.

"I just don't think you need them anymore," he said softly. Gripping his fork and feeling honest, he looked down at his dessert. "But I like spending time with you."

"I do too when you're not biting my head off about cutting carrots wrong," Gwen joked.

Alaric chuckled weakly, knowing that she didn't quite understand what he'd meant. He took another bite of his crepe and cast his thoughts about to see if he could figure out something to talk about.

"You've had a long day," he said at last. "What with Major Dalton showing up and putting up with James. Why don't you head home? I'll clean up here."

"What?" Gwen asked, clearly stunned. "You're letting me get out of cleaning? Okay, you being nice was different, but this is just plain strange. Is everything all right?"

"Fine," Alaric said. "I just think you've earned a break. Go on. I'll take care of this."

Gwen hesitated, but Alaric shot her a look and half a snarl, and she retreated, apparently knowing to choose her battles. Something was eating Alaric, but he knew she couldn't fix it. He needed time. Scooping her dessert into a takeaway box, Gwen threw one last look at Alaric, still sitting and staring at his half-eaten crepe, and left.

As soon as the back door was closed, Alaric sighed and put down his fork. He put his head in his hands and sighed. He couldn't keep tiptoeing around Gwen just because he wasn't sure what would cause her pain. He had to understand what was going on in her mind so that he could figure out how to deal with whatever it was that he was feeling toward her. He would have asked her, but he wanted to avoid that pain-filled look that she was bound to get. He wanted to help her, not cause her pain.

He reached into his pocket and pulled out the business card, staring at it without really seeing what he was holding. The words swam before his eyes, and only when he was able to recall the way that Gwen had stared, frozen in fear at the sight of her old major, did he pull out his phone and dial the number on the card.

"Hello?" The voice was unmistakably Major Dalton's, for which Alaric was grateful. He didn't want to deal with some office lackey in a matter such as this.

"Hello, Major. This is Alaric Bennet, er, the chef from The Wooden Rose," Alaric said.

"Of course. What can I do for you?"

"Well, I was thinking I would take you up on your offer. About Gwen, I mean. Is there somewhere you would prefer to meet?"

"Are you free for breakfast? There's a nice little spot near my hotel, and I've been told they have a decent cup of tea," the major said. Alaric agreed, got the details, and hung up with little ceremony. Then, tossing his phone onto the counter in disdain, he slumped his shoulders and put his fingers through his hair. The crepe he had eaten was beginning to sit poorly in his stomach.

Gwen stood in the storage room, having come back for her coat. She hadn't meant to overhear, but it was hard not to. The kitchens were silent, the floor was silent, and there was nothing to stop Alaric's voice from echoing through the building. He wanted to meet Major Dalton. About her. There could be only one reason that her boss—she had wanted to think of him as a friend, especially after tonight, but hearing what she had just heard meant there was little chance of that—was meeting with the former leader of her regiment.

Were it anyone but her, the fear would have gnawed at her insides. But in Gwen, her fear turned to resolve and anger, and a fire flared up inside of her. Without a noise, she grabbed her coat from the hook by the door and left the restaurant. She made it to her building before her anger grew strong enough to break through. With a roar of rage, Gwen balled her fingers into a fist and drove them into the wall.

The brick fractured, just at the mortaring, and so did her hand. Skin broken and bleeding, Gwen sank to her knees and cradled the injured appendage in her lap, beginning to cry. Her burden, what she had done, was for her to accept and deal with. Not a wild-haired, fiery-tongued, handsome, and caring—damn it, but he was that—chef.

8

The next morning, Alaric dressed with care and drove to the cafe near Major Dalton's hotel. He parked his car a block away from the cafe and sat there, though the clock on his dashboard was moving ever closer to the appointed meeting time. He just couldn't bring himself to actually get out of the car and go to Major Dalton, opening himself up to admit that he cared for Gwen and wanted to know about her so that he could help. He had essentially said as much the night before, but that was over the telephone and this was in person, with the major's calm, understanding, and piercing gaze fixed on him. Alaric hesitated until the clock told him that he was officially five minutes late, then he got out of the car and walked over to the cafe.

"Chef," he heard a voice call before he even had a chance to look over the place. Alaric turned toward the voice and felt extremely overdressed and out of place.

He was wearing dark trousers and a button-up shirt, the sleeves rolled up as a concession to the almost oppressive muggy heat that lay over the city despite it being still spring. Major Dalton was wearing a light pair of khaki trousers and a T-shirt that had obviously seen much wear.

"Good morning," Alaric said, walking over to the table and holding out his hand that Major Dalton did not hesitate to take and grasp firmly. A military man's handshake.

"Do you want to order some tea or some eggs or something?" the major asked, looking over at the cashier's counter with considerable interest. "I think I'm going to see about getting some toast and a couple boiled eggs."

"I think I'll settle for coffee," Alaric said. His stomach was far too wobbly for him to even consider eating. What was it about this interview—if you could call it an interview—that made him so nervous? The major nodded and rose, returning a few minutes later with two cups, one tea and one coffee, on a tray. He sat, and they both doctored their drinks as desired—cream for Major Dalton and black for Alaric—then sat in silence.

"So you're here about Gwen's, ah, problems?" the major asked, breaking the building tension. Alaric swallowed the mouthful of coffee that he had just taken and set down his cup on the table as gently as he could. He wanted to know so badly. It was becoming ridiculous how much time he spent thinking about

Gwen and how much he wanted to know her and understand the struggles she had been through. But something was holding him back.

"I... I want to know," Alaric admitted, looking at the coffee before him, thinking that even that was upsetting his stomach. "But I don't think that I should be asking you to do this. The likelihood of Gwen telling me is very slim. Still, I think...I don't know why I'm telling you this, but I think that I need to wait until she tells me herself."

There was another period of silence, but the tension was lessened considerably. Major Dalton sat back in his chair and appraised Alaric carefully, taking in the full measure of the man. When he had done this, his eyes softened, and a slight smile appeared at his mouth. The major took a deep breath and another sip of tea and nodded.

"Good," he said. A waitress who looked bleary-eyed and was obviously too tired for the morning shift brought the major's food and set it down before him, nodding in acknowledgment of the thanks that was muttered. Major Dalton picked up his knife and fork before speaking again. "I don't pretend to know a thing about psychology or whatever, but I know a thing or two about Gwen, and I know a thing or two about relationships."

"We're not—" Alaric tried to protest, suddenly embarrassed that he was talking about his potential relationship with a man he hardly knew on top of being the former commander of the woman he was interested in. He was silenced with a severe look and focused his attention on drinking his cup of coffee while the major continued.

"Not yet, maybe, but from the conversations we've had and the way that you look at her, not to mention the fact that she seems to be comfortable in your presence, I'd say you're well on your way," the man said, smirking as if amused by Alaric's embarrassment. "Relax, I'm not going to act as Gwen's protective older brother. I just care about her is all. And I wouldn't want her to end up with someone who is willing to go behind her back to try and fix things. She's been broken in the past, and she's the one that ultimately needs to mend herself. I doubt it will be easy, but she's on her way, working for a living instead of running."

"How do I even approach her about this?" Alaric asked, more to himself than anything.

"If you don't know how to woo a woman, I'm not going to teach you," Major Dalton said.

Alaric looked up, staring at the man incredulously. A moment later, he realized the joke and allowed himself to grin. Then came laughter, and the two were soon chuckling over more than just that.

"You're both fiery and temperamental—don't let her quietness fool you—but I think the two of you will get on just fine."

~

Gwen was sitting in the waiting room at the hospital, gently cradling her broken hand in her lap. Of all the days to go breaking her hand, it had to be on her day off. And if she weren't in so much pain, she would have just put a wrap on it. She had dealt with worse, after all. But her fingers throbbed at any movement, and her hand was swollen considerably, with great ugly bruises marbling the surface. She needed her hand to cook, and so she had clambered onto a bus and was now waiting to be seen by a doctor. Her only consolation was that the brick had fared worse.

"Gwen Townsend?" a nurse called.

Gwen blinked, startled, and rose before walking over to where the woman was waiting.

She looked at Gwen and consulted the chart before turning and walking back to a small exam room. "Have a seat," the woman said, sitting in her own chair.

Gwen sat.

"So what brings you in today?"

"I broke my hand," Gwen said, showing the injured right appendage. "And yes, I'm sure it's broken."

"I have no doubt of that," the nurse said, turning away from the chart to look at the hand. She reached out as if to touch it, then looked up at Gwen and refrained. "That's quite the injury. How did it happen?"

"I had an argument with a brick," Gwen answered, her voice dry and sarcastic. The nurse blinked and weakly laughed, obviously wondering at the mentality of the person sitting before her. "I just need it bandaged up."

"We'll have to take X-rays," the nurse said. Gwen started to protest, but the woman held up her hand and shook her head. "They're necessary to set the bones right."

"How long will it take?" Gwen sighed, slumping back in the chair.

"Well, you'll have to have a talk with the doctor— Dr. Hojek—but I'm fairly certain that he'll just send you to get X-rays scheduled anyway. I'll see how quickly I can set something up," the nurse said. "Hopefully, we'll have you out of here before too long."

"Right," Gwen answered in resigned disbelief. The nurse asked a few more questions and then left, leaving Gwen to wait for the doctor, cradling her hand as best she could while she tried to get comfortable in the chair. She failed. The doctor, an older Indian gentleman with the look of someone who had seen far too much life, entered, took one look at Gwen's hand, and called to the nurse to order X-rays.

Which is how, when Graham walked in an hour later after getting a call from the hospital, he found Gwen in the waiting area in radiology, her head leaned back at an uncomfortable-looking angle, her eyes glazed with boredom. "Gwen?" he asked, stepping up to her.

She jumped, as much as it was possible to jump in the waiting room chairs, then winced, her hand jostled against her leg. "What are you doing here?" Gwen asked, holding her good hand up to her head and pinching the bridge of her nose as she got over the sudden burst of pain.

"There's a stipulation in your file that if you ever get hurt, at least while Mr. Smythe is responsible for your well-being, that his office is phoned. Since I'm the office manager..." Graham trailed off and shrugged his shoulders beneath his well-tailored suit.

"Do you have your fingers in every aspect of my life?" Gwen muttered, drawing her eyebrows together.

"Pardon?" Graham asked.

"Nothing," Gwen answered. She shifted in her chair and watched the man warily. Why would he come down to see her in person rather than just calling and working out the problem from a distance? And for that matter, why was he looking at her like that? It was some sort of mixture between pity and acceptance and something else that Gwen couldn't place, and it sent a shiver down her spine. She wasn't sure whether that was good or bad.

"May I sit?" Graham asked, gesturing to the seat next to Gwen. She shrugged, and he sat, looking at her swollen and bruised hand. "What happened?"

"I had an argument with a brick," Gwen said, giving the same story she had given the nurse. She realized a moment too late that she probably should have told him something else.

"An argument with a brick," he said slowly, curiously. "I take it you won?"

Gwen blinked; was he trying to make a joke? It was an incongruous act from Graham, and she had doubted that the serious, completely focused man was capable of such a thing. Yet there it was, a joke and a slight smile at the corner of his mouth.

"Yes," Gwen said, "though it did a number on my hand."

"Will you be all right to work?" Graham asked. He leaned forward to examine the injury, and Gwen obligingly held it up, though the movement alone was enough to cause her to suck in a silent breath. She had experienced worse, she reminded herself.

"I can use my left hand. All I really need is for it to get bandaged up, and I'll be fine," Gwen said. "But the doctor insists on getting an X-ray. Something about being unable to set it properly otherwise."

"Well, that makes sense," Graham said.

"I never had to go through this much trouble whenever I broke a bone in the past," Gwen grumbled, trying to gauge the reaction of her companion. Would he protest to friendly conversation? After all, that was what they had been doing for the last minute or so, but then it could also have been him gathering information for a status report to Walter.

"I imagine things are different off the battlefield," Graham said, then flinched as if he'd said something distasteful. "I'm sorry, I didn't mean to bring it up..."

"It's fine," Gwen said honestly. This was strange. He was being considerate as well as attempting to be friendly. It was as though he was a completely different person. Gwen decided to make the most of the situation and ignore the memory that rose in her mind;

Alaric was laughing and telling her exactly what he thought of Graham. She shoved the picture away and stifled a yawn that arose in its place. She had been waiting for a long time.

"If you don't mind my asking," Graham said after a moment of not-quite-awkward silence, "what exactly was the fight about?"

"With the brick? I was…angry," Gwen said, looking at the wall across from her to avoid seeing what Graham thought of that statement.

"With whom?" Graham asked, causing Gwen to start and look at him, wide-eyed. "Well, I figure that someone must have caused you to be angry. I don't take you for the type to get angry at a lost spoon."

"No," Gwen said quietly. "I guess not."

"Gwen Townsend," a radiologist called, looking over a chart. Gwen stood, and Graham looked for a moment as though he was going to follow, then settled back into his seat.

Gwen followed the man to a room with an X-ray machine, ignored the sound of the machine as it took pictures of her bones, and then was returned to the original waiting room. Graham came with, making no mention of leaving, for which Gwen was grateful.

"So how are things going at The Wooden Rose?" he asked after they had settled into yet another set of chairs.

"I'm getting my legs," Gwen answered. "I'm almost done with the course. I think we have three more weeks, and then I can see about getting a proper job."

"Don't you have the option of staying at The Rose?" Graham said.

Gwen shrugged, knowing that there was a notation that said a student could stay on, should the head chef offer a position. She doubted very much that would happen, and even if it did, she wasn't sure she wanted to stay. She didn't like people digging into her background without her say-so. Alaric may have thought that he cared, may have thought that this was the best way to help her, but she didn't agree. She didn't want her nightmares ever coming to life. She could handle them on her own. A moment later, she realized that Graham had asked her a question and she was still without an answer.

"I suppose. But I don't know if I'm ready to stay in one place for the rest of my life. Besides, there are hundreds of restaurants in the city," Gwen said. She shrugged noncommittally. "I want to explore a bit."

"I understand that," Graham said. He shifted in his seat and folded his arms, making it impossible for Gwen not to notice that his shoulders were very shapely, very powerful. She looked away. This man was the office manager of her patron. There had to be a rule somewhere that forbade such thoughts. And besides, she didn't like Graham all that much. He was rude and cold. Or at least, he had been. Now he was being friendly and caring, and while it was out of character, Gwen didn't disapprove. It suited him.

Gwen's name was called again, and she left the waiting room one more time, this time to get her hand set and bandaged. Half an hour later, she was free to leave. Graham walked with her, his hands fisted in his pockets. When they were free of the hospital, Gwen took a deep breath and felt her body relaxing.

"Don't like hospitals?" Graham asked, narrowing his eyes slightly against the sun, which pierced through the clouds.

"There are worse things out there," Gwen said, "but I've never been a huge fan of them. There's something about the way they smell. Hey, thanks for coming and hanging out with me."

"Sure. I was happy to do it. And I'm glad that you weren't more injured. I can just imagine how angry Mr. Smythe would be with me if you got yourself...I'm sorry, I don't mean to be insensitive," Graham said, grimacing.

"It's fine," Gwen said. "I'm glad I wasn't more injured too. That would have been annoying."

"Right," Graham said.

The two stood there for a moment, the former soldier looking at the bandage on her hand and musing how things had changed.

"Um," said Graham, "if you're not doing anything tonight, there's a gala at the Ritz-Carlton by the park, and I was wondering if, well, you wanted to come with me. As my date."

Gwen blinked, looking up and drawing her eyebrows together. With her good hand, she tucked a stray strand of hair behind her ear and resisted the urge to rub the back of her neck awkwardly.

"If it's any consolation, I find him to be an annoying bastard," Alaric said. Gwen mentally shoved the memory away, only to have another rise in its place. *"Well, I was thinking I would take you up on your offer. About Gwen, I mean. Is there someplace you would prefer to meet?"*

"All right," Gwen said, smiling up at Graham. It wasn't as though he was poor to look at; in fact, with his physique and sculpted features, he was handsome. As long as he wasn't scowling, he was even more than that. And if his behavior at the hospital had been any indication, he was a nice guy when he got over his shyness masked by formality. "But if this is a black-tie sort of thing, I don't really have anything to wear."

"There're a few shops a couple of blocks over. You can put some of Mr. Smythe's money to good use," Graham said, not unkindly.

Gwen smiled, knowing as well as he did that she spent only what she needed for food and let the other portion of the weekly allowance sit in the bank.

"I'll pick you up around seven?"

"That sounds fine," Gwen said. Graham nodded, smiled, then reached out and tugged gently at another strand of her hair. She nearly gaped in astonishment, but then he was turning and walking over to his car. She barely heard the "see you later, Gwen" that he gave her, but the glance over his shoulder was enough to make her smile.

～

Alaric bid the major farewell not long after finishing his coffee. Then, unable to think of anything but the look of shock on Gwen's face as she had espied Major Dalton, he went to the one place where he knew he could be calm: the quiet and empty kitchens of The Rose.

With all the time that Alaric spent supervising his staff and teaching his students about the delicate art of cooking, he rarely had time to himself to simply create. But every now and again, when things were too bothersome—such as when he couldn't stand another night of yelling at his people or when his mother called and forced him to talk with his father—he went to The Rose when it was closed and simply spent time cooking.

This time, he was trying out different, lighter dishes for the summer. There was already a summer menu, but he thought it was time to change things up. So he pureed cucumbers and sliced celery into minuscule pieces. He put chicken stock in with the cucumber and added spices and sour cream, making a cold soup. His hands handled the knives as though they were simply extensions of his fingers. He reached for the spices naturally, not even bothering to think about what he was grabbing, just knowing that it would be there. And to complete the picture, he had a quiet symphony playing in the background. He never allowed music in his kitchens during business hours, but sometimes, when he was all alone, the sounds soothed him.

Except this time, Gwen's ghost seemed to be moving around him.

Just because he had decided not to ask Major Dalton about her past didn't mean that it didn't bother him. He was still caught up in the pain that she was feeling. She was still a mystery, and he was curious. Now that she had entered his kitchens, it was hard for him to see them without her. Even if she never let him become anything more than a friend, he wanted her around. Alaric knew he was being unreasonable, that he couldn't expect to attach himself to her, to keep Gwen at his side. That didn't stop him from wanting to try.

The cucumber soup was finished, and he reached for another pan to start on something new. Then he hesitated. "Damn it," he muttered, gripping the edges of the stainless-steel countertops until his knuckles turned white. He took a deep breath, growled in frustration, and stalked over to the freezers, determined to at least *try* and get Gwen out of his mind. He stopped as he saw the dent in the freezers that she had made and closed his eyes, drawing his mouth into a thin line.

She only lives two minutes away, he thought. That did it. Alaric didn't bother to taste the cucumber soup, just threw it into the freezer for later, turned off the lights—he couldn't start cleaning now or he would never go through with this—and left. Only as he was walking up to Gwen's building did he realize that he'd left his keys right next to his jacket.

With a muffled cry of anger, Alaric leaned his

weight on her buzzer and hoped desperately that she was there. He waited. Thirty seconds later, he tried again, muttering, "Please just be sleeping. Come on, Gwen."

"Alaric?"

He spun around, bumping his shoulder on the corner of the brick. One of them was chipped, leaving sharp points that jammed into his skin. He winced and rubbed his arm, staring at Gwen. She was standing there in dark jeans and a plain shirt, a garment bag over one arm, the other at her side, wrapped in a bandage. Her light-brown hair was down and seemed to glow in the afternoon sunlight. "What are you doing here?"

"I, er, was cooking over at The Rose, and I went outside, and I left my keys, and..." He silently cursed himself. That wasn't what he was doing there, and from the skeptical look that Gwen was giving him, she knew it too. "Actually, I wanted to—"

"Can you take this?" Gwen asked, holding out the garment bag. Alaric nodded and took it, noticing again that her hand was bandaged. She took the keys with her left hand, as skilled with that hand as she was with her right. Maybe it was an army thing. "Thanks," she said, shouldering open the door.

"What did you do to your hand?" Alaric asked, not waiting for an invitation but following Gwen inside and up the stairs to her flat.

"I had an argument with a brick," she answered

flatly. Was that anger he detected in her voice? "I think you jammed your shoulder into it."

"That explains why it hurt so much," Alaric said. Gwen gave a half-hearted shrug and opened the door to her flat. Alaric followed, swallowing nervously. He had never been to her apartment, and even though he was holding the garment bag and she hadn't exactly invited him in, this felt like he was taking a great step forward. The apartment was sparse, decorated in a style completely unlike Gwen. He looked at the pictures of the desert on the walls and wondered if they were from her time overseas.

"Thanks for carrying the bag," Gwen said, reaching out for it. The door remained open behind Alaric, and she didn't look all that thrilled to be having him standing there without a by-your-leave.

"No problem," Alaric said. He took a deep breath and told himself that if he didn't say something now, he would never get it out. "Look, I noticed your problems with the major last night and just wanted to make sure everything is okay. I c—I like you, Gwen, and I just wanted you to know that I'm here for you. And I was wondering if you wanted to—"

"Haven't you intruded into my life enough already?" she asked, the garment bag draped over a chair, her good hand gripping the back tightly. Furiously.

"What?" Alaric asked, raising his eyebrows in confusion.

"I know all about your meeting with the major.

What, you couldn't muster the courage to ask me? Or you couldn't deal with having a potential psychotic person on your team?" Gwen snarled, rounding on Alaric with fire in her eyes.

"No, wait, you don't understand what's going on," Alaric said, not even bothering to question how she knew about the meeting.

"Don't I? Next time you want to know something about me, just ask. Or better yet, leave it alone. I don't need your help, Alaric. I don't need anyone's help." Gwen raised her hand and pointed at the door. "Get out."

"Gwen, it wasn't like—"

"I said get out," she snapped. Alaric hesitated for a moment, then backed away, knowing the look in her eyes and the tone of voice as though he was looking in a mirror. If he lingered any longer, he imagined she would start really lashing out, broken hand or no. Gwen grabbed the door to slam it shut, but Alaric managed to stick his shoe in the way, ignoring the jolt of pain as Gwen attempted to close the door.

"I never asked Major Dalton about your past. I was going to, but I couldn't," Alaric said quickly before he was injured further. Then, his own temper growing, he turned and stormed away. He left Gwen's building and stalked over to The Wooden Rose, forgetting until he was standing at the door that he had no keys to get in. He yelled in annoyance.

9

Gwen stared at herself in the mirror, her expression set in a look of annoyance. She had taken a cold shower following her furious encounter with Alaric, dressed, and proceeded to do her hair with passionate, jerky movements. Now she had nothing to do but focus on the guilt that rose up in her. It was funny how a few simple words shouted as she was ousting him from her apartment could make her feel so bad.

She had been fuming the whole day and for what? A mistake, that was what.

Growling at her reflection, Gwen tore herself away from the mirror and marched to the kitchen, where she poured herself a lemonade, liberally adding ice though she didn't care for it much. It was better than reaching for the liquor cabinet. She knew what drowning her sorrows was like, and it was not something she wanted to experience ever again.

Lemonade glass in hand, Gwen slumped against the counter and touched the material of her dress with the fingers that emerged from her cast. The movement sent twinges of pain up her arm, but she ignored them. The dress was pretty, a sort of olive-green color with a high, square neck and sleeves that covered her to her elbows. She didn't fill it out perfectly, but she wasn't nearly as skinny as she had been even a month ago. Considering how much she moved, between running and teaching Allison to fight and cooking and keeping her home in immaculate condition, it wasn't surprising she hadn't gained more weight. But she could have wished for a few more curves on a night like this.

Did she even want to go out?

Gwen picked again at the dress and sipped at her cold drink—she really did hate ice—and sighed. She didn't know. Feeling like she did, it probably would have been better to stay in her apartment and watch a movie. But Graham had been so nice to her, and she had told him that she would come. Maybe being admired and being among splendor and interesting people for an evening would take the edge off Gwen's temper. She didn't think that hitting a brick wall with her other hand was the best plan.

In any case, it was too late for her to back out. Graham would be there to pick her up in about a minute, and unless she developed a serious illness, it looked as though she was going. Gwen finished off her lemonade and dumped the ice in the sink before leaving the kitchen, feeling the loss of a comfortable evening of cooking as she thought of the evening that lay ahead of her. She couldn't mope around her apartment, but to have to go dancing? She hadn't danced since she was a girl.

Someone rang the buzzer, and it became officially too late for Gwen to do anything. She forcibly shoved thoughts of Alaric from her mind and brought forth the memories of how nice Graham had been to her that afternoon. She was wearing a pretty dress and had shoes that didn't kill her feet. It *was* going to be a good evening.

"I'll be right down," Gwen said into the intercom before throwing on a jacket and moving toward the door. She found Graham waiting for her, wearing a well-tailored suit that could pass as a tuxedo but wasn't quite. He had a thin black tie around his neck and his hands stuffed into his pockets.

"You look lovely," he said, smiling appreciatively at her. Gwen smiled in return and wondered absently when the last time she had blushed had been. There was no blush now.

"Thanks," she said, following Graham as he led her to his car. He was gallant and opened the door for Gwen, and she tried to be happy, but there was a tug of annoyance. She was a perfectly capable person, a former lieutenant in the US Army, and here was Graham, acting as though she was unable to open the door. She frowned and scolded herself, *This is a date. Stop acting like an idiot.*

"How's the hand?" Graham asked, climbing into the driver's side and turning on the engine.

"Fine," Gwen said, holding it up and examining the doctor's work. She flexed her fingers as much as she was able and ignored the pain. "So what exactly is this gala for?"

"Some charity or other," Graham answered. "Mr. Smythe was invited ages ago, and as his office manager, I am required to go so that he does not spend a fortune on the auction."

"It's an auction?" Gwen asked, brushing her hand over her skirt to smooth it out and looking out the window. She didn't know anything about auctions except that rich people went and bid on things.

"I think so. Don't worry, patrons aren't expected to bid on anything. Just the price of a plate is a couple hundred dollars, so there will be a decent profit for the night." Somehow, his words didn't make Gwen feel any better. A couple hundred dollars per plate? It wasn't so long ago that she had been wandering on the streets with nothing to her name. Now she was sitting in the seat of a fairly nice Mercedes, wearing a dress that had cost nearly half her weekly allowance, going to play nice with the wealthy of New York City. Circumstances changed, but such a dramatic change was astonishing to her. And it felt strange.

"I didn't know that you had to buy a plate for me," Gwen said.

"Don't worry, there's always an extra invitation set aside for Mr. Smythe or myself. Since he isn't bringing anyone, he said that it was just fine for me to bring you. Actually, he thought it was a great idea," Graham said, looking over at Gwen and brushing his fingers through her hair.

"If you say so," Gwen said. She was silent for a moment, her gaze fixed on the buildings flying past the window of Graham's car. She heard him sigh, and then his hand was tentatively resting on her knee.

"Listen, I'm sorry if this makes you uncomfortable," he said. "I didn't think about how you would feel around such people, and...well, I was just trying to ask you on a date."

"It's fine," Gwen assured him, touched that he was feeling uncomfortable for her sake. "I know where I come from, and I know where these people come from, and I'm grateful for everything that you and Walter have done for me. I just didn't want you to spend so much money on me."

Graham said nothing for a bit, then tightened his fingers on the steering wheel and replied with a cheeky grin, "You're probably worth it."

"Probably?" Gwen teased. Graham shot her a look of surprise and, after staring at her for a moment, smiled tentatively back. Gwen turned her attention to the people and buildings of New York and watched in fascination as the scenery changed ever so subtly the closer they got to the Ritz.

The two could find nothing to talk about, and the silence became increasingly awkward. Graham already knew about Gwen's work, and she had little desire to know about his. She wasn't going to talk about her past, and he wasn't going to ask. It was to the relief of both when Graham pulled up to the Ritz. He helped Gwen out of the car—she didn't mind chivalry, but being seen as weak was something else—and the valet took the Mercedes away, leaving an unobstructed view of the hotel.

It was a beautiful building, with just the right touches of modern and classic styling and lights glowing on the people that were arriving. The doormen were standing straight and tall, and the gathering of people looked to be magnificent. Gwen took Graham's arm, and the two walked up to the doors. Inside, it was even more stunning.

"Well," Gwen said, "I'm definitely out of place."

"What are you talking about?" Graham asked, looking at Gwen in surprise. She shrugged, taking in all the bejeweled women and their dashing counterparts. "You look like you were meant to be here."

"I feel like I should be somewhere else," she said. "I'm much more comfortable in a uniform."

"Do me a favor," Graham answered, gently pulling her in the direction of a small group of women, all wearing obviously expensive dresses and jewelry that must have cost a fortune. "Relax. You have every right to be here."

"Well, Graham Ruskin," one of the women said, turning a beaming smile on the handsome office manager. She held out her hand, and Graham took it, bending over it gallantly. She was a woman in her middle years with the air of someone far younger. Her hair was piled on her head in a tousled yet elegant manner, and she had the makeup to match. This was someone with both money and power, and Gwen wanted to edge quietly away.

"You know I come to these events just to see you," the woman said.

"You flatter me, Mrs. Stewart," Graham said with a dignified smile. Gwen wondered if you had to go to a special school to learn that sort of social interaction. If so, she certainly hadn't attended.

"Of course not," Mrs. Stewart preened. "You are so much more fun than these dreary men who stand around talking about their holdings in various companies. And you know how to dance." With a smile, she turned her attention on Gwen. "If you have any sense, you'll hold on to this one!"

"Mrs. Irene Stewart, this is Gwen," Graham introduced with a casual wave of his hand. Gwen smiled as best she could and excused herself from shaking hands with a gesture of her broken appendage.

"Lovely to meet you, dear. Whatever happened to your hand?" Mrs. Stewart asked, flagging down a waiter and snatching a drink of champagne off his tray. The man was gone before Gwen could do the same.

"I had an argument with a brick," she answered, the story told enough that it was spoken without thought.

The woman stared at Gwen incredulously for a moment, then chuckled as if it was a very clever joke. "I understand completely. Men can be such brutes sometimes," she said. "It's a good thing you moved on to dear Graham. Oh, if you'll excuse me, I see Mrs. Cheston and need to go speak with her." Just like that, Mrs. Stewart was gone, gliding off to go talk with another overly made-up woman with glittering diamonds at her ears.

"I don't think I understand what just happened," Gwen said, following Graham as he moved away, threading a path through the crowds of people.

"I'm not surprised. It's difficult to understand her sometimes. I find that the best solution is to smile and drink copiously," Graham said. Gwen nodded and looked for one of the waiters with a passing drink tray. There was no way she was going to get through this evening without one.

"Gwen!" The voice was unmistakable; Walter Smythe hurried over, looking cheerful and pleased with the general splendor of the evening. He came up to Gwen and, before she could even attempt to greet him, wrapped her in a hug. She froze, every muscle in her going tense until Walter released her. He didn't even seem to notice that she hadn't responded to his hug, just started in on commenting on her dress, firing questions about how things were working at The Wooden Rose, how she liked the apartment, what she was going to do when the class ended, what happened to her hand, how she had come to be on the arm of Graham, speaking so rapidly she could barely understand.

"Things are good," she managed when he paused to take a sip of some sort of drink.

"Sir," Graham said, rescuing Gwen by going into business mode, "have you spoken with Charles Kane yet this evening? He was looking quite seriously into your company, and I know that he wanted to talk with you about one of the start-ups he has invested in."

"Kane? An interesting fellow," Walter said, looking about, completely oblivious to the fact that he had been manipulated into pursuing a different line of conversation.

"Yes, though I don't know if he's here yet. You must also make sure to approach Mrs. Worthing; she wanted to thank you for the attention paid to her son's career. I don't believe he's here, but she was standing by the fig tree last I saw," Graham said.

"Certainly. Well, Gwen, it looks as though I've got to make the rounds." Walter beamed, patting her arm. "Such is life when you have money and people want it. When you become a famous chef, you'll understand. Everyone will want to talk with you." Just like that, he was gone.

"I think I'd much rather keep to the background," Gwen said, finally spotting a waiter within reach. She was too late though. Graham managed to pick up two glasses before Gwen could even move her arm, and with the air of someone bestowing a fantastic gift, he handed one to her. "Thanks," she said.

"I don't know, you seem to manage just fine," Graham said. At Gwen's skeptical look, he shrugged and sipped at the glass of bubbly liquid. "These things take practice is all. With a few more events under your belt, no one will even know that you don't come from the same background."

"Frankly, that's something I'd rather not train to achieve," Gwen said, a scoffing smile on her lips.

Graham drew his eyebrows together and looked at Gwen curiously. "Why not? You look beautiful here, and I know you could thrive. After all, you've been through worse, no?" He sipped again at his drink, and Gwen lowered her gaze, staring into her own glass. Then Graham chuckled and put his hand under her chin, looking at her with a strange sort of pride. "It would be like *Pygmalion,* the play. Or the musical *My Fair Lady*. Surely you know it. You would be Eliza, and I'd be Professor Higgins. Only you're much more accomplished than Eliza."

Gwen did the best she could to keep her expression neutral, to push that fiery temper down. She didn't have to worry, though, because at that minute, the gong for dinner sounded, and all the guests started streaming into the banquet hall to find their seats and exclaim over their dining companions. By keeping her eyes focused on the many tables, fixated on the task of finding the plate that had the card bearing her name, Gwen was able to keep the rage she felt from showing.

He thought that she was inferior, needing to be molded into something better so that she could fool the world and be little more than proof of his capabilities. Gwen knew that many women would be pleased to be a part of something greater, taking pains to act differently to be seen as better. But she was not one of those people. She was just fine with what she was, a person who was building her own life. Just because Walter was helping her make something out of herself did not mean that his office manager could turn her into something to be stared at. She was making her way in the world. Not him. The fact that Graham was even considering such a thing was offensive and infuriating.

Gwen remained silent through the introduction by the man on the stage, through the applauding over whatever the evening's event entailed. She simply sat there while the waiters served what looked to be an interesting meal of poached salmon and roasted fingerling potatoes with French-cut green beans in a light muscatel sauce, capers resting on the fish, a lemon wedge beside the potatoes. Only when a man asked her a question over her shoulder did she return to the scene at hand.

"I'm sorry," Gwen said to the man, indicating a need for the repetition of the question.

"Of course. Would you prefer white or red wine? We have a pink zinfandel, an aged chardonnay, or a deeper port," the sommelier said. Gwen considered and went with the port, fully aware of the fact that Alaric would disapprove. She liked port, and she didn't care.

"Are you all right?" Graham asked, sipping at his zinfandel and raising his eyebrows.

Gwen picked up her knife and fork and shrugged. "A bit hungry," she said, cutting into her salmon. She didn't know why she was hesitant to tell Graham exactly what she thought of him at the moment—normally, she didn't hold back at all—but she couldn't be bothered to explain her mood. She was hungry, her mood was souring, and it looked as though the evening had only just begun. Besides, they hadn't even started the auction yet.

"Let me know what you think," Graham said, looking dubiously at his own meal. Gwen took a bite and looked around, spying three different meals that looked preordered. She chewed the salmon slowly, swallowed, then sighed and put her cutlery down. It was definitely going to be a long night with such poor fare.

"It's not the worst I've had," Gwen said, considering the potatoes on her plate. The salmon was overcooked and oversauced, and if the wedge of lemon was any hint, the potatoes weren't likely to be much better. "But I've had better."

"Don't tell Chef Maurice that," a woman on Gwen's left said, leaning over as if it was a great secret, though her voice spoke to the contrary.

"Is he the head chef at the Ritz?" Gwen asked, glad for the distraction into a world she knew. Somehow, she doubted that any of these people were going to start talking war, guns, or language interpretation, so food was as good a lifeline as any.

"He's been here for dogs' years," the woman said,

taking a stab at her own meal—a chicken marsala with white rice instead of pasta. "I think he came from Italy or Spain or some such place, and he supposedly trained at some of the best restaurants in the world, looking for the perfect flavor."

"I'm amazed he ended up in at hotel, then," Gwen said dryly. Chefs like that fought tooth and nail to be at world-class restaurants, not in hotel dining. To her surprise, the woman laughed loudly. Gwen choked for a moment on a mouthful of port, feeling Graham's hand on her back as she coughed, then looked at the woman in astonishment.

"He's wondered the same thing a few times. But I've heard him say that he's trying to educate the poor hotel people. He's a friend of my brother's, so we've had the benefit of his cooking many a time. Have you eaten at The Wooden Rose, by any chance?" the woman asked. Gwen managed not to choke on this mouthful of wine, but Gwen barely hid a snort of derision. Of all the things to ask on her night off.

"You could say that," she said, deciding that the lemon might just be for decoration and spearing one of the potatoes with her fork.

"Well, for years now, Chef Maurice has been trying to either get one of his people in there or steal one of the students that come out of there. Apparently, he and the head chef at The Wooden Rose have some sort of rivalry going on. I couldn't tell you which one was better, but don't say I said so or Chef Maurice will have my head," the woman said. She, too, took another bite of her meal, but it was plain that she relished it far more than Gwen. As suspected, the potatoes were flavored too much with citrus.

"He sounds like quite the character," Gwen said. She debated with herself on whether she would finish off her food, then stopped, horrified. Had she really come so far as to forget the feeling of hunger enough that she could consider skipping a meal paid for by someone else and cooked for her benefit? It wasn't so long ago that she'd lived on the streets, begging for enough money to buy a hot dog at a food stand. She had eaten every scrap of food she had made under the tutelage of Alaric, and faced by the prospect of being elegant and beautiful, surrounded by people who were used to getting exactly what they wanted, she was becoming a snob. Even in the army, she hadn't been like that.

"Yes, rather," the woman said.

Gwen started eating properly, ignoring the dubious looks from the woman next to her and Graham's questions about the meal. She wouldn't send it back because it was overcooked. She settled into her meal and sipped delicately at the port, hoping that the waiter wouldn't come by and fill her glass. This evening was bad enough; she didn't need to be drunk to top things off.

"Gwen, is everything all right?" Graham asked as she stabbed a green bean. "You seem out of sorts."

"I've just had a long day," she answered. "And I

think the pain medication I was given at the hospital is wearing off."

"Do you want me to see if I can find something? Perhaps an aspirin?" Graham asked.

Gwen gave a minute shake of the head.

"I have to stay for the auction, but...if you're tired, I'll call you a cab."

"Thank you," Gwen said. "I'll finish supper, but I may take you up on that."

"Just as long as you're okay," Graham said. He reached out to touch her hair again, making Gwen wonder why he acted as though he had to possess her, keeping in contact with her as much as he could. "I should have thought about that earlier, that you would be tired."

"It's fine, Graham," Gwen said, finishing the last of her salmon. "It was great of you to ask me. I really appreciate it."

The simple statement seemed to smooth all her escort's ruffled feathers, and he went back to his own meal, engaging Gwen in small talk while the other people wined and dined all around them. Gwen finished her food with determination, putting down her knife and fork just as the lights in the hall dimmed and the man returned once more to the stage, this time to introduce the auction. Gwen sat through the intro-duction and waited until there was a lull before bidders began to slip out of the hall.

"Gwen, wait," Graham said, walking swiftly to catch

up with her as she left the hall. "Let me at least call you a cab or an Uber or something."

"I think I'd rather walk," she answered, tucking a strand of hair behind her ear, suddenly annoyed with it and the way that the dress restricted her movements to something befitting a lady. She wanted to go for a run, the exertion burning any excess anger from her system.

"I can't let you do that," Graham said, putting his hand on Gwen's shoulder. She scowled up at him, the first sign of anger that she'd let him see. He stepped back half an inch, then smiled at Gwen delicately. "It's dark, and I wouldn't want you to get hurt. If only to ease my mind, let me call you a cab."

Gwen hesitated, torn between snapping that she was perfectly capable of taking care of herself and not yelling at the man who had asked her on a date, no matter that he wanted to treat her like a porcelain doll. Her hesitation was enough to let Graham pull his phone from his pocket and dial a number, requesting a cab at the Ritz. Now she had no choice. That was enough to put Gwen over the edge.

"I can take care of myself," she grumbled. "I'm not some sort of stupid, useless girl that can't manage on her own."

"I never said you were," Graham said, obviously taken aback.

"Then why do you insist on treating me as though I'm a child, ignorant of all the ways of the world and in need of your help and guidance?" Gwen said, narrowing her eyes.

"You've just been to the hospital," Graham protested, though from the alarm in his eyes, it was plain that he was fully aware of the fact that Gwen wasn't referring to her broken hand.

"Yes, fine, open the door, then. But don't treat me as though I don't know how to act in social situations or in getting home. Because you know something? I could kick your ass *and* cook it up. I'm tired of people treating me like I'm some sort of fragile thing that could keel over at any minute," Gwen hissed. She snarled, and Graham froze his forward advance. "I don't need your cab, and I'm going for a walk. Now leave me alone!"

10

"What are you doing here?" Jack asked as he slipped the key into the back door of The Wooden Rose, where Alaric was sitting, two hours after having forgotten his key inside. At least he had remembered to turn off all the cooking equipment, if the lights. "It's your day off."

"I was working on some possible new additions to the menu earlier and went outside for a bit... I left my keys in my jacket," Alaric said, hopping to his feet and following Jack inside. The manager and friend of the head chef shook his head.

"You were just working on the menu, huh? Then why do I hear Paganini?" Jack asked.

Alaric cursed himself silently for not having turned off his music. He liked classical music, but he only listened to Paganini when he was in a funk over something. This time, it just happened to be Gwen. Alaric walked into the kitchen and picked up a rag, preparing to clean.

"Come on, Alaric. I'm your friend. If you don't tell me what's going on, then I'm going to have to take drastic measures."

"Why would you think that anything would be wrong? Maybe I just wanted to listen to Paganini? Besides, I haven't yelled at my staff nearly as much lately," Alaric snarled. "Isn't that what you wanted?" He squeezed the soapy water out of the rag and hurled it at the counter, furious at himself and Gwen—and at Jack for asking too many questions.

"Exactly. I'm pretty sure that you would have told me if you were taking up boxing, or at least complained about it. There's no way that you would even consider doing therapy, so that's out, and you haven't got the smugly superior look of someone who's having sex regularly. So what's got you in a mood?" Jack asked, rolling up his shirtsleeves and grabbing another rag. He squeezed out the water and, much more gently than Alaric, set about cleaning the counter opposite his friend.

"It's nothing," Alaric insisted. He sighed and leaned his weight on the counter, trying to convince himself that it really was nothing. Still, the image of Gwen haunted his thoughts, angry at him one moment, lost and alone the next.

"Alaric," Jack said softly, pausing in his own cleaning. "Tell me."

"What do you want me to say? Hmm? That I have

completely messed everything up and am becoming obsessed with something out of reach? Or would you rather I just say I've got the flu and need some time to get over it?" Alaric snarled, straightening and curling his lip, glaring at Jack.

"If you had the flu, you wouldn't be within a mile of this place," Jack pointed out. "And obsessed? With what? Or who—oh, no. Alaric, please tell me you don't have a, a *thing* for Gwen." By this point, both men had given up on cleaning the counters, all pretense dropped. They were just friends, trying to sort out the world.

Alaric leaned against a counter and looked upward, tracing patterns in the ceiling with his gaze. "Is that so terrible? You have—what's her name—Eloise, who worked as an accountant here. Why can't I have a *thing* for Gwen?" Alaric hissed, pointedly looking away as Jack leaned on the counter opposite.

"She's your student, Alaric," Jack said flatly. "You can't get involved with one of your students."

"Says who? She's my age. It's not illegal," Alaric grumbled.

Jack shook his head. "No, but it's practically taking advantage of the poor girl. You're her mentor, teaching her to become independent in the world of food. You're teaching her to be great, and if what I hear from you is anything close to the truth and not you looking through rose-tinted glasses, then she will be. If you do this, Alaric, you're going to hold her back," Jack said.

Alaric said nothing, fully aware of the truth of

Jack's words. The fact that he said nothing, though, was telling enough.

"Shit. Alaric, I'm telling you, this is a bad idea. You're one of the best chefs in New York, and you can't afford to be distracted by a girl."

"I tried, Jack," Alaric muttered, his anger vanished only to be replaced by guilt and pain. "Don't you think I haven't tried to treat her like any of the other students? I've yelled at her more than practically anyone because she was so far behind them, but it doesn't seem to matter how much I try. I can't get her out of my head."

"Can't you just, I don't know, be friends or something? Start dating again. Get back together with Kelsey or whatever the other one's name was, Beth, just don't do this," Jack pleaded.

Alaric shrugged. Then he ran his hands through his hair and shook his head. "I tried that too," Alaric said quietly. "Somehow, I don't think this is going to be that easy."

"Let me guess," Jack said dryly, eyes fixed on his friend's face so that he could see every reaction. "You get shivers when she brushes past you, you want to see her able to deal with her demons more than you want to see her smile, you want to follow her back to her place and be welcomed in rather than shut—damn. Congratulations, Alaric, you've got it bad."

"Shut up, all right? I'm fully aware that I've got a problem when it comes to Gwen," Alaric said. He turned around and grabbed up the cleaning cloth again, desperate for something to cover up his embarrassment. "The question is: What do I do about it? I can't very well ignore her, seeing as we have three weeks left of classes. That and with Lauren going on maternity leave in two days, I'm going to need all my people more than ever. Besides, I don't think she's all that happy with me at the moment. Maybe I should just ignore her."

"I don't think that's going to fix anything," Jack said. "If what you say is true, then ignoring her is only going to make the problem worse. And what do you mean, she's angry at you?"

Alaric groaned and buried his head in his hands, muttering something through the cleaning cloth. Jack waited. A moment later, the head chef raised his head and started to explain. He told his friend everything, flicking his eyes to Jack's face every now and again, trying to gauge his reaction. From the solemn look that Jack carried, it was bad. Really bad.

"So I shoved my foot in her door, told her that I hadn't asked Major Dalton about anything because it wasn't my place, and then I left."

"You left. Just like that?" Jack asked. He glanced at the clock and moved to finish up the last of the cleaning. The kitchen crew would be arriving in a few minutes, and they would ask questions at the mess. Alaric just stood there.

"Just like that," Alaric said. "Now what do I do?"

"Wait until tomorrow and then apologize," Jack

said, giving an easy shrug of his shoulders. "That's a place to start."

"And then what, tell her that I can't get her out of my head and would she please go on a date with me? Or should I skip that and just tell her I want to sleep with her?" Alaric asked.

"I think if you can avoid talking about sex, at least for now, then you're probably heading in the right direction. And yeah, asking her on a date is a good place to start. Just don't take her to a restaurant. You two are far too into food to possibly make it anywhere without breaking down into a conversation about the preparation of the meal. Which is fine, just not for a first date," Jack said. "Now stop standing there, and—"

"Hey, Chef." Danny walked in, slinging his jacket on the coat rack by the back door. "I thought it was your night off. Are we changing up the menu?" That was, after all, the only reasonable explanation for Alaric to be there on his day off. He may have been obsessed with the restaurant, but he was aware that he needed time away.

"No," Alaric said, thinking of the dishes he had put into the large refrigerator. "I was just asking Jack a question about something. Working on figuring out what to do when Lauren leaves."

"Oh, right. I need to remember to get her a card for her baby," Danny said. "We'll be sure to cook well tonight, Chef."

"If you don't, I'm coming after you to flay your hide," Alaric grumbled, then turned back to Jack, pleading with his eyes. Before he could voice his question, the manager shook his head and raised his eyebrows.

"Not a chance, Alaric. This is your day off. Get your ass home, go to the gym, whatever it is that you do on your day off. Just don't you dare stay here," Jack snapped.

"Fine," Alaric grumbled. "See you later, Jack. And don't you dare mess up my kitchen."

"Out. Now," Jack said.

Alaric snarled his obedience and grabbed his jacket, this time remembering to make sure that he had his keys. He stalked through the back door as Lauren was coming in, growled what could pass as a greeting, and loped off to his car. Following a display of slamming his doors and revving the engine—something that annoyed Jack greatly—Alaric sped off toward his apartment, trying to think of something that would occupy his time while he tried not to think of Gwen. He started with a film, moved to examining his fridge to cook, and ended up doing exactly as Jack had suggested, a gym bag over his shoulders and trainers on his feet.

His gym was only a couple of blocks away, and he went faithfully every week on his day off, not because he enjoyed it but because he couldn't think of much else to do with his free time. And when he didn't have his students to worry about, he often went in the mornings too. The path to the gym was so familiar to him that Alaric could stew and grumble to himself without worrying about losing his way.

Tonight, though, he paused. She was in his head surely, not walking in front of him, wearing an evening gown and heels, looking rather more upset than she had when he'd seen her earlier. *Don't do it,* Alaric told himself, but it was already too late. He picked up his pace and jogged up to Gwen's side.

"Hey," he said, stepping back to avoid the blow that she aimed at his head. It was half-hearted, meant more as a warning to strangers to stay away than anything. "What are you doing out this way? And, er, dressed like that?"

"I am walking home," Gwen snapped. She growled and sped up. "Or at least, I was trying before I got lost. I have no idea where I am, and I am inches away from calling a cab. Either that or I'm going to throw these shoes through a window."

"Um, can I offer you a ride?" Alaric asked warily. Was she angry at him? Frankly, in her current mood, Alaric didn't want to find out. "I only live a block from here, and it wouldn't take long."

"That's very kind of you," Gwen hissed, stumbling as she tried to wrestle her shoes into cooperating. "But I think I can manage."

"Come on, Gwen," Alaric said as gently as possible. "It's really not that big of a deal."

"It's—dumb shoe—fine," Gwen said, marching resolutely forward. "I've dealt with—damn it—worse."

"Somehow, I doubt that. There's not much worse

than shoes like that," Alaric said, trying a joke. Maybe that would work, if nothing else. When that got him nothing but a furious look from Gwen, he shrugged and held up his hands in a gesture of peace. "Look, I'm sorry about earlier. I won't ever mention it again, if it bothers you. But can we just let bygones be bygones and act normally? You know, like friends?"

Gwen stopped walking, instead choosing to slump against a wall. "It's partly my fault. I have this thing about people trying to dig around in my life. So I guess I should also be apologizing. I'm not even all that mad about that. It's these stupid shoes, this dress, this whole night that's been driving me crazy."

"Come on," Alaric said, holding out his arm that, to his surprise, Gwen actually took. She must have been in excruciating pain from the shoes to go through that. "My building's not too far from here. Just two minutes that way." He started walking, going slowly enough that Gwen wouldn't have to hurt herself more but also moving at a decent pace, acting under the assumption that if Gwen thought he was babying her, she would kill him.

"How did you end up with an apartment down here?" Gwen asked as they reached the building. She waited patiently while Alaric opened the door, her expression betraying dismay as she realized there was no elevator. "It's a fairly nice area with lawyers and technology sorts. Not your style, I would have thought."

"Once upon a time," Alaric said, "I dated a lawyer.

This was back in my young and impetuous days, when I was just making it as a chef and able to afford a decent apartment. I thought that she and I were going to last forever, and so I listened to her when she said she wanted to live close to her work. What did it matter? I had a car, and the apartments are nice, if a bit too streamlined for my tastes."

"Let me guess," Gwen said, nodding her thanks as Alaric opened the door for her, letting her into his flat. "She dumped you."

"Actually, it was the other way around," Alaric said. "I wasn't a huge fan of lawyers determined to hang on to me for the notoriety and the sex. Though, the sex was pretty good." Alaric winced, knowing that he had just done exactly what Jack told him not to do. But Gwen had been around men for long periods of time, and his statement obviously didn't bother her. She just barked out a sarcastic laugh and smiled sardonically.

"It's a nice place," Gwen said. It was, actually. The lines of the flat were all crisp and clean, with dark muted tones on the walls, shiny tile on the floor. The furniture was a mash of styles, some obviously having been provided to the resident—these were all very modern, in bold colors—others much more comfortable and traditional in styling. It was clean but not clinical, and there were signs of life, but mostly in the kitchen and bedroom. There were plates in the sink, and the bed was not made. Otherwise, it looked to be the residence of a bachelor with a *very* successful career who would come home to a glass of fifty-year-old scotch and turn on some really bad jazz just to say he was cultured.

"It's a place to live," Alaric said, "but I'm not too attached to it."

"Then why don't you move?" Gwen asked, walking toward a leather couch that looked as though it had seen much use as a bed. Alaric gestured for her to sit, and she did.

"Want something to drink? All right," Alaric said. He went into the kitchen for a minute and returned, carrying two bottles of stout rather than the cut glass of scotch.

Gwen nodded in approval.

"It's a hassle to get out of this lease, and besides, the apartment that I wanted was recently rented out to a former army person. Such a pain, really."

"You mean...oh, sorry. Walter rented the apartment before I even knew what being clean felt like, so there wasn't much I could do. Though I'm sure he could figure something out," Gwen said, prying off the top of the bottle with a practiced twist of her hand.

Alaric gaped at her. To go from absolutely furious with him to demure and talking about moving out of her apartment just because he was interested was bizarre. And totally unlike the Gwen that he knew.

"I'm not serious. I was just teasing you," Alaric said.

Gwen snorted, sipping at the stout, and Alaric shook his head, settling into the couch next to Gwen. She had been teasing too. All right, fine. That was good. She wasn't angry at him anymore, and she was acting more like they were the friends they had come to be over the last weeks. They both sipped again at their drinks, and Gwen leaned her head back on the couch, slipping her feet out of her shoes and flexing her toes. Alaric watched, fascinated, though he noted that he didn't see any blisters or blood. Even so, shoes like that must have been painful.

"How do you make your own way in the world, completely independent and without other people trying to make something out of you that you're not?" Gwen asked, tapping her fingers gently against the bottle.

"I'm getting the impression that this question isn't purely theoretical," Alaric said, mimicking her pose, head on the back of the couch, legs stretched out. "If it is, then it's a fairly deep question to be having over a beer."

"Yeah," Gwen said. "It's not really all that theoretical."

"And this is the part where you tell me exactly what's going on," Alaric said. Gwen shot him a look, and he shrugged. "I've had friends before, Gwen. I've even had friends who were girls. It doesn't mean that you're allowed to cry on my shoulder or anything, but I know when to ask you to explain."

"You're an ass," Gwen said, chuckling. She took a long pull of her stout and settled deeper into the couch, which caused her dress to slide up her thigh enough to make Alaric want to do things other than sit there and listen. He kept his hands still and forced himself to do nothing but listen.

"I know," he said. "But it works for me."

"Right," she replied. "Fine, if you're going to ask, I may as well tell you. Graham asked me to go to a gala with him."

"What? When did this happen?!" Alaric asked in alarm, fighting the urge to grab Gwen by the shoulders and demand that she return to her senses. He thought that they had an agreement about Graham; he was an insufferable bastard, and they didn't need to deal with him anymore.

"Sometime after I overheard you on the phone with Major Dalton last night and went to the hospital to get my hand bandaged," Gwen said, wincing even as she said the words. "I fully admit that, in hindsight, it was stupid to hit the brick. But I was angry. And I couldn't very well hit you because that would just get me kicked out of this school, and I really need this."

"Actually, it's just as likely that I would have hit you back," Alaric said. "Then there would be no hard feelings, and we could have avoided this whole stewing anger and yelling bit. Got right down to drinking beer."

"You're such a man," Gwen said, rolling her eyes. "Anyway, this morning, I figured that my hand was really and truly broken and that I should probably do something about it, so I went to the hospital, where, since there is a notation in my file now thanks to Walter's meddling ways, Graham showed up after receiving a phone call."

"So what, if you get sick or something, Walter knows about it? So he doesn't lose track of his investment?" Alaric scoffed, shaking his head.

Gwen tightened her lips, considering. "I don't think it's anything quite as sinister as that. At least, Walter doesn't think so. But then, he lives in a different world than we do. It doesn't matter either way. Graham showed up, he asked me what happened, I told him I had an argument with a brick, he laughed, we talked. It was strange, him being so nice to me. I should have seen it then," Gwen said. She pressed the bottle to her head and groaned in relief.

"Graham can be charming when he wants to be," Alaric growled, the sound rumbling deep in his chest. Gwen turned her head to look at him in surprise. His mouth was etched in a deep frown, and his eyebrows were drawn together. That wasn't just anger, that was bitterness.

"I'm sensing that you two have a past?" Gwen probed.

"Yeah," Alaric said. "We can talk about that later. You still haven't finished your story. And don't you dare complain. I told you, I've had friends that are girls before, not to mention girlfriends. I know how tricky you can be."

"Wise guy," Gwen muttered. She tugged at the neckline of her dress as if it was suddenly restricting.

Alaric swallowed, knowing precisely how he could help her with that particular problem. He scolded himself and took a drink of his stout.

"Fine. He was nice, charming even, and so I agreed to go to this gala thing. Even though I've never been to an event like that. Frankly, I've never spent that much money on clothes before, and that was pennies on the dollar to the sort of people that attend those events."

"Ah, yes, the fantastically wealthy," Alaric mused. "Smiles and sparkles and very sharp knives to stab you in the back."

"That about sums it up. I have no idea how to act among these people, so I did the smile-and-say-nothing routine," Gwen said. "It worked too, until that idiot Graham spoiled everything by saying that I was like Eliza from *Pygmalion*. You know, the one where Professor Higgins takes a flower seller and turns her into some sort of fantastic lady. He was quite pleased with the comparison—"

"He was to be Professor Higgins?" Alaric asked.

Gwen hummed in agreement.

"Ouch. That's really harsh. Saying you're incapable of fitting in on your own and pretending that you need someone like him to 'guide' you."

"So I ate dinner—it was average, there was too much sauce and everything was far too overt for actual quality—and left but not after yelling at him to leave me alone," Gwen said.

"Where was this? Do I know the chef?" Alaric asked, distracted by the description of the meal.

Gwen looked tempted to punch Alaric, but her good hand was taken up with her drink, and the other was broken. "The Ritz-Carlton. According to one of the very wealthy, the chef is some sort of great admirer or great enemy. I didn't really pay attention," Gwen said. "In any case, that's how I ended up pissed off, determined to walk back to my building in shoes that look great but are really uncomfortable."

"The Ritz…hmm, I'll think about it. But hey, at least you don't have to deal with Graham anymore. And we're back to being friends, so you've at least got a decent drink out of the deal," Alaric said. He watched Gwen drink up the last of her stout and rose from the couch, taking both bottles to the kitchen, where he threw them away and rifled through his fridge, thinking that, if nothing else, he could fix a subpar dinner with a decent dessert. "Do you want some crème brûlée? I have all the ingredients, and that might smooth things over," Alaric called.

"That sounds fine," Gwen said from the doorway, making Alaric jump. He turned to look at her and all but grinned when she reached for one of the aprons he kept on a hook by the door. She tied it over her dress, looking very nice while she did so, and turned to him. "Your kitchen, Chef. Tell me what to do."

11

"Don't you dare overheat that cream," Alaric said harshly, watching as Gwen stirred the liquid in a saucepan. She flicked him a glance but said nothing, knowing perfectly well that no matter how friendly he was out of the kitchen, when he was cooking—or supervising cooking—things had to be perfect.

"The cream is fine," Gwen said, watching as a lone bubble of heat popped on the surface of the mixture. She flicked the stove off and moved the saucepan so that she could pour the cream into the egg mixture. Alaric got in the way and snatched the pan from her, muttering under his breath as he did so. Gwen shrugged and rolled her eyes. "You'd think that this was up for some prize, the way you bother."

"If I only put forth my best effort on food that is to be judged, then I am not a proper chef," Alaric said, bending over the mixture as he poured the cream into it. Gwen handed him a whisk, and he plucked it from her fingers. He growled even as she laughed quietly and retreated to a safe corner by the refrigerator, watching him work. If it were possible, Alaric was even more temperamental and prone to bursts of anger at home than at the Rose. Gwen smiled slightly and shook her head.

"I'm sure it's fine," Gwen said. "It isn't as though you've never made crème brûlée before, after all."

"It is one of my specialties," Alaric said, transferring the mixture to a double boiler he had prepped. Gently and precisely, he dipped a spoon into the mixture and began stirring it, like an artisan mixing paints. "If you want to be helpful, you can get the raspberries in there and see about chopping them up and turning them into a syrup."

"Right." Gwen smiled to herself and shook her head. She went into the fridge and pulled out raspberries, fresh and looking as though they had been purchased from a farmers market despite the earliness of the season. "Where did you find raspberries this time of year? Fresh ones, I mean."

"I know a guy," Alaric said, looking at the spoon and nodding to himself. He pulled the mixture off the stove and into the dishes, then slid the dishes into the oven, checking the temperature before turning his attention to Gwen. He froze for a moment, staring at her, his breath hitching. She turned away and focused on her task, trying to ignore the potential implications. She was holding a knife with her left hand and using the flat of the blade to squash the raspberries, getting the juices out.

"Are you all right to be doing that?" Alaric asked.

"What? Oh, my hand," Gwen said, raising the broken hand to examine it. "I don't know. The doctors would probably complain, but it's bandaged, and I've had loads worse than this."

"Doesn't it hurt?" Alaric asked, stepping over to grasp the bandaged hand lightly and look at it, as if by examining it, he could fix it.

"A little," Gwen admitted, blinking away a twinge of pain as Alaric brushed his fingers over hers, the touch featherlight and careful. "But in a couple of days, I'll hardly notice it but for the cast."

"And will you be all right to cook?" Alaric asked, looking up from studying the injury to meet Gwen's gaze.

She smiled and raised her eyebrows, straightening her shoulders as if suddenly faced with her boss rather than her friend.

"Is that all you care about?" Gwen admonished, her sarcasm hiding the hurt. She knew that it was silly to think otherwise, that first and foremost Alaric was her employer and teacher, that he would and should care about her ability to perform her job before he should care about her well-being, emotional or otherwise. She watched then, astonished as Alaric raised her hand, his eyes never once leaving hers.

"Not in the slightest," he said, kissing the tips of her fingers. As before, pain flared through Gwen's hand, but she ignored it, startled into trying to analyze all the possible implications of Alaric's words. The safest was that he was simply her friend, worried about her and feeling slightly guilty for having caused her to break her hand even indirectly. The most thrilling, the one she only admitted to wanting in the quietest reaches of her mind, slipped swiftly out of friendship and into something much deeper and much more interesting. It was this that caused her skin to tingle at Alaric's touch.

She didn't know whether to smile or look stern, and the room seemed to heat as she struggled to decide. Alaric's eyes shifted for a moment, then grew wide.

"Shit," he cried, leaping forward and past Gwen to the stove. The edges of Gwen's dress, as she had been close to the still-burning cooktop, had started to smolder and caught on fire. She turned and searched for the nearest way of putting out the fire. Alaric was being no help, dancing around as he was, trying to pat out the worst of the flames with a kitchen towel.

Gwen lunged for the sink, hurling herself into it as if she was playing a game of musical chairs. She reached around and turned on the faucet, the hissing that followed indicating that the flames had been put out. Smoke, smelling terribly of burned silk, filled the air, and Gwen's heart finally started to slow. She stared at Alaric, who stared back, both at a loss for words. Then, with her dress completely wet and ruined by this point, half of the back skirt being lost to the flames, Gwen started to laugh.

"It's not funny," Alaric tried to protest, though he was doing poorly at concealing his own laughter.

Gwen snorted at that and tried to pull herself out of the sink. She floundered and failed, too caught up in hysterics to manage such coordination.

"Stop laughing," Alaric said, grabbing onto her arms and pulling.

"It's hilarious," Gwen said, yelping as Alaric pulled too hard and she practically flew out of the sink. The pair were thrown off-balance. They slipped to the floor and stayed there, unable to stop laughing. Gwen was lying on top of Alaric's chest, her legs entangled in his. He had one hand covering his eyes as his face was twisted in mirth. As soon as Gwen stopped for breath, she realized the awkwardness of her position and attempted to roll off Alaric. Her legs got caught in his, and she succeeded in doing nothing more than wasting her breath and moving the pair of them about an inch.

"Here," Alaric said between breathless laughs, his face flushed with more than just lack of breath. He pulled one way, Gwen pulled another, and the two managed to disentangle themselves. Gwen let her laughter die as she sat up against one of the counters. Still grinning, she did her best to ignore the way that being pressed against Alaric felt. It felt more than nice. He was her friend; he had given her no indication that he wanted more. She would live with that, though once she had accepted the fact that she was interested, her blood wouldn't stop singing for another touch.

"In all my life, even through all the shit with the army, I have never set myself on fire," Gwen said, brushing her hair out of her eyes.

Alaric moved to sit on the floor next to her and looked on in amazement. "Really? I've done it loads of times, just never in my house. I think it's a prerogative of cooks to catch on fire at least once in their lives. You seemed to know what you were doing though," Alaric said, still breathing hard enough to give a sort of flush to his skin.

"I've got a good head for emergencies," Gwen replied. She rubbed at the dress and let out a single deep breath, leaning her head backward against the counter. "I don't suppose you have some clothes I can borrow? I feel a rather awkward draft where there shouldn't be."

This set both of them off again, laughing like a couple of heady teenagers alone for the first time without a parent looking over their shoulders. Alaric finally managed to rise, and he helped Gwen stand, using the counter for support.

"Come on," he said, "I think I have some sweats and a shirt that might fit you."

He led Gwen to his bedroom, rifling through his closet and trying to find something that wouldn't look terribly indecent on her. Considering that the crème brûlée had just gone into the oven and needed another hour after that to cool, she didn't want to tempt him further. Finally, thrusting a pair of old pajama pants and a black T-shirt at Gwen, Alaric hurried her into the bathroom, looking pointedly away from the damaged part of the dress. Gwen twisted to undo the dress and tripped, knocking over some things on the counter.

"Are you all right?" Alaric asked, knocking twice on the bathroom door. Another *thud* and furious grumbling. "Gwen?"

"I can't get this dumb dress off. The zipper's all messed up with the burned material, especially since it's wet," Gwen said through the door. "I think it fused together."

"Do you want some help?" Alaric asked. Gwen muttered a yes, and Alaric opened the door. It wasn't complete chaos, but it was close. Gwen had managed to get the zipper about halfway down her back, but she had knocked over the tissue box and the cup Alaric kept on the counter. The rest of the dress was twisted about so that she could try and reach the zipper and see what she was doing at the same time.

"This dratted thing is just being difficult on purpose," Gwen snarled, unable to work the zipper with both hands and, despite the laughter of a few minutes previous, feeling as though she was inches from tears.

"Hold still," Alaric said. Gwen did so, and he stepped forward, swallowing as he looked at the ruined back of her dress. It was impressive that Gwen wasn't hurt. What hadn't been burned was wet and, as a result, sticky. He worked with featherlight fingers, brushing against her skin as little as possible and doing his very best to not touch her any more than necessary.

Gwen shivered as he brushed against her skin and didn't move when he yanked at the zipper to get it moving. He finished unzipping her with a whisper of his fingers on her skin, then she was free, slipping her arms through the sleeves and stepping out of the ruined fabric as it fell to the floor. When she turned to find the clothes Alaric had loaned, she froze.

Alaric stood there, completely immobile and staring unabashedly as though he couldn't stop. His hand was stone still as he held out the T-shirt, and he couldn't seem to draw himself away from taking in every inch of her. She was still wearing underwear, but that wasn't helping her think clearly. He stared as though he could see through to her soul. She shivered once, and the spell was broken.

Alaric reared backward. "Oh, crap. Sorry! I'm sorry —I didn't mean—It's not that—sorry!"

Gwen took the T-shirt, beyond the point of blushing for her modesty. "I lived a considerable amount of time with a bunch of men, Alaric. Relax." She dressed, Alaric with his back to her still babbling apologies and sounding as though he was going to melt into a puddle of shame if he didn't stop soon.

"Hey, enough, all right?" Gwen said, putting a hand on his shoulder. Alaric stiffened, and Gwen had to forcibly turn him around to prove that she was fully dressed and perfectly fine, despite his ogling. "It's not a big deal."

Alaric muttered something that sounded like, "It's a pretty big deal." Perhaps not wanting to have to embarrass himself any further, he fled to the kitchen. Gwen entered the kitchen as he was throwing raspberries into a small saucepan and reaching for the control to turn on the heat. He moved quickly, his actions jerky and far from the normal grace that he used when cooking. His shoulders were tense, and he grumbled quietly to himself.

A disaster. This whole thing was a complete disaster.

Gwen stopped Alaric before he could turn on the flame, her hand doing nothing more than touching his. He still froze.

She turned him to face her and raised her eyebrows at the stove. "That's what got us into trouble in the first place," she murmured. Alaric tried not to look confused, though he was a bit distracted by the way that his pajama pants slipped down her hips, leaving a patch of exposed skin between them and the shirt. He was also distracted by the way that Gwen advanced slowly, backing him into a corner.

"I, ah, thought that we should make the syrup before the, er, crème brûlée was done in the oven. Then we could chill them both and, well, watch television or something," Alaric said, trying to distract himself and Gwen—but mostly stop the way that his heart was pounding, his thoughts screaming at him to take ahold of her right then and there—with cooking. She hadn't been a chef for her whole life and wasn't so easily distracted.

"Alaric?" Gwen said, stopping inches away from him, her eyes slightly lidded and a smile twitching at the corner of her mouth.

"Yeah?" he said.

"Shut up." Gwen stood on her toes, despite the fact that he wasn't that much taller than she was, and kissed him square on the mouth. Maybe it was because he had wanted this for a long time—at least it felt like a long time—and was so used to restraining himself, but Alaric did not move. Gwen pulled slowly back and looked up at him with a wicked smirk. "That wasn't so bad, was it?" she purred, the sound more like a growl than anything. It was more than enough to send shivers down Alaric's spine.

"No," he breathed. "No, it wasn't."

Then he attacked, bringing his hands up to cup Gwen's chin and prevent her from pulling back as he kissed her. It wasn't soft and calm but needy and desperate. Gwen didn't complain, not even when his hands slipped from her face and started roaming, sliding up and down her side, brushing skin and pressing into the small of her back. She reacted with equal pleasure. Alaric growled into her mouth. She moaned in return.

When Alaric switched their places though, pressing Gwen into the corner and bearing down on her, she let out a cry of shock and pain and pulled back. Immediately, Alaric leaped away, looking at her with horror. "Shit. Gwen, I'm sorry. You started…I couldn't…"

"It wasn't that," Gwen said, her face screwed up as she tried to deal with the pain. "My hand got jammed against the counter." She pressed her lips together in a thin line, her skin ashy and pale.

Alaric waved between going to help and staying away where he couldn't hurt her.

"Ow."

"I'm so sorry," Alaric said. "Are you going to be okay?"

"Yes," Gwen said, taking a few deep breaths. "But I think I should perhaps sit down."

"Of course," Alaric said. He gently put his arm around her shoulder, leading her to the couch where Gwen sank into the cushions as if her legs were going to give out. She took a few deep breaths and leaned back, her eyes unfocused. She sat like that for a few minutes until her breathing got under control, and then she turned to look at Alaric.

"I don't suppose you have any pain pills?" Gwen asked. Alaric didn't even bother answering, just jogged to the bathroom and pulled out some aspirin before returning with them and a glass of water. Gwen didn't bother with the water, just threw the medicine into her mouth and swallowed, wincing as she did so. "Right," she murmured. "I think you're going to have to finish the crème brûlée on your own."

"We don't have to—"

"You're not going to waste a decent dessert are you?" Gwen asked, looking more alarmed at this than the sudden injury of her hand. This alone assured Alaric that she was going to be all right. He laughed in relief.

"No, I suppose not." He turned to the kitchen when Gwen made a sound in her throat. He looked over his shoulder, and she was staring at him with a look of annoyance. He frowned—what had he done *this* time—and she held out her good hand. Alaric took it and was pulled forward until Gwen could sit up and kiss him soundly. Alaric pulled away a minute later, the oven timer having gone off the only reason for his retreat.

"Better?" he asked with the air of a cat before a bowl of cream.

Gwen nodded. "Good."

Alaric returned to the kitchen and pulled the crème brûlée out of the oven before putting it straight into the fridge. And with a shadow of a smile on his face, he cooked the raspberries with a very mild liqueur, sugar, and vanilla to make a syrup. It was a good thing that he had cooked for years, his hands able to create without much direction of his mind, because he was completely preoccupied.

Gwen had kissed him.

His thoughts and dreams over the last while had finally come to pass. Jack's worrying had been for naught, and now, well, it seemed as though the whole world had opened up to him. He didn't know what it was exactly that Gwen and he shared, but it was nice. It was better than *nice*. His fingers twitched as he stirred the syrup, and he wanted to hurry things up and get back to doing whatever it was that she wanted. He knew he was being stupid; you didn't rush cooking. And he had been with other women before. He didn't understand why this was different, felt so different.

After what seemed like an interminable amount of time, Alaric finished the syrup and put it into the fridge to cool along with the custard. He would give it another twenty minutes before pulling it out and crisping the top with his blowtorch. Until then...he went out to the living room, preparing to sneak up on Gwen and make her produce those very satisfying noises that she made when he was touching her.

He found her stretched out on the couch, her broken hand resting gently before her, the other pinned beneath her head. She was sound asleep.

"Damn," Alaric muttered, watching the even in and out of her breath. He grabbed a blanket from another chair and draped it over her, unable to resist moving her hair to rest behind her ear. The crème brûlée would be good another time.

Glancing at the clock, he saw that it was barely half past eleven. He would be up for another couple of hours on a normal night, and he was far too awake to even consider going to sleep. He couldn't very well turn on the television because he didn't want to wake Gwen. Then she might be more comfortable in his bed while he slept on the couch.

"Will you let me move you without waking up?" Alaric asked her. She simply slept on. He decided to risk it and, as if he were lifting a child, picked Gwen up off the couch and carried her to his room, putting him in his bed and tucking the covers around her. She murmured slightly and turned over, stretching as she did so. "This wasn't quite how I was planning on getting you in bed," Alaric said with a dry laugh.

He grabbed a spare pillow and went back out to the living room, closing his door behind him. Then it was little more than watching television for the next while, trying to distract himself from the figure in the other room. He failed.

Somewhere around two in the morning, as he half dozed and half watched the figures flickering on the screen before him, Alaric jerked awake to the sound of a noise. He stared at his bedroom door, fear making his hearing acute. Had Gwen woken? Was she in pain? The sound came again and he cursed, digging around in the cushions of his couch to find his phone. Who would have the nerve to call him at two in the morning? His mother, that was who.

"Mom, do you have any idea what time it is?" Alaric asked, throwing his arm over his eyes.

"Since when are you not awake at two in the morning?" his mother replied, her tone somewhere between scolding and affectionate. Alaric sighed, deciding if this was going to be one of the good conversations with his mother or one of the bad. It all depended if his father entered into the conversation.

"It's my night off. I can go to bed earlier on my night off," Alaric replied. "The question isn't why *I'm* up this late, it's why you are. And why you're calling me this late."

"It's about your father," his mother said. Alaric groaned; it was going to be a bad conversation.

"Whatever he wants me to do now, it's not happening. And I don't care what he's doing to make you get in contact with me, it's not happening. Ever," Alaric snarled, now more than fully awake and angry.

"For goodness' sake, Alaric, he's not trying to get you to do anything. I'm inviting you to his retirement party," his mother said. "And if you know what's good for you, you'll come. He's retiring in three weeks, and you will be there."

"No, I won't," Alaric said. "He doesn't want me there."

"He does, Alaric," his mother pleaded. "He's been asking questions about you, about how your restaurant is going, and reading all the stories in the news about it and you. You know your father. He's stubborn as a mule—a trait you inherited—and he won't call. But it would mean a lot if you were to come to this party. Please, Alaric."

"Mom, I'm busy," Alaric said. "I have the school ending about that time, and there's no way that I can get time off. And you live halfway across the state, so I'd need at least two days. I'm head chef. I can't just get time off."

"You just don't want to see your father. Or me, for that matter," she replied, sounding hurt.

"No, Mom, of course I want to see you," Alaric tried to soothe her, but from the sounds on the other end of the line, it wasn't working well.

"But you won't come see me if your father is there. Do you really hate him that much?"

"No, Mom. Things just aren't as simple as me showing up and saying, 'Congratulations on your retirement.' If you remember, he's the one who threw me out of the house. Not the other way around," Alaric said, the memories he tried so hard to forget coming to the forefront of his mind. His father, lip curled in disgust, his mother cowering in a chair as she recovered from getting slapped out of the way for interfering.

"Be the better man," she said. "Three weeks. Just say you'll come. You don't have to stay at the house, and you only have to see him for a short time. You can even bring a friend, if it's that terrible. Just please come."

"N—" Alaric started, sitting up straight again. This time, the noise was coming from his room. It sounded like cries of pain, quiet and muted but still there.

"Alaric? Are you still there?" his mother asked.

"Yeah, all right, I'll be there. I have to go," Alaric said and hung up, seconds before the screams started. He ran to the door, tripping in his blankets as he did so. He cursed loudly, and Gwen screamed again. Alaric fumbled with the doorknob for a moment, growling as he did so. He managed it, finally, and threw open the door, expecting to see Gwen sitting there, wide-eyed and afraid. Instead, she was sound asleep, her expression twisted into something beyond terror and pain. She looked as though the world was being ripped out from beneath her and there was nothing she could do.

Nothing he could do either.

"Gwen!" Alaric said, shaking her. She resisted, even in sleep, and she was strong. Alaric shook her harder and got an elbow to the center of his chest as a reward. Coughing, he retreated and stared at Gwen. Luckily, her need to fight had woken her from whatever dream she had been having. She stared at Alaric in confusion, a definite expression of fear around her eyes.

"Alaric?" she asked tentatively, balling her left fist in the covers, starting to tremble slightly. After having her hand broken, her night ruined by an annoying prick, and being set on fire, it was a dream that was her undoing? What was it in her mind that was so terrible?

"It was just a dream," he said, moving closer to her again, wondering if she would even accept him trying to comfort her. But his movements set her off, and she closed the gap, burying her head in his shoulder. Alaric wrapped his arms around her and let her stay there, trembling, until she calmed down. Even when she stopped shaking, she didn't move. He was glad for the comfort. He should be comforting her, not taking comfort from her, but her screams had shaken him more than he cared to admit.

"How did I get here?" Gwen asked finally, smoothing her hand over the sheets. "I remember sitting on your couch."

"You fell asleep. I figured you'd be more comfortable on the bed, so I moved you and took the couch," Alaric said. "Sorry if it was an intrusion or anything."

"No," Gwen shook her head. "It's fine. I just...I don't often sleep in a bed. The couch or floor keeps me from having..."

"Dreams," Alaric prompted. He tightened his arms around her, horrified at the fact that she had to sacrifice her own comfort for the sake of a decent night's sleep. "I understand."

"Not dreams," Gwen murmured, almost too softly to hear. She turned and pressed her nose to the point where Alaric's neck met his shoulder. "Memories." Alaric stiffened slightly, and Gwen attempted to pull away. He forced himself to relax and ran his fingers through her hair, keeping one arm wrapped securely around her shoulders.

"Gwen, I'm sorry," Alaric said, kissing the crown of her head. "I'm sorry that you have to go through this."

"It was my fault," Gwen said, bitterness plain in her voice. She curled her fingers into Alaric's shirt and began shaking again. Only after she started breathing raggedly did Alaric realize that she wasn't afraid or angry, she was crying. "I'm the one who caused it, so it's only right that I pay for what happened."

"It wasn't your fault," Alaric growled, annoyed at her for thinking such a thing.

Gwen laughed sardonically, the sound of her sniffing ruining the effect. "How do you know? You don't know what happened, and you couldn't possibly know. Unless you did get Major Dalton to tell you what happened," Gwen said, growling even as her tears wet Alaric's shirt. She tried to pull away again, but he held fast. She might have been strong, but Alaric was in the position of advantage here.

"No, I don't know what happened. But I know that something so terrible would never be your fault. You are the most careful and gracious person I've met in a long time. So it can't be your fault."

Gwen snorted in derision and sidled away from Alaric, this time slipping from his grasp before he could stop her. She leaned against the headboard and wrapped her arms around her knees, pulling them into her chest. "That's because I've learned from my mistakes," she said, propping her chin on her knees.

Alaric slid over the bed to sit next to Gwen, though he sat with his legs stretched out and his hands folded in his lap. "I wish I knew what was so terrible that you can't forgive yourself."

"Not now," Gwen said, leaning to rest on Alaric's shoulder. Obligingly, he put his arm around her and rubbed circles on her arm. "Sometime, maybe. Just not now."

"All right," Alaric said. "I won't push you." He thought he should say something else, like maybe *"you're not alone"* or *"I'm here for you,"* but the words got caught on his tongue. Instead he sat there in silence, just glad for the proximity of Gwen. They sat like that for a while, neither speaking, neither moving, neither falling asleep. Alaric took a deep breath as the silence got too oppressive. "My mom called."

"What, earlier today?" Gwen asked quietly, unwrapping her knees and stretching out until she was reclined on the pillow. Alaric joined her, keeping his arm around her shoulder, though her head was lying on his arm and her hand was resting on his chest. He thought he could feel the heat of her flesh through his shirt, and he wanted to act. It seemed to be an inappropriate time though. Especially after he had introduced the topic of his mom.

"No, after you went to sleep. She wants me to show up at my dad's retirement party," Alaric said.

"I thought that your dad had kicked you out of the house," Gwen replied.

Alaric was quiet for a moment.

"Sorry. Just, you told me at breakfast that you had left and didn't get along with him."

"'Don't get along with him' is a bit of an understatement. But I was coerced into going to this stupid party. He'll be there with all his crowing lawyer friends and the socialites that I never liked. Mom's sort of depending on me to show up." Alaric knew that agreeing had been the only way to dismiss his mother and get to Gwen, but he wished he hadn't. The choice between a party and Gwen was an easy one. It didn't mean that agreeing to attend didn't niggle.

"Any chance you can get a desperate plea from Jack that you be at The Rose during the party?" Gwen asked.

Alaric shook his head.

"That sucks. What about developing a serious illness?"

"In the next three weeks? I don't think so," Alaric grumbled. "No, I have told Mom that I would show up, and so I will. Where I will proceed to get drunk for the entire weekend and do my best to stay away from my dad until the last possible moment."

"The entire weekend? This is lasting for more than a day?" Gwen asked. She bit her lip.

The Wooden Rose would suffer without their chef for two days, and he wasn't sure that he would like doing without for that long. Or without Gwen. Especially not since they had started whatever it was that they had started. He enjoyed kissing her. Her teasing him.

"They live in upstate New York, and I wouldn't be able to get there and back in a day, not if I'm expected to spend time at this party," Alaric said. "Trust me, every way that I look at it, it sucks. Except I get to bring a friend."

"Jack will be thrilled," Gwen said, fighting a smile.

"A weekend with you drunk and him being pounced on by socialite women decades older than he is."

"Jack won't go," Alaric said. "He made that mistake at my dad's seventieth birthday party four years ago. He has vowed never to go near my parents ever again. Something about the fact that he walked away with a ruined suit and something very close to a black eye. Oh, and there was a lizard."

"Your father hit Jack?" Gwen exclaimed in astonishment, drawing back to look at Alaric.

"No, a cousin who decided that a friend of mine must be just as idiotic as I am." Alaric chuckled at the memory, though there was the sting of pain there as well. "But Jack won't come with me. Actually, I was wondering if you wanted to come."

"I certainly hit back," Gwen mused. "And usually harder."

"Exactly. Besides, people would be less inclined to mess with a woman, I would be avoiding the daughters of these terrifying people that keep hanging around—probably hoping for money, but they'll settle for an affair with a world-class chef—and you wouldn't even have to put up with men treating you like a home improvement project." Alaric paused in rubbing Gwen's shoulder to shift and look at her. "Say you'll come?"

Gwen propped herself up on her elbows. "You're serious!" she said, looking at him incredulously. She flopped back onto the pillows. "I thought you were joking."

"When it comes to my parents," Alaric said in a voice that was meant to be serious but was riddled with mocking laughter and sarcasm, "I never joke. Yes, of course I'm serious. There's no way that I'm going to do this alone, and I want you to come with me."

"So you're trying to make me suffer on your account?" Gwen asked, swallowing a yawn. "What did I do to you?"

"No! That's not what I mean," Alaric said. He grumbled under his breath and sighed. "I need your help, all right? I want you to come because I can't—literally can't—do this alone. And if I have to go into battle, I'd like to have you as my backup. I just messed that phrase up, didn't I?"

"It wasn't too bad," Gwen said, sounding sleepy. "And I appreciate the offer. I'd like to help you, I really would."

"I'm sensing a 'however' coming," Alaric said.

Gwen stretched slightly, yawning. She shook her head as much as was possible without lifting it off the pillow. "I'm desperately trying to think of a bad side to this. The fear that I'll end up like Jack is the only one I can come up with. And we both know that I'm tougher than he is by a long shot," Gwen said. Alaric snorted good-naturedly and flinched when Gwen thumped his chest. "I hit a brick, thank you very much. So, no, there's not a 'however.' I'll go."

"Really?" Alaric asked. Gwen murmured assent. "Thanks. I was expecting this to be much harder."

"You have so little faith in your skills of persuasion?" Gwen asked. She fished around until she managed to grab the covers that had been tossed aside and pulled them up around her, settling in.

"You haven't met my parents," Alaric said. "Now go to sleep, all right? I'll go sleep on the—"

"No," Gwen said, pulling her voice from sleepiness to alarm. If she hadn't been pinned by the covers and Alaric's arm, she likely would have sat up straight. "Don't go. I don't want to...remember again."

"Hey, I won't let that happen," Alaric said. He kissed Gwen's head, and she replied with a faint smile and by relaxing into the bed. It didn't take long before she was asleep again. Soundly and deeply asleep. Alaric lay for much longer, simply enjoying the fact that he held Gwen in his arms. It seemed as though he had been waiting for this for a time longer than he had even known her. How many women had he gone through trying to find the one that fit? He didn't necessarily want to marry her right away—he didn't even know if that was in the cards for him—but the fact that he could enjoy just being there with her and have no thoughts about what was going to go wrong next was, well, nice.

Sometime around three, Alaric managed to drift off as well. And he smiled to himself, closing his eyes. Neither he nor Gwen had to be in to The Rose until nearly noon. It would be nice to wake up to her in his arms. He knew nothing more than that until morning.

~

There came a crashing sound, a suppressed curse, and a dull *thud*. Alaric sat up, blinking off the sleep and noting that it was still fairly dark. He automatically looked to the place next to him and frowned; where was Gwen? Had she gotten up to get something to eat? What time was it, anyway?

He glanced at the clock and scowled: 5:30. He never got up this early, not even when he had been working the morning shift at a restaurant during his teenage years. Even when Allison had called, worried about Gwen, she'd had the decency to wait until it was light before waking him up. But this? Groaning, Alaric lay back down and rolled over, trying to ignore the obvious sounds of life that were coming from the kitchen.

He lay there for fifteen minutes before giving up on the concept of sleep and rolling out of bed. Alaric shivered, unused to dealing with the cool morning air that filtered in from the windows. He trudged to the bathroom, took one look at himself in the mirror, and wanted to bang his head against it. His hair was sticking up at odd angles, and he desperately needed a shave. His eyes were bleary, and he was fairly certain that the shadows there had nothing to do with staying up late but rather with getting up early.

Alaric sighed, splashed cold water on his face, growled into his towel as he dried off, and shuffled his way into the kitchen, where Gwen moved about, looking far too awake for that dreadful hour. She wore an apron, her hair had been neatly done in a tight bun, and he was pretty sure he smelled his soap on her skin. She had taken a shower? "What time did you get up?" he muttered, his voice rough.

"About five," Gwen answered. At least she had the decency not to sound cheerful and chipper. Alaric might have clocked her for that. "I didn't mean to wake you," she said, an apology hidden in her voice. Alaric was tempted to snap at her, give her snark, but he simply sighed, blinked a few times, and slid his arms around Gwen's waist.

"It's all right," Alaric said. "As long as you're cooking. Coffee?"

"In the pot," Gwen said, leaning back into his embrace. It pleased Alaric to know that what had happened the night before wasn't some sort of fluke. He wanted to try and kiss her but figured that it was a bit too early for that. Gwen might have been awake and showered, but he wasn't. No need to start the morning off with bad breath and a scratchy face.

"I'm going to grab a shower," Alaric murmured, resting his chin on Gwen's shoulder. "Will this be done in a few minutes? Should I wait?"

"No, go ahead. It'll take another ten minutes before everything is sorted. Besides, I don't want you falling asleep in the middle of my breakfast. Go on," Gwen nudged him away, and Alaric obeyed, showering and changing into a pair of jeans and a plain shirt and shaving before he returned to Gwen. When he did, he was flabbergasted.

She had set the table. As in full cutlery, actual

plates instead of the paper ones he kept for his usual breakfast, glasses, and a pitcher of orange juice (he hadn't even known he *had* a pitcher)—a full breakfast set out on platters with shiny serving tools and everything. He usually just scarfed a bowl of granola or had some toast and eggs. This was, well, fantastic. "You sure go to a lot of effort for breakfast."

"Only when I'm trying to butter people up," Gwen said frankly. She sat and without ceremony began to serve herself eggs, toast, sausage, fruit, everything. Alaric joined her, glad that his waking up early hadn't been for naught. He wouldn't complain too much to a breakfast like this one.

"Are you trying to butter me up? Why?" Alaric asked. "I figure I'm the one who needs to get into your good favor, considering what I asked of you last night."

"Ah, yes, the family," Gwen said. "I suppose I could have just taken that as payment for what I'm going to ask you, but a good breakfast never hurt. Besides, I'm hungry, and I'm going to need energy for later."

"So what is it you need from me?" Alaric asked, smiling at the taste of coffee on his tongue. It was dark and sharp and just how he liked it. And it had the added benefit of waking him up in the morning. "Telling Graham off? Though I don't see how that could possibly merit such a breakfast. Or perhaps putting James in his rightful place. He is still being a jerk, right? Not that I can really get rid of him, considering he is a decent cook and has been attending to my instructions as best as someone like him can."

"Nothing quite so complicated," Gwen assured him. "No, I need a lift back to my apartment."

"What? Now?" Alaric asked.

To his relief, Gwen shook her head. "No, in about half an hour or so. I have my self-defense lessons with Allison this morning, and I don't think I have enough cash for a cab. Oh, and I left my bus pass back at my place when I went out last night. I guess when you're invited to a gala, you don't think you'll need an alternate means of transportation," Gwen said. She looked at Alaric sheepishly, and he was tempted to laugh. But she had gone to all the effort, and she seemed serious enough about the matter.

"All right," Alaric said. "Sure. Though I don't see that a lift to your apartment is worth this breakfast."

"Ah, well. It's early, and you were nice enough to let me stay last night, and well, I was hungry," Gwen said.

Alaric nodded in understanding, smirking as he did so. "This wasn't made strictly for my benefit, was it?"

Gwen shook her head. "Though even if I weren't terribly big on breakfast, I would probably have still made some. You know, as a thanks for letting me stay over and so forth."

Alaric didn't know what to say to that, so he just shrugged, piercing a piece of sausage with his fork. They ate in companionable silence for a few minutes before he spoke, "So do you want to go on a date with me?"

Gwen was halfway through a sip of coffee and

spluttered, coughing. She recovered a few moments later but looked at Alaric as though he had tried to kill her. He blanched. Maybe he had gotten the wrong impression last night? But she hadn't been drunk, and she had initiated it. So what was the problem? Maybe it was the fact that he was asking at six in the morning.

"Sorry," Alaric apologized. "I didn't want to make you, er, choke."

"It wasn't that," Gwen said. "It was more a sudden and glaring realization that everyone at The Rose will be fully aware that we are, well, something. I thought that practically living on top of a bunch of men with the ability to squash most people like flies and also a very healthy sex drive—" Alaric was the one to splutter at Gwen's words, but she continued, ignoring him. "—would be bad enough. But the kitchen team gossips like no one I've ever met before."

"Ah, yes, sorry," Alaric said, shrugging. "I mean, we could try to keep it quiet, if you'd prefer."

"I don't think that's going to work very well," Gwen said. "Jack has been keeping a very close eye on you for a while now, and I'm certain that Bob and Sarah are determined to imitate your every move."

"So you noticed," Alaric said dryly. He was used to people looking up to him for cooking and acknowledging his relative fame in the cooking world, but being copied like some sort of idol was disconcerting. "I've been biding my time until classes end, but I honestly can't wait until these things are done.

Normally I have such a good time with this, but this year... It's been stressful."

"Sorry," Gwen said. "I'm sure this isn't helping."

"What? No. Actually, this is helping a lot. I thought that if I had to wait until these classes were done before, ah, expressing my interest that I might go crazy. Or I'd actually have to listen to Jack and start taking up boxing," Alaric said.

Gwen raised her eyebrows. "Boxing," she stated flatly. "I don't mean to question your masculinity or anything, but you don't seem to be the boxing type. Trust me, I've been around a few of those."

"No. I don't see much point in beating the stuffing out of another guy who has done nothing to you. Or a bag. Punching bags are even worse," Alaric said. "They can't fight back."

"They're called heavy bags," Gwen said. "And they only work so well. It's hard to train seriously with them unless you're certain your opponent will never hit back, let alone move around. That's why sparring and getting actual combat time is so critical."

"It sounds dangerous," Alaric said. He looked at Gwen's broken hand and turned his attention to his food. He knew that she had been through some horrible stuff, but the thought of her actively seeking out a fight just so she could practice, no matter if her opponent was looking for practice too, was sobering.

Gwen got a far-off look in her eye and blinked, her fork and knife held as if forgotten. "It is," she said, her voice somewhere between vacant and forceful. "But

I'd rather deal with the danger than ever feel victimized because I couldn't defend myself. It's amazing what knowing you can hold your own will do for a person."

"Like Allison?" Alaric asked. Gwen nodded. They both remembered that night, the one where Gwen had stepped in and Alaric had realized for the first time that she wasn't some worthless charity case, trying to make her way in a world where she didn't belong. "She seems to be doing well."

"You should see her at our sessions," Gwen said with a smirk. She raised her eyebrows and lifted her glass of orange juice to her lips. "She fights like a wildcat."

"I don't suppose you'd let me sit in?" he asked because he was curious; just because he didn't care for boxing or whatever didn't mean that self-defense wasn't something useful. Besides, it would be nice to see Gwen in a setting outside of cooking and lounging about after ruined evenings. Doing something she knew better than most.

"Sure, but you'd have to put up with being made useful," Gwen said. "I could use an attacker."

"What?" Alaric asked, the way that Gwen asked making him not so certain that he wanted to know or participate any more. "What is an attacker?"

"Exactly what it sounds like. You'll be attacking, I'll be defending. Don't worry, you won't get hurt. At least, nothing that will last more than a few minutes," Gwen said. She straightened in her chair, and Alaric got the sinking feeling that this was not going to end well for him.

"Uh, all right," he said. "We should probably leave soon?"

"Yeah, sure. Hey, relax. Just think of this as your payment for me going with you to meet and endure your family."

"I knew that would be coming back to bite me sooner or later," Alaric grumbled. He pushed back from the table and rose, moving to find containers in which to store the leftover breakfast. He did that while Gwen cleaned the dishes and then, after changing into some workout pants because Gwen smirked when he asked if jeans were all right, got in the car. The drive to Gwen's building was uneventful, though it was interesting to see how long he could go without flicking his eyes over to admire how well she wore his spare clothing. The bit of flesh that showed due to the loose pants didn't hurt either.

Gwen hopped out of the car as soon as he parked and ran up to her apartment to change. She emerged minutes later wearing something much more formfitting and far more distracting for Alaric.

He swallowed. "All right, so we just wait for Allison?"

Gwen nodded. She looked around and stepped forward in one fluid, completely confident motion. "I forgot to kiss you good morning," she breathed before wrapping her arms around his neck and pressing her lips to his. Alaric groaned and leaned back against his car, mindful only of the fact that she was letting his hands wander wherever they wanted. And they *wanted.*

"Well, good morning."

Alaric stiffened at the new voice, but if he expected Gwen to leap back like some sort of guilty teenager, he was disappointed. Because she stayed there, her body pressed very nicely against his, her eyes lidded in pleasure. She simply turned her head and smiled at Allison.

"Good morning to you too," she said. "Right, shall we go?"

13

"What happened to your hand?" Allison asked as she walked with Gwen. Alaric was trailing behind, and Gwen was sure she felt his eyes on the back of her neck and other parts of her body. It didn't help that Allison was obviously curious about what was going on between the two of them, not that it was difficult to guess, considering what she had witnessed.

"I had a fight with a brick," Gwen gave her well-practiced answer. "Don't worry, we can still work on things. You just won't be attacking me. This way, I can see how well you do against someone else. A man."

"Won't I get, oh, I don't know, fired or something?" Allison breathed, loud enough so only Gwen could hear. She smirked and nodded at the small park they were approaching. The ground was just as likely to be hard there as it was outside of Gwen's building, but it wouldn't cause quite as many nasty abrasions. And fewer people would stare or possibly call the police.

"Alaric?" Gwen turned to him. He raised his eyebrows expectantly. "Will Allison get fired if she beats the crap out of you?"

"Probably not," Alaric said. "As long as you don't tell anyone about it," he added with a sneaky grin. Allison whipped her head around and gaped at her boss. Gwen did too. She hadn't even known that he *had* a sense of humor, let alone was willing to show it with others. Of course, she hadn't seen a spark between them until they were all over each other either, so perhaps she shouldn't have been surprised.

Gwen and Allison went over to their usual spot, a piece of ground that was relatively flat with no trees, rocks, or people to get in the way.

"So remind me," Gwen said, stepping into a fighting stance and holding up her hands. Allison mirrored her. "What did we do the day before yesterday?"

The two started moving around, shuffle stepping as though they were fencing but not anything quite so fancy. After a few moments of this, Allison tentatively shot a hand out to try and touch Gwen's shoulder. The former interpreter blocked it easily and responded with a lightning-fast counterstrike that Allison nearly blocked, Gwen's cast brushing against the smaller woman's shoulder. "Um, choke holds," Allison said, striking again. This time, Gwen simply slid her shoulders off-line, leaving her opponent's hand grasping at thin air.

Gwen and Allison continued to play tag, trying to land hits on the other person, until they were both warm, their faces flushed. There was another two minutes of this to get them breathing hard enough before Gwen called it quits. "Right. Right. We'll work on choke holds from behind, then. For now, just do some shadow fighting. I have to let Alaric know what we'll be doing."

Allison did as she was told, looking like she knew exactly what she was doing. Gwen smiled, the motion small. It was good to see Allison so confident and capable in herself, especially after how poor the first few weeks had been. Even Alaric was watching with his jaw lowered, his eyes wide. She walked over to where he was watching and stretched her arms. It was good to be moving, to be stretching. Fighting.

"I hope you don't expect me to do that," Alaric said, pointing to where Allison was throwing punches at the air, dodging and dancing about.

"No, but I do want you to be able to at least use a proper fighting stance," Gwen said. "So stand straight and lean your weight forward until one leg flies out to catch you from falling." Alaric did so, looking rather silly in doing so. His left leg jumped forward, and he looked at Gwen, who nodded. "Good. Now do what I do."

She watched him as he tried to copy her movements, settling into a fighter's crouch and holding his hands as she directed him to. After two minutes of this, Gwen burst out laughing. Allison stopped her shadow fighting and turned to look at Gwen. She was standing with one hand across her belly, her head thrown backward in mirth. Alaric was looking at her with a mixture of annoyance and tolerance.

"Now you understand why I don't play the student," Alaric grumbled, straightening.

"No, no. You were...um, close," Gwen said. Alaric scowled. She chuckled again and stepped next to him. "Do what I do," she murmured, slipping into a crouch. He obliged, copying her movements. "Good," Gwen said, turning so that she was standing in front of him, her stance mirroring his. She brought up her hands as though she meant to fight, and he did the same, protecting his face and still keeping her in sight. Gwen nodded. She took one quick step forward, her left foot leading, her right foot following, forcing Alaric to retreat in the opposite manner.

"See?" Gwen said. "It's not so bad."

"Somehow, I don't think I'm quite cut out for this fighting thing," Alaric grumbled, though he looked pleased at Gwen's praise. The two straightened, and Gwen turned to her student who had been watching with a sort of smirk.

"What?" Gwen asked. Allison shook her head. "All right, fine. So here's how this is going to work..." She showed Allison the bar-arm choke, bringing her arm across the other woman's throat and holding her in place. They reversed roles, and she explained how to get out of it, going over the technique multiple times until Allison could do it nearly perfectly with Gwen, going at a slow speed to keep from hurting Gwen's hand. While she was teaching, she was completely focused on her task, almost unaware of Alaric standing only a few feet away. The only time she became more self-aware was when her injured hand got in the way. Even then, she only let her frustration flicker across her features for a moment before adjusting and moving on.

When Gwen finally turned to Alaric, he was so engrossed with watching her—his eyes lingered on her figure, which she didn't necessarily disapprove—that he didn't hear her call him the first time.

"Alaric!" she said again, trying not to sound annoyed. It was flattering, sure, but there was a time and a place for such things. Fight training was *not* the place.

He jerked to attention and gave her a sheepish look.

"I need you to attack me."

"Huh?" he said.

"I need you to attack me. Just to show Allison what this looks like before you attack her. All you have to do is put me in a bar-arm choke. Your forearm across my neck," Gwen said.

He looked at her skeptically.

"If you don't want to, then you're welcome to leave. Otherwise, make yourself useful."

It was a rule Gwen knew he applied to his kitchens,

so he didn't argue with her order. He stepped up behind her and, with about as much awkwardness as possible, put his forearm around her neck, his other hand resting on her shoulder. He stood as far back from her as he could, as though being too close would cause more problems. "All right, now what?" he asked.

Gwen sighed. "You're going to have to act as though you actually want to attack me, or this is going to be a pointless exercise."

"I don't want to hurt you," Alaric grumbled, though he shuffled a few inches forward.

"Fine, fine, let me out. If you're not going to do this properly, I'm going to have to convince you," Gwen said.

Alaric released her and waited to see what she would do. Gwen did not waste a moment, just darted around behind him and put him in the choke hold she had been demonstrating that morning. He stumbled backward, the pressure of her forearm tight across his neck, her other hand controlling his shoulder as much as guiding him where she wanted him to go. He panicked, struggling blindly and scrabbling at her arm. Gwen did something to his feet and lifted her arm off his neck, his body unstable enough that he stumbled backward. He hit the ground a moment later.

Gwen didn't waste any time, straddling his stomach and keeping him in place no matter how much he struggled. Her expression was grim, her lips curled as if she was a fighting dog, her eyes blazing. Alaric froze, unable to do anything, eyes wide. An instant later and she was calm, leaning forward to press her lips gently against his. "You won't hurt me," she murmured, kissing him deeper. "I promise."

"I hate to interrupt," Allison said, sounding as though she had swallowed a few laughs. "But if we could continue? I have to be somewhere in an hour, and I still have to shower."

"Very well," Gwen said, standing as quickly as she had knelt, her hand held out to Alaric. He took it and pulled himself to his feet, still looking dazed, though whether that was from the attack or the kiss, Gwen couldn't say. She hoped it was both. "Now will you attack me properly? I won't hurt you."

"Yeah, right. I'm going to show up to work all bruised, and I will have to tell everyone that I got beat up by a girl," Alaric growled playfully, this time putting his arm around Gwen's throat as if he meant it. At least, he tried. Somehow, she didn't think that his heart was really in it. He let out a grunt as Gwen's elbow nudged his stomach, lightly for her but still enough to make him breathe sharply. She pulled his arm down in a quick jerk, stepped under it, and pinned it behind his back so that his shoulder would be wrenched if he moved too far one way or another.

He spluttered uncomfortably for a few moments, struggling blindly against her attack. If he continued to pull and turn the way he was, Gwen would end up dislocating his shoulder or breaking his elbow. She released him, hands instinctively up to defend.

Alaric didn't even seem to realize that Gwen had

purposefully released him. He just lunged, uncoordinated and unskilled, which was enough for Gwen to realize what he was doing and step aside.

She didn't even bother to fight back as he turned again, doing his best to hit her. She simply held up her hands, open and calm, a gentle message for him to stop. She hid her alarm behind a carefully schooled expression, one that she had used when translating dangerous conversations for her people. She let him approach her, obviously furious about something and obviously not seeing her but something else. She was prepared for when he swung at her, blocking his blow easily. He kept attacking; she kept blocking. Until he hesitated.

"Alaric," Gwen said, her voice breaking slightly as she said his name. She silently cursed herself for getting emotional over such a thing, but it hurt to see him that way. Something had triggered this—she didn't know what, but she had a guess—and as easily as it had been triggered, it was gone. Almost like one of her attacks, she thought in the quietest recesses of her mind. Except with her attacks, the ones that lasted hours, she actually caused damage, to herself and to the others that had tried to stop her. Unbidden, an image of the room where she had stayed for a few months after the attack in Afghanistan came to her mind. She shuddered.

Alaric saw the shudder and immediately retreated. "Shit. Gwen, I'm sorry. I didn't think that... Shit." He backed up into a tree and used it to balance himself, obviously unable to control the sudden shaking that came on him. Gwen took a deep breath and turned to the wide-eyed and terrified Allison.

"We'll finish this another time," Gwen said softly. The blonde woman nodded and fled, moving as quickly as she could without seeming like she was running from the scene. Then, ever so carefully, Gwen approached the base of the tree where Alaric now sat, his head buried in his hands. She sat next to him, and he stiffened.

"I'm sorry," he said again. "I've never... I get angry, sometimes, but it's mostly in the kitchens, and it's never so...I don't know what came over—"

"Who was it that hit you?" Gwen asked quietly. Alaric raised his head and looked at her with furrowed brows, his hands tangled in his hair. He was obviously distressed, and Gwen didn't want to push him. She took another deep breath and tried to remember what her own psychologists had said. "You weren't attacking me," she began. "You wouldn't attack me. You were attacking whoever it was that...made you feel weak, that made you feel as though you were trapped and couldn't defend yourself. You were attacking the person who made you feel—"

"Vulnerable," Alaric cut in, his voice like ice. He turned his gaze away from Gwen and looked at the grass instead. "Yeah. You're right."

"So who was it?" Gwen pressed, leaning her shoulder against his. He responded by unfurling his arms and putting one around her shoulders, pulling her close as if she would leave him for what he had done. "Who was it you were attacking? I—I shouldn't push you. It's not my place," Gwen said, thinking of her own secrets she didn't want revealed.

"You'll find out soon enough anyway. My father," Alaric said softly. "He was the one who hit me, who, well, abused me. It was only once physically, but unless I did what he said, then the emotional abuse started."

"You're very frank about it," Gwen said after a minute's pause. "More than I would be. Am."

"It's because I've come to realize something," Alaric said, leaning back against the tree.

"What's that?" Gwen asked. She looked up at Alaric, tempted to brush the strands of black hair out of his eyes.

"He's a real bastard, that's what," Alaric said. Gwen blinked in surprise, then chuckled. She stopped as soon as she realized what she was doing, but Alaric turned to grin at her, and she started laughing again. It didn't take long for Alaric to join her. They laughed for a few minutes, the fight completely forgotten, tempers soothed and ruffled feathers smoothed back into place. Things were just as they should be.

"All right. You win. That's a pretty decent reason for being frank," Gwen said. She stretched, and Alaric loosened his hold on her, letting her stand. "Come on, we should get back. I have to at least change into something a bit more work appropriate, and I'm sure you have to do the same."

"Right," Alaric said. "Work." He rose and followed

Gwen from the park, catching up to her and slipping his hand into hers. "Sorry about attacking you like that. I didn't know that I would, well, react so poorly."

"It's nothing I haven't seen before," Gwen shrugged. "Some people just have memories blur together when they fight. They don't remember who they're fighting, just the reason that makes them fight. For some it's revenge, others protection, still others do it just because they're good at it. Doesn't matter."

"Some of your friends were like that?" Alaric asked. The question was innocent; Gwen knew that he wouldn't pry into her past unless she wanted to offer it. He didn't care about that. She was shocked, then, when she actually answered.

"I knew a soldier," Gwen said softly. "Damon. He was sort of your rough-and-tumble, go-get-'em type. Fiery. He was a damn good soldier, but when he got into hand-to-hand combat, he was nigh uncontrollable. He was back in his youth, fighting to stay alive against his stepfather and stepbrother. They would have killed him if he hadn't fought. Eventually, it got so bad that he was put in a sharpshooting squadron, an advance force. He had a gun, not his fists. I don't know which was more deadly."

"Was he one of the ones you lost?" Alaric asked before he could stop himself. He cursed out loud as Gwen stiffened, stopping in her tracks. He froze as well, unable to think of anything to say that would make what he had done better.

"It's not important," Gwen said, her voice like ice. She started walking again, and Alaric hurried to catch up. They said nothing, the conversation between them over and done with. It didn't take long before Gwen's flat came into view. She dug her key out of a pocket and trudged up to the door. Alaric hesitated, wondering if he should follow her or drive back to his own flat. If he followed her, she might yell at him. But if he went back to his flat, it would be acknowledging that something was now between them. He didn't think he could stand having another barrier between the two of them. He had only just gotten her to lower hers.

She didn't argue as he came up to her flat, just as she didn't argue when he immediately went to her kitchen while she went to change. He ran his fingers lightly over the pots and pans, wondering how much of Walter Smythe's money was spent on these things. As far as he was concerned, it was high time that the philanthropist put his money toward something useful, like cooking. Not that what he did wasn't useful, just far from practical. Alaric considered cooking her something, but she had already made them breakfast, and in another hour, he would need to be at The Wooden Rose for classes.

"Hey," Gwen said, standing in the doorway to the kitchen. "I didn't mean to snap at you."

"It's fine," Alaric said. He smiled appreciatively at

the clothing Gwen was wearing, only because she didn't seem to understand just how much he was enjoying it. She wore tight trousers that showed off every curve and muscle and a blue blouse that rode up and showed a slim patch of skin whenever Gwen moved. "It's not like I haven't done worse."

"Yeah. But if we're going to do, well, *this*," Gwen said, "then we're going to have to stop biting each other's heads off every time one of us does something even remotely bothersome."

"All right, we'll work on it," Alaric said.

Gwen nodded, apparently satisfied, and slipped into the kitchen to reach for the tea kettle. She was stopped when Alaric cornered her, putting his hands on her hips. He lowered his head and kissed her hungrily before moving to her jaw, her neck, the collarbone that showed through the neck of her shirt.

"Gwen," Alaric said, groaning in pleasure as her hands started slipping up and down his shoulders.

"Yeah?" she breathed, her breath hitching as Alaric nipped at the corner of her jaw.

"Go on a date with me?" he asked. "Our next day off. Or sooner, if I can get Jack to switch the schedules around.

"All right," Gwen answered. She gave a slight moan as Alaric's hand slid under her shirt, dancing along the tops of her trousers. She responded in kind, slipping her hands under his shirt as if she couldn't get enough flesh. He helped, pausing long enough to tear away the offending piece of fabric before kissing her again and letting his hands start on her buttons. "Alaric," Gwen whispered between his assault on her mouth and shoulder.

"Hmm?" he managed, wondering what could be so damn important.

"We don't have enough time for this," she said a minute later, her touch gentle on his shoulder.

"Sure we do. We have an hour before we have to be at work. And The Rose is only across the street. Awfully convenient, wouldn't you say?" Alaric managed to get out in between pressing kisses to Gwen's neck and jaw.

"We have half an hour," Gwen corrected him, gasping as he pressed in closer, touching her breast, which was barely covered by her now exposed bra. "And you have to get dressed. I don't have any men's clothes in my flat for you to borrow."

"I'll use one of the spare uniforms at the restaurant," Alaric said, cupping Gwen's jaw in his hands so she wouldn't be able to interrupt again.

She let him do that for a bit before speaking again, this time in little more than a whisper blurred by pleasure. "There are spare uniforms at the restaurant?" she asked. Alaric murmured assent, and Gwen purred in submission. "All right, then," she said. Alaric growled his pleasure and attacked. It was neither slow nor gentle. He felt as though he had been wanting this for a very long time and he wasn't going to have her tear this away. A thought occurred to him, and he paused, making Gwen groan in annoyance.

"You do want this, don't you?" Alaric asked. Gwen looked at him in complete surprise. Her chest was moving up and down in a most alluring manner as she caught her breath. Her hair was no longer held back in a military-style bun. She had her hands on the waistband of his sweats, and her eyes were direct and piercing.

"Yes," she snapped. "Now stop struggling and hold still." Alaric ignored the last statement in favor of the first, stepping forward to completely trap Gwen against him. She growled and sat up on the countertop, hooking her legs behind his back. He started, feeling her pressed against him like that. They came together again, all scrambling hands and desperate kisses. Somewhere in the process of things, Gwen lost her bra and Alaric his pants. He struggled with her trousers, and Gwen broke contact long enough to slip them off her legs, shapely and muscular, before pulling Alaric back toward her.

They moved together as one being, their hips rocking in tandem. They didn't seem to know where one began and the other ended, just that they were. And when it was done, the emotional high lingered, their breathing heavy. They were content to lean against each other for support, staying close. Gwen was the first to break the silence.

"Damn," she said, throwing her head back and shaking out the last of her bun.

Alaric smiled and ran his fingers through her hair.

"I needed that," Gwen said, returning the favor and

trying to smooth some of the strands of black hair that had fallen into his eyes.

"We'll have to do it again sometime," Alaric said. Gwen nodded, smirking. Finally, when the clock told them they had no more time, they pulled apart to pick up discarded clothes, then opted for quick rinses of their hair and faces before leaving for work.

That was the day when all of the staff came in to discuss new menu options and taste various dishes to approve or improve. The students had never before been allowed to participate in the event, always given most of the morning off. But, as the classes were near ending, they had finally gained the right to be present. Which meant that when Alaric and Gwen walked in together, the whispering started immediately instead of not until the restaurant actually opened. Jack was the first—apart from Allison—to figure out what was going on. He looked at Alaric with raised eyebrows. His head chef just returned the look and, in case anyone was wondering about the extent of the relationship, slung his arm around Gwen's shoulder.

14

"I'm going to have to lay down some basic rules," Jack said as he cornered Alaric.

The Rose was open for the evening, and things had been going smoothly, for the most part. There had been some of the usual grumbling as Alaric proved to be just as ruthless in his critique, despite having a relationship with Gwen. Apparently, everyone thought she would mellow him out. They were quickly proven wrong.

"First off, no sex in the storeroom," Jack said. He grinned as Alaric shoved an elbow at his stomach. "I guess I don't have to worry about the free food bit, since she works here and all, but keep it moderate, all right?"

"Shut up," Alaric grumbled. Gwen was too busy roasting a haunch of lamb to pay attention to what Alaric was doing, so there was no worry of her overhearing. Even so, Alaric sent a worried glance in her direction.

Jack simply laughed and clapped his friend on the back. "It took you long enough. And I didn't have to insist you go to anger management classes. So everything works out," Jack said. He dodged a swipe from a metal spatula and went out to the floor. Alaric returned to his own dish and tried to stay annoyed at his friend but couldn't. He was too thrilled with the reality of what had happened. Things were working out, and he wasn't even all that worried about attending his father's retirement party in three weeks' time because Gwen would be going with him. He saw Bob making a rookie mistake in slicing the green onion and snarled out a warning.

Yes, things were going very well.

Gwen, though, was not quite as sure. She was pleased to have a relationship with Alaric—just the thought of it sent tingles of pleasure up her spine—but the looks from the other students were enough to be more than a bit annoying. James was the worst of the lot, glaring at her throughout the day and doing his very best to trip her up as she worked. He had somehow managed to get his workstation next to hers that evening and was continuously getting in her way, reaching across her stove for a different ladle or some ingredient that he "needed." He jabbed at Gwen with his elbows whenever he could, and finally, as she struggled to make do with her left hand and James kept getting closer, inhibiting her movement, she snapped.

"If you have a problem," she growled, "just come right out and say it. I don't take well to sabotage."

"Fine," James leered, turning over a fillet of salmon before rounding on Gwen. "You think that banging the chef will get you a job here? Will make things easier? Well, you can bet that I'm going to fight this. There has to be some clause in our contract that prohibits sexual relations between students and teachers. Or maybe I should just complain to my lawyers, who would be happy to have this fought. You're pathetic, doing this to get what you want. I won't fall for it."

"I'm not doing 'this' to get a better shot at landing a job here," Gwen said flatly. She began basting the lamb with her sauce and watched with a sort of sadistic pleasure as James's salmon began to sizzle a bit too loudly. "I'm dating him because I like him. And no, there are no rules prohibiting it. You can go ahead and shut up because no matter what you say, I'm not going to stop just because you don't like it. If you weren't so convinced that you were better than the rest of us, maybe you would understand why I'm doing this."

"You insolent little—" James said, narrowing his eyes.

"James, that salmon is burning," Alaric roared from across the kitchen. Sure enough, it was. Alaric's timing couldn't have been any worse though. All it did was reinforce the impression that Alaric was going to keep looking out for Gwen, giving her special treatment while attacking the others because of it. It would never occur to James that perhaps he was at fault.

Gwen did her best to swallow the sharp retort that was rising in her throat. She had to at least try and keep the peace. This was a new thing for both of them, she reminded herself. They had to work at it, test the boundaries, figure out what was all right and what wasn't. Before that, they had to make it through the evening. As usual, The Rose was busy. Alaric was kept dancing around the kitchen, checking on various dishes and barking orders at his staff. Gwen was busy in her own right, doing her best to keep up with the orders and to make sure that she didn't mess up the dishes. Maybe it was because she was thinking of what would happen after the night was over, but things seemed too busy for her. She felt the evening was too fast and yet too slow. She desperately wanted to catch her breath, but every time she glanced at the clock, only seconds seemed to have passed. It was infuriating.

Finally, *finally*, the night drew to a close, and all that was left was cleaning. Alaric went to talk with Jack about getting more supplies, and the regular kitchen staff cleaned their various workstations and left, leaving the students to finish up the general cleaning. Allison and Sarah chatted pleasantly while they tackled the floors, and Robert and Thomas begged off to go meet their wives for a late drink. Eventually, even the cleaning got done, and Gwen was more than happy to throw her rag in the dirty bin and grab her jacket.

James shoved past her, his shoulder ramming into hers, making sure that he hit her broken hand against his hip. Gwen curled her lip in discomfort but made no sound, instead just shrugging into her coat.

"Have fun with your sleeping around," James hissed. He strode off to the back door with his head held high and a muttered "whore" as he left. Gwen waited until he left before shaking her head.

"Idiot," she murmured, rubbing her shoulder.

"Are you all right?" Alaric asked, stepping up to grab his own jacket. He let his hand brush Gwen's cheek, and he frowned, as though he was looking for obvious signs of abuse from James. "Has he been giving you problems? I could—"

"Don't even say it," Gwen warned. She pulled back from Alaric's touch and looked up at him, her gaze firm. "I don't need help in this."

"But I—" Alaric started.

Gwen shook her head, setting her jaw. "This is not your fault," Gwen said. "It's just idiots like him being unable to look past their own egos. And I can handle it."

"If he's causing problems in the kitchen, I should do something about it," Alaric insisted. He held open the door for Gwen, and she slipped through, watching him lock up. "It's my job."

"No, it isn't," Gwen said. "This is nothing more than James being an idiot. I can deal with it. I have to deal with it on my own. If you start fighting my battles for me, things will only get worse. Trust me, I can take care of myself."

Alaric looked uncertain, but he slipped his keys into his pocket and followed Gwen across the street to her flat. Thankfully, he didn't offer his help again. She fumbled with her keys as she opened the door and groaned in relief as she finally closed the door behind them.

"I don't think that I've ever had such a long night at The Rose before," Gwen said.

Alaric twined his arms around her waist. "That's because you had something to look forward to." She smiled and turned to face him, blinking languidly. Gwen kissed him, biting down gently on his lower lip before pulling back, a mischievous expression on her face.

"That might have had something to do with it," she agreed. Alaric grinned and leaned in to kiss her again when she pulled away. He grumbled in annoyance but let her be as she put her keys away and took off her jacket before hanging it on its hook. He did the same, draping his jacket over hers, and then waited so they could get back to what they had been doing. Instead, Gwen pressed the button on her answering machine. Alaric frowned.

"One new message," the machine said in its computerized voice. Another voice started, and it took Gwen a moment to recognize it. When she did, she glared at the machine in frustration. "Hey, Gwen, it's me. Er, Graham. I'm calling to apologize for yesterday evening… I didn't mean to upset you, uh, about the whole not being able to manage on your own thing. It…just sort of came out. I mean, you looked great last night, and well, I think I was just trying to come to terms with the fact that, er, a month and a half ago, you were just barely getting settled into things. You were so uncertain, and now, well, you're completely different. I'm just screwing this whole thing up. I was going to have some sort of eloquent apology planned, but now I'm just making a mess of things. If you're not really pissed at me, do you think that we could try and do this again? I mean, just meet for lunch or some—"

The machine beeped. "End of messages."

Alaric stood there, shifting his weight uncomfortably. "How about I put on the kettle for some tea?" he asked.

Gwen blinked as though she was just remembering his presence and nodded. When in doubt, make tea.

Gwen didn't move for a minute, afraid she'd lose the tenuous control she had over her emotions right then and do something stupid. Like break her other hand. She took three deep breaths and reached for the answering machine again, deleting the message. He didn't know what he was doing? Yeah, and she was a dancing elephant. She heard Alaric moving around in the kitchen and hesitated. She didn't want to talk about what had just happened, and if she went in there, talking would be necessary. Maybe not immediately, but it would have to happen. She tore off her shoes instead before picking them up and taking them into her room. The kettle started whistling.

Gwen took another deep breath and shook her head. She was going to have to face it at some point. Her anger wouldn't last, and when it was gone, things wouldn't look so grim. Maybe some practical way of dealing with Graham without infuriating herself would present itself. Maybe she could just pretend that it hadn't happened and that she was not being accused of being a slut by her coworkers so that she could get ahead. Maybe she could have a normal life with a normal boyfriend.

She lifted her eyes to one of the pictures of the desert as she undid her hair. A knot of guilt and pain wrapped itself around her stomach. "Normal?" she scoffed. "Yeah, right." Still, she smiled as she walked into the kitchen and saw Alaric standing next to the teapot. He was in the middle of putting together what looked like a fairly elaborate snack platter—fruit, cheeses, crackers, cakes, and some cookies Gwen had made the other day.

"I didn't know if you were hungry or not," he said, turning to look apologetically at her. "But I was, so I sort of raided your fridge."

"I'm starving," Gwen admitted, stepping forward to snatch some food off the plate. "Thanks." They stood there for a minute, eating and sipping at the tea. Gwen knew that Alaric was holding back on asking how she was doing, and she was desperately trying to come up with something to say that would relieve the awkward tension in the room. Finally, she could do nothing but lean back against the counter and look over the rim of her mug. "We're pathetic, aren't we?" she asked.

"What?" Alaric said, widening his eyes in astonishment as he talked around a cracker and cheese. "We're not pathetic! Why would you think that?"

"Because we can't think of a single thing to say to each other right now. You don't want to bring up Graham, and I don't want to talk about James, so we're stuck standing here and eating food, pretending that absolutely nothing is wrong and somehow making it perfectly okay that we're going to end up having sex in a bit," Gwen said. She sipped furiously at her tea and scowled into the drink.

Alaric chewed slowly before he responded. "I wouldn't say that," he said carefully. "I mean, I would *like* to have sex with you right now, but I'm all right with talking too. There're plenty of things we can discuss that are outside the realm of Graham and that idiot I'm meant to be teaching." He took a mouthful of his own tea and met Gwen's gaze, as if daring her to deny his statement.

"Like what?" she asked, picking up another cracker and putting a slice of apple on top of it.

"Like asking questions. Like if you could travel anywhere, where would you go?" Alaric asked.

Gwen looked at him skeptically. He sighed and reached out to tuck a strand of her hair behind her ears, the gesture more intimate than anything they had previously done, and—she blushed—they had done a fair bit.

"Things like that are called getting to know one another," Alaric said. "It's typically what people, especially couples, do."

"Smart-ass," Gwen said.

Alaric nodded and continued to look at her expectantly.

"I don't mind the idea of traveling, but every time I've had to do it in the past," she started, "I've been going to train or on tour. Right now, I think I just want to get my life together. I mean, after this whole school thing ends, I still have to find a job and figure out how I'm going to live. I don't want to...I can't end up back on the streets."

"I forgot," Alaric said. "It must have been hard."

"The interesting thing about living on the streets is that no matter where you are, you know what to expect. The people around you, the other homeless, they'll look out for you. Only after they've looked after their own skins, mind you, but if there's anything to spare, they'll be sure to help. Everyone else is your enemy." Gwen shrugged as if it was no big deal.

"Was it really that bad?" he asked softly.

Gwen knew that he was just trying to make sense of her, but the words still stung. How could he, a world-class chef and the son of a wealthy man, understand what sort of hardship it was to live minute by minute, hoping that you would be able to find a place to sleep away from the rain and the cold and that you might be able to scrounge together enough change to afford a full sandwich and a cup of coffee?

She mentally shook herself. It wasn't his fault that he would never be able to empathize with her life. And she wouldn't wish him to. It was hard enough having gone through it herself; Alaric didn't need to experience it as well.

"It's over and done with," Gwen said in answer to the question both had left hanging in the air. "Now I can look to the future. Now I have something to look forward to. I just have to get a job."

"I don't think getting a job will be too much of an issue," Alaric said.

Gwen smiled at the compliment.

"I'm serious," he protested. "You may not have grown up with cooking, but you are quite talented. You're keeping up with the other students, and they've been doing this for years. You've got a natural talent for this, Gwen. You'll be able to make it."

"I hope so. I've heard that getting hired at a decent restaurant is like going to war," Gwen said, doing her best to keep her tone light. "Of course, I've done that, so maybe it won't be so bad."

"You'll be just fine," Alaric assured her. "If you don't believe that, then you'll never get anywhere. Besides, with a kitchen like this, you could probably open a home catering business and manage just fine."

"Oh, yes, I want to go through all that trouble," Gwen said, drawing one side of her mouth up in a smirk. She shook her head. "I think I'd much rather just get a nice job somewhere. It wouldn't have to be too fancy, nothing that would grant me world-class status, just something decent. Of course, I'd have to get paid enough to keep this apartment."

"Ah, yes, there is that," Alaric said. "When I started out, my father was convinced that I would never be able to make enough money to buy an apartment. He continuously scolded my mother for slipping me money on the sly so that I would keep afloat. She denied it, of course, and I did just fine. Though I really don't care for the one I have."

"Why keep it, then?" Gwen asked. She rinsed out her tea cup and stretched, reminding Alaric that it was rather late at night—for normal people, that was. He wanted to start peeling clothes off Gwen and take her to bed. It would be slower, much more like lovemaking than the frantic sex they'd had earlier that day. Even as he thought about it, he could feel her touch on his skin and the way that she'd left burning trails where her fingers had been. He shivered and forced his mind back to the question at hand. Immediately, he scowled.

"Because getting out of the deed is a pain. It was bought at a time when I was dating a lawyer and figured that, should I ever need to get out of the deed, the lawyer would help. You know how that worked out," Alaric said. He put down his mug rather more forcefully than he would have under normal circumstances. Gwen made a sympathetic noise in the back of her throat and stepped forward to wrap her arms around his waist. It was meant to be comforting, but Alaric was beginning to think in a whole different direction.

"Poor thing," Gwen said, her voice laced with sarcasm. Alaric laughed and brought his hands around Gwen's waist to where her shirt met her trousers. Lightly, he brushed his fingers over the patch of skin, smiling with success as Gwen's breath caught.

"Yes, I'm horribly maligned," Alaric said. He kissed Gwen, nipping at her lips. She grinned under his ministrations and pressed him back against the countertop. Before he could react, she had undone the buttons of his shirt and was slipping it back off his shoulders. He was glad that it wasn't the sort of shirt that slipped over the head. Her mouth was far too interesting for that.

"We shall have to fix that," Gwen said as Alaric broke away to deal with her own shirt and trousers. All she got in response was a growl.

This time around, their lovemaking was just that. It was slow and sensual, with more touching and exploring than desperate need to relieve the pressure that had built up in both their bellies. Everything became blurred together and yet completely distinct, each moment melding into the next seamlessly and yet being framed distinctly in their minds. Somewhere in the middle of everything, they were coupled and caught in the throes of pleasure. And neither noticed when they slowed to quiet caresses and the simple pleasure of just lying in each other's company.

Alaric glanced at the digital clock on Gwen's nightstand, her head propped on Alaric's chest while his hands rubbed circles into her back: 2:27. She should have been asleep, he knew. She had to get up in four hours and get ready to train Allison, but she was still awake. For now.

"Tell me about your family," Gwen murmured, her voice blurred by her unwillingness to move so that she could speak properly.

"You know about my family," Alaric said.

Gwen shook her head minutely, shifting so that her weight rested more independently on the bed. "Not your immediate family. The people that will be showing up to your father's retirement party," Gwen said. "Do you have any crazy uncles or cousins I should know about?"

"Well, there's Aunt Harriet," Alaric said. Gwen made a noise that told him to continue, and he did. "She is my mother's sister, ten years younger. She married young and to a man twice her age with a fortune that was impressive, even given her pedigree. He died about five years after they married, and she inherited everything. She then proceeded to travel the world, collecting odd artifacts, behaviors, and people. I remember when I was ten, she showed up for an unannounced visit with a Bulgarian street magician on her arm. He was just about the strangest thing I have ever seen, with tattoos and piercings in all places except his hands and above his neckline. He said that if he ever had to appear in court, he needed to present a good image for the judges, so he kept his body art contained. Then he proceeded to pull some cards from his pocket and attempt to teach me how to swindle my schoolmates. He was the one who taught me about alcohol, and Aunt Harriet convinced me never to smoke. She let me have a cigarette once, probably just after the magician offered me whiskey, and I nearly choked to death. Father was furious."

"She sounds like quite the character," Gwen said, her voice finally taking on a sleepy quality.

Alaric nodded.

"We didn't have any crazy Aunt Harriets," Gwen said. "Instead, I had a cousin who was maybe three years older than I was. Ricardo. Illegitimate child but part of the family. I thought he was the coolest kid in the world and did my best to get him to pay attention to me. He did, but only as an annoying kid sister. Called me Squirt."

"Squirt," Alaric said. "Didn't he realize that you could beat the daylights out of him?"

"No," Gwen answered. Her voice was beginning to slur with drowsiness, and Alaric knew that it wouldn't be long before she dropped off to sleep. "He was bigger than me, and he had an earring. I didn't care about being annoying. As long as he was paying attention to me, it was all right. Eventually, he ran off with the daughter of the local garage owner. I was devastated.

Of course, I joined the army the next year, so obviously it didn't have a lasting impact on me."

"Good. If you'd hung out with him much longer, you would have gotten involved with one of his cronies, and then where would I be? Probably yelling profanities at my students and mourning the fact that I dated Marcie, the lawyer," Alaric said.

Gwen murmured something into his chest that sounded like "you do that anyway." He smiled.

They lay like that for another ten minutes before Alaric got enough nerve to speak. "Gwen?"

"Hmm?" she murmured. She was awake, but only just. Another moment and she would probably drop off.

"When the school is done, come work for The Wooden Rose. Work in my kitchens. Work for me," Alaric said.

"All right," Gwen said. She took a deep breath and then, just like that, she was asleep. Two minutes later and Alaric was as well.

15

—————

Morning came and found Gwen frying eggs, scowling as she tried to figure out what it was that she was missing. Something important, maybe something someone had said or done. Did it have to do with Allison? She didn't know. Or perhaps her doctor had said something about her broken hand. She ground her teeth together as she tried to remember what it was that was bothering her so much, her hands automatically moving as she flipped the eggs. She took a deep breath and released it, turning off the heat under the eggs. Maybe Alaric would know.

Right on cue, he stumbled into the kitchen, looking bleary-eyed and much the worse for wear. Gwen could survive on four hours of sleep; it was fairly plain that Alaric couldn't. She opened her mouth to ask him if he knew what it was that was bothering her, and he simply held up a hand, trudging to the cabinet above the kettle and getting out the coffee and French press.

He had only been in her kitchen a short time, and he already knew where the coffee was. Gwen was pleased.

She waited until he was three sips into his coffee before speaking. "So I've got this feeling like I've forgotten something important...you wouldn't happen to know what it is?" she asked.

Alaric shrugged, inching closer to where Gwen was putting together plates of food for breakfast.

She rolled her eyes and slid one to him. "Because it's driving me crazy."

"I have no idea," Alaric said, taking the plate to the table, where he began to scarf down food. For someone with such a high appreciation of food, he really didn't understand the purpose of breakfast. "Of course, I can't think about *anything* this early in the morning. I don't understand why you do this," he complained.

"Because I have Allison to train and because I like getting up early. It makes me feel as though I have utilized more of the day instead of sleeping for a good part of it. Besides, I have time to cook breakfast," Gwen said.

Alaric muttered something around a mouthful of toast.

Gwen shrugged. "You could have slept in, you know."

"Yeah, well, it's hard to sleep in when you're in the shower. Thoughts like that get me up fairly quickly," Alaric said.

Gwen didn't realize what he was saying for a few moments, then she whacked his head gently.

Alaric looked up at her with a grin. "Come on, sit down. You did make breakfast, after all. You might as well eat something."

"I just can't get over the feeling that I've missed something," Gwen said, though she dutifully took her place at the table, her fork and knife wavering over the plate.

Alaric waited until she actually took a bite of food before replying. "I'm sure it will come to you. As far as I know, it's just a normal day. I had planned for us to work on some of the new summer dishes before The Rose opens. Everyone else is fairly familiar with them, since we've had them before, but you students should get to make them at least once before tonight," Alaric said. "It's weird to think that the summer season, at least food-wise, starts tonight. Soon we'll have to contend with tourists and people who don't know what they want."

"We have to do that anyway," Gwen pointed out, eating properly now that she'd started. "You just like to blame tourists for all your problems with customers."

"They're the most annoying," Alaric said. "But at least we can expect them to be annoying. No, what really gets to me are the amateur reviewers with their blogs. They come in expecting something completely different from what we can give them and then rant about it. Low-key as they are, one bad review from them can put people off The Rose for a long time."

"So we'll just cook well," Gwen said. "We always do."

"No," Alaric countered, pointing at her with his knife, "we *try* to cook well. It works most of the time but not always."

"With you continuously looking over our shoulders, I don't see how we can do otherwise," Gwen said.

Alaric blinked, considered his coffee, and then looked at Gwen again. After stifling a yawn, he picked up his knife and fork, then paused.

"Was that sarcasm?" he asked.

Gwen nodded.

"It's too early for this sort of thing." He yawned again, and Gwen chuckled.

Gwen finished off her breakfast and stood, walking over to kiss the top of Alaric's head before putting her plates in the sink and leaving to finish getting ready. By the time she returned, Alaric was on his second cup of coffee and still looking as bleary-eyed as ever.

"I'll be back in a while," Gwen said. "I really think you should get to your place and pick up a change of clothes or something. So I'll see you at The Rose, all right?"

"Are you kicking me out?" Alaric teased.

"No, just suggesting you pay attention to personal hygiene," Gwen said. She jumped out of reach of Alaric's poorly aimed blow and grinned, stalking away like a satisfied cat.

For the first time in a while, Allison was there

before Gwen. The blonde woman stood as though she was expecting something: her arms were folded, and she had a perfectly formed "tell me everything" look on her face.

"All right," Allison said as the two of them walked to the park. "Tell me everything."

"I don't know what you're talking about," Gwen said primly.

Allison snorted in derision. "Okay, fine. I'll play along. I show up yesterday and there you are inhaling Alaric's face. Like, our *boss*, Alaric. Alaric Bennet, the world-class chef who is known for his inflamed temper and his cooking skills, not his sociability. But I leave it because I'm not going to bring it up in front of him," Allison said, waving her hands as she talked. They reached the park, and the two women took their customary stances, starting the warm-up. Allison continued to talk. "So then he goes all haywire on you, and you have to do some seriously fancy fighting to get him to stop. I leave, you show up at the restaurant with his arm slung around your shoulder, looking as though you just had some very satisfying sex—oh! You did, didn't you? You had sex with Alaric Bennet!"

"Shut up," Gwen groaned before Allison could continue her tirade. She stopped the initial warm-up and sighed. "Shadow fighting," Gwen said. Allison raised her eyebrows expectantly but did as she was told. Gwen waited for twenty seconds before replying, "Yes, all right, fine. I'm dating Alaric."

"I knew it!" Allison exclaimed, dodging good-naturedly as Gwen turned to aim a weak blow at her head. "I mean, you were getting all those extra lessons from him at first, so it was either going to be that you ended up hating each other or sleeping with each other."

"There was a betting pool, was there?" Gwen growled, suddenly feeling as ornery as Alaric when someone cooked something wrong.

"No," Allison said, hurrying to assure her friend. "Just a couple of the girls speculating whether or not you two would end up together. Lauren was convinced that you were sort of tailor-made for one another, but Sarah and—"

"Lauren!" Gwen said, pausing. "How could I have been so stupid?"

"Um, well, since you didn't really know about it, then I suppose it wasn't that difficult to consider," Allison said. Gwen shook her head, giving up on the warm-up. Allison stopped as well, breathing hard despite—or perhaps because of—her conversation.

"No, I meant that it's Lauren's last night, isn't it?" Gwen said. "She's going on maternity leave for an unknowable amount of time."

"Yeah," Allison said, still unsure of what the issue was.

"I knew I was forgetting something important," Gwen said. "It's been bothering me all morning. I still haven't gone to get her a going-away present."

"Oh, right," Allison said. "You can just contribute ten dollars to the pot. We're going in to get her a nice stroller, and Bob is picking it up today. As the only one with children, we figured he would know what sort of stroller is a good one."

"Okay, great," Gwen said. She stretched a bit and then turned to Allison. "So since we got interrupted yesterday, shall we work on those choke holds?" The small woman nodded, and the two got to work.

Alaric wanted to linger over his meal, waiting until Gwen got back before heading out. He knew, though, that he did need to go get some fresh clothes, and then there was the matter of formalizing her new position at The Rose. He still couldn't believe she had agreed to such a proposition. He had figured that he would have to wheedle and beg her to even listen to his offer, let alone accept without any argument. Granted, she had been mostly asleep at the time. Even so.

He did the dutiful thing and cleaned up the kitchen, making sure to put everything in its place. Then, simply because he was there, he looked around her apartment. He told himself that it wasn't prying; Gwen had left him there to finish up as he wished. He wasn't going to go through her drawers or anything, just look. There wasn't much to look at though. The furniture had been picked out by one of Walter's people, and even after months of living there, Gwen hadn't added her own personal touch. The only things that were even remotely significant were the pictures on the wall. All desert scenes, all slightly blurred or of amateur quality. Possibly from her time in the Middle East? He didn't know. Alaric resolved to buy Gwen some kitschy knickknack as soon as he could, just to remove the *monotony* of everything. She was far too bright to live like she did.

He had one last look around the place to make sure he hadn't forgotten anything and was halfway out the door before he thought that he should leave her a note. Something personal to come back to. Alaric grabbed a piece of paper from the stack by the answering machine and searched around for a pen. "Come on, Gwen," he muttered, sifting through drawers of fiercely organized items to find a pen. "You have everything arranged just so and you couldn't leave a pen out?" Alaric reached for a small drawer in the kitchen that looked as though it might have been put in as an afterthought. If a pen was anywhere, a drawer like that would be the place.

He froze. A photograph, just the one, shiny but worn as though it had been kept in a pocket for a very long time, the edges tattered like they'd been handled frequently, looked up at Alaric. He saw a pen lying right next to the photograph, and he knew that he should leave it. Just write the note to Gwen, deal with the details about getting her the job, and everything would be fine. But this photograph had people in it. Alaric looked around, checking to make sure that he was the only one there, though he knew Gwen would be out for at least another hour, then picked up the picture.

It was set in the desert, with the only scenery being rocks and some sort of hills in the background. The sky was a blazing blue, and it could have been the backdrop for a Valentino film from the twenties. Except for the group of people standing in the center. There were six of them, all men but for Gwen, who looked as though she fit right in, minus the weapons. They wore combat clothing, their uniforms dirty and obviously well used but still whole. All wore helmets on their heads, covering their hair but leaving their faces more expressive for it. They had guns clipped to the large utility vests they wore, the muzzles pointed down. They were soldiers, equipped for war. But they were still smiling.

Alaric leaned against the counter, staring at the picture in amazement. Gwen had never smiled like that, not even around him. The man on her left, a man of average height but with muscle and power that made it plain you didn't mess with him, had his arm slung around her shoulder, and she had her arm around his waist. The man on her right leaned in toward her, his head tilted to touch her helmet. The others all leaned in toward the two in the middle. Gwen and...who was he? Alaric turned over the picture, hoping for names. All that was written was "The Hellcats" in a hand unfamiliar to him. He turned it over again, staring at the people there. Hellcats. They didn't look like Hellcats. They looked like a family, wound together and dependent upon one another and perfectly content with that.

Swallowing the lump in his throat, Alaric replaced the picture and took the pen, doing his best to force a cheerful manner as he wrote the note. The picture kept flashing in his mind. Gwen had been so happy. She had been dirty and her face had been hollower, but she'd been confident and sure of herself. The Gwen in the picture could have taken on the world and won. His Gwen? She smiled, sure. She seemed to be confident, certainly. But there was a part of her that was in that picture that was missing from her smile, from her gaze. It was plain only when she hesitated over her knife, when she backed down from a fight with James.

His Gwen, Alaric realized, was broken.

He glanced at the clock on the wall and grimaced. He had an hour to get to The Rose and start instructing his students on the new menu. And in that time, he still had to go take a shower and somehow convince Jack that hiring Gwen to replace Lauren was a good idea. Alaric winced as he thought this; he should have realized earlier that Jack wasn't going to go for his plan. But it was Alaric's choice, wasn't it? *Damn*, he thought. He didn't know.

Grumbling, Alaric stalked out to his car and left for his flat, doing his best not to let his temper get in the way of driving (though he might have scared a few pedestrians on the way). Twenty minutes later and he was back at The Wooden Rose, fumbling to get his key into the lock while holding a bag of pastries to bribe Jack. Alaric couldn't bake, despite many experiments, and he knew that Jack liked pastries.

"Need some help?" Jack asked, walking up behind his head chef and friend with a smirk on his face. He took the bag of pastries Alaric thrust at him and watched, amused, as the ornery man opened the door. Jack took out a pan au raisin and nibbled on it, following Alaric inside. "So how was your night with Gwen?"

Alaric rounded on Jack with a furious look in his eye, "It is none of your business what I do with—damn it, Jack!" His friend was laughing, doing his best not to get crumbs all over his office. He swallowed his bite and smirked.

"You have to admit, you asked for it," Jack said. Alaric growled something unintelligible and rude and reached for the bag. He had eaten well at Gwen's, but suddenly the task before him was looking exhausting. He would need food for it. "What's wrong?" Jack asked, finishing off the pastry.

"Why would you automatically assume that something is wrong just because I snapped at you?" Alaric asked around a mouthful of croissant. Jack pulled out the chair from behind his desk and pointed at the one opposite. Alaric sat after Jack did and the two considered each other like dogs testing the boundaries.

"It has nothing to do with you trying to bite my head off," Jack said casually. "You do that all the time. It has everything to do with the fact that you brought pastries and didn't complain when I took one and ate it. That means they were for me, and you don't bring me pastries unless something is wrong. So what's wrong?"

Alaric polished off the croissant and looked at his friend with a guilty expression. Jack had been his boss for years now, but he had been Alaric's friend for longer. He sometimes forgot how well Jack knew him, just as he sometimes forgot that he couldn't have made it this far without Jack backing him up. He was a good man and Alaric treated him like just another person in his kitchens—that was to say, not well. He supposed that after coming to the realization that Gwen was broken and that he wanted to help her, he was analyzing his interactions with all his friends. He didn't want that haunted look in Gwen's eye to be his fault. He didn't want his shortcomings to hurt other people. Not that such a desire would stop him from snapping at anyone who decided that cooking food properly wasn't necessary, but still.

"It's Gwen," Alaric said.

Jack sighed and leaned back in his chair, reaching for another pastry. He looked at Alaric with a masked expression, which meant nothing good.

"You two can't have broken up already," Jack said. "You are both very, well, temperamental, but I wouldn't think that would stop either of you from—"

"We didn't 'break up,'" Alaric muttered, looking at his hands. He explained about the picture as well as he could without an actual copy and did his best not to break down in front of Jack. He hadn't realized how hard this was for him until he tried to talk about it. His voice grew quieter and rougher as he talked and eventually gave out altogether.

Jack looked at his friend, eyes wide and a little concerned. "Gwen will talk about it when she's ready. Don't forget, this is new for her. She's had a hard time, and for all we know, this is just the beginning of her rebuilding her life. She came from the streets, right? After some sort of accident or something. Just give it time, Alaric. I'm sure she doesn't mean to keep things from you."

"I know. She's even *said* that she'll tell me eventually; she just needs more time. I'm the one who isn't okay with that," Alaric groaned. He put his head in his hands and pulled his fingers through his hair. Leaning back, he remembered why he was there in the first place, pastries in hand. "I wasn't going to talk about this now. I need to talk with you about Lauren's replacement."

"Right. Tonight's her last night. She's a good cook. We'll miss her. I was thinking that you could manage without a replacement for a while, at least until the school is done. Then we can put out an advertisement and see about holding interviews—"

"I want Gwen to do it," Alaric said firmly, lifting his head to meet Jack's gaze. He hoped that the direct approach would mean that Jack wouldn't argue. When he saw how much Alaric wanted this, then things would be sorted out and agreed upon. He was gravely mistaken.

Jack rose out of his chair like it was on fire, his expression livid. He leaned forward, putting his hands first on the desk, then folding them and finally settling with waving them furiously at Alaric. "Are you insane?" he hissed, keeping his volume under control likely only because he was aware that the students would be arriving soon and that there was only a door and thin walls between them and him. "Do you have any idea what you're doing?!"

"I know that she's perfectly capable of doing it," Alaric said. "She's a natural in the kitchen, Jack. I haven't been giving her lessons for a while, and you know she came in here with only the skills to boil pasta and cook a chicken—barely."

"I don't give a shit how talented she is, Alaric. You're *dating* her. You're the head chef of this restaurant. A five-star restaurant, if I may remind you. We can't just go around hiring your girlfriend because she's a decent chef and because you two are fucking about," Jack snarled.

Alaric drew his brows together and felt his own anger rising. Jack didn't understand. "She's not just a decent chef, Jack," Alaric said, his voice rumbling. He was inches away from exploding. "She's one of the best students I've ever had."

"And this decision has nothing to do with the fact that you two are sleeping together," Jack said in a low voice.

Alaric started to deny it and then shook his head and pointed his finger at Jack. "You know what? Yeah, it does. I like her. I'm sleeping with her. I would love to have my girlfriend working under me. But more than that, Gwen deserves this chance. Sure, she could get a job in another kitchen, but with the army as the only job on her resume, she wouldn't get very far. A year from now? She'd be working in some corner bar, feeding tourists who don't even know what a proper burger and fries dish is meant to be, let alone actual food. She's a damn good chef, Jack. And she's the only one out of all the people I've ever taught that I would think about offering this to. She's perfect for this job and you know it. You just want to keep her away because I'm dating her. You don't think it will work. You don't think that I can do it." Alaric started to turn for the door, fed up with the doubt that was being thrown his way. He was determined to help Gwen as best he could, and if this was the only way that he could, then by God, he would do this for her.

"Alaric, sit down," Jack said, his voice radiating authority and offering no option for Alaric to disobey. Jack hated using that voice on Alaric just as much as Alaric hated hearing it. The sound was reminiscent of Alaric's father and had it been anyone other than Jack using it, Alaric would have punched him. He was still considering it, but Jack sat as well and rubbed the heel of his palm into his eyes.

Alaric sat and folded his arms expectantly.

"I don't think you *can't* do it. I think that you're

trying to do this for the wrong reasons. Yes"—Jack held up his hand to stop Alaric from protesting—"I understand that this is a great opportunity for her. I even recognize that she's a good cook. A great one, with some work. The problem is that you want to be some sort of hero to her. You know full well that Gwen is independent and not keen on asking anyone for help. You want her to need your help. You want her to depend on you. She isn't going to like this, Alaric."

"You think that I'm doing this because I want Gwen to act like I'm some sort of savior?" Alaric asked in disbelief. "I just want to help her!"

"I know," Jack said. "She likes you, obviously, or she wouldn't be dating you. But she hasn't asked for your help, Alaric. If you think this is the only way to give her a chance in life, then by all means, hire her. It is your kitchen, your staff. But you're a bloody fool if you do this."

"I'm hiring her," Alaric said darkly, standing to leave. "And that's the end of it." He turned and stormed out the door, ready to pound into the first thing he saw. His students were already gathered and awaiting his instructions, Gwen sitting with Allison and Bob, smiling and laughing as if everything was perfectly normal and good. His anger fluttered as he looked at Gwen, and Alaric, with one last furious look at the door where Jack was standing, gave up on being angry in favor of smiling beneficently at her.

Gwen looked up at Alaric with a raised eyebrow. James was scowling as he watched the interaction between the two, but he made no move to argue. *See? Alaric wanted to point out to Jack. Things are just fine. Even James isn't going to make a fuss about Gwen's place here. I don't see why you want to.* When he turned to look meaningfully at his friend, though, Jack was gone, the door to his office closed behind him. Alaric sneered and turned his attention back to his students.

"Right," he growled, "let's see how well you pick up the summer menu."

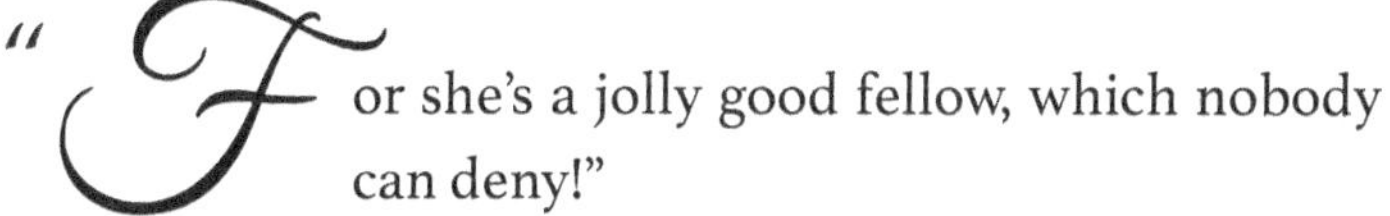

16

"For she's a jolly good fellow, which nobody can deny!"

Lauren smiled at the people around her, who were singing wildly off-key and doing their best to make everyone cringe. She patted her round stomach and shook her head at her well-meaning coworkers. Gwen shook her head at the antics.

"That's really sweet of you," she said once the song had finished, mostly to prevent them from starting another. Danny and Tom were already well into the bottle of champagne that had been passed around, and it looked as though Sarah was going to succumb as well. The only person besides Lauren who didn't have a glass was Gwen, who stood with one hip leaning against the countertop, a smile on her face. "Thanks again for the stroller. Michael and I were going to go out and get one this weekend."

"Well, now you don't have to," Bob said enthusiastically. Alaric raised his eyebrows at Lauren, and she laughed. They would all be sorry to see her go, Gwen knew, but it was nice to see that she would be happy in her new life. Alaric had told her that if she wanted a job after a while, she would be welcome to come back. Lauren had smiled and patted her belly gently before nodding and going in to the party.

The Rose had been closed for an hour now, and everyone was still chatting happily, eating the cake that Jack had ordered and making it fairly clear that they weren't going to leave for a while. Gwen was the only one who seemed inclined to leave, something about the celebration hitting a sour note in her. Maybe it had something to do with the fact that she was missing her own family, or perhaps it was the look that James kept sending her way. She thought, though, that it was more to do with the knowledge that the last time she had sung that song, the subject of her attentions had been dead less than a week later.

"Hey," Jack said, coming up next to Gwen and ignoring the glare Alaric threw his way. "Are you all right? You seem sort of out of it."

"I'm just tired. And I'm not halfway drunk, like everyone else," Gwen said, showing off her glass of mineral water. Jack smiled knowingly and sipped at his own drink without looking self-conscious, a feat few could pull off.

"You don't drink?" he asked.

Gwen shrugged and shook her head, putting her water on the counter and picking up her plate of half-eaten cake. She poked at it unenthusiastically and kept her gaze focused on it when answering. "My father was a drunk," Gwen said. "And when I tried to turn to alcohol to fix my own problems, things got worse. I figured it was safer to just not bother except for the occasional glass. I just don't feel like it, tonight."

"You are far wiser than most," Jack said.

Gwen smiled in thanks at the praise and speared a bite of cake with her fork.

"Which is why I wonder if you really considered what you were doing when you accepted Alaric's offer."

"Of going with him to see his parents?" Gwen asked, drawing her brows together. She shrugged nonchalantly. "I've dealt with worse things than disapproving fathers. I think I can handle it. Besides, he seems to genuinely not want to go. I might as well try and support him."

"That's very gallant of you," Jack replied, frowning as though Gwen had answered the wrong question. "But I was talking about The Rose."

Gwen looked at him in confusion.

He widened his eyes and stared at her in shock. "You don't...know?"

"Know what? Is Alaric getting promoted? I wouldn't think that would be possible, given that he's already head of the kitchens," Gwen said. She took another bite of cake, and Jack looked at her as though he had killed her dog. Okay, now she was worried. He took Gwen's elbow and steered her gently away from the other people. They were speaking quietly enough that the likelihood of them being overheard was fairly slim. Still, Jack didn't seem to want to take a chance.

"I thought Alaric had discussed this with you," Jack said. "About the job."

Gwen scowled. "Oh, right. He thinks that I won't have any problems getting a job after this school ends. I think otherwise. I don't really want to end up working at some Chinese place in the West End."

"Gwen, you don't understand. He wants to hire you *here*. To take Lauren's job, be her replacement," Jack said. Gwen stiffened. Jack withdrew his hand and shifted his weight. Gwen knew that expression; it was the one where people found a sudden urge to get very far away from her. Fast.

"I knew I was forgetting something important," Gwen said, her voice like ice though her expression was exactly the same. Jack took a cautious step backward, his own expression one of anxiety. Alaric came over just then, holding a bottle of beer and looking suspiciously between Gwen and Jack. He threw an accusing look at Jack and put his arm protectively around Gwen's shoulder, as if that would be enough to dispel any animosity. This time, Gwen stiffened, and Alaric flinched as if he'd been struck.

"Are you all right?" he asked Gwen, the bite of anger in his voice clearly directed at Jack. Shouldn't she be the angry one? Shouldn't she be raging at Alaric? Even as she thought it, her temper rose and snapped.

"You bloody idiot," Gwen hissed, rounding on Alaric. There was a lull in the conversation the others were holding, and Gwen frowned. She didn't want to create a scene, not in front of Alaric's people, not in front of people she had to work with. And the look that Jack was giving her reminded her too much of the look that some of the psychiatrists had given her after the incident. Alaric was looking at her as though he had been shot—she knew the look well—and her hand was tightening on the fork she was holding, her broken hand twitching as she restrained from decking Alaric.

"Gwen?" Alaric asked, hesitantly putting his hand on her shoulder. "Are you feeling okay?"

She should have answered no, should have said she was feeling ill, could he please take her home, but she didn't. Instead, with the eyes of everyone in the kitchen on her, she made a visible effort to relax and smiled. "I'm fine," she said, putting down the plate of cake and picking up her water instead. As she sipped at the bubbling liquid, those watching couldn't help but shudder. Behind the natural-looking smile were the eyes of a wolf.

Alaric let the matter drop, putting Gwen's sudden mood change down to being tired after a long day. She had, he remembered belatedly, only gotten four hours of sleep the night before. That on top of working with Allison, being in a hot kitchen for the greater portion of the day, and trying to learn the new summer menu would be enough to make anyone tired. Maybe he should sleep at his own place tonight, let her get some genuine rest. Having convinced himself of that, he returned his attention to the party and to Lauren.

An hour later, Alaric was one of three people left, cleaning the counters and disposing of paper cake plates. He was annoyed because Gwen had vanished and because she hadn't told him she was leaving. He would give her some slack, he determined. She was new to this whole relationship thing. She would—they both would—need to get used to doing something for two people rather than just one. Still, he would have figured that Gwen would have said something.

"Danny, go home," Jack ordered, taking the rubbish bag from the sous chef. "You look dead on your feet."

"Right, boss," Danny said, gladly relinquishing the bag and grabbing his jacket from the hook by the door. "See you tomorrow."

Jack waited until the door clicked into place and turned to watch Alaric furiously clean a spot on the stove that had been there for a year, simply worn in by time. "You should go home too."

"What I should do is go find Gwen, make sure that she's all right," Alaric said. "I knew she looked ill."

"I don't think that was what was bothering her," Jack said, clearing the last of the plates into the bag. "She was more angry than ill."

"How would you know that?" Alaric seethed,

throwing down his rag in disgust. "Because she'll talk to you rather than me?"

Jack recoiled, staring at Alaric in shock. "You can't seriously be jealous of me," he said in disbelief. "Alaric, don't be an idiot. Gwen—I don't think of her that way, and I know she doesn't think of me that way. I wanted to make sure that she knew what she was doing getting into this job, nothing more."

Alaric's shoulders relaxed slightly, and he let the original irritation take the place of jealousy. "Yeah, well, she does. She can handle it. You're the one that—"

"She didn't know anything about it!" Jack shouted.

Alaric looked up at his friend in astonishment. Jack never shouted. Even when he was being particularly idiotic and causing mayhem in the kitchens, Jack never shouted at him. The only time Alaric had even heard Jack raise his voice was when things were too loud for him to be heard clearly. Alaric's initial shock over Jack's shouting gave way to bemusement as he comprehended the words.

"Of course she did," Alaric said. "She agreed to it last night."

Jack simply sighed and rubbed the bridge of his nose. "You should go and talk with her," he said in a defeated voice. "I'll finish clearing up here."

Alaric didn't argue; he grabbed his jacket and slipped it on, making sure he had his keys in his pocket. "She agreed to it, Jack. This will work out for the best. You'll see," he said. Then, with a determined spring in his stride, Alaric left.

Jack looked despondently at the bag of rubbish in his hands. "Just as long as you're not trying to prove that to yourself," he called after Alaric.

When Alaric rang Gwen's buzzer, she was just getting out of the shower, her hair tied up nicely in a towel, a dressing gown wrapped snugly around her. If there was one thing that would help assuage the frustrations that came with dealing with men, a good cup of tea was it. A long, hot shower worked almost as well. She heard the buzzer and knew exactly who it was. For a minute, she considered not answering. She was more than furious with him, and he could do with a bit of discipline. That being said, she didn't want to ruin her relationship with Alaric before it really began. Shutting him out might do just that.

Gwen let him up, opening the door just as he finished climbing the stairs. He looked tired, haggard, and annoyed. As he saw her, some of his tension melted away. She tried very hard not to feel flattered by that. She wasn't shutting him out, but she was still angry.

He greeted her with a kiss, slipping his arms around her waist and pulling her close. "You left without saying anything," he said as she pulled away to close the door. "I thought you were looking a bit ill earlier, but you should have said something. No one would have minded that you had to go." He put his hand to her forehead. "Are you feeling better?"

"I'm not sick," Gwen snapped, pulling away from his touch forcefully. She stalked into the kitchen and looked for something to do that would keep her from pummeling him.

Alaric followed, watching as she put on the kettle and rifled through the fridge.

"I'm pissed."

"Was it James?" he asked, growling at the thought of that man hurling insults at her.

Gwen straightened and looked at him, her lip curled in disdain, a container of custard in her hands. Alaric waited for a response, then realized that the look, the one that radiated barely controlled rage, was his answer. Except that it was directed at *him*.

"Gwen, what's wrong?" he demanded. "I can't do anything if you won't talk to me!"

"Oh, like you talk to me?" she snarled, throwing the custard to the counter and flinging open a drawer to get a knife to open it. "Like you tell me that I'm going to be Lauren's replacement? Or maybe it's just easier for you to assume that I'll be fine with it and that you can go ahead and arrange my life for me. That is what you're doing after all, isn't it?" Gwen stabbed the custard container viciously before depositing the knife on the counter when the container was full of holes enough to be poured into a bowl.

Alaric took a step backward. "You said that you wanted to do it," he said in a small voice. Jack had been right; she didn't know. He thought that she would have remembered the conversation—if you could call it that when she was dropping from exhaustion and he had only asked one question—but he'd been was wrong. "You agreed."

"When was this?" Gwen demanded, keeping her back turned to him as she worked on preparing the custard. She snatched a nectarine from the fruit bowl and chopped it into chunks before practically throwing the pit away into the trash.

"Last night," Alaric said, the sinking feeling in his stomach growing. "After we were talking about our families."

"Oh, you mean last night when I was tired enough to say anything and not remember it in the morning?" Gwen said, her voice scathing. She finished with the nectarine and turned toward Alaric. Her eyes were not angry, as he'd expected. They were hurt, distrustful, as though he'd betrayed her. "I told you that there was something I was forgetting this morning," she accused. "Why didn't you tell me?"

"Because I didn't know that you didn't remember!" Alaric said, doing his best not to see the hurt in her eyes. It wasn't his fault. He couldn't have known that was what she was referring to. Why was she so angry about the job in the first place? He was trying to help her!

"And you didn't think that something so crucial to my life as a job might have been the 'important thing' I was asking about? Is my life something that you can just arrange for your own pleasure? Should I completely fix my schedule to suit you? Or would you like something else from me?"

"I was trying to help you," Alaric growled, giving in to the temper that he had been trying to hold back. Why didn't she understand? "I was trying to give you a decent shot at having a career as a chef. I thought that was what you wanted, after all. You were attending my school to learn how to be a chef so you could get off the streets, isn't that right?"

"Yes," Gwen said. "I want to be a chef. I want to be off the streets, making my own money rather than depending on Walter to give me funds. I want to forge a career for myself. I don't need you doing it for me. I can fight my own battles, Alaric. I've been doing it for years."

"Yes, and see where it got you!" Alaric yelled. Gwen didn't flinch or recoil at his volume, instead straightening her shoulders and staring him down. He wouldn't realize until later that she was preparing for battle. This was not a fight she would lose. "Damn it, Gwen, I'm trying to give you a chance here. You don't have enough experience in the world of food to make it very far. You need a job like this on your resume if you're going to get anywhere."

"I may need a job," Gwen said, her words more forceful than loud. "But I don't need you to *hand* it to me. I can earn it for myself. I can, despite what you may think, have a life without depending on other people to create it for me. I've functioned for years without you, Alaric. You said it yourself, I'm a good cook. I *can* get a job, create a career, on my own."

"Obviously, you can't!" Alaric shouted. "You needed Walter to pick you up out of your own misery and the despondency of the streets to give you this chance. You're not arguing with *him* about this. Yet you seem to find fault with the fact that I'm trying to do the same thing. Is it because I'm not rich? Or does it have to do with the fact that I'm dating you? Or maybe it's just because I'm your boss."

Gwen bared her teeth at Alaric, her eyes sparkling with malice. "You just can't get over the fact that I was homeless, can you? It's just one more failure to hang over my head. Yeah, all right, so I needed Walter to give me a hand and get me started, but I earned my way into your good graces without his help. He wasn't trying to hand me a life. He was just giving me a chance to earn it. You, on the other hand, seem to think I'm incapable of doing anything without help. 'James is causing problems? Here, let me deal with it. You're going to need a job after classes end? I can fix that for you.' Alaric, you're not giving me a chance to prove myself!"

He opened his mouth to retort, to say that was exactly what he was doing, but he knew it wasn't true.

He wanted to make Gwen's life easier and to help her become a great chef. He knew that she was capable of being great and didn't see the need for her to prove it. She did though. She needed to prove it to herself as well as to the world. Just because he saw that she was great didn't mean she saw it or Jack saw it. It just meant that he saw her potential. He couldn't show her without her doing something. He was, in a word, wrong.

Alaric took a deep breath as he tried to shove away the last vestiges of his anger. He leaned against the table and put his arms down, giving up. "Yeah," he murmured. "You're right."

Gwen faltered; she had been prepared to fire another retort at him. She was flushed with her anger running through her veins, and she wanted to fight, to force him to see reason. Here he was, though, backing down. Conceding the fight. She blinked and pulled back, some part of her closing off.

"I'm sorry," Gwen said softly. "I...I know you were just trying to help. It's just that's not helpful to me."

"I know. I wanted to fix things for you," Alaric answered, coming up behind her and snaking his arms around her waist. He rested his head on the towel wrapped around her hair. "Sorry," he said, ducking his head to kiss the corner of her jaw. "Am I forgiven?"

"Yes," Gwen sighed. She relaxed into his hold and

leaned her head on his shoulder. "You'd better tell Jack to start organizing interviews for the job, then. I'll prepare my resume, and—"

"I have a better idea," Alaric said. "This way, you can earn your way into the job. No trickery, no being soft on you. Just plain, raw talent."

"Encouraging," Gwen said with a sarcastic snort. She poured out the tea and picked up the bowl of custard, digging in a drawer to grab two spoons.

Alaric had just eaten cake at Lauren's party, but he didn't refuse. It was a peace offering more than a meal, and who was he to turn down custard with fruit? Halfway through the custard and tea, Gwen began to yawn.

"You should get some sleep," Alaric said, taking that as his cue to start the washing up. Gwen protested and rose to help. "Stop," Alaric grumbled, shoving her back as gently as he could. "I've been something of an inconsiderate prick tonight, so the least I can do is get the washing up sorted out. Besides, you've been on your feet since what, six, six thirty?"

"Something like that," Gwen muttered. Alaric raised his eyebrows expectantly, and Gwen muttered something under her breath. "Fine, fine," she repeated. "I'll go to bed. I don't have any pajamas, but I think I have some old sweats that might fit you."

"I'll just head back to my apartment," Alaric said.

Gwen frowned and, in an uncharacteristic motion, put her hands on her hips, accentuating her scowl.

Alaric smirked. "You can't seriously have energy for that."

"Well, perhaps not," Gwen said, "but that isn't all that beds are good for."

"Come on, Gwen," Alaric said, finishing the washing and turning to face her. He leaned back against the counters and crossed his arms; he wasn't going to give in, and there was little she could do to make him. "You're tired, and we've just had a fight, so maybe we should sleep separately tonight. I haven't got a change of clothes with me anyway, or a toothbrush. It's not like we'll have to wait ages to see one another. Just the...what are you doing?"

"Showing you what you're missing," Gwen said in her best imitation of a coquette. It wasn't very good, and Alaric would have laughed if he hadn't been engrossed in what she was doing. It started with her undoing the towel that held her hair. The brown locks fell to her shoulders in an unmannerly rush, tangled together and still slightly damp. It was a very interesting look, Alaric mused silently, sort of the fresh-out-of-shower look (which, he supposed, was reality). Then she stretched, her body straining against the now far-too-thin fabric of the dressing gown. Alaric shifted his weight. When Gwen started undoing the ties around her waist, turning her back and looking at him over her shoulder, he was done for. He pounced before she could even get the dressing gown all the way off.

"I thought you didn't have the energy for this," Alaric said, kissing as much flesh as he could get, using his teeth and tongue as much as his lips. Gwen arched beneath him and simply purred, tangling her fingers in his hair.

"Ah, but I'm not doing the work right now, am I?" she said. Alaric had to give her that; he was the one picking her up and carrying her to the bedroom, kissing her while she slowly and carefully divested him of his clothing. "Just go slowly," Gwen murmured when Alaric disentangled himself to throw his trousers on the floor and dim the lights.

"I think," he said, nipping at the soft skin of her breast, "I can manage that."

17

Alaric was going crazy. Not literally, but he was fed up with getting next to no sleep. Tonight, he would be sleeping at his own place in his own bed. It had nothing to do with the sex. He could deal with things if it were just sex. But even when they managed to drop off to sleep, Gwen would be thrashing about half an hour later or just be awake. In three days, she hadn't started screaming like she had at his apartment, but he knew it was just a matter of time. And her being sleepless meant that he got no sleep as well. He wasn't trained as a military interpreter or soldier. He wasn't meant to be working on four hours of sleep or less.

Just thinking about it made him feel guilty, but he couldn't stand it. He hadn't believed Major Dalton when the man had said that Gwen was more volatile than before, and even the knowledge that something—the death of her squad—had removed a piece of her couldn't have prepared him for what reality was like.

Alaric had believed that getting her to open up to him would be the worst of his problems. After all, she seemed perfectly normal? How bad could her PTSD be? Some days he doubted that she had it. Then came the nights.

Whatever she squashed down during the day reared its ugly head at night. And there was nothing that Alaric could do that would stop it. Now, with three nights of very little sleep under his belt, he wasn't sure he would ever be able to. He just needed *peace*.

Hopefully, after what he had planned for today, Gwen would be too happy to worry about why he wanted to sleep at his place. Without her.

Alaric ran his hands through his hair to get it under control before he turned his attention to the kitchen. Gwen was off either doing something with Allison or going on a run. He couldn't remember which event was for that day. Part of the reason why he needed a decent night's sleep. It didn't matter; he had left shortly after she had, going to The Wooden Rose to get everything prepared. Considering how advanced his students were, they didn't do much in the way of lessons. Not that they would ever stop learning—no one, in Alaric's opinion, could ever stop learning about how to cook. He was just running out of things to actively teach them. Today would be different. If he was right, it would take most of the day to get what he wanted sorted out, and then he had to deal with the actual restaurant. So, despite the fact that it was barely eight in the morning, he was busy.

"When you said you were getting here early," Jack grumbled as he walked through the door with a large cup of coffee in his hand and a look that said he was feeling as tired as Alaric felt, "you weren't kidding."

"This is going to take long enough," Alaric said. "I don't want to have to think about getting everything prepped when people get here."

"Are you sure this is the way that you want to do things?" Jack asked. "I mean, putting out an ad in the *Times* would have been easy enough. A 'competition' between your students seems a bit extreme."

"It's an 'audition,'" Alaric corrected, "and this is the only way that I know how to convince Gwen that she's the one who should be getting this job and I wasn't just trying to be nice and help her out. Besides, if these people were good enough to get into my classes, they're probably the only people I'd consider hiring anyway."

"Right. So even if this doesn't turn out the way you want and you end up having to concede the matter to James, your *least* favorite of your students for all he's a good cook, then you'll be satisfied?" Jack asked.

Alaric glared at his friend from where he was pulling out fresh fish and other seafood and setting it in a large cooler in the center of the room. "I'd beat him into shape if that were to happen, but it won't because Gwen's going to win, so there's no point in worrying about it," Alaric said. "That's that."

"Right. And asking me to call in Walter to be a judge had nothing to do with the fact that you want to stack things in Gwen's favor," Jack said. He leaned against a counter and watched Alaric set out more ingredients and thereby limit what his students had to work with. Only what was set out would be fair game. Everything else was up to the creativity of the chef.

"He's an unbiased judge when it comes to food. He's also the least snobby person about food that I've ever met, so he won't judge based on silly things," Alaric said. "Like the quality of beer used to braise a lamb flank or—"

"Or question the quality of someone's dish who hasn't been cooking nearly as long as the others," Jack finished.

Alaric scowled and pointed rudely to the freezer. "Go get some meat," he snarled. "And stop making this more difficult than it needs to be. I'm tired, I'm irritated, and if you don't start helping, I'm going to move very quickly into the 'pissed' category."

"We wouldn't want that, now would we?" Jack said. Alaric replied with some very choice phrases that made Jack grin in response. The manager ducked into the freezer to go do what he had been told.

Gwen ran. She wasn't sure if she was running toward something or away from it, but she ran like her life depended on it. The thought crossed her mind that she had been running for a very long time, long before The Incident and long prior to joining the army. She should have been used to it—the mindset, not the act

—but something in her rebelled. She wanted to stop and take in the world around her, to live without worrying about who was looking for her or what secrets she needed to keep.

She kept running.

Being with Alaric was nice, she mused, settling into her fourth mile. She didn't feel as though she had to watch her step quite as much, though there were moments. Like this morning, when she got up and he simply looked at her and turned over, going back to sleep. It was her restlessness, she knew. It was getting to him. Her inability to sleep, and more importantly to sleep with him, content to have his arms wrapped around her and feeling safe, rankled him. She hadn't felt safe for a very long time. Hence, she supposed, the running.

If she didn't get a proper night's sleep, she knew that she would drive Alaric crazy. Only he wouldn't admit it to her because that would be admitting failure. Instead, he would take it out on his kitchen staff and others around her. But not her; he treated Gwen delicately, carefully, as if he was worried that something in her might break. (Or was already broken? She wondered about that, sometimes.) That didn't mean that the two of them didn't argue, just that he did it with more care than usual. Gwen could tell, despite his care, that his nerves were wearing thin.

They needed a night off from each other. Alaric needed sleep, and Gwen? Well, she needed to figure out how to get him to stop mincing his words and minding his step around her. Maybe Allison would be up for a night on the town. Gwen would ask about it, see if they could schedule it for their next day off. They could go see a show, have dinner somewhere nice. Maybe go to a club. She considered the pulsing music and pressing bodies and shivered, her heart suddenly racing and not from the running. Clubbing would be out.

Gwen slowed as she reached Central Park, her stride changing to a walk as she found herself among the well-groomed gardens and nicely paved footpaths. Even though it was early, there were still people meandering about, pushing strollers or talking with other people. Gwen couldn't help but watch them, completely oblivious to the world around them apart from a casual glance or brushing a bug away. A few were even just enjoying the sunlight.

Did they know? Did they know how much people payed to grant them their freedom? To let them walk around with to-go cups in their hand, chattering away on their phones and determined that the world revolved around them? She wondered if she had ever been that content, able to let the world keep moving while she lived. She doubted it. Even as a girl, she had seen things pulling the strings and shaping the world in subtle—or not-so-subtle—ways. She had gone to fight for the chance to preserve the ways she believed in, and look where it landed her.

Constantly running and unable to sleep for longer than a couple hours at a time without seeing images of horror. At least she had Alaric. He belonged to the category of the oblivious, but Gwen wouldn't want it any other way.

"Hey, watch it," a man snapped at her as she barely avoided barreling straight into him. She had been dancing to avoid the mother and her stroller walking the other way, and the man had appeared from around a corner, moving quickly and talking on his phone. He held his now-empty coffee cup with the air of someone who was on his last straw. The coffee had, luckily enough, not spilled on him, though Gwen had been splattered a bit. Most of it was on the ground, and from the way that the man was now glaring at Gwen, she figured that he considered it her fault.

"I'm sorry," Gwen said. "I'll get you—"

"Don't you have any respect for other people?" he seethed, straightening to his full height and staring Gwen down. She scoffed mentally; no one was able to stare her down and win. Except perhaps Major Dalton, but that was another story. "Why don't you look where you're going?"

"I've already apologized," Gwen said. "I can buy you another coffee, but I don't really think it was my fault."

"Wasn't your fault?" the man growled, the sound grating and furious and not anywhere near as effective as Alaric's growls. "Get your head out of your ass, lady. *You* ran into *me*."

Gwen was truly annoyed at this point. She took a deep breath to keep from snapping and held up her hands defensively, trying to show him she meant no harm. He took one look at her broken hand and flicked his eyes back to her face, somehow even more angry with her movements. "Look, I'm sorry. I was trying to avoid the stroller. It was an accident, and I'll get you another coffee," she said. She was inches away from biting his head off.

"I don't want a coffee from you," the man sneered. He straightened his suit jacket and half turned. "It's people like you that make our country slip into degradation."

Gwen should have let it go. She knew that. She had refused to be annoyed by his comments about her anatomy, refused to be infuriated by his insinuations that she was an idiot. But that was taking things too far. With a shift of her weight, the lowering of her hands, and a straightening of her posture, Gwen no longer looked defensive. She looked downright threatening.

"People like me?" she asked, her voice low and dangerous. "And what sort of people would that be? Because from where I'm standing, people like me are the only thing between you and a whole heck of a lot of chaos. Are you willing to go strap on one hundred pounds of gear and tramp through the desert to fight people who are more than eager to blow you up? Or translate while a gun is being aimed at your friends? How about killing boys barely old enough to drive a car, let alone fight in a war, just because they're pointing guns at your head? And then giving up every-thing you ever loved because people cut corners and didn't get the right information? Then how about living on the streets because no one knows what to do with you? People like me causing things to go downhill. I don't think so."

She didn't wait around to find out what the man had to say to her tirade. Gwen simply turned on her heel and walked away, her stride eating up ground so as to make sure that no one, especially not people like him, could follow her and attack her. She was tired of being put down because she hadn't been born into a world where things were handed to her. She worked and fought for everything in life, including her beliefs. Nothing was going to change that. It didn't mean she couldn't be angry at the people who thought otherwise.

After a good distance, when Gwen figured that the man couldn't see her or wouldn't be watching for her, Gwen started up her run again. She had originally thought to stop somewhere in that part of the city and get a decent breakfast, but her anger fueled her body, and she simply ran all the way back to her apartment. It was only when she opened the door and narrowly avoided the urge to slam it shut that Gwen realized her legs were trembling.

What was she now that she wasn't a soldier? An interpreter? All that man had seen was a woman out for a run who probably didn't care about endurance or strength as much as she did her figure. She could have been anyone. She wasn't distinguishable, and she wasn't anything out of the ordinary. Not that she had joined the military for the purpose of being special or recognized as a hero. She had just wanted to have some sense of worth, and that had been taken from her. She was a chef now, Gwen reminded herself. But she didn't even know if she had that. After the classes at The Rose drew to a close—they were nearly there already—she would have to search for a job. And she had refused Alaric's help, so the likelihood of her getting a decent one was, well, slim.

Gwen looked at the clock on her oven. It was nearly eleven, and she still had to take a shower and make herself generally presentable before heading over to the restaurant. She stripped and stepped under the hot water, letting it run over her still-trembling muscles while she considered things. She liked being at The Wooden Rose. She enjoyed her relationship with Alaric. She didn't mourn her old life every second of every day. That should have been enough, but it wasn't. Because every time she closed her eyes, the ghosts of her past—Damon in particular—were staring over her shoulder, reminding her of her inadequacies and failures. She would never be good enough; she couldn't help but make mistakes, and they were the sort that couldn't be fixed.

"Stop feeling sorry for yourself, Townsend," Gwen snarled at her reflection, the bathroom steamy around her. She glared at her image and then, in an act of defiance, turned her back on it. She might never be good enough, but that didn't mean she couldn't enjoy what she was capable of. And at that moment, it meant going over to The Rose, kissing Alaric until he turned blue, and then cooking up a hell of a storm. It would have to be enough.

She arrived just after James, which meant that her impression of the kitchens was slightly marred by his own exclamations of awe. Alaric had said something about going in early to get a few things sorted out, but this was just...wow. There were ingredients set out in organized categories: meats, fish, fruits, veggies, spices, liquids, etc. The workstations were set up with the same tools instead of the widely different things that different tasks required on an average evening. It looked, to Gwen's eye, like one of the cooking competition shows on television.

"Alaric," Gwen said, spotting him standing in a corner with a look of pride on his face. He grinned at her and raised his eyebrows. She didn't bother asking what was going on since he wouldn't explain until everyone was present. Instead, she reached up, cupped his jaw in her hands, and pressed her lips to his. "Hi," she said.

"Hello to you too," he answered, promptly wrapping his arms around her waist and kissing her again. "Should I ask what got you in a mood for such a public display of affection?"

"I ran into an idiot in the park, and he got me soundly pissed," Gwen said. "I just thought I should put my anger into something more productive."

"I won't complain," Alaric said, kissing her again for good measure. He nipped at her lips, and she nearly melted into him, her troubles forgotten for the moment. Alaric pulled away and released his hold on her waist before pulling her out of the corner and into the center of things. Not everyone was there yet, so he waited, putting his arm around her shoulders instead. "What happened to make you so angry? Is there some idiot I need to beat up, or do I just need to call you a lawyer?"

"Ha," Gwen said, digging her elbow lightly into his gut. "I didn't hit him. I was sorely tempted, but I didn't. He just got mad at me for trying to avoid a stroller and accidentally spilling his coffee in the process. He yelled, and I defended, then walked away."

"Good girl," Alaric said.

Sarah was the last in the door, and after a quick look around to make sure that everyone was present, Alaric disentangled his arm from around Gwen's shoulder and took up a position at the center of the group. He looked at each of them, taking his time and making everyone shift uncomfortably. That look, the calculating and assessing one, was never a good sign.

"All right, everyone," Alaric said with a smirk. "What do you see?"

"An interesting setup," Thomas said, breaking some of the tension in the room.

Alaric pointed at him. "Smart-ass," he said. "But you are partly right. From now until exactly one hour before opening, everything that you see in this kitchen is all that you'll be able to use. The freezer and store-rooms are off-limits. You can't go searching for more tools, different ingredients, anything. The reason for that is that I want you to show me what you can do. Lauren, as you all know, left a hole in my kitchen staff, and one of you is going to get the opportunity to fill it. Since I can't just pick based on my own whims and have to actually satisfy my manager and the people that eat here, we're going to have a friendly competition."

"You must be joking," Allison said. Alaric fixed her in a severe stare so that she shifted uncomfortably and folded her arms defensively. "It's true though. You want us to compete, like those television shows, for a job?"

"Basically, yes," Alaric said. "Though I could do this just because I'm still your teacher and you still have to do what I say for another week. If you don't want the job, just say so now, and you can be left out of the competition."

"I already have a job lined up," Bob said after a moment's hesitation.

"I do too," Jennifer said. "Bellton is promoting me."

"I've gotten a nice offer from a place a couple miles from here," Robert chimed in. "Though I wouldn't mind watching."

"Anyone else?" Alaric asked, looking around at the remaining people. They all shook their heads, the air of competition already having them inching away from their colleagues. "All right, then. Here's how this works. You have an hour to put together each course. Appetizer, main course, dessert course. There will be three judges to determine whose dish was the best of the round. The person with the most wins gets the position. In the interest of goodwill, though, you won't know the results until the very end."

"Who are the judges?" James asked, eyeing a workstation.

"Walter Smythe, Jack, and"—Alaric hesitated for a moment, looking displeased—"Graham Ruskin. I will, of course, be tasting everything, but I'm not actually allowed to judge. So any questions?"

"Are there any specifications we need to worry about for the meals?" Sarah asked, ever practical.

"Your only limitation is sticking to the ingredients presented here," Alaric said. "And if you run out? Figure it out. Right, if that's everything, then get to work. You have exactly one hour from now."

Gwen did as she was told, staking out a workstation and picking up ingredients as quickly as she could, trying to get food before her peers did. She managed to grab nearly everything she needed and was in the middle of chopping some peppers before she stopped to think about what was going on.

A competition? For a job? It was absurd. And she knew exactly why Alaric was doing it. Of *course* she wanted to work at The Wooden Rose. It would be marvelous. But she wouldn't take a handout from Alaric, not without proving herself. This was his idea of a compromise. She didn't have to prove herself to him for the job but to other people. She had to fight for the position. She could do that. She excelled at fighting, earning, her way in the world. Then, with a facetious smile on her lips, Gwen hoped that Alaric was prepared to deal with the fact that James might win instead of her.

She redoubled her efforts, mind already turning to different combinations, recipes, techniques. James would not be allowed to win.

18

"I've prepared a pepper and mango salsa with a mint puree and roasted crisps," Gwen said, standing before the panel of judges, her posture straight and rigid, her arms behind her back, her stance balanced. She looked every inch the proper soldier except for the fact that her hair was far from meeting military regulations, her clothing was that of a chef, and her nose had a smudge of flour on it that no one was willing to point out to her. She looked as though she had finally found a place to fit in. That alone made Walter smile.

Then, of course, there was the fact that he had been asked to sit in on this competition and judge the food. There were worse ways to spend an afternoon. Graham had complained about the afternoon being wasted the whole drive over and was still looking slightly sulky, though he had perked up at the sight of Gwen. Walter dutifully tasted the appetizer that Gwen had made and closed his eyes in pleasure. Who knew that something so simple could taste so good? It even had a slight bite to it to remind you that it was a salsa you were eating, not your grandmother's bean dip. Walter had tasted four appetizers already, and he was thrilled.

"This is great," Walter said, reaching for another mouthful of the food. His hand was slapped away by Jack, who looked at him with raised brows. "What? I want more."

"You have a whole set of main courses and desserts to try," Jack said. "I think you should hold back on the food."

"Don't worry," Gwen said with a smirk, "I made extra. I'll have Alaric put it in a doggy bag for takeaway."

"You're a good girl," Walter said and waved Gwen away with a flick of his hand. She gave a half-mocking bow and turned, heading back to the kitchens. The other chefs were waiting, some pacing, others standing with folded arms.

"Done?" Alaric asked. He had already tasted Gwen's dip and was in the middle of keeping James and Allison from biting each other's heads off. The two chefs were bristling at each other, and while saying nothing, they looked to be close to blows. Gwen nodded, and Alaric let his shoulders relax for a second.

"Right," he said, his voice carrying through the kitchen. "Enough chitchat. Time to move on to your second course! Any ingredients already used up will not be replenished. You have exactly one hour."

Just as before, Gwen lunged for various ingredients, snatching a salmon steak and some potatoes before the others could. She grabbed lemons, pepper, truffle oil, and various other things and began to cook. It never seemed to occur to her to be tired. Alaric watched as she moved gracefully, seemingly ignoring the implications of the competition. Or maybe she was just that good. The other students' activities didn't seem to faze her at all. She just cooked. Her concentration was such that she ignored everyone else around her. James muttered to himself while grilling a rack of lamb, and Allison was shifting her weight nervously, looking about at what everyone else was doing while cubing chicken. The others cooked with equal or less fervor, just thinking about the next minutes. And Alaric watched it all.

The hour passed quickly for him, consumed as he was with watching his students create. It was what he liked more than anything about cooking. The creation of something wonderful from ingredients that wouldn't amount to anything on their own. The ability to take pieces and make a whole. It was magnificent.

He watched others creating food with as much pleasure as he got from doing it himself. Well, nearly. Even watching James, whom he didn't care for personally, put together pieces of what looked to be a savory lamb dish with some sort of kale side dish was an experience worth enjoying. Gwen, though, was his favorite—and only part of it came from the fact that he just liked watching her.

It took him a while to figure out what she was making, but when he did, he had to fight to keep from laughing. Fish and chips? One of the most simple, common dishes around, and here was Gwen, using it to—hopefully—win herself the job. Granted, most fish and chips shops didn't sear the salmon to perfection with hints of saffron and fennel, nor cook the fries in truffle oil and put rosemary on top. Still, despite the trappings, it was a classic dish. And a bold statement.

But wasn't that everything about Gwen? Bold statements, no backing down, no hiding. She wasn't one to tiptoe around a topic just because someone complained. She believed what she believed, said what she thought, and meant every word. Behind that was the flash temper and a steel core. Alaric was pleased to be able to recognize her moods because it gave him the satisfaction of claiming he was getting to know her, to break down the barriers around that core. If only she would stop putting them up, things would be great. He had a plan for that though. One that involved getting her alone and willing to be vulerable so they could have a proper discussion. For that, he would need an Incident, and there was only one person he knew that could create an Incident better than anyone else. His father.

She was coming to the party in a week and a half.

He had asked her because he'd been hoping for her support in dealing with his family, but Alaric wasn't one to pass up an opportunity when it danced in front of him. He would take her, and knowing his family like he did, things would likely get ugly. If they didn't, so much the better. When they did, he would be ready with the strong liquor and the glasses.

He shook his head to clear away those thoughts. It wasn't manipulation, he told himself as he watched Sarah put a duck breast on a plate. It was simply careful questioning. Considering that Gwen was driving him crazy, keeping him up for half the night, and refusing to talk about things, he figured it was worth it. He wanted to know her, every bit. And more than anything, he wanted to know the person in the photograph she kept in her kitchen drawer. The one with the smile. Alaric was so caught up in his musings that he nearly missed calling time. He muttered a curse to himself—Gwen's problems were proving to be quite the distraction—and barked out, "Time!"

Immediately, everyone stepped away from what they were doing, some looking around in pride, others staring at their dishes as if willing them to get better or be different.

James took one look at Gwen's plate and sneered. "Couldn't think of anything more interesting than fish and chips?"

"Everyone likes a good fish and chips," Gwen replied, her voice steady. "Mine is better than most."

"Somehow, I don't think that's going to get you very far in this business," James said, folding his arms. "This is a five-star restaurant. Five-dollar meals aren't served here."

Gwen didn't rise to the bait and merely shrugged. Maybe it was the fact that she had argued with the man in the park earlier or maybe she was finally seeing a way out of her difficulties with her job, but she allowed herself to fully ignore James. He was nothing more than an annoyance, and his opinion didn't matter anymore. She looked over to see what he had made and looked with interest at the grilled lamb and a creamed kale slaw, both drizzled with some sort of sauce. James saw her looking, and his smirk only deepened.

"Right, our judges are ready, and we'll begin. The same order as before, so Thomas, you're up." Alaric held open the door to the kitchens and followed Thomas out, the dish carried steadily in Thomas's hands. Gwen would have watched, but she didn't think her nerves would stand up to it. Sure, she was ignoring James and pleased with the result, but that didn't mean she wasn't worried about her chances. These people were in Alaric's school because they were good. Better than good, they were great chefs. She was pleased to have been able to keep up with them, but that didn't mean she would be able to win in a head-on competition against them. She could hope; her chances weren't great. That didn't mean she wasn't going to fight.

"Enough," Gwen muttered to herself. "You're overthinking things." She looked around for some distraction and settled on Allison. The petite woman was pacing back and forth in front of her workstation, looking at everyone's dishes and frowning. She had created a wonderful, thick chicken-and-corn chowder spooned out over crisped toast, and just the scent was intoxicating. Gwen meandered over.

"This is nerve-racking," Allison said as Gwen leaned against the counter next to her friend. "I thought it would be just like a typical day, cooking and seeing what we could come up with, but this is much worse."

"Your chowder looks great," Gwen said.

Allison smiled in return and managed to calm herself down enough to stop pacing.

"Is there any extra?"

"I feel like I made enough to feed a small army." Allison gestured to the pot still simmering on the stove. "I thought I would use more of it in plating, but with the toast, I don't think it should be too overwhelming, and—"

"I was just hoping I could snag a bowl," Gwen said.

Allison grew red and, if possible, even more agitated. "I don't think...it's just that...perhaps you shouldn't," she stuttered.

Gwen had already reached for a spare bowl and

spoon and paused, looking at the other woman. "It is edible, isn't it?" she asked.

Allison nodded.

"Were you planning on using it for something else? Because if you wanted to save it, I'm fine with that. I mean, I can always see about cooking up a grilled cheese, but this looked so good, and it's lunch time and..."

"Fine, go ahead," Allison said, breaking into a smile at Gwen's hopeful look. Gwen grinned in return and served out the last of Allison's chowder. Just like that, the tension in the kitchen seemed to break, and everyone, including James, decided that it was a good enough time for lunch. Those who had leftover food from their preparations shared it, and those who didn't threw together a few small dishes. Thomas returned, looking as though a great weight had been lifted from his shoulders, and Sarah went out.

"So," Gwen said, putting down her now-clean bowl and watching Allison eat the leftover fries she had made. "I was thinking that we should go out sometime."

"What? Like a girls' night?"

"Exactly like that," Gwen said. "Next day off we get, go out and eat at a nice place, go to the movies or theater or a symphony or whatever it is that people do on nights off. We would have to stay out until at least one in the morning. It would be fun."

"I had considered getting out of the city on the next free day, but that works just as well. All right, I'll look around and see what we can do, since you're very clear on the options," Allison said sarcastically.

Gwen shrugged.

"Gosh, it's weird to think that we only have one more day off before the last week begins. I've gotten interviews at a couple of places, but I don't know where I'll end up working. I mean, I'd like to work here, but I don't think the chances of that happening are too high. Don't give me that look," she scolded Gwen. "I know my limitations, and I know my skills. I'm a damn good cook, but there are people better. You're one of them. And don't even think about trying to protest because I won't hear a word of it."

"Then I won't protest. You are a damn good cook too though. That chowder was proof," Gwen said.

Allison snorted and shook her head good-naturedly.

"I hope that you get a really good position."

"There's a new restaurant opening in the theater district," Allison said, "and they've put out advertisements for head chefs. I'm interviewing there and really hoping I get the job. It's meant to be one of those fancy little places where everything is modern and makes no sense except to the artists who designed it. But I've seen a couple of sample menus, and should I get the job, I think I can do really well there. I'd finalize the menus, of course, but it would be nice."

"When's the interview?" Gwen asked.

"Two days. Jack's already given me the afternoon to go and interview, and I've been promised really nice references for my resume from my last job and from Jack. I would have asked Alaric, but since his school is already on my resume, I didn't want to pester him. And he scares me," Allison admitted.

Gwen chuckled. "He's not so scary," she said. "You just have to ignore the fact that he yells a lot."

"I think there's slightly more to it than that, but I'm also not dating him," Allison pointed out.

Gwen shrugged, smiling and watched as Sarah returned and James went out. Once he returned, it would be Allison's turn and then her own. She met Alaric's gaze as he held the door for James and offered a secret smile, her eyes narrowing seductively. Alaric looked startled and seemed unsure as to what to do. He ended up simply following James out, leaving Gwen and Allison laughing.

"I have to admit, it is fun being able to tease him," Gwen said. "Though considering how much we work, getting the actual *dating* bit in is difficult. We haven't had a proper date yet."

"So then, what, you two just talk on your way to and from The Rose and have a quick make-out session in the storerooms?" Allison asked. The way she phrased it made it seem like some sort of illicit romance between school children.

Gwen laughed and shook her head. "No, we talk at my apartment—it's closer—and there's no making out in the storerooms. Jack won't allow it. We just make do with sex. He can be quite creative when he wants to be," Gwen said.

Allison spluttered and shook her head fervently. "Okay, I'm glad you're enjoying the sex, but there are some things about my current boss, teacher, whatever, that I don't need to know," Allison said.

Gwen smirked and folded her arms triumphantly.

"Still, putting sex aside, you should go out on an actual date. I mean, that is more or less the whole point of dating. You'll burn out otherwise."

"Which is why I suggested a girls' night. To keep me from burning out. And I think he needs a break from me for a day or so," Gwen said. Before Allison could ask, she explained, not wanting to make a big deal out of things. She wouldn't be able to know that by trying to make nothing out of something, she was cementing its importance. "I don't sleep all that well on a good day, and he's getting tired of not sleeping the whole night through. Sex aside, that is. Besides, even I, incredibly tolerant though I am, can't spend every waking moment with Alaric. I need a break too."

Allison pursed her lips together and did her best not to worry, forcing her voice to match Gwen's light-hearted tone. "Don't you think that, considering you've only been together about a week, needing a break from each other already might be indicative of, well, something more?"

Gwen's expression darkened into a scowl. "I don't. But thanks for the thought, doctor. You'd better straighten up. Looks like you're up."

Allison looked as though she was about to say more, but Gwen was right. James had returned, and

Alaric was gesturing impatiently toward Allison. She looked at Gwen and sighed, picking up her chowder and leaving the kitchens to go present her dish. James stood at his workstation, cleaning lazily and looked rather pleased with himself. Gwen wanted to stand and sulk, but she forced herself to do as James was doing and go clean up her workstation. There was still the dessert course to make, and she didn't need to be wasting any time on cleaning. She couldn't very well go after ingredients just then, but she could make sure that everything was ready.

"Are you sure your fish and chips are going to pass muster?" James asked, his voice containing far too much innocence to be sincere. "It's probably a little too simple for the taste of the wealthy philanthropist and his snobbish office manager."

"I think you don't know how to please people," Gwen countered. "Simple dishes are always better."

James simply raised his eyebrows and turned his attention to his cleaning.

Gwen wanted to act as nonchalant as he did, her anxiety nothing more than impatience for the next round to start, but the voice in the back of her mind was telling her to listen. Walter may have been a happy-go-lucky sort of man, easily pleased and content with a dish of fish and chips—gourmet though it was—but Gwen had spent a night trying to fit into the circles that he and Graham walked and while not exactly failing, hadn't succeeded either. They were used to the best that money could buy, and even if her meal was a five-star version of a classic dish, was it good enough to be considered the best? When placed next to James's delicately grilled lamb and creamed kale or Allison's chicken-and-corn chowder with cilantro and fresh garlic, would a plate of saffron salmon and truffle oil fries really pass muster?

Gwen knew that Alaric had put together this competition for her benefit, so she could prove herself worthy of this job, but there was still an element of doubt in things. What if she wasn't good enough? What if, as she had proved spectacularly in Afghanistan, she was incompetent? Then where would she be? She sighed and threw her cleaning rag in a bin. She knew exactly where she would be: in a crowded and greasy pub cooking burgers and plain versions of fish and chips for people eager for the ale to flow and the next trivia night to begin. She was good, but she wasn't good enough. Not if Walter and Graham and Jack didn't like her dish, not if it was too simple.

She looked over at her dish. Under the heating lamps, the fish and chips were still steaming and looking good. Gwen knew she had done well with that. She had put together flavors that worked well together, cooked everything to perfection, and it would be delicious. Simple? Maybe. Like she had told James, though, sometimes simple was better.

Even as she was thinking that, Allison returned, a smile on her face. Her chowder must have gone over well, or she was simply relieved at being done with that part of the competition. Gwen picked up her dish

—she would stand by it, simple and common or not— squared her shoulders, and walked out of the kitchen doors. She threw Alaric a smile and considered sauntering, just to annoy James, but refrained.

"You look pleased," Gwen said of Walter, noting his wide smile and the relaxed look that Jack wore. Graham didn't seem to be quite as pleased with the proceedings, but considering that he wasn't checking his phone or looking for a way out, Gwen figured that things were all right. She did notice the angry look he shot between her and Alaric and chose to ignore it. Graham was a grown man; he could very well get over her rejection.

"I get to sit and have food served to me, figuring out which one is best," Walter said, smiling up at her. "I've had worse days."

"All right, then," Gwen laughed, setting the meal before the judges. "I'd better tell you what I've got for you."

"It smells great," Jack said. Gwen raised her eyebrows—was he supposed to be commenting like that?—and shrugged.

"It should suit," she said. "I've made you an exotic twist on a classic dish. This is a salmon fillet pan seared in a saffron and butter sauce with just a hint of red pepper. To pair that off is a helping of fries cooked in truffle oil and dusted with salt and rosemary."

"You made fish and chips?" Graham asked. He didn't sound impressed. Gwen did her best not to get annoyed at him, though she couldn't help but shift her weight so her hip was cocked and put her hand on it.

"I thought," she replied in her calmest tone, "that after such fancy fare, you might want something simple, relaxing. I'll confess that it's not quite like what you'll get from the touristy pubs, but—"

"It's great," Walter said around a mouthful of salmon. "Just what I wanted." He speared a fry with his fork and popped that into his mouth as well, chewing and smiling with his eyes closed.

"I'll admit," Jack said, "that it is nice to have something not quite so...intricate after all these meals. And you did well; the saffron is a nice touch, and the pepper gives it enough kick to bring out the other flavors."

Gwen inclined her head in thanks and straightened back into her relaxed position. She watched as Walter snagged another few fries with his fork before Alaric whisked the plate away, muttering something about there still being dessert. Gwen nodded at the three judges before turning and going back to the kitchen, her heart much lighter. She even enjoyed the way that Alaric's hand rested on her back, leading her with a gentle touch. She wasn't one for being led, but considering the way that his fingers splayed over the small of her back, sending pleasant tingles up her spine, she wasn't going to complain.

"You know the drill," Alaric said. "One hour. Desserts. Same order as before. Chins up, people. You have a job to fight for. Go." His words sparked a sort of frenzy, and the kitchens buzzed to life. This was the last leg of the race, and everyone knew it. Most of the ingredients had been used for the first two courses, but there were still enough sweet options to be used for dessert. Gwen hesitated over some fresh berries, trying to decide whether she wanted to make a light crepe with a berry compote or something else. Then Sarah's hand moved some ingredients about, and Gwen saw them. A bag of chocolate chips. Spurred on by the taunts that James had thrown about her last dish, Gwen picked them up and saw a jug of milk still full in its cooler.

She knew exactly what she was going to do.

The hour seemed to pass incredibly quickly for all involved in the competition. Feeling the need to outdo the others as well as themselves, everyone made their desserts as gourmet and intricate as possible. Apart from Gwen. When the time was called, each was too nervous to even mingle with the others, so they simply stood before their desserts, waiting for the chance to present before the judges. Thomas went out with a vanilla-hazelnut ice cream; Sarah with a custard topped with a crisp, sweet wafer; and James with a raspberry, white-chocolate mousse, and finally Allison went to present her own flambéed pears with a cinnamon sauce. They each returned looking triumphant or relieved. Then it was Gwen's turn.

She picked up the tray with her dessert on it and marched out the door, ignoring Alaric's look of surprise at her creation. Jack was listening intently to something that Walter had to say while Graham checked his phone, looking miffed. Gwen didn't bother with the small talk, just put her tray down and distributed the dessert among the judges. There was complete silence as each man stared in astonishment at the food before him.

"This is…," Graham said, sounding neither annoyed nor miffed, just completely taken aback.

"A cookie," Walter agreed.

"With milk," Jack added.

Gwen nodded. There on the plate before each judge was a large, still-warm chocolate chip cookie, the chocolate slightly melted, the cookie fluffy and inviting. Sitting next to each plate was a tall glass of plain white milk. "Enjoy," Gwen said, smiling.

19

"Here's to new jobs and new futures," Allison said, holding up a small shot glass filled with amber liquid. Gwen tapped her own glass against Allison's and grinned.

"Cheers," she said, and the two tossed back the liquor, setting their glasses on the table with a satisfying *clink*. The hard liquor out of the way, both women turned to their ale and the appetizer set between them. They were at a fairly nice, though not too over the top, pub and were drinking in the buzz of energy in the air as well as the liquor. The evening had only just begun, and Gwen was determined to get a good buzz going before they went out to the concert that Allison had chosen.

Gwen picked up a piece of the pita bread and spooned a dollop of the crab dip onto the bread. "So tell me the name of your restaurant again?"

"Outside the Box," Allison said with a laugh. "It's a

terribly artsy sort of name, but it suits the place perfectly. Oh, Gwen, you'll have to come for the grand opening. Bring Alaric or just come on your own, whatever. It's just about everything I ever dreamed."

"What, working in a modern—no, sorry, *contemporary*—restaurant with youths who have too much style and clients who are too pretentious to know any better? It had better have good food, at the least," Gwen said. Allison rolled her eyes, but both women were smiling.

"All right, fine, so the actual place is a bit much, but being 'executive chef,' as it says on my contract, is exactly what I wanted. I get to pick my own staff, build up my own kitchen. I'm living in a dream, Gwen," Allison said, getting a happy, faraway look in her eye. Gwen waved a piece of pita bread in front of her friend's face, startling Allison and getting a laugh out of her.

"I'm happy for you," Gwen said. "And for me. I got the job. Damn it, but I got the job."

"Yes, working for the most difficult chef anyone has ever met. I imagine you'll be too busy battling words to get much cooking done. If he doesn't figure out some way to break Jack's rule on the no sex in the storeroom," Allison smirked.

Gwen laughed and shook her head. "It's unsanitary. And besides, who would want to have sex in there? It's too cold," she said, shivering for emphasis. The two nodded knowingly and laughed again. Things, as far as Gwen was concerned, were good.

She had gotten the job at The Wooden Rose due to her own skill and hard work. She would be working next to Alaric, continuing the relationship that had been built up since her arrival at the restaurant, albeit slightly more intimately. She had even gotten a very agreeable salary, enough to pay rent on her apartment and live well within her means. She would no longer have to rely on Walter, generous though he was, for her living. Gwen had successfully picked herself up, dusted herself off, and made something of her life. Now, she was sitting in a pub with Allison, drinking to their futures and looking forward to a night of music and dancing. Things were as great as they could ever be, considering.

There it was again, Gwen thought. That *considering*. The memory of what had happened, always hanging over her shoulder, reminding her that her life was built on death, especially of those she loved. It would never be a perfect life because there was no way that Gwen could ever reconcile what had happened. But at least she was learning to live with herself and with the pain. She was managing.

"Great," Allison said dryly, startling Gwen out of her thoughts. She looked to where the blonde woman was gesturing and saw a pack of people, mostly men, moving through the doors of the pub, loud and raucous, raising the level of noise in the pub to something nearly unbearable for conversation. The newcomers moved in a pack, talking together and mingling with one another, though they were beginning to spread out. Gwen caught sight of a patch on the sleeve of one man's leather jacket and groaned.

"Let's settle up and get out of here," Gwen said, setting down her glass and sliding out of her chair. Allison didn't argue, though she looked slightly confused.

"It's not that bad," she said, following Gwen to the register and the waitress managing it. "I mean, sure, it's a little loud..."

"No, it's just that I don't really want to hang around these guys," Gwen said, raising her voice slightly as they got closer to the group hanging around the bar.

"Why?" Allison asked. "Who are they?"

Gwen turned to answer and ran into something solid. She found herself looking up into the eyes of a man, well built and ruggedly handsome with an air about him that said he knew it. She narrowed her eyes slightly as he did a very slow once-over. "Jarheads," she growled.

The man started in surprise, and his arrogant look turned to one of mocking surprise. He laughed and turned to a man standing just behind him, ordering a drink. "Oho, lookie here, Matt. We seem to have found a military girl. Not a Marine, to be giving us that name."

The man Matt turned and appraised Gwen in the same manner, slow, arrogant. She felt her temper rising.

"Well, who do we have the pleasure of addressing?" Matt asked, his voice a dangerous sort of growl. Gwen felt Allison step closer, and she knew that they had to get out of there or Gwen would do something incredibly stupid. "You are most definitely not in military dress," he said, nodding his head at Gwen's tight dress, leather jacket, and heels—which were comfortable, despite their dangerous points. "But you talk like one of us."

"None of your business, jarhead. Come on, Allison, we're out of here," Gwen said. "We'll go somewhere a bit classier and see about getting away from Marines on leave." By this point, the tension among the three was palpable, and Allison didn't argue. She was still learning on the whole self-defense point, and Gwen, while extremely capable, still had a bandage around her broken hand.

"Come on," Matt said as Gwen shoved past him. "You won't even give us a hint? Air force? Or are you army?"

Gwen stiffened, causing Matt and his friend to break off into mocking whistles. She told herself that it would be safer to leave, to go and find a different restaurant and laugh it off with Allison, then go to the concert and forget about it. She was retired. Didn't need to answer to anyone, especially not about her army background. But when people went around using derogatory terms about her army, her people, she wasn't keen on walking away.

"Gwen, let it be," Allison said, tugging on her arm. "Come on, just walk away."

"Yeah, walk away, army bas—" Matt's friend said,

cutting off as Gwen spun around, her eyes blazing and her expression grim.

"That's Lieutenant Army Bastard to you," Gwen snarled, glaring up at the man and baring her teeth like a wild dog. She balled her hands into fists and gave a gasp of pain as the broken one twinged. She relaxed it immediately, but her whole hand felt like it was on fire. She had probably messed it up, gotten the bone to shift or crack again. Allison was at her elbow in an instant, guiding Gwen away.

"Leave them be, Gwen. It's not worth it," Allison said. Gwen didn't bother to resist; Allison was strong and determined. She did her best to ignore the loud catcalls and leers that the Marines sent after them and only ended up with herself angrier and feeling as though she had failed to defend the name of her army.

Only when they were two blocks away from the pub did Allison let go of Gwen's arm.

Gwen pulled it in, wrapping it around her and cradling her broken hand in the crook of her elbow. "I'm sorry," she murmured. "I... shouldn't have let myself get so riled up, but it's hard to ignore old rivalries."

"Gwen, you didn't even *know* the guy," Allison said, exasperated. "You can't have a rivalry with someone you don't know."

"Yeah, you can," Gwen said, hunching her shoulders as she remembered the things she had been told about the other members of the military. Everything was spoken with respect—always respect those who put their lives on the line for their country—but there was a sneer, a snide comment, masking that respect. When it came down to a fight, the military would fight together. Otherwise, they preferred to be kept separate. "It's just how things are, Allison. Civilians...they think differently. Don't understand."

"Is that what I am to you, Gwen?" Allison asked, putting her hands on her hips. "A civilian?"

Gwen pinched the bridge of her nose and leaned against a building, suddenly feeling tired and worn down. She had been so excited for girls' night too. "No," she said after a moment. "I'm sorry, really. I've thought that way for so long. I knew it was better to let it go, walk away, but I've been trained to do otherwise. I couldn't help but get riled up."

Allison leaned against the wall beside Gwen, nudging the former soldier with her shoulder. "Hey, it's not the end of the world. And let's face it. You have a pretty wild temper. We're probably lucky you didn't bash the guy's nose in and get your other hand broken."

"His nose wouldn't have broken my hand," Gwen said with a wry, slightly guilty grin. "If I had gone straight for his jaw, maybe I would have done some damage. But his nose was far too soft. And if we had been in there any longer, I would have started a fight. Thanks, Allison."

"No problem. That's what friends do," Allison said. "Now what do you say we find somewhere else to get a good meal and a nice drink before we head over to the concert? We still have enough time to find someplace."

"Sounds good," Gwen said. They did just that, settling on a restaurant where the noise level was more than manageable and the staff friendly and discreet. There was no chance that the Marines would come in there. Then, feeling free and loose, Gwen and Allison headed to the concert, dancing to what was meant to be some sort of alternative rock. It was catchy and had a good beat for dancing, so Gwen didn't really care whether or not she liked it. At the end of the night, she went back to her building and closed the door behind her with a smile. The incident with the Marines had been almost forgotten—though she would have to go to the doctor to see if she had messed her hand up again—and it had been, on the whole, a good night. She almost wished that Alaric were there to sit with her over a cup of tea and ask how it had been.

That was getting to be a bit too much, Gwen thought and shook her head. She didn't need Alaric to revel in her own happiness. She was perfectly capable of enjoying herself without him, and the fact that she came home to an empty flat was a good thing, not lonely. Maybe she should get a dog, she mused, then immediately rejected that idea. She didn't have time to take care of a dog.

"Have a cup of tea and go to bed," Gwen said to herself. Her words rang through the empty apartment with a note that she hadn't heard or felt before. She growled and cursed herself. She was *not* lonely. She had just been on a very nice excursion with her friend, and everything in her life was good. She had a job, friends, a decent relationship with someone who needed his space as much as she needed hers. Was that wrong? she wondered. After all, he liked being with her and had only started sleeping every other night at his place because she insisted that if he didn't get a decent night's sleep, he would go crazy. Things were good. She didn't need to look for more. And yet there was that note in the back of her mind that was waiting in anticipation for the next day when she would be working side by side with Alaric and sharing his bed by night rather than being alone.

Gwen dumped the majority of her cup of tea down the drain, disgusted with herself. She was usually so far away from being able to make connections with people that she didn't need to worry about keeping her boundaries up. Now that she actually had a connection, a relationship, it was time to start reminding herself where those boundaries were. She feared that if she got any closer to Alaric, she would start telling him the answers to those questions that he was delicate enough not to ask. She knew that he wanted to know about her past, about the things that haunted her. He had told her as much, after all. She also knew that if she were to tell him, the look in his eyes whenever he was with her would be one of two things: pity or horror. She wasn't sure she could handle either, and that was the problem.

Gwen tossed and turned for the majority of the

night, managing to slip into sleep sometime around two and waking two hours later, shaking, her body coated in sweat, her throat hoarse from calling for the help of her squad or screaming for them to wake up. She leaned against the headboard and pressed the heels of her palms to her eyes, forcing herself to take deep, cleansing breaths.

It was over. There was nothing she could do.

"Then why do I still hurt?" Gwen asked herself, tempted to curl up and weep her problems away. She didn't because she had tried to do so in the past and knew that she would only end up feeling worse. So, with the weight of death riding on her shoulders, Gwen climbed out of bed and put on her exercise clothes before lacing up her running shoes and heading out. Running didn't seem to be enough, but she didn't know of anywhere else to go. None of the boxing gyms would be open so early, and she couldn't bring herself to go to Alaric. As Gwen ran out of her building's parking lot, she thought about a place that she hadn't seen for six months. Her stride lengthened as her legs grew used to the pace, and she went to the darker parts of the city.

An hour later, her shirt sweat through and the sun just barely beginning to rise, Gwen jogged to a stop, her nerves tingling with awareness. She hadn't been back to this place in so long—not since Walter pulled had her off the streets—that it was like looking at a house that you had once lived in but sold long ago. Esplanade and Pelham two streets that had once been little more than a place to sleep, a spot to meet up with other of her kin or to possibly get a meal from one of the food trucks that occasionally acted charitably in the area. Then she had belonged there, been one of the rulers of that area. People knew of her talents in fighting and her unwillingness to put up with any crap and stayed away or got hurt trying to muscle in. She didn't interfere too much and was respected in her right. Now she was well fed and wearing exercise clothes that cost more than these people saw in a month. The bandage on her hand told them that she was on her way to being a victim, if not one already. She may have had that same stormy fierce look about her, but very few would have recognized her as the Gwen that had once lived there.

Despite the early hour, the people that were living there were stirring. Some were still asleep, dead to the world unless someone messed with their belongings. Others wandered over to the trash bins, hoping that there was something there that hadn't been before they went to sleep. A couple were just sitting, backpacks or dogs lying by their sides, eyes wide and vacant as if they were unable to see the terrible reality into which they hand landed. A few spotted Gwen, and one was bold enough to advance.

"What's someone like you doing out here so early?" a grimy and bearded man asked, his shoulders hunched from everything but age. "It's not safe for someone like you. There are unsavory characters about."

"I can take care of myself," Gwen said softly, recognizing the man. "Hello, Tiger."

"Wha—how do you...Gwen?" the man asked, straightening slightly as he peered at Gwen from beneath busy and unkempt eyebrows and greasy, wild hair.

She gave a half smile, the corners keeping well away from her eyes as she surveyed him in turn.

"Well, I never thought I'd see you again, not after that rich guy pulled you off the streets. What did he promise you? Money, obviously, but what else? Life as his mistress, a gift for one of his family members or business partners, posing as someone else to get a payday?"

"No, Tiger," Gwen said. "He offered me a life earning for myself. Living for myself."

Tiger didn't say anything for a minute, just watched Gwen solemnly. Eventually, he nodded and gestured toward the others who were beginning to stir in earnest, especially now that Gwen's presence had been noted. "Come on," he said. "Let's go sit down. You can tell us all that's been going on, and we can provide you with company. I'd offer you a cup of tea, but you know how things are."

"Yeah," Gwen answered, following Tiger back to his spot and sitting on the duvet that served as bed and home for him. "I know how things are."

Having spent most of her time while homeless on the corner of Yates and Fair, Gwen was familiar with most of the people that lived there. A few simply nodded their heads in greeting as she passed, and her name was whispered. Others gathered themselves closer to Tiger's space and stared at her as if they couldn't believe she was actually present. Gwen greeted every one of them by name and, following their customs, didn't talk until one of them asked a question. Then the floodgates opened.

She told them everything.

It wasn't that Gwen trusted these people more than she trusted Alaric or Allison; it was that she knew them just as well as she knew herself. They wouldn't care one way or another whether she had doubts about her life, and they wouldn't tell anyone for anything. She didn't mention what had happened before her time on the streets, and they didn't ask. It was good to be able to talk to people who understood the challenges that life presented and knew what happened when you failed. There were only two places to go once you had hit bottom as these people had: death or up. So Gwen told them everything pressing on her.

"He's going to want more out of our relationship than I can give him," Gwen said of Alaric. "There are just some things in my past that I can't tell him. He wouldn't understand. No one would understand. The things that I've had to do, the people I've hurt. He thinks that I need to tell him, that we can never be really happy together unless I've told him. So I build up the walls and try to let him know that I care for him, really. I just know that it's not going to be enough."

"Do you know it or fear it?" a grizzled, old woman asked, her skin more wrinkle than expression and her hair only gray because the white was too dirty to show through. The others affectionately called her Maman, and she had been giving Gwen—and, in fact, most of the community—advice since Gwen had first arrived.

Gwen blinked and looked Maman in the eyes, trying to read her own soul in their depths. Finally, she murmured, "I don't know," and Maman nodded her head in wise understanding. Gwen took a deep breath and wrapped her arms around her knees, pulling them close to her chest. "It's just that I thought things were going so well. Then last night, Allison and I were in a pub, and these people walk in. They were Marines, on leave, and I didn't want to deal with them because, you know, military rivalries..."

The others muttered their understanding. A good number of them were former military or connected to it in some way. They knew, even if those rivalries were put aside on the streets.

Gwen continued, "So I told Allison that we should go, and then we ran into one of them. It was just like being back on tour. All the same attitudes, the same jargon, the same feeling of someone watching you all the time, no matter that you were in camp. For a second, just a split second, I thought that I was back there, and I wanted to pound his head in for calling me an army bastard and declaiming *my* people. I was inches away from it too. Allison had to pull me out of there. Now I just don't know, things seem different. Like I was reminded of things that I shouldn't have tried to forget in the first place. I wanted to go to Alaric when the night was over but not because of this incident, because it had been a good night... I can't let him in. He wouldn't understand." Gwen looked desperately at the people gathered around her. Tiger was silent, and even Maman seemed to be at a loss for something to say.

One of the quieter ones, even by the standards of the homeless, spoke up, his skin not quite as wrinkled as some, tanner than others, his eyes still holding the sparkle that told of hope for a different life. "You love him," he said, his fingers tapping out a rhythmic beat on his leg. "And that scares you because you don't think that he'll accept you once he learns what you've done."

"No," Gwen protested, shaking her head fervently. The man stared at her, his fingers tapping away without thought as he looked at her, just as some people rocked gently or muttered conversations under their breath. Gwen looked between him and the eyes of the others, hoping that someone would agree with her denial.

She *couldn't* love Alaric. Everything was going just fine with their relationship, with the casual nature of things between them. She didn't expect anything out of him, and while she knew that he wanted to know about her past, he didn't expect anything more than that out of her. Love brought a whole new layer of things into the mix, and Gwen wasn't prepared to deal with that. She couldn't love him.

Gwen tried to convince herself of that as she sat there, but in the end she gave up. The man was right. Every word he had said was right. Very carefully, so as to hide the tears that began building in her eyes and the slight tremble to her chin, Gwen lowered her head to bury it in her knees. She felt Tiger put a hand on her back and rub it comfortingly, a gesture that meant more to her than anything that had been said. These people were on the streets and had created a community to reflect that, but they didn't encourage contact. That was reserved for people with real families and real lives.

Suddenly, everything that had happened to Gwen in the last six months became that much more real and meaningful. She had been offered a new life, a chance to pick herself up from the bottom of all possibilities and build herself up. She had a job, a roof over her head, and food in her belly, friends and someone she loved. The past may have shaped her, but it didn't matter anymore. It was left only for her to shut it in a box and put it in the furthest reaches of her mind. Gwen looked up and met the gentle gaze of Maman. She would do just that.

20

"Do I really have to wear the suit?" Alaric asked, tugging uncomfortably at the collar at his throat.

Gwen rolled her eyes and stepped in to undo the first two buttons, letting her hands linger on his shoulders.

"We're just driving out today. The party isn't until tomorrow and I doubt very much anyone will care whether or not I show up in jeans or a suit."

"Except for me. I care."

The time since Gwen's revelation on the streets, Maman and Tiger at her side, had passed in what seemed like an instant. She had come to terms with her feelings for Alaric and then made certain that she did not reveal the intensity of her emotions by getting into an argument with him almost the moment she had returned from her run. He had stopped by her building to coax her into having breakfast with him at a restaurant he had just discovered, only he'd found her away. After checking with Allison—in bed with the beginnings of a headache from drinking too much and staying out too late—and trying Gwen's cell phone, he had begun to panic. She had arrived at her flat forty minutes later, out of breath and dirty.

Alaric had panicked.

Since then, Gwen had found it becoming increasingly easier to acknowledge that she was in love with Alaric and make sure that he didn't know and she didn't say. Though as she stepped back to admire her work, watching him shift his weight in discomfort while wearing a very well-tailored suit, she acknowledged it would be a challenge.

"The whole point of you going to this retirement party is to appease your mother and impress your father. Therefore, you show up in a suit. Trust me, successful people—chefs included—wear suits. I'm wearing a dress, so you can't complain," Gwen said, brushing a hand over her own clothes.

Alaric raised his eyebrows and pulled his eyes over Gwen's figure very slowly and carefully, making sure that not an inch was left unexamined. She, to his mild disappointment, did not blush.

"No," Alaric said after a minute, his voice low and bordering on a hungry growl, "I suppose I can't."

Gwen was wearing a dress that hugged the curves she had and emphasized the muscle that made up the rest of her person. It was a startling shade of deep purple, and with her hair brushing her shoulders and her legs covered in silk stockings that Alaric had enjoyed helping her into—with a few distractions— she looked like a very successful and frankly beautiful woman. Her eyes, though, said that there was more than that, if only because they held the shadows of pain and the hint of steel beneath the surface.

"Go get your bag," Gwen ordered, "or you're going to make us late."

"I don't mind," Alaric said. "Besides, it would be nice to get out of this suit for a while."

Gwen put up a hand, halting him as he took a step forward, her expression set and determined. "Not going to happen," she said firmly. "We just got you into that suit, and I don't have the inclination to fix my hair after you mess it up. We are going to leave now, and we are *not* going to be late. Your mother is expecting us."

Alaric sighed, curling his lip in annoyance at the fact that he really had to go through with this and the knowledge that Gwen was, again, right. The retirement party had seemed like a vague unpleasantness before. With the truth of its presence looming before him in the form of two small weekend bags that he and Gwen had packed, the unpleasantness turned into something much worse: dread and a headache. The only bright point that he could see was that Gwen would be at his side, suffering with him. He ran his fingers through his hair and sighed. "Fine. Fine, have it your way. But I get to pick the music on the drive," he said, growling. Gwen made a face but didn't argue.

The two picked up the bags and went out to Alaric's car, stowing them in the trunk. Gwen put the cooler with provisions for the trip—should either of them get hungry or thirsty on the way up, run out of food during the party, or need a snack where there would be no shops—in the back. Alaric turned on the car, sat for exactly forty-seven seconds, and debated calling the whole thing off, then put the car into gear and started the journey to his parents' house in upstate New York. He knew, just as soon as he had turned the radio to a station playing modern rock music and saw Gwen take a slow, deep breath, that it was going to be a long trip.

They remained in relative peace for the amount of time it took them to get out of the city before breaking out into bickering. It started, as most things do, with Alaric's choice of music.

"Can we play something a bit less...boring? The same four chords make up every single one of the songs we've heard so far," Gwen said. "Maybe there's a station playing the classics. You know, Dire Straits, Toto. Or the blues. Just something a bit more musically interesting."

"We agreed that I get to choose the music on the way there," Alaric snapped. "And it's not about the chords, it's about the variations on those chords and the lyrics behind them."

"Oh, so the 'na, na, nas' actually mean something?"

Gwen asked, the sarcasm in her voice so thick that Alaric had to fight not to snarl something cruel. He took the sudden flare of temper out on a car that had just passed him on the left, muttering incoherently at the driver.

Gwen watched all of this silently and waited for a response. Alaric made no move to reply or change the station, so she grumbled and turned her head to watch the world pass by outside the window, obviously doing her best to ignore both Alaric's bad mood and the music filling the car.

"All right, enough. I should probably warn you about some of the people that you're going to meet this weekend," Alaric said after about ten minutes of no conversation. He turned down the music, catching Gwen's attention, and she turned her head in his direction.

"I thought you had already warned me about everyone. Your father—"

"The ass," Alaric supplied, making Gwen roll her eyes and shake her head, though she did it with a smile. "It's true," he grumbled.

"Beside the point," Gwen replied. "You warned me about him, about your crazy aunt—Harriet, isn't it? And from what I understand about your mother, she's not too bad but gets coerced into doing things that you or she doesn't like. Anyone else? Business partners, perhaps?"

"Ah, crap," Alaric said. "I forgot about all the business associates that are bound to be there. Considering that I'm the wayward son, lost cause and all, I haven't had much contact with them. But the ones I have met are all pretentious and annoying. This is going to be a long weekend."

"I can deal with pretentious and annoying," Gwen said. "And besides, it's not as though we're trapped there. We have your car. Worse comes to worst, we can hightail it out of there and go back to the city for the remainder of the weekend. I'm sure Jack wouldn't complain; he has let two of his chefs go away on vacation, no matter how short it may be."

"Right... Are you sure you don't want to turn back now?" Alaric asked, tightening his hands on the wheel. Gwen shook her head and reached across the gear shift, putting her hand on his knee. "I know, I know," Alaric muttered. He squeezed Gwen's hand and was disappointed when she pulled away. They lapsed into an easy silence, and when Alaric turned to check if Gwen was watching before turning up the volume on the radio, he saw that she had unbelievably fallen asleep.

Her head lay against her hand, propped up as her elbow rested on the windowsill. Her mouth was open just slightly, and as Alaric failed to avoid a pothole in the road, it became apparent that she was deeply asleep. *Finally*, Alaric thought. What with Gwen's order that they spend every other night away from each other to save his sanity and let him get some sleep, he had become aware of just how much she *didn't* sleep. The three nights he spent continuously by her side were one thing; then, they had both been distracted until late—or early, depending on the view. Only when he'd returned to his own apartment and fallen exhausted into bed had he understood how little sleep he had been getting. Ever since, it had been his goal to get Gwen to sleep more; if he was going crazy, he couldn't imagine what damage it was doing to Gwen, who had been having problems for a while. If he had known all it would take was a prolonged car trip, he would have driven her to Canada and back.

Alaric was tempted, as he approached his parents' house, to keep driving and not bother waking Gwen up. It wouldn't be the end of the world if they were late, and he would much rather have Gwen sleep than deal with his family. He should have known, though, that she had some sort of sixth sense regarding these things. As soon as he began the turn onto the road to the house, she stirred and woke.

She stretched and looked about. "We're here," she said. It wasn't a question.

"Unfortunately," Alaric said and turned the car into the drive. Gwen looked at the house in awe. It wasn't a manor house, per se, or a mansion, but it was extravagant, and it was grand. The grounds were well landscaped, with strategic splashes of color drawing the eye onto the next piece of designed and manicured land. The house itself was old stone, darkened with age and looking as though it bore the weight of wealth. It was a monied house, and with an Audi and BMW in the drive, there was no doubt as to the status of the family that lived there.

"Home sweet home," Alaric said sardonically, cutting the engine with an annoyed jerk of his wrist.

"Oh my," Gwen replied, staring at the house with wide eyes. Alaric nodded grimly.

The sound of the car must have alerted the people inside because as soon as Gwen got out of the car and walked around it, the front door opened, and a woman ran out. She was shorter than Alaric by a fair amount, and she was round where her son was lean, but there was no denying the family resemblance. She had his same dark-blond hair and sharp eyes, though hers were welled with tears. She wore a suit of deep royal blue and her shoes looked as though they had just been purchased; there were pearls at her ears and her throat. None of that prevented her from running across the drive and nearly tripping on the gravel to throw herself at Alaric.

"My boy!" she cried, wrapping him in an exuberant hug. He took a deep breath and returned the hug, though his enthusiasm was nowhere on par with that of his mother. "Alaric, I'm so glad you're here. It's been so long."

"You can visit, Mom," Alaric said. "Just because I won't come here doesn't mean that my place is closed to you."

"Oh, well," his mother deferred, waving her hand dismissively and averting her gaze. It was this that brought Gwen to her attention. Mrs. Bennet took one look at Gwen and widened her eyes in surprise. "You're not Jack," she said, then shook her head and put on a smile. "I'm sorry, I didn't mean to cause offense. I'm Caroline Bennet, Alaric's mother."

"Gwen Townsend," Gwen said, extending her hand.

Mrs. Bennet took it gingerly and shook.

"I take it Alaric didn't tell you I was coming?"

"Well, I told him he should bring someone, I just thought he would...I'm sorry," she apologized again, a faint blush rising to her cheeks. Alaric put his arm around Gwen's shoulder, an act that caused his mother to purse her lips in alarm.

"Jack wouldn't come back after what happened last time. And I thought that you would like to meet Gwen. She's, well, er," Alaric said, trying to put what they had into a word that didn't sound so immature as "girlfriend."

"We're dating," Gwen stepped in. She saw the quick flash of panic in Mrs. Bennet's eyes and winced. "And Alaric didn't tell you that either, did he?"

"No," Mrs. Bennet said in a quiet voice, looking ashamed that she had been read so easily. "I didn't know. I wish I had, or I wouldn't have invited Melissa..."

"Damn it," Alaric snarled, making his mother recoil. Gwen squeezed Alaric's arm in a warning gesture, making sure that he felt it before releasing him and returning her friendly gaze to his mother. "Sorry," Alaric muttered. "Mom, why did you feel it was necessary to invite my ex-girlfriend to this thing?"

"I thought...well, I didn't know that you were dating anyone, and she was the only one of your girlfriends that was willing to put up with your father, so I thought that when you came, she might..." His mother trailed off as if realizing the impropriety of her statement. She pressed a hand to her head and blinked rapidly, clearly fighting off tears. Alaric was still dealing with his own anger and didn't notice his mother's distress.

"Mom, I broke up with her for a reason. And she put up with Father because she's a lawyer," Alaric said, not bothering to check the volume of his words. Gwen squeezed his arm again, this time not releasing her grip even when Alaric winced.

"I wouldn't worry too much, Mrs. Bennet," Gwen said with an easy smile. "I've put up with your son yelling at me in the kitchens. I think I can keep him under control when dealing with ex-girlfriends. Besides, I'd like to meet her, to thank her for getting him into such a wonderful apartment."

Mrs. Bennet smiled at Gwen's words, though the smile was watery and looked like it could fade at any moment. "Please call me Carol. You work with Alaric?"

"I was one of his students, but now I work at The Wooden Rose full-time. It's very fulfilling, apart from being yelled at if I so much as overcook the salmon," Gwen teased. Alaric started struggling slightly in her grip, and she squeezed harder before releasing him, completely ignoring the annoyed look he threw at her. "I hear that he got his passion for cooking from you."

"Oh, he did not," Carol said, the smile becoming more solidified on her features. "I just dabble in the kitchen is all. I've forgotten my manners! You two have probably been driving for hours. Would you like some coffee? I've got some fresh baked bread and cucumber salad if you're hungry. Come in, come in!"

"That sounds wonderful," Gwen said, and leaving Alaric to handle their bags on his own, followed Carol inside the grand house. "You have a lovely house," she said. With that, Carol's smile became fixed, and Gwen was led through a history of the house and all the recent renovations or decorations. The two women, much to Alaric's amazement and slight discomfort, became immediate friends.

Somehow—Alaric wasn't going to ask how his mother had arranged it—they managed to avoid seeing his father until supper that evening. If Alaric could have gotten away with it, he would have taken Gwen out to dinner in the town, but that wouldn't have gone over well. He had to try and make his way through the weekend without any serious infractions. He failed within the first ten minutes.

Gwen and Alaric were called to dinner by Carol, who insisted on pouring them both drinks and serving appetizers. Alaric excused himself almost immediately to see how the appetizers were being prepared. Gwen imagined he just wanted to be somewhere familiar.

"Now," Carol said, filling Gwen's wine glass with a deep-burgundy liquid. It was, apparently, very old and very expensive, but when Gwen tasted it, she could find nothing to distinguish it. "I don't want you making yourself uneasy about this. I imagine Alaric has told you a few stories about his father, but he is a good man. He can be difficult at times and, well, a bit overbearing, but he's not a bad man."

"I'm sure I'll manage," Gwen said.

Carol watched her with a worried expression and sighed before looking around the dining room as if to make sure no one else was in earshot. With Alaric in the kitchen overseeing the plating of the appetizers, there was little doubt of that.

"Watch your step," Carol advised. "I will simply say that Alaric inherited his temper from his father, and he didn't even get the full force of it. You've probably experienced that, what with his yelling in the kitchens— I've heard he can be quite the fearsome boss."

"I have," Gwen said. She had purposefully neglected to mention her previous employment, planning on saving it for the right time, but suspected that it would have to be revealed sooner rather than later. She wasn't about to let a difficult old lawyer intimidate her. "And I assure you that I wouldn't be involved with your son unless I could handle his temper. I've had worse."

"Oh," Carol said, blinking in confusion and jumping when Alaric returned, following the man carrying the tray with a watchful eye. Gwen shouldn't have been surprised, considering the grandeur of the house, but the presence of servants continued to startle her. More had been hired for the party, so the house was busier than usual. Even so, it was...different than what she had come to expect. Her social standing, at least before she'd been plucked up by Walter, was below that of the people catering to her needs. She tried not to be uncomfortable and only partially succeeded.

"And make sure that the lamb is basted with that rosemary and vegetable stock in exactly ten minutes. Don't put the orange peel in until the last five minutes of cooking or the flavor will be overpowered," Alaric instructed the man who set the appetizer platter onto the sideboard.

The servant nodded thanks for the instructions and disappeared through the door before Alaric could do something like remind him how to cut the lamb.

Gwen sighed and picked up her wine. It was going to be a long weekend.

"These people you've hired are decent," Alaric told his mother, picking up a glass with scotch. "But they could use a bit of help."

"Not from you," Carol said with a shake of her head. "You promised that you would stay out of the kitchens during this event. You have to keep your pretty Gwen company, after all."

"She's as likely to retreat to the kitchens as I am," Alaric muttered, reaching for one of the small dishes and piling it with tidbits from the platter of food. Gwen was about to mention that it might be wise to wait until his father arrived when the door burst open, and a stately man walked in, glowering strongly enough to have Carol wincing, Alaric frowning, and Gwen straightening her posture.

He was every part of Alaric that was not his mother, all the lean and hard pieces that had never been tempered. His hair was steel gray and swept back from his forehead in an elegant wave, his eyes and face lined deeply from years of severe expressions. He wore a suit that was well cut and more expensive than the clothes his wife wore. The most dangerous part about him was the cunning that rode in his eyes. He was, Gwen determined, a formidable ally and an even more formidable enemy. She was immediately on her guard.

At the sight of Alaric and Gwen, Mr. Bennet stopped, his glower deepening. "What are you doing here?" he asked Alaric, his voice ringing with deep, enthralling tones that would be quite deadly in any negotiation.

"You didn't tell him I was coming?" Alaric asked his mother, his lip curling in distaste.

Carol opened and closed her mouth as if struggling to find words and ended up simply shutting down, her eyes slipping to the floor in defense.

"I can't think of a more terrible plan," Alaric said.

"Carol?" Mr. Bennet asked, raising his eyebrows expectantly at his wife.

She jerked as if struck and poured a drink before walking over to her husband. Gwen wanted to frown in disapproval, but she forced herself to remain calm and serene.

"Why did you bring him here?" Mr. Bennet asked.

All right, enough, Gwen thought. It was time for her to act. "Your lovely wife invited Alaric and me here for your retirement party. I offer my congratulations on that point. You must have been quite successful in your practice to manage such a lovely house."

"And you are?" Mr. Bennet asked pointedly, taking a long sip of his drink while keeping his eyes fixed on Gwen. He obviously didn't suffer propriety. Fine, she could be direct as well.

She set her wine on the sideboard and strode forward, her demeanor changing as she did. By the time she stood in front of Alaric's father, she was no longer Gwen the chef, dressed well and enjoying the hospitality of her boyfriend's family, but Lieutenant Townsend of the US Army, geared for battle. She didn't think herself small and felt pleased that Mr. Bennet blinked in astonishment at the change.

"Gwen Townsend," she said, extending her hand. "I'm involved with your son."

"Nathaniel Bennet," the man replied, ignoring Gwen's second statement.

She held the grip for a second longer than necessary before smiling pleasantly and returning to her drink. Alaric smiled weakly at her, looking stunned. Gwen handed him his drink before taking her own.

"Carol?" Nathaniel asked again, this time the question more urgent than before, though he did manage to quiet his voice somewhat.

"I thought it would be good to have him out for the party. He's done so well with his restaurant, and you're retiring, and...well, it would be nice," she said. Nathaniel opened his mouth to say something, which wasn't likely to be very kind, when the doorbell rang, breaking through the tension in the room like a knife.

"We'll discuss this later," Nathaniel growled to his wife. He drained the last of his drink in one quick jerk and went to see to the door. Carol smiled fleetingly at Gwen and Alaric and followed her husband, like a dog trailing after its master. Gwen said nothing, only snatched a tidbit from Alaric's plate and popped it in her mouth.

"That could have gone better," Alaric said, draining his own drink in a move very similar to that of his father. Gwen nodded, but there was a quiet amusement in her eyes. "Don't give me that," he grumbled, wrapping an arm around her shoulder and pressing a quick kiss to her forehead. "I am well justified in getting drunk."

"I never said otherwise," Gwen replied primly. Alaric shook his head and disentangled himself from her embrace to pour another scotch.

"Smart-ass," he said. Gwen laughed, the sound strange and unfamiliar in the dining room, that appeared to be more used to seeing arguments and anger than joy. Even that was short lived. Gwen's laughter fell silent as the door swung open again, letting Nathaniel back in the room, his wife trailing behind with her arm through that of another younger woman. She was tall, leggy, and wearing a dress that left absolutely nothing to the imagination while still remaining—mysteriously—professional. Her reddish-brown hair hung in a thick sheet down to her waist, and she carried herself with the ease of the knowingly attractive.

Before any introductions could be made and anyone else could do something, the woman moved forward in a quick stride, her dangerous-looking heels eating up the ground to bring her to a full stop before Alaric. She didn't waste a moment, just put her hands on either side of his face and pulled him to her, greeting him with a very deep, very intimate kiss. The woman pulled away, a wide smile somehow only making her more attractive. "Alaric! It's been too long since we've seen each other. I've missed you!" she simpered.

Alaric gaped, swallowing nervously and too aghast to say anything other than, "M-Melissa."

Gwen narrowed her eyes, setting down her wine glass before it broke. This was not going to end well, especially not for the ex-girlfriend.

She had to fight not to attack Melissa, telling herself that it would do her no good to be petty. Melissa had no idea about Gwen; after all, she had been invited to the party for the express purpose of being there for Alaric. When she thought about it like that, Gwen did her best not to laugh. Carol Bennet had called a woman to be a, to be blunt, sex buddy for Alaric. It was telling about Melissa that she had taken the offer to heart. So, instead of jumping forward to defend her standing, Gwen picked up the wine glass again and took a very relaxed sip.

21

If Alaric was expecting Gwen to step in and save him from overaffectionate ex-girl-friends, he was disappointed. He beat a hasty retreat and stood by Gwen, expression flickering with shock as she did nothing more than sip her wine. It wouldn't hurt for her to be slightly jealous, he felt. He ran his hand through his hair and struggled to come up with something to say. He couldn't ask what Melissa was doing there as he knew she had been invited. He couldn't ask what she thought she was doing with that kiss because it was fairly obvious. He settled on making a strangled noise in the back of his throat, all that would come out.

"Alaric," Gwen said, finally coming to his rescue and slipping her arm through his. He seized it like a lifeline. "Why don't you introduce us?"

That seemed like a terrible idea, but he could come

up with no others. "Erm, Melissa, this is Gwen, my, uh, girlfriend. Gwen, Melissa."

The other woman blinked in surprise and took a long look at Gwen. Then, smiling without guile and having the grace to blush, she said, "Oh my. I'm so sorry!"

"No problem." Gwen smiled back, making Alaric blanch. "Alaric needs to be flustered every now and again. It's a change from him snapping at me."

"I know exactly what you mean." Melissa chuckled, beaming at Carol as the older woman gave her a drink. Alaric blinked in shock, feeling completely out of place as the woman he was currently involved with and the one he had been previously involved with started talking as though they were actually getting along. Somehow, the five of them sat at the table, and as Gwen and Melissa laughed over something, he knew it was going to be the longest weekend of his life.

Family dinner lasted far too long, in Alaric's view. By the time Gwen and he made it back to their room— at least his mother had the sense to room them together—he was exhausted from trying to keep up on the conversation between his mother and the other two women. His father, for which he was extremely thankful, had said next to nothing during the whole meal, only breaking that silence when Melissa had started talking about her work. Alaric had said even less, drinking enough hard liquor to give him a nice buzz. So when he closed the door behind Gwen, leaving them essentially shut away, he smiled at her and reached to wrap his arms around her waist, thinking of alleviating his pain in her.

"Oh no, you don't," Gwen said, putting a hand on his chest and pushing back gently.

"I'm hurting, Gwen," Alaric pleaded. "Can't you see that?"

"I see someone who is trying to make himself feel better about being assaulted by his ex-girlfriend by having sex with his current girlfriend," Gwen replied, raising her eyebrows. "Here's a thought, why don't you talk about it?"

"I don't have a problem except for the fact that I'm being put upon by all sides," Alaric pleaded, though he was quickly becoming annoyed. "There's nothing to talk about."

"That's crap," Gwen said, fisting her hands on her hips. "I know all about your problems with your father, and I have no doubt that you have problems with Melissa. I know you're annoyed at having to be here at all, and I know that this evening didn't turn out like you expected."

"Seems like you know all there is to know," Alaric growled, turning away from her and unbuttoning his shirt. He pulled the old shirt he had packed from the bag and stripped down to his boxers, growling all the while.

"It doesn't matter," Gwen said flatly. "Because you are still annoyed, and you still need to talk about it. Just because I've been informed of your issues in these various areas doesn't mean you can slide by with saying nothing and expecting me to just sit here and let you be frustrated. That's sort of the whole point of a *relationship*, Alaric. You tell me what's bothering you. I tell you what's bothering me. We may have to pry that information out of each other, but we talk."

"I don't want to talk," Alaric said. "I've had a long day, and I'm tired. I know you'll just stay up for another four hours anyway, but I'm going to bed."

"See?" Gwen said, following him when he grabbed his toothbrush and stalked into the bathroom. "You're annoyed. You're bothered. Now talk about it. Unless you think this relationship is one-sided and I'm the only one who has to talk about things. Or if you're just in this for the sex."

"What?" Alaric recoiled, the toothbrush halfway to his mouth, toothpaste flecking his lips. "No! How can you think that this is just about sex? After all the shit that we've gone through? I sat with you on my couch while you complained about Graham, helped you once your nightmares started. I set up a contest so that you would have a chance at a job right next to me, and you can question that this whole thing is just about sex?"

"That's the thing, Alaric. I don't know. You are more than happy to prod me and pester me until I give in and tell you just about every intimate secret in my past and present. But when I try and get more out of you besides the fact that your father is an ass and you don't have a good relationship with anyone in your family or that you won't tolerate weakness in the kitchens but will put up with it anywhere else, you just shut me down," Gwen said. "I want to know what's bothering you. I want to—I need to—know these things, Alaric. So instead of shutting me out and just trying to assuage me by taking me to bed, why don't you talk about it?"

"Fine," Alaric said, reaching for a towel to wipe his face. He glared openly at Gwen, and there was a pull to his neutral expression that revealed just how angry he actually was. "Fine. You want me to tell you what I'm thinking? I'm pissed because my mother didn't see fit to tell my father that I was showing up for his retirement party and didn't even bother to apologize for it. I'm pissed because my father is and will remain, as you say, an ass who is more interested in his drink and his power over my mother than even *attempting* to make any conversation with me—and slighting you by doing so. I'm pissed because my mother, and my father, think that I am so hopeless in my current life to invite my ex-girlfriend; she was the only one of my ex-girlfriends that they actually liked, and that's only because she's everything I'm not. I'm pissed with her for actually showing up. And I'm pissed at you because you think that this is going to help anything."

Gwen sighed and, instead of reaching out to comfort Alaric as she likely knew he would only shove her away, wrapped her arms around herself. The movement made Alaric wince, and it was as though a knife had just been stabbed in his gut. Was he really so selfish as to expect Gwen to tell him everything and hold all of his baggage back? Sure, it was a pain to talk about, and he didn't need any psychoanalysis, but she wasn't one to psychoanalyze in the first place. She just wanted to be there for him like he was with her. That was touching, and now he was yelling at her for it.

"I can't say that I don't feel for you, because I do," Gwen said, forcing herself to meet his gaze. "But honestly, I think you're taking things just a little too far. You knew before coming here what this was likely to be. You knew that your father was, *is*, an ass and—don't bite my head off for this—that your mother is completely under his control—"

"She is," Alaric acknowledged with a sardonic snort. "There's no point in yelling at you for that."

"All right. Anyway, you knew all of these things before coming, so there's no point in getting angry over the fact. Just ignore what they think and want from you and enjoy yourself. You...well, you're getting yourself riled up over something that you can't prevent. Why try?" Gwen said. She pressed a hand to her head.

Alaric blinked and stared at Gwen. He understood what she was trying to convey, but the method was almost comical. He couldn't help himself and broke out into a smile. "You...want me to take up, what, Buddhism? Taoism? Yoga?"

"You're such a pain," Gwen said, laughing in return. "I don't think you'd do very well under any of those regimens. I can't even imagine you trying to do yoga."

"I've done yoga," Alaric said.

Gwen raised her eyebrows incredulously.

"Seriously! I was...oh, I must have just gotten out of

culinary school or was about to. There was this college sophomore that looked really good in those tight yoga pants. I asked her out, we dated for a bit, and somewhere in there, she convinced me to come with her to one of her yoga classes. I went mostly because…" He trailed off, thinking that it might not be the best time to be bringing up another one of his exes with Gwen, but she just waved her hand, expression fascinated.

"No, go on. I want to hear this. And I won't be offended that you found another girl attractive. You've dated other people. You've probably even had sex with other people. I'm not going to strangle you because of it," Gwen smirked.

Alaric shook his head. "Well, when you put it like that," he continued. "All I'll say is that she looked very interesting when bending into a pretzel. I made it through the one class and swore never again. Actually, it was the yoga that made me break up with the girl."

"Poor sophomore," Gwen said with a chuckle. Alaric stepped forward to undo the zipper on the back of her dress. This time, she didn't protest, only kissed the base of his throat gently.

"Yeah," Alaric said, running his hands down her back and watching with pleasure as the dress pooled around her feet. "She was heartbroken for about a week. I heard she started dating this guy not long after. Very new age type. He even did yoga."

"Perfect," Gwen said.

Alaric nodded and pulled the straps of her bra off her shoulders, smiling as Gwen shivered. "I hope you don't expect that this conversation is going to prevent me from getting quite drunk tomorrow," Alaric said.

Gwen laughed and twined her arms around his neck, burying her fingers in his hair. "In all probability," she said, "I'll be joining you."

Alaric made a satisfied sound in the back of his throat and took Gwen to bed, completely uncaring that his parents were only a few doors away. All that mattered was the woman in bed with him, her fingers doing magical things to his skin and the sounds coming from her only spurring him on. He didn't care, either, that she would likely be awake long after he was asleep or that, if she did sleep, he would be forced to deal with her fitful rest. All that mattered was the moment at hand.

Gwen did manage to sleep, though it was interrupted, and she tossed and turned as if unable to get settled. Alaric slept much deeper, having slowly grown used to her interrupted sleep. But when, sometime around five in the morning, Gwen's weight disappeared from the bed, Alaric cracked open his eyes and sought her out. He saw a light from underneath the bathroom door and tried to assure himself that she was just taking a shower or something. When she emerged a minute later, though, dressed in exercise clothes and carrying her running shoes in her hand, he forced himself to wake.

"What do you think you're doing?" he asked, sounding groggy and worn.

Gwen jumped and turned to look at him, holding a

hand to her chest. "You nearly gave me a heart attack," she accused.

He made no reply.

"Don't worry, I'm just going out for a run. I'll be back in time for breakfast."

"You are *not* going out for a run," Alaric said, clearing his throat so that he sounded slightly more awake. It didn't work well as he yawned a moment later. "You don't know this area, and it's...seriously? It's 4:45 in the morning, Gwen."

"I run around the city at just about the same time, and you've never had a problem before," Gwen pointed out.

Alaric shook his head and threw back the duvet, grumbling as the cool morning air hit him. "That's different," Alaric said. "You know that area. You don't know your way around here."

"So what you're saying is that you're not worried for my safety but for my sense of direction?" Gwen asked.

"Are you serious? You could take on some of the worst people in New York City, and all that you'll have to contend with here are the neighborhood cats," Alaric said. "If you'll just wait a few minutes, I'll come with you."

Gwen was laughing, a sound that had excited pleasure hours ago and only caused annoyance now. He was beginning to think she thought he couldn't do anything. Just to prove that he could, Alaric got out of bed and stretched, his muscles groaning at the early-morning demands.

"You're willing to come on a five o'clock run with me? That's sweet, Alaric," Gwen said, pacifying his bad mood immediately. She stepped up to him and kissed him gently, her lips tasting like strawberries, which confused him as he had no idea where that could have come from. "You don't have any running shoes."

"Ah," Alaric said. It was true; he hadn't packed any sneakers, and the only reason he brought clothes that would suit for running was for sleeping. He had figured that he wouldn't be needing exercise clothes for the weekend as he planned to get out as quickly as possible. Gwen, on the other hand, seemed to have planned ahead. He wondered what else was in that weekend bag of hers. "Right."

"Tell you what," Gwen said. "Put on those loafers, and we can go for a walk. You can show me around, and that way you won't have to worry about me getting lost."

"Or we could skip this foolish going outside thing and go back to bed," Alaric said, pulling Gwen back when she tried to pull away. She laughed again, making him smile, and shook her head.

"Too late. I'm already dressed," she said. "Come on, you won't die from morning air. And if you're good, I'll make you my famous Belgian waffles."

"My mother said that I had to stay out of the kitchens," Alaric said, but he was already moving toward the bathroom. "I think we can break that rule, though, for waffles."

Gwen nodded, and Alaric got dressed. He tried to

use cold water to wake himself up and only succeeded in getting his face wet. Rumbling, he hoped that the exercise with Gwen would make him slightly more amenable to facing the world. They went out through the house, sneaking so as not to wake anyone and slipping out through the side door. After half-heartedly chasing Gwen down the drive and slowing to a walk, slipping his fingers into hers, Alaric had to admit that there were worse ways to wake up. Of course, if it had been a mere two hours later, things would have been exponentially better.

They walked all over the area, Alaric pointing out the various houses and describing the people that lived there. The man delivering the newspapers waved to them, looking startled to see someone else up and about at such an hour. And as predicted, the neighborhood cats were on the prowl, seen only as a patch of fur here or there or a streak running across the road. The sun was fully up by the time that they returned to the large house, and Alaric was more than ready for a large cup of very strong coffee and waffles.

They met instead with Alaric's father, already dressed and looking rather severe, in the kitchen with a plate of eggs, tomatoes, mushrooms, sausage, a pot of tea nearby.

He was holding the newspaper and folded it accusingly as Gwen and Alaric wandered in. "Where have you been?" he growled, the sound somehow elegant as well as biting.

"We've been out walking," Alaric said, throwing the kettle on the stove with more force than necessary. "Gwen wanted to see the area, and I didn't want her going alone."

"I'm an early riser," Gwen said, glancing at the clock and noting that it was barely seven.

Nathaniel tightened his mouth in a scowl but could apparently find no fault with their actions. He turned back to his paper and gave a humph as the only reply. Gwen exchanged a glance with Alaric, who looked just as surprised, and proceeded to make waffles. Even though the kitchen wasn't empty didn't mean she was going to be deterred. Besides, it wouldn't hurt to get Alaric to relax slightly around his father. Making waffles seemed to be a decent way of going about it.

Alaric was tense, only speaking when Gwen asked him whether there were any strawberries or where the flour was. Eventually, in the course of forcing him to whip the batter or slice up fresh fruit to boil down to a warm compote as topping, Gwen managed to get him to act at least somewhat more natural. Nathaniel sat, back tense and expression set, reading his paper methodically, not saying a word or looking up at any of the things that Gwen did or said. She set a plate of waffles on the table and poured glasses of orange juice, served Alaric, and then turned to Nathaniel.

"Do you want a waffle?" she asked.

The older man seemed startled by the fact that

Gwen was even speaking to him, let alone offering him food. He carefully sipped his tea and furrowed his brows ever so slightly before turning to reply. "No, thank you," he said, returning his attention to his paper as if expecting that to be everything.

"Are you sure?" Gwen asked, waving the plate of waffles through the air, the steam coming off them tantalizing. "I make a pretty tasty waffle," she said. Behind her, doing his best not to look like he had swallowed something unpleasant, Alaric cut into his breakfast with a determined focus that exactly mirrored that of his father reading the paper.

"Quite sure," Nathaniel said, shaking his paper to straighten it out, saying clearly that he was not and would never be interested in the waffles. Gwen merely shrugged and set the plate back on the table before serving herself a waffle and spooning the compote over top.

"Suit yourself," she said and proceeded to eat, stopping to converse with Alaric on subjects like the increasing price of truffles or whether or not to try a lemon crab salad as a starter on the new menu. Nathaniel left shortly afterward, and Gwen and Alaric merely finished breakfast.

They were interrupted by Carol coming to rope them into helping set up for the party. It looked to be a beautiful day with no rain in the forecast, so tables were set out on the vast lawn, covered with pristine white table-cloths and set with blue-and-yellow dishes. After the twentieth such table—which could seat six—Alaric began to question, again, the wisdom in coming.

"How many people can my mother expect to come?" Alaric asked as he and Gwen wrestled the twenty-first table into place.

Gwen shrugged and went to fetch the chairs.

"I mean, I realize that my father was a well-known lawyer and had many clients that were more friends than clients, but there can't have been that many people! And that they would all come to this absurd event is just, well..."

"Absurd?" Gwen supplied. Alaric threw a napkin at her, and she dodged, the lemony fabric falling to the ground.

"Alaric Mathew Bennet, I had better not see you let my good napkins fall on the ground!" Carol's voice rang out like a whip.

Gwen had discovered that when the woman wasn't under the thumb of her husband or worried about being rebuffed by Alaric, she could actually be quite fierce. Especially, as it turned out, when preparing a party. Melissa was close behind Carol, carrying a basket full of shining cutlery.

She was already dressed in a slip of a dress that brushed her thighs and left little to the imagination, struggling to manage setting up while tottering along in heels that were hugely impractical. Gwen was still wearing her workout clothes, and Alaric, while dressed in pressed trousers, had left his shirt plain and his hair tousled. In another hour, they would both go dress properly. Melissa, Gwen discovered, despite her looks and charm, was not the most capable person.

"Of course not," Alaric muttered under his breath, picking up the napkin and making a show of examining it for blemishes. He folded it carefully and put it on the table while Gwen arranged the chairs to her satisfaction.

"How much do you want to bet Melissa will fall over and break one of those precious heels before the party even starts?" Gwen asked softly, for Alaric's ears only, as she watched the woman totter around a table, bending awkwardly to set out the cutlery.

Alaric snorted in derision and shook his head. "That's not fair. There's no point in betting at all," he said.

Gwen appraised Melissa and agreed.

"Come on, let's go get the last table, and then we can take a break." They did just that and were just about to admire their work when Carol let out a noise that sounded like something between a laugh and a crow of dismay. Gwen turned, wondering what could have caused the woman to make such a noise and desperately hoping that it was Melissa having broken a heel. She saw, instead, that it was a man, dressed to the nines in a crisp blue suit and bearing a wrapped gift under his arm. He looked vaguely familiar, but it wasn't until a second man materialized at his shoulder, wearing an Army Service Uniform that Gwen knew very well—Major Dalton—that she recognized the first man.

"Damn it," she growled.

Alaric turned to her, frowning at the unexpected cursing and examined her hands to see if she had done something like drop a plate. He spotted the guests and his demeanour straightened, but he didn't look alarmed. Then Alaric obviously recognized Major Dalton and understood Gwen's curse.

"We can leave if you want," he said, already grabbing her elbow and steering her away from the area.

She shook him off. "No, it's not Dalton. It's the man he's come with. Someone I hoped very much never to have to see again in my life," Gwen said. "Dr. Joseph Rawlins, psychiatrist."

Suddenly, Alaric's problems with his ex-girlfriend, bothersome father, and clingy mother seemed to be nothing more than flies buzzing around his head. He thought it was time to drag Gwen away and make her reciprocate on last night. They needed to talk.

22

Alaric and Gwen spent the next hour doing their best to avoid Dr. Rawlins and Major Dalton while still appeasing Carol and staying out of the way. Gwen appeared to be highly aware of the fact that Alaric was desperate to ask questions of her, wanting to know what connection she had to the psychiatrist—as if he couldn't guess. But more than that, he wanted to know about her past. She avoided all his attempts to corner her, instead offering to help his mother and Melissa with any last-minute details. Every time Alaric approached, there was a hint of panic in her eyes. Not much, but enough to have his throat tightening in worry.

Finally, as she was slipping into her dress and Alaric changed his shirt for a proper dress shirt and tie, he cornered her. "Are you going to tell me what this is about, Gwen?" he asked, zipping up the back of her dress while she held her hair out of the way.

"We've been over this before," Gwen said. "I'm…"

"If you say you're not willing to talk about it or that it's not a big deal or anything of the sort, then so help me we're going to have a problem," Alaric snarled, grabbing Gwen's shoulders to spin her around. If he expected to see effrontery in her gaze, then he was disappointed. All he saw was the typical steel that meant she was building up her walls. "You piss me off last night and demand that I tell you what's going on, even if it really was no big deal, because that's what you do in a relationship, and then turn around and hold things back? That's rather hypocritical of you," he hissed.

"Some things," Gwen said, her voice not sharp and furious like Alaric's but piercing as ice, "have no bearing on the present."

"That doesn't mean you don't talk about them!" Alaric threw up his hands and took a step away from her so he could turn in a circle and try and order his thoughts. "And don't you dare say that's what's going on here because that's crap."

"It's the truth," Gwen said flatly, crossing her arms over her chest and turning toward the window, the simple action revealing just how upset she actually was. "My connection with Dr. Rawlins has nothing to do with my life anymore. It doesn't affect anything I do; it's in the past, and there's no point in bringing it up. So take my advice and let it go."

"Bullshit," Alaric said. Gwen turned her head to

glare at him, and Alaric jabbed his finger at her, repeating, "Bull. Shit. You want to know why? Because I've spent hours listening to you toss and turn in bed or go without sleep because whatever it is that happened still haunts you and won't let you get a decent night's sleep. You don't talk about what happened because it still hurts you. You won't even consider having a connection with people from your past because it brings up memories of whatever it is that happened to you. Tell me that the screams you do your best to hide have nothing to do with it."

Gwen blinked away a sheen of tears and pressed a hand to the base of her throat, but she said nothing, making Alaric all the more furious and determined to wrench the truth out of her. It was time to do away with secrets, to tear down all those boundaries that they had set up between them. Some of it was his fault, he could acknowledge that now. He had been too focused on her problems to consider that he was being selfish in holding his own back. It had taken being confronted with his ex-girlfriend and watching Gwen do her best to befriend the woman for him to realize that. Now it was Gwen's turn. He cared far too much about Gwen for her to shut him out and pretend that everything was fine, that she was Wonder Woman and could take on anything and everything and she didn't need him fighting for her. Everyone needed someone.

"See, this thing, this *relationship*," Alaric spat the word, making Gwen realize what a mockery of the word she had made, "goes both ways. My past is here in the form of my ass of a father, and yours is here in the form of a psychiatrist. I've told you about my past, but you won't tell me about yours? That hurts, Gwen. It hurts that a stranger knows more about you than I do. But if you don't want to talk about it? Fine. Fine. Just don't come asking after me if you're not willing to talk about you."

With that, he turned and stalked out of the room, slamming the door behind him.

Gwen jerked at the sound and straightened her spine, clenching her fist and determined to do anything but cry. She was stronger than that. She had been through hell and come out in one piece—sort of—and she could hold herself together after arguing with Alaric. That didn't stop the pain from flaring up, making her want to lie on the bed and curl into a ball until it subsided. Who knew that the heart-wrenching reality of watching the person you loved walk away could feel so much like being shot? No, Gwen thought, allowing herself to sit on the edge of the bed, she had been shot before. This woas much worse.

He didn't understand. She loved him, absolutely, completely, and entirely. That was why she couldn't tell him about her past. It would, undoubtedly, change the way that he looked at her, and she wasn't sure she could survive that. Having him turn away from her, not because of anger but because of disappointment, would kill her she was sure.

Gwen swallowed the desperate sound that was rising in her throat. Sooner or later, she would have no choice but to tell Alaric, but she couldn't bring herself to do more than stare disconsolately at the patterns in the rug on the floor. She wasn't sure how long she sat like that, unaware of everything but her own dilemma. Eventually, the sounds of the party outside broke through, and Gwen blinked, reality returning to its normal shape. She rubbed her collarbone and sighed. She had to make things right with Alaric, and she had to go see to his needs. Right now, he was facing his past alone, and she had promised to support him. She had made that promise, and she wasn't about to abandon one of her comrades in need.

That wasn't the right term, Gwen thought, pressing the heel of her palm to her head. "He's your boyfriend, not a soldier," she told herself. She had to move, had to get out of there, before other things started blurring together and she started to relive the event that haunted her nightmares. It was terrifying in the dark, but in the daytime, when she thought she was safe, it was much worse. Gwen forced herself to stand, put on her shoes, and strode from the room, focusing on finding Alaric.

Outside, the party was in full swing. Music—soft, comfortable jazz—floated from speakers that had been set up sometime after Gwen's disappearance. People in expensive clothes and shining jewelry stood in groups, glasses of high-quality alcohol in their hands. The men stood with practiced slouches that said they didn't care what others thought because they were among the powerful. The women laughed in charming tones, tossing their hair and watching everybody from the corners of their eyes, waiting for an opportunity to grab up an interesting bit of information or prove their standing by speaking the right word into someone's ear. Most of them, Gwen assumed, were former clients. The lawyers were the group gathered around Nathaniel, all wearing suits of a similar cut and design, laughing at something. Dr. Rawlins was nowhere to be seen. Alaric was far easier to spot.

He had been cornered by Melissa, standing near a table where drinks and snacks had been set out. A glass of dark-amber liquid was in his hand, and from the way that he kept sipping at it, Gwen knew it was soon to be empty. Melissa smiled, attractive and charming and intelligent enough to be underhanded and subtle in her conversation. Gwen didn't dislike the woman—though she thought that Melissa's motives for showing up left something to be desired—but there was no doubt that Alaric was uncomfortable.

She strode up to him and wrapped an arm through his, pushing away the hurt when he stiffened slightly. "I never got to tell you just how much I like your dress," Gwen said to Melissa. Before the woman had a chance to respond, Gwen turned her head to Alaric. "You look like you could use a refill. And I could use a drink.

Come on, let's go see what we can find." With a slight tug, Gwen pulled on Alaric's arm and dragged him away from the ex-girlfriend, leaving to go search for a drink.

Alaric remained quiet while he followed Gwen to the makeshift bar at the opposite end of the lawn. He waited while she filled his glass and poured her own and didn't even blink when she drained the glass in one quick jerk.

Then she turned to him, brows drawn together and eyes full of regret. "I'm sorry," she said.

"It's all right," he replied, wrapping an arm around her waist. "I just wish you would tell me these things, Gwen. What happened in your past is so much of who you are. I want to know that."

"And I'll tell you," she said, making him straighten in surprise and anticipation. "Just not right now. I'm not... I don't think I can do that right now. Give me time?"

"As much as you need," Alaric said, kissing the top of her head. Gwen relaxed into his hold, and he topped off her glass. "Come on, you've got some catching up to do. I'm on my third drink, and I haven't even had a conversation with my father or any of his business partners. I'm planning on getting truly drunk before this thing is over."

"If you want to get me drunk," Gwen said, dutifully taking a long sip of the scotch, "then you're going to have to do quite a bit more than three drinks. I've outdrunk men twice my size."

Alaric laughed and shook his head in disbelief but let the matter drop.

~

Reconciled, both found it easier to avoid certain people with the excuse and company the other provided. Anytime that Alaric's father got too close, Gwen would steer him in the direction of the buffet or, more often, the bar, claiming to need a drink. Alaric provided the same service in regard to Dr. Rawlins and Major Dalton, though it was slightly more difficult to avoid someone who wasn't actually keen on avoiding you.

"Gwen," Major Dalton called out, making Gwen stiffen and toss back the last mouthful of another drink. Alaric could tell she was feeling buzzed by this time and imagined that another hour would do to get her quite drunk. He couldn't figure out whether that was a good thing or bad, but that might have had something to do with the amount of alcohol he'd imbibed. The important thing was that Major Dalton was coming her way, and with him having seen her, it would be impossible to slip away.

"Major," she said, not bothering to smile. Alaric remembered the last time that the two had talked, the major had all but accused Gwen of being suicidal. That was a conversation that hadn't gone particularly well.

"You're looking well," he said, nodding at her. Alaric didn't get the impression he was complimenting her dress. He remembered the discussion they'd had about Gwen, not too long before.

"She has put on weight, and there's a definite energy in her that wasn't there before."

"But," Alaric prompted.

"But I've seen her at her best, and she's nowhere close..."

"As are you," Gwen said. "I'm surprised to see you here. I didn't think you enjoyed the company of lawyers." Her tone was short and clipped, though her words weren't as enunciated as usual. Then again, she had just finished her fourth scotch.

"I don't particularly, but one of the psychiatrists from the military hospital was asked to come, and I was invited to attend," Major Dalton said.

Alaric did his best to hide the tick that suddenly developed in his jaw. One of the psychiatrists was "asked" to come, right. Major Dalton knew exactly who the psychiatrist was in relation to Gwen, and he likely only wheedled his way into attending the party because it was hosted by Alaric's family. If Walter hadn't kept the major appraised of Gwen's and his relationship, then Alaric was a sous chef.

"I hope you enjoy the party," Alaric said, doing his best to smile. "If you'll excuse us, I think—"

"Well, I'll be," a new voice said, the smooth tones making chills run up Alaric's spine.

Beside him, Gwen stiffened and dug her fingers into his arm, and a single tremor made the hand holding her glass shake once before becoming perfectly, unnaturally still. Her expression, though, was completely blank and neutral, betraying nothing of her thoughts.

"Lieutenant Gwen Townsend. I didn't think I'd see you again after you were discharged. How are you?"

"Dr. Rawlins," Gwen said, her voice, like her expression, perfectly neutral and even. Alaric found the sound chilling and unnatural. "I did not expect to see you here."

"I was invited by a friend of mine at one of the law firms that represents the hospital. It was a welcome change from the hospital, so I came. And I'm glad I did. I get to see you," he said, blinking at Gwen from behind his square glasses. Alaric wanted to punch him.

"Fortuitous," Gwen said. "If you'll excuse me, I have to go powder my nose." Just like that, she slipped out of Alaric's grasp and walked away, her stride even and unfaltering, her posture straight. Alaric looked at the spot where she had been holding his arm and swallowed a wince. He would have some pretty bruises there tomorrow.

"She's quite the character," Dr. Rawlins said, nodding after Gwen. "I'm glad to see she's adjusting. One of the hardest cases I've ever dealt with in my career. Poor thing."

"I think I'd better find my mother," Alaric said, his voice bordering on extremely rude. He nodded at the major and walked away, not bothering to even pretend to look for his mother. Instead, he followed Gwen's path to the house and found her standing at the back door, regarding the brick beside the door with a determined expression.

Alaric came up behind her. "I'd prefer it if you didn't punch the brick. I don't want to have to take you to the hospital, and my father would be furious with me for breaking the house."

"I'm still recovering from the last time I did that," Gwen said, holding up her hand. The cast had been taken off, but she was still wearing a brace and was more careful with the appendage than usual. Her voice was still that eerie calm tone, and Alaric shifted nervously. "I was thinking about murder, actually."

"Please don't," Alaric said. "How about we steal one of those bottles of wine from the bar and go up to the room? We can skip out on the rest of this stupid party, my father be damned." He half expected her to refuse, to be the strong, unwavering soldier that she became whenever things were threatening. He did not expect her to nod and wipe her eyes with the back of her hand, brushing away glistening tears.

"I feel so stupid," Gwen said around a growl. She let her shoulders slump and didn't protest when Alaric wrapped his arms around her waist.

"There's nothing for you to feel stupid about," he said, kissing her hair. "You had no idea he would be here. It's not your fault."

"I hated that man," Gwen said. "After I was admitted to hospital, I was made to talk with him for hours each day, putting up with group therapy and basically wallowing in my mistakes. It was the worst thing that they could have done for me. When Major Dalton showed up at The Rose, surprised to see me alive, I wasn't shocked. I was inches away from killing myself at that damn hospital. But I made it out, and I started over, and now here I am, faced with *that man* again."

"Hey," Alaric said, turning her around so he could cup her face and look into her eyes, "it's all right. There's nothing to be upset about, Gwen. He has no hold over you, and you have nothing to prove to him or Major Dalton. Understand me?"

She bit her lip and blinked away more tears but nodded dutifully.

"Good," Alaric growled. "Now come on. I'll steal the wine, and you go upstairs and get into your pajamas."

"Can you get some food too?" Gwen asked in a small voice. "I don't want to have to come back down."

"Anything you want," Alaric said and gently shoved her away. She only hesitated for a moment before going inside. He watched her retreating form to make sure that she was, in fact, going upstairs, then slipped back into the throng of people. He snatched a wine bottle and some glasses, then considered the array of food before him. His mother had been strict in her choice of food for the party; there was nothing more substantial than chicken and prawn kebabs with mango and pineapple. It was all snack food, tidbits designed to be eaten at a table or while standing and talking. Grumbling, Alaric went inside to the kitchens and grabbed a loaf of bread, some fruits, cheeses, a few of the pieces of food that had been deemed unfit to be served to guests, and whatever desserts he could find in the fridge. He stuffed everything into a bag and went upstairs, not relaxing until he closed the door behind him.

What he found was Gwen lying on the bed, the back of her dress unzipped and her pajamas laid out. She stared blankly at the wall across from her and only stirred enough to lift her head and look at Alaric as he entered. When he finished setting out the food and pouring the wine, he carried her a glass.

She pushed herself up and sighed, taking the glass and drinking deeply. "I'm not being much fun," she murmured.

"That doesn't matter," Alaric said. "Besides, I was as happy to get away from the party as you were."

"I suppose," Gwen said. She took another long sip of the wine and hiccuped slightly. "Do you know what?"

"No, what?" Alaric asked, laughing at the sound. She nudged him with her shoulder, and he laughed harder, covering his mouth as she hiccuped again.

"I think I'm drunk," Gwen said.

Alaric nodded in understanding. With all that had happened to him in the last couple of days, he felt he was perfectly justified in getting drunk. He extended the same courtesy to Gwen.

"Well, it's partly your fault."

"I'm not surprised," Alaric said.

Gwen raised an eyebrow and settled back on the bed, leaning her head against the headboard and taking a deep breath. "You shouldn't be," she said. "After all, you dragged me along to this...event. And you introduced me to your parents. You started it too. The drinking thing. You started it."

"That I did," Alaric said wisely, acknowledging the fact with another sip of wine, which Gwen mirrored. She set down the glass and crawled over to where Alaric had set out the food, picking up some fruit and bread before returning to the bed. "Anything for me?"

"You have to get it yourself," Gwen said primly, the words starting to blur together. Yes, she nodded, biting into the apple, she was drunk. Even as she acknowledged the fact, a slight smile appeared on her face, widening when Alaric shifted closer to her and plucked up the second apple, biting into it.

"I got it myself," Alaric said, his own words running together. Gwen sighed dramatically, then laughed, the sound louder than she would normally dare.

"Damon used to do that," Gwen said, nodding at the half-eaten apple "Steal my food. He would attack just as we were sitting down to mess. I could barely get in a single bite before he pilfened—no, that's not right; plefered...damn it, I can do this...pilfered my food," Gwen said each syllable carefully, more worried about the fact that she was having difficulties speaking than she was about the content of her words.

"I didn't steal it," Alaric said, doing his best to appear calm and collected, though his heart was pounding. Gwen was talking to him about her past. She was talking about Damon—one of her squad mates, possibly even the man in the picture—and not hesitating to do so. "I'll pay you back."

"He would do that too," Gwen said, stuffing a piece of bread into her mouth. "Promise to pay me back. He did too. Always with some sort of contraband food that we couldn't normally get on base. He was going to get me some chocolate that night...if it hadn't been for the stupid cat, I would have gotten it too."

"Cat?" Alaric asked, unable to believe his luck. She was talking about everything. She was going to tell him what had happened without his prodding or begging. Sure, she was drunk—and he felt mildly guilty about taking advantage of that—but she was coherent.

At Alaric's words, she scowled and took another sip of wine, snorting in displeasure. "We had everything planned out," she said, her words clearer and laced with pain. "The insurgents were holed up in a...a... bunker thing, and it was our job to corner one or two. I would translate and hope that our informant was r- right when he said they were amenable to talking. Walker and Bonehead and Johnnie and D-damon. I got held up 'cause that stupid, *idiotic* cat got in the way. I c-couldn't yell at it 'cause they might hear and shoot us, not knowing we w-w-were the good guys. And Damon got imp-patient and stepped around Johnnie. Stepped on a bloody IED, b-blew himself up. Captain Samson was s-still alive, and he was shot at b-by the insurg-g-gents. I couldn't help 'cause I was knocked d-down by the explosion. They were dead, every last one of them, and I w-woke up in that damn hospital with the face of that moronic Major Dalton looking at me. It's all my f-fault, Alaric! I couldn't move, and they all died because of it!"

The stutters in Gwen's speech plainly weren't from drunkenness by the end. They were from the fact that she was barely holding herself together. Tears were streaming down her cheeks, and she had barely managed to set down the wine glass on the nightstand before wrapping her arms around her waist and bending nearly in two. Alaric was stunned, unable to say anything as Gwen moaned her pain. It wasn't her fault; how could it be? He set down his own drink and put an arm around her shoulder, brushing his hand over her hair. She looked up at him, her eyes full of unshed tears, already starting to turn red from irritation. She met his gaze and sucked in a sharp breath, recoiling from him.

"Gwen!" Alaric said, reaching for her.

She pulled back further.

"Gwen, what is it?" he asked, alarmed.

"That look...*that* is why I didn't want to tell you," she breathed, her eyes locked on Alaric's.

"What look? Gwen, I don't understand what you're talking about," Alaric said, moving his weight toward her to try and pull her to him, to comfort her and assure her that everything was all right and that it wasn't her fault. He stopped when she moved off the bed, standing in a stance that, even for the uninitiated, was obviously dangerous and furious.

"Pity," she said, her voice cracking.

23

Gwen focused on the steady drum of water on her back and held her knees close to her chest. She was in the shower, letting the warm water wash away any last traces of alcohol and clear her mind. Mostly, though, she was in the shower because it was far easier to ignore Alaric's pleading from behind the locked bathroom door than otherwise. His voice still carried through the door, and Gwen squeezed her eyes shut and hunched her shoulders, focusing on the beat of the water.

"I don't pity you, Gwen," Alaric insisted, his head pressed against the door. "All I wanted was to understand what sort of pain was in your past, and I do now. It wasn't your fault! You couldn't have known there would be a cat, and there was nothing you could have done that would have changed things. Damon was the one who stepped out of line. Not you. You had nothing to do with it! It wasn't your fault."

Gwen wished that he would stop repeating that. It was the same thing that Dr. Rawlins had told her over and over and over again while she sat in his office on a chair that was plush and uncomfortable. He had insisted that what had happened wasn't her fault. Damon was the one who'd stepped out of the cleared space. He had set off the IED that had alerted the enemy to their presence, preventing the opportunity to talk and come to a peaceful arrangement. Gwen had been there to make peace. Damon's misstep was what had killed her squad. None of that explained away the fact that Gwen was still alive, and if it hadn't been for her getting tripped up by a cat, a *stupid cat*, then everything would have been fine. They would have cleared the building and had a conversation...and she would still be in the army, risking her life every day instead of here, in a mansion owned by her boyfriend's parents.

"You have to come out of there eventually," Alaric said, pulling Gwen out of her thoughts.

She turned the heat up on the water.

"And when you do, maybe you'll understand that I'm not going anywhere."

Gwen said nothing. She heard a thud from the door and assumed that Alaric had hit the wood.

"Fine," he snarled, anger clearly growing. "Fine, if you want to believe that it was your fault because you couldn't figure out how to move a cat without making noise that would alert the people willing to do anything to survive, including kill you, to your presence, then go ahead. You made a mistake, Gwen. That doesn't make you worse than everyone else; it just makes you human. And you know what? You built yourself up again, created a new life for yourself. But if you want to dwell on the one thing you can't change, so be it. When you realize that you can't live in the past anymore, let me know. Until then, I'll be outside."

Alaric rose from leaning against the door and stalked out of the room, ignoring the array of food that he had set up for Gwen and himself. Unlike Gwen, he didn't have the privilege of washing away the effects of the alcohol, and he was still drunk—or mostly drunk. Having your girlfriend accuse you of disappointing her in exactly the way she'd imagined you would, even though there was nothing you could have done, tended to brush away some of the buzz. He wasn't likely to drink anything else for the remainder of the evening though. Some things needed to be dealt with sober.

His father was not one of those things.

"Ah, so now you emerge," Nathaniel said, standing at the foot of the staircase, the knot of his tie loosened ever so slightly and the first button of his shirt undone. That was enough to signify that the party was over. Alaric was not sorry to have missed it, though now he would have to find some other excuse for keeping out of the room he shared with Gwen.

"I'm going for a walk," Alaric said flatly.

"Not until you've answered for your actions,"

Nathaniel replied, his lip curling into a sneer. "I had people who were wondering where you were, who had seen you and were waiting for a chance to talk with you. And you go and vanish without so much as a by-your-leave. That was extremely rude of you, boy."

Alaric curled his fingers into fists and did his best to breathe deeply. He was already angry from dealing with Gwen, and he *really* wasn't in the mood to argue with his father. That invariably made things worse, and he didn't have time for worse. "Right, well, sorry," Alaric spat. "I was trying to help Gwen through something."

"Using your little girlfriend as an excuse to shirk your social duty is weak, Alaric. It borders on pathetic," Nathaniel said, his voice dripping with contempt. Alaric narrowed his eyes; Gwen was being a pain in his ass at the moment, but at least he could understand why. His father was being a pain in his ass for no good reason other than he could.

"Gwen has had a few issues she needed help with," Alaric said. "Whereas I have no social duty, at least not with your friends. I doubt very much they cared enough to ask after me or even recognized me. I'm tired of you pushing me around because you think I owe you some great debt for being my father. That's not such a boon, *Dad*. You are controlling and domineering and just plain spiteful. So what if I didn't become a lawyer? I have done extremely well for myself without your help. Shove off."

"You dare," Nathaniel said, his voice low and

threatening, his eyes glittering with malice. "After all that I've do—"

"You haven't done anything," Alaric cut in, "except hurt me and Mom. If I have to choose between you and your so-called social duties or even any familial ties and the girl I love, I choose her. Every. Time. I'm going for a walk. Gwen and I will be gone tomorrow." Alaric shouldered his way past his father and stalked out the door, ignoring the furious shouts that followed him. When he was halfway down the drive, he let out the roar of frustration that he hadn't known he had been holding in.

Alaric was fed up with dealing with his family issues. He had been slapped around—physically and emotionally—one too many times, and he was done. No more would he return to the house in upstate New York and pretend that he was part of that family. He had no obligations to them like he had to Gwen. He had been so busy trying to help her this weekend that he had hardly bothered to pay attention to his family problems. It was difficult to wallow in self-pity with her around. She was what mattered to him now, and it had taken seeing her in pain to understand that. He— Alaric froze, one foot poised above the edge of the foot-path as he realized the implications of what he had said.

He loved Gwen. He was in love with Gwen.

The words had just come out when yelling at his father, and he hadn't even realized how true they were. It was surprising that he hadn't realized it before. After all the time he had spent with her, during their lessons or just talking or on a date or anything, he knew that he cared about her. But he hadn't known the extent of his feelings until then. He was in love with Gwen. And that made it all the more difficult to see her in pain.

"All right," Alaric said, easing backward until he was leaning against the wall next to the footpath. "You're in love with her. What are you going to do about it?" The obvious choice was to rush back to the house and demand that Gwen let him in so that he could profess his feelings for her and thereby force her to accept what had happened. He wasn't sure he would be in love with the woman who hadn't gone through that, and she would simply have to understand that. But he wasn't sure that going back there just then was a good idea. She was hurting from his—unknowingly given—pity. He might just make things worse if he went back there.

Alaric hesitated, looking at the road before him without seeing it. He loved her. That didn't make him all-knowing or wise. He had no idea what the right thing to do was. He sank down onto the edge of the footpath and cradled his head in his hands. Just a moment ago, he had been thinking about how much better she was than him at dealing with his familial issues and now this? It was slightly overwhelming. More than slightly. It changed everything. It was as if something in his mind had just shifted into place, and suddenly the things that had seemed to matter didn't, and those that he had tried to ignore took on the greatest importance.

For so long, Alaric had tried to understand what it was in Gwen's past that had made her the way she was. He'd wanted to understand what it was that haunted her and made her retreat behind her wall of steel just to face the world. Now he did, and with it came the knowledge that he didn't care if it was her fault or not; he loved her in spite of it. He wanted to be in her future, not let her wallow in her past. It was sudden and jarring and put everything into perspective. Alaric straightened and stood, pulling his fingers through his hair. Everything might have clicked into place for him, but Gwen was still back at the house, looking through a haze of her past. He had to make her see.

He turned back toward the house, taking the driveway at a run. Alaric went through the front door without fear of seeing his father or mother. His father would be nursing his wounds in his study, and his mother was undoubtedly busy with tearing down the party. He took the stairs two at a time and burst through the door to his room just as Gwen was emerging from the bathroom, one of his dressing gowns wrapped around her with a loose knot, her hair hanging in wet strings around her face.

She froze when she saw him, obviously looking for signs of pity in his face, her shoulders hunched as she searched. That act of uncertainty made Alaric all the surer that what he was doing was good.

"Gwen," he said, holding out his arms ever so slightly.

"I'm a fool," she answered, going to him. The words weren't meant as an apology to him but as a chastisement to herself for her past mistakes. She thought it was her fault that her squad was gone, and that she was a fool for thinking otherwise. That didn't mean she couldn't accept the comfort Alaric was offering.

"No," he said, kissing the top of her head and wrapping his arms tightly around her waist. "You're just human."

"That doesn't change things," Gwen answered. "I'm still to blame."

Alaric hesitated, instinct telling him to convince her otherwise. He took a deep breath and curbed the desire to make things easier for her. He loved her because she was strong and able to fight her own way. When she was hurting and curled in on herself in frightened weakness, he couldn't just make things better. She had told him as much in no uncertain terms many times. He had to stand by her and lend a hand when she stood. He shook his head. One realization about the nature of his feelings was making him a sentimental idiot. He couldn't start overthinking things now.

"Maybe," he said at last. "I wasn't there, so I don't know. But even if you were to blame, there's nothing you can do to change what happened." Then he smiled slightly, the look profound and real, the words to soothe her wounds coming to the forefront of his mind as if called. "You have to keep living, Gwen, if only because they can't."

She stiffened but did not pull away. "I don't think it's quite that simple," she said, her voice somewhere between a growl and whisper.

Alaric shrugged and tilted her head so he could look her in the eye. "I think it is," he said. "So what's it going to be? Are you going to wallow away in this room because you can't face the fact that you're still alive, or are you going to embrace the life you have and come back to the city with me? Live for them, Gwen. Live the lives that they no longer have. Whether or not it's your fault is something we may never be able to figure out. It doesn't mean you give up."

Gwen stood there, searching Alaric's eyes for the answers to her own questions. Finally, she sighed and pressed her nose into his shoulder. "I guess it doesn't," she said. Part of her wanted to rebel and fight, to yell at him that he didn't understand what she had been through, didn't understand that there was no way to fix death. People were dead because of her, and there was nothing she could do to amend that; therefore, she needed to pay for her mistakes, her crimes. The other part of her, the part that had pulled her out of the streets and accepted Walter's offer and created a new life for herself—that part told her that Alaric was right. Just because Damon, Captain Samson, Walker, Bonehead, and Johnnie were gone didn't mean she had to stop trying to live as though she'd died that day too. That was the part that spoke loudest.

"Glad you figured it out," Alaric said. Things were far from over. But it was a start, and for figuring out the rest, she would have him standing right beside her. For now, though, it was enough. "Now, how about we finish off that food and go to bed. I would say we could drive back tonight, but I'm still drunk and I don't think you're in any mood to drive."

"First thing in the morning?" Gwen asked, pulling away to sit on the bed and pick up her discarded plate. She retreated into the calmer, less serious conversation thankfully. Her heart felt as though it had been laid bare. She needed time to heal and to consider things before figuring out what to do next. She crossed her legs, and the dressing gown slid up far enough to be considered indecent.

Alaric grinned slyly. "Well," he said, joining her on the bed and taking the plate carefully out of her hand. "Maybe not *first* thing."

She laughed. It wasn't loud or boisterous or even completely joyful, but it was a start. That was what mattered.

Morning came, and despite Alaric's protests, Gwen dragged him out of bed so they could leave just after seven. They did not run into Nathaniel or Carol, for which Alaric was thankful. He considered going to find his mother to say goodbye and thought better of it. He loved her, but he had been manipulated too many times. He wrote a note instead: *Gwen and I are off to the city. You can stop by any time. Alaric.* Then he and Gwen were away, back to New York City, back to The Wooden Rose, back home.

"Do you think Jack managed to survive the weekend without us?" Gwen teased as they spotted the city on the horizon. Her voice wasn't as happy or relaxed as it had been on the drive out, but that was to be expected. Neither of them were what they had been, and they certainly weren't relaxed, but they had seen the depths of their souls. They were still recovering.

Alaric tensed ever so slightly, thinking up scenarios of what tragedies might have befallen his restaurant during his absence. "If one pan in my kitchens is out of place, I'm going to wring someone's neck," Alaric said.

"I wouldn't worry too much," Gwen said. "Danny has been working for you for nearly three years. I'm sure that he'd have sorted things out while we were gone. If there were any problems, that is."

"Every time I go away for more than one night, things get completely out of order, and I spend ages trying to put it back together again," Alaric grumbled. "Last time, they mislaid a whole order of duck breasts. A whole order! I can understand a few, but a whole order is just beyond me."

"All right," Gwen said, "I'll make you a deal. If they've lost an order of duck breasts, salmon fillets, or even the entire collection of black truffles, I'll replace them from my own salary."

"Now that you've said that, nothing is going to happen," Alaric said.

"That's just how things work," Gwen replied, apparently completely assured. She smiled as Alaric muttered complaints under his breath, and they made it into the city. It was barely lunchtime when Alaric pulled into the parking lot across from The Rose. He helped Gwen carry her bag up to her apartment and reluctantly went down to the car and drove to his own. Only the knowledge that he was wearing a slightly wrinkled suit and the desire to make something in his own kitchen could persuade him. Otherwise, he would have happily joined Gwen in the shower.

He made a panini and ate it while staring out the window to his flat, wondering just how difficult it would be to get out of the deed. Melissa had made it incredibly complicated because there was some sort of price benefit she claimed he would get. Maybe she would want to buy it off him, as she had been the one to covet it in the first place. Of course, that would depend on whether Gwen wanted him to move in with her. He loved her and figured he could put up with just about anything if it meant he got to be with her all the time, but did she feel the same way? He supposed that he should start looking for a ring and thinking about asking her if she loved him. That would solidify things for the both of them. First things first, though: he had to figure out a way to tell her. Oh, and there was the fact that he was introducing a new dish at The Rose.

Alaric smiled. Two things he couldn't live without—Gwen and cooking—and here he was with both of them. "To hell with it," he said to the last corner of his panini. Throwing the sandwich in his mouth, Alaric chewed even as he raced down to his car and drove to Gwen's apartment. The building seemed to have taken on a glow since he'd last seen it, and even though he knew that he was looking at it through the haze of his hopes, it was nice. Alaric leaned on the buzzer.

The door clicked open, and he raced up the stairs, making it to Gwen's flat before she could get her door fully open.

Her eyes were wide and slightly worried, "Is something wrong? Did your flat get burgled? Did Jack lose an order of duck? Damn it, Alaric, tell me!"

"I love you," Alaric said, pushing past her and into the flat. He had intended for the statement to be slightly more romantic, a bit softer and perhaps followed with a kiss, not growled out as though he had just been woken up.

"Oh," Gwen said, closing the door behind him. "Ah."

"Is that a problem?" Alaric asked, fear that she would reject him putting a bite to this tone.

"No," Gwen answered, moving into the kitchen and leaning against the counter. She tucked a strand of brown hair behind her ears and folded her arms. "It just makes things easier. Because I love you too."

Alaric blinked, startled for only a moment before the realization of what she had said struck him. He couldn't help himself; he grinned and kissed her. Hard.

He didn't notice that there was a new picture on the fridge, one with six people smiling as if they hadn't a care in the world.

ACKNOWLEDGMENTS

As always, there are a number of people who must be remembered in the making of a book. The first is my cover designer, Fay Lane, who seems to be able to put together a cover in just about any genre, with all the direction I can give her. (Which is, admittedly, not much as my skills with graphics cover the occasional doodle.) Your work always continues to amaze.

The second person I need to acknowledge is Lyss Em, my editor, who took this book that I had written ages (read years) ago—and then rewritten this last summer—and then turned it into a proper novel. She fixed the mistakes that I was too close to this work to see and was a pleasure to work with. Any mistakes that you may see here are, therefore, my own because I was too silly to see them even after she fixed them.

And I must, of course, acknowledge all the people who stood by me while trying to make a go of this author thing. Without you, my readers and family, I would be who knows where. So, to all of you, thank you.

ABOUT THE AUTHOR

Evelyn Grimald has been writing since she was a girl. When she wasn't reading, she was going about inventing stories to keep her entertained at social events like parties and dinners. Since then, she has pretended to be a touch practical and went to university, where she got degrees in linguistics. As it turns out, practicality proved to be a useful thing and now Evelyn applies her knowledge of language to writing stories.

Evelyn lives a quiet life reading and writing, which her cat and dog both appreciate. When not writing, she is walking, sewing, or reading, exploring so many of the worlds which books provide.

You can find more about Evelyn and her books at her website: https://evelyngrimald.com

ALSO BY EVELYN GRIMALD

The Houndskeeper, an historical romance

The Wooden Rose